A VOICE EMERGED
FROM THE DARKNESS.

"Troubled, aren't you?"

"Who's there?" Stefan called out.

A figure stepped from the shadow of a twisted elm, so close that Stefan found it unbelievable that the man could have approached him without being heard.

"A fellow wanderer in the darkness," the man said.

"This isn't the safest place to wander," Stefan said.

"This is an uneasy place," the man responded.

"What do you know of what happened here?" Stefan asked.

"Murder," the man said. "Murder most foul."

"If you know anything about the murders, I think you should tell me." Stefan had to raise his voice above the sound of a train passing below them.

The man was laughing. "So typical of the police, so little subtlety, so little heed of the consequences the truth might bring."

"You'd better explain yourself, or we're going to take a trip to the station."

Something akin to panic gripped Stefan for no apparent reason. He felt sweat in the small of his back, and he tasted fear, like blood, in the back of his throat.

The man turned to Stefan as the train whistle screamed. "What would you do if you knew? What could you do?" He took a step forward, and Stefan tried to draw his gun, but he was suddenly paralyzed by an unnatural fear. "The truth would destroy you. . . ."

S.A.Swiniarski

✝The Flesh,
✝The Blood,
and ✝The Fire.

DAW BOOKS, INC.

DONALD A. WOLLHEIM, FOUNDER

375 Hudson Street, New York, NY 10014

ELIZABETH R. WOLLHEIM
SHEILA E. GILBERT
PUBLISHERS

First Printing, July 1998
1 2 3 4 5 6 7 8 9

DAW TRADEMARK REGISTERED
U.S. PAT. OFF. AND FOREIGN COUNTRIES
—MARCA REGISTRADA
HECHO EN U.S.A.

PRINTED IN THE U.S.A.

This book is dedicated to Michelle,
the love of my life—*Loads.*

ACKNOWLEDGMENTS

I'd like to thank everyone who went over this MS at the last minute; Sally Kohonoski, Geoff Landis, Charles Oberndorf and Mary Turzillo. I'd also like to thank the authors of a number of books that I found useful while writing this; especially Steven Nickel for *Torso: The Story of Eliot Ness and the Search for a Psychopathic Killer*, John Stark Bellamy III for *They Died Crawling and Other Tales of Cleveland Woe*, David D. Van Tassel and John J. Grabowski for *The Encyclopedia of Cleveland History*, and Ian S. Haberman for *The Van Sweringens of Cleveland: the Biography of an Empire*. As always, any errors within are strictly my own.

Prologue

---⊗⊗⊗---

April 1934-September 1934

THE LADY IN THE LAKE

1934

1

Her name was Laila, and it had been over two weeks since she had fed. Death lingered in the shadows of the iron room where they kept her chained, naked, to a seat bolted to the floor. She could not remember another time when she had felt this vulnerable, and she had a very long memory.

The metal room, her prison, was a small chamber with slightly curving walls, ocher with rust stains. There was one light, the bulb wrapped in a hooded cage above her. The hood's shadow cloaked half the room in darkness. Oil and diesel fumes hung in the still air.

She was on a ship; the sound of the waves and the rocking of the room around her told her that. That was all she knew. She didn't know why she was here, or why her captors had not yet killed her. All she knew of her captors came from the few stray bits of German she'd overheard before hunger had completely dulled her senses.

They had known enough to take her in the day, while she slept. They had known enough not to confront her when she'd first awakened in this room.

It seemed an age ago, that first awakening. She had been able to escape the chains and attack the walls of this prison. But there were limits to her strength, even before the hunger had gnawed away at her. Her captors would wait for exhaustion to take her, then chain her again while she was unconscious.

For the first five days it had gone like that, until she had lost the strength to free herself from the bonds.

It made no sense to her. They had her trapped. If they meant to kill her, they could have done so a dozen times over. Why the torture? Why allow her to exist, allow the hunger consume her body? Why not simply cut out her heart during one of her lengthening periods of delirium?

She was coming out of an extended period of semiconsciousness when she sensed a familiar presence. At first she believed she was hallucinating, because the presence was from so long ago. Her senses were dulled. It couldn't be what she thought, no matter how familiar the scent of his blood might be.

He was dead—dead so long that she might have been the only one alive left to remember who he was and how his blood smelled.

She raised her head to face the darkness. Hunger had dimmed her once-sensitive vision until she could only make out a shadowy form beyond the pool of light centered on the seat she was chained to.

The presence did not recede. However impossible it seemed, the scent knifing into her mind was not a hallucination.

It was real.

He was real.

For the first time in two weeks she spoke, her voice a sandpaper whisper. Her lips cracked, weeping fluid as she mouthed the name . . .

"*Melchior* . . ."

"Such a long time," his voice came from the shadows. "Such a long, *long* time." The voice was slightly different, but she could feel him behind the words. His mind was like a choking fog filling the room, asphyxiating all that wasn't his.

"You . . . died . . ." The words came hard for her.

Melchior laughed. His laugh was condescending, someone laughing at a child, someone who hated children.

"You mean they were supposed to kill me."

She found her voice. She shouted at him. "You defied the only law we have!"

His voice was like a velvet garrote. "Your Covenant? It was an exercise in self-castration. I thought, once, that I had taught you better. Anyone who willingly cedes power deserves none."

Melchior walked into the pool of light so Laila could see him. He had changed his appearance. He was taller now, his hair was blond and longer than any man wore it nowadays. But his eyes had not changed. His irises were colored somewhere between violet and brown, a color close to that of clotted blood.

In his right hand, he carried a long knife.

"What has their precious Covenant done for those who condemned me? Who is left of them? Saul? Gildas? Kabir? All dust now, all but you—" He knelt and touched the tip of the blade to where a scar traversed her abdomen. "You still choose to bear the scar where they removed our child? You're overly sentimental."

"You will never understand, will you?" she hissed at him. "Without the Covenant we would *all* be as dead as Saul, Gildas, Kabir, *and* your son."

"We were kings once," he said. "I held more power when I was condemned than any one of you dreams of today."

She looked away from him and said, "What do you want?"

"What is mine. What was taken from me."

"They won't let you—"

"Who won't let me? Who, aside from you, knows who I am?"

Laila felt a knot of terror. There was no one else. Even out of those few that were as ancient, there were none left that would have felt his presence, known the scent of his blood. Only her, who had once called him master, and had spit on what she thought were his ashes.

He drew away from her, as if he knew her thoughts. He probably did. Laila steadied herself and gathered as much of her will as she could, her own presence, together in the face of her old master. "You care nothing for the Covenant. Why didn't you have your men kill me?"

Melchior smiled. If the Black Death could smile, its expression would resemble Melchior's. "Should I say I was sentimental? That I wished you to join me in my new kingdom as you were mine in the old?" He shook his head slowly. "No."

Laila watched his grip tighten on the handle of his knife.

"No," he repeated. "You defied me, and this moment has been a long time coming." He bent so his breath brushed her cheek. "You were saved for me, Laila."

She barely had time to see what was coming before the blade swung.

2

Wednesday, September 5

It was still summer, but the dark clouds boiling off the lake seemed to carry the first knife-edge of winter. Detective Stefan Ryzard found himself looking up every few minutes as he walked through the park toward the beach. Occasionally he grabbed the brim of his hat to keep a particularly strong gust from blowing it away.

From the look of the sky in the direction of the lake, dark as a fresh bruise, they were in for one beaut of a storm. The threatening sky had done a lot to thin out the late-season crowd at Euclid Beach Park, and it was too easy for Stefan to believe he walked the broad avenues alone. The wind seemed to suck up every sound except for the rumble of a coaster, a noise that could easily be faraway thunder, and the insane laughter of the mannequin outside the funhouse.

The mannequin was a cartoonish female figure looming over passersby. As he passed, it rocked back and forth with an amplified laugh. Between the manic laugh and the cartoonish paint makeup, the thing reminded Stefan of a drunken prostitute, tragic and frightening.

He walked past it, and the rides, and the Humphry Popcorn stand, until he reached the pier and the walkway along Euclid Beach. Here it wasn't deserted. Kids, most younger than fourteen, lined the railing overlooking the beach. Half of them had climbed up on the rail and were craning their necks as if a baseball game were being played on the beach below. Standing behind the kids, adults milled around, watching over their heads. Most had the manner of waiting for a streetcar, a few whispered to each other, and a few— the ones with the least pretense, and coincidentally the most shopworn clothes—wore expressions of undisguised curiosity.

Stefan pushed his way through the crowd to the stairs leading down to the beach. At the bottom a lone uniformed policeman blocked his way.

"Sir, you have to watch from up there." He waved a baton toward the spectators.

Stefan fished out his badge and said, "Detective Ryzard."

The uniformed cop looked at the badge and shifted the direction of his baton. "Oh, everyone's up the beach over there. And Inspector Cody wants everyone keeping an eye on the shoreline, in case anything else washes up."

Stefan nodded. "Has the wagon shown up yet?"

The cop shook his head. "Nope, everything's still like they found it."

Stefan stepped down, past the cop, and let his shoes sink into the sand. The soles of his feet felt an anticipatory itch. Grit was going to fill his shoes before he walked ten yards.

"Watch it," the cop said. "Ain't pretty down there."

Stefan said, "Thank you, officer," and walked down the beach. He wasn't too worried about what he was going to see. He had seen plenty of bodies in his career. He had been a patrol officer in the Roaring Third before he made Detective. Even today, that assignment was something out of Dante, and during Prohibition it had been far worse.

The Third was poor, violent, and just this side of completely lawless. Stefan had started in a place cops usually ended up. Coming from the Third made all the stand-up cops wonder how bent you were, and it made the bent cops—who assumed everyone else was bent—wonder what kind of screwup got you assigned to the Third in the first place.

In his stint there, he'd seen more bodies than most funeral directors. Corpses had lost their impact on him through sheer repetition.

A knot of people were assembled a fair way down from the Euclid Beach pier. About half were uniformed officers, about half wore suits. They all seemed subdued, as if something about the crime scene or the oppressive weather made everyone leery of raising their voices.

When he got within twenty yards, one of the suits waved him over. "Detective Ryzard!" he called. Stefan recognized

Inspector Cody. He was holding the brim of his hat and shouting at Stefan through the wind. His tie had gotten loose, and every few seconds would flap toward shore.

Stefan waved acknowledgment without shouting back. The small crowd parted to let him walk up to the crime scene. He got there in time to see what was left of the victim bathed in the flash from a police photographer.

The flash dazzled him for a moment, and for a few seconds a part of his mind too primitive to know cameras waited for the rumble of thunder.

"Washed up sometime last night," Inspector Cody said, "during the last high tide."

Stefan nodded, and raised a hand toward his nose as the near subliminal smell began sinking in from the remains. It smelled of the lake, but there was an odor of corruption that turned his stomach.

He bent to look at what Lake Erie had disgorged onto Euclid Beach. It was discolored and wrapped in seaweed, so at first it was hard to make the mind perceive it for what it was. From a distance it could have been a twisted piece of driftwood. This close, the texture of the purpled flesh made it hard to make that mistake. Even this close—Stefan took out a handkerchief and raised it to his mouth, bending until he was barely a foot away from the surface of the skin—it was hard to tell what this had once been. The mind was used to seeing the human body as a whole; if it saw disjoint pieces, it was as functional units, arms, legs, head.

It took nearly a minute for Stefan to see the remains as part of a human body, even though he had some idea what to expect before he drove down here.

"Who found it?" he asked, unable to turn away. He could see it now, the curve of a thigh, the bend of a hip. His mind finally acknowledged that he was looking at the lower half of a woman's torso, severed at the abdomen and at mid thigh. He could now mentally place the bones and muscles in their proper relationships.

It was the most appalling mutilation he'd ever seen.

"A gentleman named Frank La Grossie," someone answered his question. "He was out for a walk this morning and almost tripped over it."

Stefan slowly unbent and turned to Cody. "How often do things wash up from the lake like this?"

Cody shrugged. "More often than I'd like. Who knows, it could be some med school's cadaver."

Stefan looked up at him and said, "Half a cadaver?"

He shrugged. "The cuts struck me as awful neat."

Stefan looked at the body again, at the wounds where it had been separated from the rest of itself. It did seem that the wounds were too neat.

This body had not been torn. The separation had been done deliberately with some sort of blade. That much was obvious, even as corrupted as the corpse was. "No idea how old it is?"

"We have to wait for the coroner to look at it."

Stefan nodded and walked around the remains, stepping aside occasionally for the photographer. After a while, Stefan asked, "Have you noticed it?"

"Noticed what?"

"Fish, something, should have eaten pieces of this while it was in the water. And it looks to've been in the water a long time."

A uniformed cop spoke up, "Maybe it's burned? The color looks like someone messed up burning the body."

Yes, if the color's charring instead of decay, that'd explain that. But it didn't *smell* like someone's fresh attempt to dispose of a body.

"There's another thing," Stefan added. He waved a hand over the corpse. "No flies."

Cody shook his head and muttered something that sounded like, "Christ."

The flash of a bulb came from behind him, and Stefan turned to look at the photographer. "What's over there?" he asked.

The photographer took the stub of an unlit cigar out of the corner of his mouth and pointed at the sand midway between him and Stefan. "Dead bird," he said, "probably nothing."

It was a seagull, partly buried in sand the lake had washed in. There was no indication of what had killed it. Stefan looked up and saw the seagull's fellows massed far down the beach, awaiting the coming storm. For a moment, Stefan had the oddest sensation that every gull's back was turned to their fallen comrade, as if the dead one had committed some unpardonable sin that even death could not forgive.

Stefan turned back to the thing that used to be part of a human body and wondered if its presence seemed as ominous to the others as it did to him.

He had seen lots of bodies. He had thought that such scenes had lost the ability to disturb him. They hadn't.

Looking at the body, Stefan felt threatened. His faith had been shaken in a way he hadn't felt before. For a moment it seemed that the light of God had abandoned this stretch of Euclid Beach, and his own presence made him a participant in some unholy sacrament.

"Who would do this to someone?" he whispered to himself.

Cody waved at the lake, a slightly darker shade than the sky, and said, "Like I said, most likely something a medical school disposed of. Second most likely, some Capone type chopping up the victim to make it hard to identify. Who knows how long it's been floating out there? It could have drifted all the way from Chicago."

Stefan nodded, though it seemed more likely that the body floated out of their own Cuyahoga River.

Eventually the coroner's wagon showed up for the body, and there was little left for them to do but walk up and down the beach and look for more pieces. No more showed up.

Not there.

3

Thursday, September 6

The discovery of the lower part of a human torso on Euclid Beach was exceptional enough to be printed in one form or another in the *Plain Dealer*, the *Press*, and the *News*. Out in North Perry, halfway on the other side of Lake County from Cleveland, a gentleman named Joseph Hejduk came to the Central Station to tell them about some remains buried on his property.

On the drive out there, with a couple of uniformed cops, two detectives, and two shovels, Stefan listened to Hejduk explain how a nearly indescribable carcass had washed up on his property, how he had called the sheriff's office, and how a deputy had told him—on the phone, without ever seeing the remains—it was probably a dead animal and that Mr. Hejduk should bury it.

Mr. Hejduk wasn't someone to argue with the sheriff's department. But he'd been having nightmares about the thing he buried for the past two weeks. When he had read about what they'd found on Euclid Beach, he knew, he said, "That I bury no animal there."

Darkness and rain slammed into them as Mr. Hejduk drove his ten-year-old Studebaker to a stop next to his property. The uniformed cops grabbed the shovels as Mr. Hejduk led them out into the storm, and to the remains of a small mound of earth at the edge of a wooded area.

Stefan helped the uniformed police dig, trading places as people took breaks from digging in the cramped space. Inspector Cody continued to question Mr. Hejduk about what happened, making the occasional unkind observation about the Lake County Sheriff's Department.

The digging was hellish in the wind and rain. They only

had the light from flashlights shining above them. The scant light seemed to do nothing but make the shadows even more impenetrable. Mud pulled at Stefan's feet, and water weighed his coat down on his shoulders. Everything smelled of damp earth, and after about an hour and a half of digging, a familiar decayed odor.

By the time they found what Mr. Hejduk had buried, Stefan had stopped breathing through his nose.

One of the uniformed cops called out, "I've found something."

He was standing in the far end of a hole that had taken on the proportions of a grave. Stefan was at the other end, and when the flashlight beams swept over to shine at that cop's feet, Stefan realized that end of the hole was a foot or two shallower than his.

The cop was scraping mud away from something with the blade of his shovel, and Stefan could tell that the remains couldn't be more than three feet long. If it had been a human-sized corpse, Stefan would've been standing on part of it.

He leaned over, hoping that the deputy had been right, but knowing, from the smell, that he hadn't.

The blade of the shovel scraped black clumps of earth off of something that looked even blacker. Like the thing on the beach, it took a while for Stefan to perceive the unearthed object for what it was.

The uniformed cop reached a point where he was satisfied, or had seen enough, and backed away, letting the rain wash the rest of the mud off the carcass. He tossed the shovel up on the ground next to the hole and climbed out, calling for the stretcher.

Stefan kept staring at what the cop had unearthed. He felt the same sense of unholiness here, a sense of God's abandonment.

In the hole was another piece of a woman's body, the upper torso this time, missing the head and the arms at the shoulders. It suffered the same discoloration, but looked oddly preserved for having spent the last two weeks or so in the earth.

Stefan pulled himself up out of the hole when they came for the body. He emerged just in time to hear Mr. Hejduk tell Cody about the dead birds he'd found around the remains on the beach.

The next day Coroner Pearce fitted the remains together and declared them a match. He also ruled out the body coming from a medical lab. From the muscular contractions in the neck area, he concluded that decapitation was the cause of death. The discoloration wasn't from someone trying to burn the corpse; it seemed to be, in fact, the result of some sort of chemical preservative impregnating the victim's flesh. The coroner couldn't identify the chemical, but it explained the odd preservation of the body after what was estimated as six *months* in the lake and perhaps a month or two before that for the actual time of death.

The coroner described the woman as having been more or less average height and build, thirty-five years old or so, whose only unique distinguishing feature was having had her uterus surgically removed some years prior to death.

The lake was dredged, but no more pieces of the "Lady of the Lake" were found. Detective Stefan Ryzard spent much of his time over the next three months combing missing person's records for someone matching the Lady's remains. Despite following leads as far as Canada, the Lady was never officially identified, and it would be over two years before Stefan would know her name.

Book One

<hr/>

September 1935-June 1936

THE KINGDOM

OF HEAVEN

1935

1

Stefan Ryzard paced in an alley behind a drugstore in his old neighborhood around East Fifty-Fifth and St. Clair. He didn't like being here. It brought back too many memories. It had been years since he lost Mary and Jacob, and every time he came near the place where he'd spent the first thirty years of his life, he was reminded of the loss. Reminded of God's infinite indifference.

Being here with a body whose murder had little hope of being solved did little to relieve Stefan's sense of abandonment.

The body lay in the midst of half a dozen ashcans. He'd been finished off with a single high-caliber round in the forehead. The body had been dumped here, Ryzard suspected, as a warning to someone in the neighborhood—bumped off by one of the criminal mobs that had been running amok in this town since Prohibition. Stefan might find out who the triggerman was, might even discover why it happened, but as for evidence, or an arrest—

It wasn't going to happen.

So far, after sending uniforms out to canvass the area for three buildings in every direction, they hadn't a single witness who even thought they'd seen anything useful.

All he was doing here was marking time until the wagon showed up for the body. He hoped they'd get here soon; he wanted to get out of here. He didn't like the way the past seemed to stick to this place, sucking him in. In another few hours he might start walking back to St. John's, where he hadn't been since the funeral.

If they'd show up, he could get all of this out of his mind, get the report on this written up before lunch, and then maybe he could move on to some productive police work. If there was any such thing in this town.

"Detective Ryzard?"

Stefan turned to face the voice, which came from the entrance of the alley. A young man was there, giving him a quizzical look. Stefan's first thought was: *federal agent.* He looked like one of Hoover's boys, too damn neat.

Stefan nodded.

"Pleased to meet you." He walked over to Stefan and extended his hand, and for a moment Stefan thought: *lawyer.*

Stefan didn't take the offered hand. "Who in blazes are you?" Another thought crossed his mind, this one the most annoying: *reporter.*

"This is a crime scene, son. Are you supposed to be here?"

The young man looked crestfallen and lowered his hand. "I think so, sir. You are Detective Ryzard? They sent me here to meet you from the Central Station."

Last thought: *trainee. They've assigned me a goddamn trainee.* Stefan shook his head. "You have a name?"

"Nuri," he said after a moment of apparent confusion. "Nuri Lapidos. Sorry, I'm new here and—"

"They assigned you to me so I can show you the ropes, right?"

"I guess that's more or less it."

Stefan shook his head. "They could have warned me," he muttered to himself.

There was an oddly fatalistic sigh from Nuri, and he said, "If there's a problem, I can wait by the car."

"No, there's no problem."

Nuri Lapidos took a few steps around Stefan and looked down at the end of the alley where the corpse lay. "So what have you got here?"

"Why don't you tell me?"

Nuri looked up at him, then crouched by the body where it was sprawled. "He was dumped here, wasn't he?"

"Why do you say that?" Stefan prodded him.

"Position of the body, and no sign of blood from the wound on anything but his clothes." He kept staring at the body. "An execution. They had the poor bastard on his knees when they shot him—a garage or a parking lot from the oil stains." He pointed at the guy's pants where some dark stains peeked from beneath the blood.

He pushed back a sleeve and looked at the guy's right wrist. "He was tied or handcuffed. There's signs of abrasion."

Stefan nodded, "That's not bad."

Nuri stood up. "He was on his side long enough for lividity to set in, probably the trunk of a car." He stepped back next to Stefan. "He looks like a boxer. The fella's got heavy scarring on his hands, and on what's left of his face. You can see his nose's been broken more than once."

"Yeah," Stefan said with a touch of irony in his voice, "a boxer."

Nuri shrugged. "Well, someone who beat people up for a living."

Stefan nodded. The victim was some hood's pet gorilla, and someone had more than likely plugged him to get at his employer. Stefan looked Nuri up and down and revised his initial impression of the man. He was young, but not as young as he looked. The neat clothes and the overly open expression distracted from his gaze, which bore an intelligence that most of Stefan's colleagues lacked.

Stefan extended his hand and said, "When the wagon gets here, let me buy you lunch."

Sol's Diner was a little hole-in-the-wall place on East Ninth, a stone's throw from the nightclubs on Short Vincent. The proximity to all the glitz made the place seem that much darker, even in midday. Stefan didn't care; at times he preferred the dimness, and it was a small price to pay for Sol's corned-beef sandwiches.

He sat across from Nuri in one of the booths near the back. As they waited for their order, Stefan asked, "So what brings you to my little corner of Cleveland?"

Nuri gave him a quick grin. "I hitched a ride in a squad car."

"Yeah." Stefan leaned back and loosened his tie. "You know that's not what I mean. College educated, aren't you?"

"The damage shows?" Nuri chuckled. "Mama really wanted a lawyer." He pinched his fingers and held them up. "Mrs. Lapidos' little boy came this close. Somehow I drifted from criminal law to criminology, and here I am, degree and all."

Stefan shook his head. "A cop with a Bachelors—"

"Masters."

"You know, when I first saw you, I had you pegged for a federal agent. Why aren't you one of Hoover's boys? It probably pays better."

Nuri chuckled. "Oh, yeah, I can see the newsreels now, 'Nuri Lapidos, the Jewish G-man.' No, I don't think I'm what J. Edgar is looking for."

"Oh, sorry."

Nuri shook his head. "Don't be. I wanted to be part of a real police department anyway."

The waitress came and slid plates in front of them.

"Well, the department's *real,* all right," Stefan said, picking up his sandwich and taking a bite out of it.

Nuri had only ordered toast and coffee. He took a triangular slice and dipped it in his cup. "That sounds a little bitter."

Stefan set down his sandwich. "It *is* bitter. Some days I just pray for a little shame in this city. I swear, sometimes it seems that half the department is taking payoffs from someone."

"You're exaggerating."

Stefan shook his head. "Just wait until you collar someone with connections and see him walk out of the building before you finish the paperwork. Officers, detectives, judges—"

"You weren't kidding when you said the investigation on the guy in the alley wasn't going to go anywhere?"

Stefan nodded. "There's no way we're ever going to get something like that prosecuted in this county, maybe nowhere in the whole state. Assuming we even find out who killed him." Stefan took a sip of his own coffee. It went down like molten lead, solidifying into a weight in his stomach. "Whatever happens in this town, someone in the department is being paid to look the other way. Hard to believe, but I think it's gotten worse since they repealed Prohibition."

Nuri shook his head.

"You think I'm kidding? When we were dry, a hell of a lot of people made a lot of money in liquor. A *lot.* Regular cops got used to looking the other way. One bad law corrupted this whole city, decivilized us until law itself became devalued. Now we don't even have the excuse of a bad law."

Nuri shrugged. "So Prohibition was a bad idea. I doubt anyone'd argue with you there. You make it sound as if Cleveland was the reincarnation of Gomorrah."

Stefan sipped his coffee. "Sometimes I wonder."

2

Edward Andrassy sat in a bar as night descended, waiting for an old man. It was ironic. He had spent most of his adult life waiting for old men of one sort or another. If not for himself, then for the women or the boys who occasionally worked for him. It was a life few would envy, and he had spent the last few months trying to get out of it. He had been offered something that was pretty much unbelievable, and priceless if it were true.

Eternal life, he thought, sipping beer that was strangely tasteless now.

Listening to Him the first few times, it seemed so simple. It was impossible to say no, even when He started feeding them His blood. It wasn't even hard to call Him Master after that. What bothered Andrassy was when it came to others' blood.

He was still human, apparently, bound to Him, but not close enough to ignore the taste of someone else's blood in his mouth.

Now he waited for an old man, someone an age older than anyone he had ever met save his Master, Melchior. He hoped that this old man would be able to tell him a way through to where he was going, a way that wasn't lined with so much death.

The man he was meeting was his Master's enemy, but Andrassy was past caring. He had seen all the people who had come under Melchior's control become less and less human, more and more extensions of Melchior. Even Flo, who had started off the most human, even she was less moved at the carnage that Melchior fed them upon.

Andrassy set aside the beer, unfinished. He watched the

sky darken outside and wondered how many sunsets he would see.

Eventually a presence filled the crowded bar, a pressure at the back of his neck that told Andrassy that the man he'd been waiting for was here. One of the blood who didn't belong to Melchior. It was reassuring to think that there were others that weren't of his master; it meant that the Master's way wasn't the only way.

A hand touched his shoulder, and a voice said, "Let us walk away from here."

At the touch, it seemed that Andrassy had entered a world that only contained him and the old man. The bar and the crowd inside it seemed to fade away, and no one noticed their exit. The old man he left with was named Anacreon, and Andrassy suspected that he was one of the most powerful ones of the blood in this city. Physically, he didn't look like much. He was short, dumpy, middle-aged.

The old man was nearly six hundred years old.

Andrassy didn't believe that just because the old man said so. He believed it because he could feel the centuries in the old man's presence. He believed it in the sense of power he had next to him. He believed it because in Anacreon's presence was the only time he didn't fear his Master. In Anacreon, he saw someone who could protect him, someone who might be on a par with Melchior.

They walked through the streets of the Roaring Third, past the bars and tenements, past the hustlers and the prostitutes. None paid them attention, as if they weren't quite real.

As they walked, the old man spoke, "You must tell me everything you can now." The old man was insistent, and waves of the old man's will pushed against Andrassy's.

But Andrassy wasn't stupid, and he wasn't going to cave immediately. He had enough of his own will to act against his Master; he wasn't going to give anything to the old man without something in return. The old man wanted Melchior, and information was all Andrassy had to bargain with.

"You know what I want," Andrassy said.

"You don't realize what you ask."

"I want what He'd give me, without the strings. You

want me to roll over on someone without getting something in return?''

The old man shook his head, "You ask me to warn your Master before I have anything to convince the Council to move against him.''

"I gave you the corpse. Ain't that enough?''

"For me,'' he said, "Laila's death is enough. Your Master has violated the Covenant in a grievous manner. But for me to act without first convincing the Council would be little more than another violation of the Covenant. Taking you over the threshold now would warn him of what is to come.''

"So why am I talking to you, old man?''

Anacreon turned and placed his hands on Andrassy's shoulders. The touch was like a lightning bolt through his body. Andrassy's mouth snapped shut as he felt the strength behind Anacreon's withering gaze. Under that stare, Andrassy felt as if his shoulders were being peeled apart.

Despite a gaze that struck Andrassy like a blow, Anacreon did not raise his voice. "Listen. You are thrall to this killer. You will not be free until he is dead. As for what you ask, you have it already. Enough of the blood runs through your veins that were you to fall now to mortal death, you would be reborn. Reborn a thrall. All I need is the Council to act against him, and when he is gone you would be born of your own blood. *Give me what I need.*''

They stood like that, and it seemed hours before Andrassy realized that the street life had abandoned them. The streets were empty of people now. They stood between a deserted warehouse and a vacant lot. Andrassy had never felt more alone.

"What do you want?''

"Very first— Your Master. In his secret heart, what has he named himself?''

Andrassy's lips moved to form the word, but he never had a chance to speak it. From the darkness around them, the wind carried a whispered name, "Melchior.''

The old man let go, and Andrassy fell to the ground as if those hands were all that had been holding him upright. Anacreon turned around, facing down the street so fast that Andrassy barely saw him move. He faced an area of deepening shadow at the end of the street.

"You think to surprise me?" The words floated on the wind, sinking so deep into Andrassy's brain it hurt. He felt it in the pit of his stomach, in the way his heart tried to tear free of his chest. His Master was here, and Andrassy had led Him here.

Anacreon faced the darkness, and his body radiated strength, a bright flare of unseen light. His body twisted like water, muscles rippling, bones shifting. "Melchior," the thing that was Anacreon said. "An old name."

"Yes," replied the wind.

"An arrogant name," Anacreon said. The old man was no more. What stood in his place was a form that was somewhere between an angel and a demon. Its skin seemed to glow with an inner light, and its claws seemed metallic in the streetlight. The perfection of form was painful for Andrassy to look at.

"The last name you will hear."

Anacreon spread its wings, and the darkness descended upon him.

The light and darkness tore at each other. Andrassy, on the ground, felt every blow as if it was falling on his own body. He should have moved, run, done anything to get away from what was happening. But he stayed there, frozen.

Melchior seemed little more than a shadow. But Anacreon's metal claws tore into it and tore pieces away. For a few eternal moments, it seemed that his Master was no match for the angelic thing wrestling him. Then something changed. The shadow seemed to wrap itself around Anacreon's head, and there was a gleam of metal that wasn't from any claw.

Something tore through flesh and Andrassy closed his eyes.

In the darkness he heard something drink.

Andrassy didn't run. There was nowhere he could have gone. When he opened his eyes, his Master stood there, over a body that was just the old man again. In his hands Melchior held Anacreon's head. Scars raked across Melchior's body, flesh torn so badly that it was a miracle that he still stood. As Andrassy watched, the wounds closed up.

"That was . . . inconvenient," Melchior said. "You brought me to this too soon, Andrassy. I'm still gathering myself. You will have to pay." He walked up to Andrassy, and his will clamped down on him. In the man's mind there were no longer any thoughts but those of his Master.

He would be punished, and the Master's children would feed.

3

On Sunday, the Church descended on Stefan's Gomorrah. Cleveland, one of the midwestern strongholds of Catholicism, was host to the Seventh National Eucharist Congress. A religious fervor gripped the city in a mood that was more appropriate to a Rome or a Jerusalem.

Few were immune from the force of the event, whatever their faith. Tens of thousands of onlookers crowded Euclid Avenue, lining the streets to watch the procession. They packed the sidewalks, in some cases spilling onto the lawns of the remaining handful of old mansions on Millionaire's Row.

No one objected to the tide of immigrant labor trampling once-luxurious lawns. The mansions that didn't stand vacant were mostly occupied by some charitable institution that closed on Sunday.

As the procession marched past the remnants of nineteenth-century aristocracy, only one of the grand old houses turned other than a blind eye toward it. A massive stone structure, isolated from its cousins on the avenue, a building that seemed to resist the oncoming century by a combination of inertia and force of will.

High in one of the third-floor windows, a man who called himself Eric Dietrich, one of the first millionaires to occupy Millionaire's Row since the end of the Great War, stared down at the procession.

"All they need is a wounded Christ dragging his cross in front of them," he said.

The man seated in the room behind Dietrich winced and said, "Please, can we do without the blasphemy?"

Dietrich turned and faced the man, smiling slightly. "You

are in my house, Mr. Van Sweringen. If I say they should nail a Christ up in Public Square in front of that Tower of yours, what right have you to complain?"

Oris Paxton Van Sweringen sat in the dusty wing-backed chair and glared at Dietrich. It had been a long, long, time since he had to endure people talking to him like that. He and his brother were two of the most powerful men in the United States.

Except, for the moment, they weren't. All Oris Van Sweringen could do was nod politely and agree, "Yes, this is your house. But you could be more accommodating to a guest."

Dietrich let loose a humiliating laugh. Oris shrank under the weight of it. It was as if this man, this evil bastard, had seen into his mind and had taken all the laughter, all the derision that had ever been heaped upon the odd pair of brothers and had focused it into a single sound.

Oris couldn't take it any longer. He stood. "I think this will be all, Mr. Dietrich."

Dietrich walked away from the window, shaking his head. "Are you in a position to walk away from me, Mr. Van Sweringen?"

Oris stayed silent, his face burning. He knew he should be talking through a lawyer. He knew he wasn't at his best one-on-one, especially without his brother's support. "You can talk to our lawyers," he said, trying to force some iron into his voice.

Mr. Dietrich kept walking around the room, forcing Oris to turn to remain facing him. Framed by furnishings out of the last century, Mr. Dietrich seemed almost spectral. He was six inches taller than Oris, with pale skin that, by contrast to the muddy colors of the old furniture, almost appeared bleached. His face was framed by hair of near-invisible blondness.

Dietrich stopped walking and tapped his fingers on an oak sideboard. His fingers smeared arcane patterns in the dust. "Why would I wish to talk to an intermediary?"

"You've made a rather complex offer, Mr. Dietrich," Oris said, regaining some of his composure. "We need some time to evaluate it. It needs to be handled by our lawyers and accountants. We're talking about the control of a three-billion-dollar—"

"I know exactly what we're talking about." Dietrich's voice was as cold and characterless as the skin of a corpse. He ran his hand across the sideboard, erasing the marks he'd made in the dust. "I know how adept you and Mantis are at manipulating the illusion of money. You stand upon a mountain of paper." Dietrich slowly turned to face Oris. "No lawyers. No accountants."

Oris shook his head. "This is different than the license we granted you. That was just space in the terminal, right-of-way on some track. That was something a handshake could settle. This is so far beyond that it is beyond comprehension."

Dietrich spun around and stared at Oris. His eyes were purple-red, which Oris had always taken as a sign of albinism. Right now those eyes seemed to burn. The feeling was so intense that Oris felt his skin heat up. He reached up and loosened his tie.

"Enough," Dietrich said. He didn't raise his voice, but the word felt like a blow.

He took a step toward Oris.

"What will happen in New York if you do not have the capital? If your backers fall through?" Dietrich made a dismissive gesture with his hand, spreading a cloud of dust that settled slowly to the ground.

"They'll come through. We've drawn up contracts—"

"More paper," Dietrich said. "If I say so, you will go to New York naked."

"You have no right to interfere—"

Dietrich laughed. The sound burned into Oris' skull. "You have two choices. Agree to my terms, and you will go to the auction seven days from now, make your bid, and walk away with most of your empire intact. Or walk away from me, find your backers changing heart, and go to New York penniless." He took a step closer. Oris wanted to back away, but he couldn't move. "I am leaving for New York tonight. You will answer me now."

Oris felt the world crumbling away beneath him. Everything he and Mantis had built was teetering on a precipice. The whole empire—railroads, real estate, the corporate glue that held it all together—was being torn from his grasp again. It was humiliating enough to admit to J. P. Morgan that they couldn't meet the debt that bloomed in May, to watch as the bankers organized their public auction of everything the Van Sweringens had struggled to build. But the brothers had consented, after organizing a plan to retain what they had built.

Oris was supposed to go to New York on the 30th on behalf of a newly incorporated entity under the Van Sweringens' control. They already had the financial backing necessary to bid on the collateral being auctioned. It was a deal that had taken months to put together.

And now this shadow investor, a man who dealt in cash and handshake deals, was telling Oris that all that preparation was for nothing.

He wished Mantis was here. Facing this man without his brother for support was more than he could take. "We spent months putting the deal together. How could you undo it?"

Dietrich stared into Oris' eyes, and Oris couldn't turn away. There was a searing heat deep inside them, an intensity that terrified him and held him spellbound. "You are going to incorporate Midamerica with money from Mr. Ball and Mr. Tomlinson. How accommodating do you think their heirs would be?"

Oris wanted to back away. He wanted to *run*. He wanted anything other than to be here facing this man. But no matter what he wanted, he couldn't move. He couldn't even turn away or lower his gaze from Dietrich's burning stare. Every shred of doubt he had about Dietrich's will, his intent, his ability to carry out on his threats—all of it was torn away from him. Oris believed.

"You shall accept me as the unwritten part of Midamerica, won't you?"

Oris nodded, unable to speak.

As if the gesture broke a magic spell, Oris was suddenly able to move and break eye contact. He stumbled away toward the sideboard, leaning on it with one hand and rubbing his neck with the other. He was out of breath and felt as if someone had been trying to strangle him.

"Why?" he asked in a hoarse voice. A crystal decanter sat on a tray on the sideboard. He grabbed it with a shaking hand and filled a glass. It was water. Oris drank it, wishing for something stronger. "Why torment us like this? You have the resources to take it whole yourself. . . ."

Dietrich laughed. "You hired a man whose sole job is to keep your name out of the papers. You should understand when someone wishes to keep his privacy. That mountain of paper you built your empire upon, it provides me with shade from unwanted eyes."

Oris put down the glass and nodded. "Send me whatever arrangements you want, Mr. Dietrich. I'll be going now." He picked up his jacket from a chair by the door. It came away gray with dust.

"One last thing," Dietrich called after him. It was the cold conversational tone again, the corpselike voice that made Oris' skin crawl.

Oris stopped in the doorway and said, "What is it?"

"Never assume that I will take secrecy over power."

Oris shuddered as he left.

Stefan Ryzard was driving home to Lakewood after a long day of public service. All the talk at the Central Station was about how the Catholics were taking over the city, and Stefan was glad to escape. It wasn't the talk about the Eucharist Congress that bothered him, so much as the event itself. It was as if the descent of faith upon the city somehow brought his own deficits into greater relief.

It was after eleven now, and darkness had claimed the city for its own. Nothing seemed to stir this late on a Sunday. The stillness was probably why, as his car approached the Detroit-Superior Bridge, he noticed something out of the corner of his eye. There was ominous movement down Huron, toward the Flats of the Cuyahoga.

He rolled to a stop where Huron descended from Superior. Below, where Huron bottomed out on the shores of the river, Stefan saw a congregation of the derelicts and vagabonds who populated Cleveland's industrial bottomland. Normally it wouldn't rate any attention, it was a sign of the times, like a peeling NRA poster.

But there was something definitely wrong about the collection of tramps down there.

Stefan stopped the car and checked his revolver before he got out. He stood at the top of Huron, looking down, trying to interpret what he saw. Half a dozen men formed a semicircle around a lone figure. Some of the men carried boards, bottles, and one carried a length of pipe. The focus of their attention was a colored man who had backed up against a wall facing them.

Stefan descended, at first thinking he was about to break up a nasty lynching. But as he closed on the scene, he realized that whatever was going on here, it wasn't that simple.

The men in the circle, while they gripped their makeshift weapons as if they had murder in their hearts, had fear in their eyes, and were backing away. The man at their focus seemed terrified, whipping his head around, staring wild-eyed at his potential attackers. But as Stefan approached, it seemed almost as if he was looking *beyond* the men with the weapons.

Stefan walked down the center of the street, constantly shifting his attention, looking for any additional people. He could feel the tension in the air. Whatever was going on was near to exploding. He stopped a few dozen yards from the scene, his revolver out but pointed at the ground.

"What's going on here?" he called out, in a steady tone that he hoped wouldn't startle someone into a regrettable action.

The circle of men kept backing away from the colored man. A few of them glanced toward him, but quickly returned their attention to the man huddled against the wall.

"Don't get too close to him," said the man with the pipe, "That's one crazy jig—he fractured Larry's skull!"

Stefan scanned the semicircle and saw that one of the men did have blood splattered around the side of his head, apparently a chunk torn out of his ear. Stefan looked at the Negro and saw that the man was unarmed, and looked on the verge of panic.

"He's out there!" the Negro said, pointing a steady finger somewhere beyond the men encircling him. The arm he raised was splattered with blood.

One of the men raised a two-by-four as if to club away the pointing arm. Stefan raised his revolver and said, "Everyone calm down and drop the weapons."

The one with the busted ear turned and said, "Who the hell do you think you . . ." His words trailed off when he saw the revolver. The bottle he carried slipped from his hand to shatter at his feet, spattering his pants leg with the dregs it'd contained.

"The name's Ryzard, *Detective* Ryzard. Now drop all the weapons."

"Look," said the first one who'd spoken, gesturing with his makeshift club, "This nigger—"

Stefan leveled the gun at the man. *"Drop it."*

He backed away and dropped the pipe he carried. The others followed quickly, scattering their improvised weapons.

"I don't care what happened," Stefan said, "but I want all of you to beat it. *Now.*"

"But he—" the one with the ear motioned at the man they'd surrounded.

Stefan gestured with his head, keeping the gun steady. Slowly, way too slowly for Stefan's taste, they started moving away. All of them kept watching the terrified man, as if he were suddenly going to erupt into some sort of life-threatening attack.

Within a few minutes he was alone with the man, who looked as crazed as ever. He was still whipping his head around, staring wild-eyed into the darkness. As if the fellas who'd encircled him weren't even relevant.

Stefan took a deep breath and said, "Okay, now what's the problem?"

The man turned his face toward him, the wild eyes staring into his own. It was as if this was the first time the man had noticed him. It was also the first time that Stefan had gotten a good look at the man. The look wasn't encouraging. His face, from the cheekbones down, was shiny and wet. His teeth were stained dark red, as if he was coughing up blood.

"The devil is out here," he said. "His bulls are walking the tracks." He slid back along the brick wall, and with every step he seemed to shudder a little, as if he were in pain.

"Sure, sure." Stefan smiled in a way he hoped was reassuring. He put away the revolver. This fella did seem to be half out of his mind. Stefan raised his hands, "But the tracks are down there. You're up here."

The man kept edging away, but his movements lost a little of their jerky, panicked edge.

"Those men I chased off, were they beating on you?"

The man shook his head as if he didn't quite understand. "Get thee behind me, Satan."

Stefan kept inching toward the man, trying to keep from spooking him into running. "I work for the Cleveland Police Department, but I'm no devil. I was an altar boy."

The man started crouching, as if he thought Stefan meant to attack him. Stefan stopped approaching. The man shook his head and said, "Wicked, wicked."

This close, the man looked really bad off. He was bleeding out of his mouth, his nose, and his ears, and his overalls were spattered with blood in a way that Stefan found particularly disturbing. He had the feeling that the man was leaking his life away in front of him.

He began cursing himself for chasing away this man's attackers. If they were responsible for what happened, Stefan would never forgive himself.

"I have to get you to a hospital," he said softly, and took another step. The man scrambled away and made a sound that was more a keening than anything else.

After a moment, Stefan said, "Our Lord, who art in heaven . . ."

It worked. Some of the wildness leaked out of the man's eyes, and he seemed, for the first time, to be able to really see Stefan. Stefan kept talking, "Hallowed be thy name. Thy Kingdom come . . ."

Through the prayer, he managed to walk up to the man without him scrambling away. When he reached him, and put a hand on his shoulder, the panic had been replaced by an expression of extreme weariness. The fear had been all that was holding him up. By the time Stefan reached him, he was collapsing to the ground, and it was all Stefan could do to get an arm around him.

The last coherent thing the man said was, "Pray for me."

By the time Stefan got him to the car he was unconscious and barely breathing.

Hours later, in a hallway at St. Vincent's Charity, Stefan leaned back in a chair and waited. He didn't realize he had fallen asleep until he heard a doctor calling his name.

"Detective Ryzard "

Stefan jerked his head upright, and the chair—which had

been leaning back against the wall—obliged him by tilting forward, the forward legs hitting the linoleum with a crash.

"Yes, yes." Stefan emerged from the chair, which seemed intent on pitching him onto the floor. One hand reached out to shake hands with the doctor, the other grabbed his hat which was spilling out of his lap.

The doctor took his hand and said, "I understand you brought the man in."

Stefan nodded.

"You don't know the man's name? Have any idea who he is?"

"No, I don't." Stefan smoothed his hair and replaced his hat. "How's he doing?"

"I'm sorry, he didn't make it." The doctor looked back down the hallway from where he'd come. Stefan looked at him and realized how young the guy seemed. Dark hair, Errol Flynn mustache, he looked like some actor pretending to be a doctor.

"Didn't make it," Stefan thought. *Weak set of words, right up there with "passed away."*

"How did he die?" Stefan asked, feeling a growing anger at the men he'd chased away earlier in the night. Also anger at himself for letting it happen.

"Well, it isn't going to be a police matter, if that's what you're asking."

"What?"

"Natural causes. He died because we couldn't get his internal hemorrhaging under control in time before he bled to death."

"I grabbed this fella from a circle of club-wielding nuts, and it's *natural causes*?"

The doctor nodded. His eyes held a grave expression that seemed older than his features. "No one laid a hand on him as far as I can tell. No external trauma at all, no bruising, abrasions, broken bones— The man was sick, and suffered severe bleeding into the lungs, stomach, intestines—"

Stefan took a step back and said, "Good lord, what did he have?"

"I don't know, which is why the patient's history is important." He shook his head and sighed. "But you just picked him up off the street, right?"

"Screaming about how the devil was after him."

"He was delirious? Delusional?"

"That's a word for it."

The doctor shook his head again. "Maybe that might give me a lead on what was really wrong with him, before someone decides it was all TB and I shouldn't be wasting my time on it." He patted Stefan on the shoulder and said, "Go home, get some sleep."

"Okay. You're *sure* it's natural causes?"

The doctor nodded. "Believe it or not, people do die of that in this town."

Stefan turned to leave and the doctor said, "One more thing. If you see anyone with similar symptoms, or find out anything about his history, could you contact me. Doctor McCutcheon."

Stefan nodded. "Is whatever this is contagious?"

"I don't know."

Stefan shook his head and said, "I'll give you a call if the Devil starts chasing me."

As he left, he wondered if, in this town and with his job, he would be able to tell.

4

Edward Mullen worked long hours as a security guard at St. Vincent's. It wasn't a great job, but it was a job, and deep into the night it was peaceful. He sat behind a desk by the morgue, leaning his head on his hand and waiting for his shift to end.

The area was brightly lit and chilly, the tile walls reflecting light without heat. Mullen was used to it. Occasionally he would look up at the clock on the wall behind the desk and find that it was only another five minutes toward the end of his shift.

Nothing ever happened down here. The most exciting thing to happen this night was when they'd rolled down a fresh body.

Mullen was yawning, at about four in the morning, when he caught a shadow out of the corner of his eye. It was the size of a man, and was moving through the hallway.

Mullen stood up to greet the visitor. He was about to say something, but he was suddenly wrapped in an unaccountable feeling of dread.

The shadow strode through the hallway, shedding the bright light as if it never actually touched him. Mullen only had the impression of a tall man with long hair.

The man stopped in front of Mullen's desk and looked down at him. It was as if the man had carried his own darkness with him, wrapping himself in it. Mullen had a sense of pale skin and blond hair, but he didn't really see it. What he did see was the figure's eyes. The eyes, colored red-violet that faded almost to black, seized Mullen's attention. He couldn't look away.

"You have something that belongs to me," the figure said.

The words settled across Mullen's brain like a brand. He knew that he stood in the presence of something evil. All he could do was nod.

The figure waved a hand at the doors which led to the morgue. The room beyond was empty of people, but Mullen heard movement inside. He heard the scraping of metal, and then suddenly the doors swung open.

Walking through them was the Negro, naked, blood still caked around his mouth and chest. Mullen recognized the corpse that had been wheeled in earlier in the evening. The body moved like an automaton, and Mullen wanted to shrink away.

Edward Mullen was frozen to the spot.

The shadow reached out a hand with long fingers and touched Mullen's face. The touch burned like ice.

"You will tell everybody a story. You will not mention me."

Edward Mullen looked deep into those blood-colored eyes and couldn't conceive of refusing. At that point Mullen believed he was in the presence of the Devil himself.

At around six in the afternoon, Nuri Lapidos rode the Shaker Rapid home. He was just getting comfortable with the routine, a new city, a new job. Detective Ryzard was proving an able, if somewhat somber, introduction to the city and the department. Though the more he saw of the city, the more grateful he was for managing to find an apartment in the suburbs.

He was riding home, sometime between five-thirty and six, when the train began slowing down. Nuri looked up from the paper, slightly relieved to be distracted from the depressing stories coming out of Germany, and looked out the window. It wasn't easy, he was on the aisle, and the man next to him was already craning his neck to see the commotion ahead that was causing the train to slow.

His seatmate wasn't the only spectator. The train was passing through a valley, and before Nuri saw anything of the commotion on the tracks, he could see spectators lined up on the tops of the cliffs overlooking the tracks.

Nuri stood up, and finally could see the ground ahead of

the train. He expected some sort of workmen fixing the tracks, but instead, he saw police. Three or four uniformed officers, and at least two detectives wandering around the underbrush at the side of the tracks, beneath a brush-covered hillside.

Curiosity had always been Nuri's curse. He got up and made his way down to the conductor.

He pulled out his badge, "Can you stop the train and let me out here?"

The man scowled and looked at the badge. "You want out, here, now?"

Nuri nodded.

"Sheesh, well, I guess you paid your dime." He pulled on a lever and the train started to slow even more. Before it'd rolled to a complete stop, the doors opened. "There you are, beat it."

Nuri had to take a jump that almost cost him an ankle on the gravel. He stumbled away from the train as it began speeding up. Through the still-open door he could hear the conductor. "Give people a badge, and they think they own the damn railroad."

Nuri watched the train slide by the scene ahead of him. He edged away from the tracks and started walking up to the two detectives. One was already starting toward him, apparently to see what the Rapid had disgorged.

They met about a hundred yards from the center of attention. "Can I help you?" the man asked. He was tall man with a mustache, and he looked as if he was already irritated by the massing spectators.

"Hello," Nuri held out the badge which was still in his hand, "Detective Lapidos, I was wondering if I could help you?"

The man extended a hand. "Orly May, and I guess you can. Me and Emil just got here about ten, fifteen minutes ago—well, let me show you."

Detective May led Nuri to the focus of all the attention. Two men May said were Erie Railroad police were talking with the other detective, Emil. It was obvious what they were talking about before May led him into earshot. About ten feet from the policemen lay a man's body, naked except for a pair of black socks.

At first he thought that brush was concealing part of the

body, but as he closed on the scene he could see that the head wasn't hidden by brush. It wasn't there. As if to add insult to injury, the corpse had also been emasculated.

Nuri shook his head at the sight. Bodies he had seen before, but the mutilation made it more disturbing than it should have been. He felt light in the stomach. "That's the first one," May said to him. "What's really creepy about all this is the lack of blood."

Nuri nodded. The corpse was remarkably clean of all the violence done to it. "Almost as if the killer washed the body off before dumping it here." As May nodded, the rest of what he said sank in. "You said 'the first one'?"

"Over here," May said, waving him over to a patch of thick scrub about thirty feet away from the corpse.

Nuri could smell it before he saw it, an acrid tinny odor that made his nose itch. Rounding the bush, Nuri saw the body of a shorter, older man. Laid out as carefully as the other body, arms at the sides, feet together. Just like the other, this man had been beheaded and castrated. Unlike the other, it looked as if the man had been dead for a much longer time. He mentioned it, and May nodded. "Both killed somewhere else, at different times. Which means the killer kept this one around for a while."

Nuri suppressed a shudder and asked, "You ever see a body decompose like this?"

The body did seem oddly discolored, reddish, as if severely sunburned. The skin had become almost leathery. "Maybe some sort of preservative chemical," May said, "so he could keep the body longer."

Nuri took a step back and felt something crunch under his foot. He jerked, afraid he had stepped on some part of the body. He lifted his foot and breathed a sigh of relief.

"What is it?" May asked.

"Nothing, just a dead sparrow." He kicked the thing, and its wings splayed like a fallen angel's.

"Watch it," May said, "We want to be careful we don't miss any evidence—"

May was interrupted when one of the railroad police called out, "I've found a head!"

The valley was called Kingsbury Run, and it cut through the east side of Cleveland like a knife scar between down-

town and east Fifty-Fifth. It held the tracks that carried the
Shaker Rapid lines, and all the passenger trains that passed
through the Union Terminal, from the Chesapeake and
Ohio to the Nickel Plate. At night it was an unlit haven
for those transients with enough fortitude to risk the darkness and dangers of jumping a moving freight car in the
gloom. During the day it was populated by strays, children,
and dogs.

After five-thirty on September 23, 1935, a new population came to Kingsbury Run. Dozens of Cleveland police,
detectives, and railroad police, began walking the tracks to
discover anything related to the two headless bodies. The
unrealized fear was that another corpse might turn up;
the unrealized hope was that they might find some clue to
the identity of the murderer.

They found the rest of the murdered men, the heads
buried close to the bodies, and the genitalia had been
tossed casually to the side, as if an afterthought by the
murderer.

By evening, the police search up and down the Run had
attracted an endless crowd of spectators lining the crest
overlooking the murder scene. The ritual of the murder
investigation was observed as intently as the procession of
Catholic faith had been the night before.

Stefan Ryzard was one of the detectives who were not
converging on Kingsbury Run. He had other business.

He stood leaning against the wall of an interview room
while, sitting, handcuffed in a chair, was a man named
Larry Alessandro. On the side of Larry's head was a white
bandage covering his ear, the center darkened slightly
with blood.

"You ain't got no right to hold me here!" he said for
the dozenth time or so. Stefan simply nodded and said, "So
you've told me. But you are here, Mr. Alessandro, so why
don't you just tell me what happened."

"Look, the nigger bastard attacked me, look!" He jerked
his hands and ended up shrugging his shoulder at the bandage on the side of his head.

"The man's dead, Mr. Alessandro. Show him some
respect."

Larry Alessandro spat at Stefan's feet. "I ain't got to show respect for no nigger living or dead."

Stefan looked at the spot of moisture on the floor. "Spitting in public is a misdemeanor, Mr. Alessandro." He looked up and said, "It spreads TB."

Larry opened his mouth and Stefan said, "Shut that trap for a moment and let me explain something to you. We have a dead body, and as long as I have someone to hang for it, all the paperwork comes out nice and tidy. I like nice and tidy paperwork."

"But—"

"You have to give me a reason not to shove you into a hole where everyone can forget your ugly mug ever existed." Stefan walked up and leaned over Larry and said, "Like what happened. Tell me."

"He attacked me—"

"You keep saying that. I want details, Larry. I want your life story from the point you first saw this man."

"Goddamn it," Larry muttered. "You want to know what happened? I'll tell you what the fuck happened. Me and a bunch of other guys were minding our own business down in the flats. Under the bridge, passing the bottle around, and something starts screaming at us—"

"Who was screaming?"

Larry ignored the question. He had started the story, and the words were tumbling out. "It was the worst noise I'd ever heard. The sound of an animal in pain, like a dog that'd had its back broke. But you could tell a man was making the sound. Didn't end, it just kept getting closer and closer. Before we could tell what direction that sound was coming from, this blood-soaked jig jumps out of the darkness at me."

"He was already covered with blood?"

"He screamed something about the devil in me, or the devil in him. How he had to get it out. Then he proceeds to bite my fucking ear off. That boy just wasn't right in the head. The others pushed him off of me, and if you saw the way he was looking at all of us, you'd have started picking up pipes and bricks yourself. But we never touched him. We circled around each other, none of us wanted close to the bastard, the way he looked."

Stefan looked at Larry and decided he believed him.

What he said matched the scene he had come upon last night, and it matched up with what the doctor had said about the death of his John Doe.

"Had you ever seen this man before last night?"

"No."

"Where did he come from, what direction?"

"What the fuck does that matter?"

"It matters to me, and I think that's all you have to worry about right now."

Larry shook his head and shrugged. "From the south I think, back toward where the tracks feed into the tower."

Stefan went over the story a few more times with Larry, then he had an ambulance come to the Central Station and pick him up. Larry wasn't too enthusiastic about going. He was even less enthusiastic when Stefan told him that the man who had bitten him had been deathly sick. But Stefan managed to package him for the trip to St. Vincent's despite his objections. Even if what John Doe had wasn't something as contagious as TB, Larry needed his ear fixed.

Stefan found himself hoping it was TB, even though he'd been exposed to all that blood. TB or some other unexceptional, earthly sickness. John Doe's pronouncements about the Devil made Stefan uneasy.

When he went back up to his desk, he saw Nuri Lapidos there, talking on the phone.

"I thought you went home already—"

Nuri held up a hand and spoke into the phone, "Yes. Yes. I'm sorry, honey. Something came up, on the trip home in fact. Well, it's sort of gruesome. These two bodies—okay, I won't tell you any more." Nuri looked up at Stefan and shrugged. "Maybe another time. Love you, too, bye." Nuri hung up the phone, and looked up at Stefan. "I *did* start home. Missed a date, too."

Stefan looked and saw that Nuri's normally impeccable suit was splattered with mud, and his trouser legs were covered with burrs. "Where've you been?"

"I've had a thorough introduction to a new part of town, Kingsbury Run, searching for body parts."

"What?"

"You haven't heard? I thought the story'd be all over the station by now."

"I've been busy," Stefan said, "questioning a witness about a death last night."

"Well, we have two pretty mysterious deaths down by the railroad tracks. Two men, heads and privates cut off, the bodies cleaned of blood and laid out neatly as you please by the tracks."

"Lord save us." Stefan sat down at his desk.

"The coroner has the bodies now." Nuri shook his head and pulled a package of cigarettes out of his pocket. He offered one to Stefan.

Stefan shook his head, and Nuri took out a cigarette for himself. He lit it, and took a deep drag. "Why do that to someone?" Nuri muttered, more to himself than to Stefan. "Why mutilate a corpse?"

"There is evil in the world." Stefan looked down at his desk. There was a note slipped in at the corner of his blotter. Stefan pulled it out.

"Yes, I know," Nuri said. "But evil usually has some rationale behind it. Someone has a reason."

Stefan nodded, reading the note. There'd been a phone message for him while he was questioning Alessandro. It took him a second to place the name, "Sean McCutcheon." Fatigue had eroded some of his memory. Then it came to him, the youngish doctor last night, Errol Flynn mustache. It hadn't registered at first because the note omitted the "Doctor." The note was vague, just a name and phone number. Stefan wondered if it meant that Doctor McCutcheon had identified the cause of death.

Nuri was still talking, watching the smoke collect above his head. "It's the work of a crazy man. That's the obvious conclusion."

Stefan picked up the phone and started dialing. "You don't think it is?"

Nuri shook his head. "When it comes down to it, it ain't my case. It's just that I have an eerie feeling. There was a methodical, almost ritualistic feeling to the scene, like it was some sort of warning."

The phone started ringing, and after a few moments Stefan heard a muffled, "Hello?"

"Doctor McCutcheon?" Stefan said.

There was a mumble and a rustling on the other end,

and Stefan could picture the doctor crawling out of bed. What time was it anyway?

After a few minutes the doctor spoke, "Yes, yes. Detective Ryzard?"

"Yes." Obviously he'd been expecting the call. "I'm sorry if I woke you up."

"No matter. Just came off of a long shift, that's all." He yawned, "But I thought you should know what happened."

Something in the way the doctor phrased that made Stefan uneasy. It must have shown on his face because Nuri sat up and looked at him. "What's the matter?"

Stefan waited a few moments before he said, "What happened, Doctor?"

"The man you brought in last night. His body is gone."

There was a minute or so of silence before the doctor said, "Detective? Are you still there?"

"Yes," Stefan took a few more moments to let the words sink in. "What do you mean *gone?*"

"The body's gone missing. Somehow the hospital lost it."

"How do you *lose* a body?"

Nuri leaned over and asked, "Who lost a body?"

"I'm as mad as you are," Doctor McCutcheon said. "I don't know. But the fact is, the body is gone. The guard down in the morgue swears that someone from the coroner's office came by with all the right paperwork and signed out the cadaver. But the coroner's office says they didn't, and no one can find the paperwork."

"So someone stole it?" Stefan asked. *Who would* steal *a body?*

"Someone *stole* a body?" Nuri asked, his voice taking on a layer of incredulity.

"I don't know," the doctor said. "Who knows if the guard's telling the truth? He's lying about the paperwork; he could be trying to cover up some sort of administrative incompetence. The hospital's put him on leave until they straighten this out."

"What's the guard's name?" Stefan asked.

"Mullen, Edward Mullen. You can contact him through the hospital if you need to." The doctor yawned. "That's all I have for you. Sorry about the mess up."

"Thank you, Doctor." Stefan slowly hung up the telephone.

5

Thursday, September 26

Stefan Ryzard sat in the upper deck of Municipal Stadium, among a crowd of 150,000 people, trying not to think of death or Edward Mullen. The crowd was a strange mix, men in suits and hats next to men in overalls, young women in flowery hats, old women with beaded veils and black dresses. It was a random mix of everyone in the city, everyone linked only by the common gestures, the common responses, standing and sitting as one.

Below him, lit by electric arcs, sat the altar, tiny with distance.

The words of the mass echoed throughout the stadium, the priest's Latin distorted by the public address system. Midnight mass was supposed to be the culminating religious event of the Seventh National Eucharist Congress.

Stefan had wanted to reaffirm part of his crumbling faith. He had thought of going to St. John's, seeing his old pastor, Piotr Gerwazek, but he had never managed it. He hadn't been to a mass since Mary's funeral, and it had been so long now that he was afraid to see people he knew, afraid of the questions that Father Gerwazek might ask.

When he heard of the great mass here, he thought he might slip back into his faith anonymously, in the midst of a crowd of strangers. Somehow it didn't work like that.

He sat with thousands of people, here for the mass, and couldn't help thinking of them as spectators rather than worshipers. The setting was dissonant, too. This wasn't God's house, at least not the God to whom the wine below was being raised. The religion practiced here had Mel Harder pitching, and Earl Averill playing center field.

He sat and watched the ceremony, trying and failing to

gain any sort of connection with what was going on down on the field. The effort left him feeling, more than ever, that God had walked away from him, and from everything around him.

He left before they began communion.

Absent the thronging crowd, the parking lot was desolate. As Stefan walked away, he could still hear the words of God, amplified and reechoing, with no one out here to listen.

Stefan got into his blue Ford V-8, shutting the door on the sound. He drove slowly, as if he were sneaking away.

Almost inevitably his thoughts turned to death. The bodies that had been found in Kingsbury Run had distracted the city from thoughts of faith. The day the Congress had opened, people talked about how close the city had seemed to come toward God. It had taken a mere twenty-four hours for the mood to shift. The *Plain Dealer* was calling it the most bizarre double murder in Cleveland's history.

It was almost as if the bodies had been left as a warning against the arrogance of believing oneself so close to God.

Stefan turned east, away from home. He wasn't quite ready to face his empty apartment yet. His thoughts were too dark. He wove through the east side of downtown, passing the nightclubs and the lights of Short Vincent. He thought of stopping, but he didn't. Someone would recognize him, and because he was a cop, they would ask him about the murders in the Run.

He had no answers for them.

And no one cares about the man who died in the back of my car.

It was an evil irony that the man he had taken to the hospital had died the same evening as the headless men in the Run. The more spectacular murders had stolen any eulogy that the anonymous man might have had. Despite the disappearance of the body, it wasn't even an official police investigation. He was a nameless colored tramp—none thought him worth the trouble.

Even Edward Mullen the guard that had lost the corpse, seemed incredulous that Stefan was making such a fuss about the missing corpse. Stefan had taken him to the Central Station, and questioned him, and got nothing more than the repeated story that the coroner's office had picked the body up. In the end, he'd gotten nowhere and had let the man go.

Even so, Stefan had felt something dark had touched the man, something he was hiding. But it wasn't something Stefan could put a finger on, much less prove.

It was another fragment of evil that Stefan couldn't do anything about. Another empty case that would go nowhere. Another mystery ignored and filed away. Another victim who would be forever mute—

Almost out of some sense of predestination, Stefan found himself driving toward the dead end of East Forty-Ninth. Up ahead, beyond the end of the street, was the gully of Kingsbury Run.

He parked the car and stepped out into the cool night air.

He stepped over the barrier at the end of the street and began walking along the top of the bluffs on the southern side of the run. After a while he stopped. He stood on top of a hill overlooking the bottom of the Run, sixty feet or so below him. The scene below was inky black, except for where a lone railroad signal tower cast an eerie glow around the tracks below him.

Stefan had lived in Cleveland all his life, but he'd never known that this plot of ground overlooking the waste of Kingsbury Run was worthy of a name. However, in the last three days, Jackass Hill had attained a measure of fame. The bodies had been uncovered just below where he stood, discovered by a pair of teenage boys playing in the rugged terrain.

Stefan stood there a long time, letting thoughts of futility drain from him. He stared into the impenetrable darkness, as if there were some insight to be found there, some relief. If he had been younger, he might have prayed.

Clouds above him erased every feature of the sky, the only light in heaven the reflection of the city's electric glow.

A voice emerged from the darkness. "Troubled, aren't you?"

The sudden break of the stillness startled Stefan. He whirled upon the voice, his hand darting toward the holster at his shoulder. "Who's there?" he called out. His voice, at least, was firm, not revealing his sudden startlement.

A figure stepped from the shadow of a twisted elm, so

close that Stefan found it unbelievable that the man could have approached him without being heard.

"A fellow wanderer in the darkness," the man said, spreading his hands. "Nothing more."

In the distance a train whistle screamed into the night.

Seeing the man, Stefan stopped reaching for his holster and changed the movement of his hand into a brushing of his jacket. "This isn't the safest place to wander," Stefan said. At first, Stefan thought the man might be a tramp, here to catch a ride on the passing freight. But there was something in the man's manner that seemed to run counter to that impression.

It wasn't his clothes. He had the overalls of a laborer, and a dark porkpie set far back on his brow. But there was something in his bearing that set him apart from any of the unemployed army that the times had loosed upon the city. Hard times had beaten itself into the posture of such men, but the man facing him had a confident stance that bordered on arrogance.

"Then why do you wander here?" the man asked him. He spoke with a sly smile that Stefan didn't trust. It was a smile that changed into something else by the time it reached his eyes, eyes that were cold, remote, nearly colorless in the dimness.

"Unease," Stefan said, more of an answer than the stranger merited. He turned around, finding the stranger's gaze uncomfortable.

The man placed his hands in his pockets and stepped up next to Stefan. "This is an uneasy place."

Below them, the sound of a train grew louder, a screech and a roar in the darkness. Its light began to wash the eastern distance, preceding it.

Stefan doubted many tramps would try and hop this train here. This *was* an uneasy place now. "What do you know of what happened here?"

"Murder," the man said. "Murder most foul, as in the best it is, but this most foul, strange, and unnatural."

Stefan looked across at the man.

He shook his head, "I was an actor once, a long time ago. Ah, that things have come to this."

"What things?" Stefan asked. He had a feeling that he

had run across someone who knew about the murders. Instinct tensed him, readying him for a fight, or a chase.

The train's whistle screamed again, close enough that Stefan could hear motion in the sound. He turned to face his companion again, memorizing the profile as the other spoke.

"Things I cannot discuss with you." There was an ironic smile on the man's face. As the train shuddered by below them, its lamps washed them in a white light. For a moment Stefan had a complete unobscured view of his companion.

His brows, and small pointed beard were black, like holes cut into his face. His mustache was fading to gray at the sides. His flesh was a perfect, even white, no marks, no scars, not even a shadow of a beard beyond the edges of his goatee. His eyes were a deep gray.

"If you know anything about the murders, I think you should tell me." Stefan had to raise his voice above the sound of the train passing below them. Boxcar after boxcar rolled by, each of them mute and remote.

The man was laughing, a soft chuckle that somehow cut through the rumble of the passing train. "So typical of the police, so little subtlety, so little heed of the consequences the truth might bring."

"If you . . ." Stefan's words stopped in his throat when he realized that he had not told this man he was a detective. His hand began reaching for his gun again. The train below seemed to have found the rhythm of his heart, the rachet of the rails marking the time of his pulse. "You'd better explain yourself, or we're going to take a trip to the station."

Something akin to panic gripped Stefan. He felt sweat in the small of his back, and he tasted fear, like blood, in the back of his throat. There was no accounting for it; the man he faced had made no threatening moves.

The man turned to Stefan as the whistle screamed again.

Stefan's hand found the butt of his gun and froze there, the metal ice-cold against his sweating palm.

"What would you do if you knew? What could you do?" He took a step forward, and Stefan tried to draw his gun. "The truth would destroy you." He took another step, and Stefan was paralyzed. The fear fed upon itself, so unnatural that the fear itself became a fuel for panic. The man placed a finger upon Stefan's lips. "Shush, my dear policeman."

It may have been the touch, or it might have been that the fear—like a dike—could only hold back so much potential action before it broke. In either event, Stefan's paralysis broke, and he stumbled backward, drawing his gun and leveling it at the man before him.

"Don't you move!" Stefan called out, little caring that the strains of fear cracked his voice.

The man shook his head. "Oh, dear me." He lowered his finger, which had been left in midair. "You would be a strong-willed one, wouldn't you?"

"Keep your hands in view," Stefan shouted over the noise of the passing train.

The man spread his hands and said, "Now that you have me, what will you do with me?"

"Who are you?"

"I could tell you anything, so call me Iago."

Stefan kept backing away from the man, Iago, and tried to keep his gun arm steady. "What do you have to do with the murders?"

"Your imagination fails you if that is all you can think to ask." Iago's hands still were spread before him, but his posture, his *presence,* seemed threatening. "The deaths we speak of break a Covenant that I may not violate by telling you any of me or mine. But I can tell you that these are not the first or last, a thing you already know, Stefan Ryzard."

"How do you know my name?"

"It is written in the air before you," Iago said. "Mark me well, policeman. Hell is coming. Find Andrassy's whore; she is not yet bound to my vows."

Stefan shook his head. The panic seemed to recede, and his judgment was returning. "Come on," he waved the barrel of the gun slightly, back in the direction the car was parked. "I'm taking you down to the station, you can talk there all you like."

The train still passed below them, boxcar after boxcar—Iago lowered his hands and said, "I am afraid you aren't going to do that." He moved too swiftly for Stefan to credit. One moment he was standing immobile before him, the next he had leaped out over the hillside.

Stefan followed his motion with the gun, yelling, "Stop

S. A. Swiniarski

or I'll shoot!" A wild bullet chased his words, aimed nowhere near Iago, who had already landed at the foot of
the hillside where the bodies had been found. Stefan was
scrambling down the dark hillside before the gunshot's ech-
oes had been swallowed by the train's passage.

Scrub tore at his legs as Stefan struggled to keep upright
in the mad scramble down the hillside. He could barely
watch his footing, much less the retreating Iago.

When he reached the foot of the hill, he looked along
the moving body of the train. Iago was ahead of him, a
hundred yards away or more, running alongside the train,
matching its speed.

Stefan started running after him.

"Stop!" he yelled again. This time, his shot was well
enough placed. Iago fell next to the tracks with the impact.
Stefan halved the distance between them as the last car
passed him on the tracks.

The moment that car had passed Stefan, Iago got up.
Surprise made Stefan fire two more shots, and despite the
distance now quartered between them, neither had any effect on Iago.

Iago ran, pacing the train, and leaped at the second-to-
last car. By then the train had outdistanced Stefan, making
it impossible for him to follow. Stefan slowed until he
reached the spot where Iago had fallen. The train was already small in the distance, only visible by its lights. The
sound of its passage faded into the night.

"He timed it just right," Stefan muttered. "Probably
never was hit."

He shook his head. The speed of Iago's movement still
seemed incredible, but less so in retrospect. Stefan felt
more and more that it was himself who wasn't acting up
to par.

He turned to walk back to the hill, and his car, when he
stepped on something next to the tracks. He had to crouch
down to see what it was in the darkness.

It was Iago's porkpie hat.

Next to it, a small pool of blood stained the gravel.

Stefan picked up the hat and turned to face where the
train had gone. He could still hear it in the distance.

6

The auction rooms of Adrian H. Muller & Son was known as the securities graveyard. It was here that creditors tried to dispose of the assets of their defaulted debtors. It was where old corporations went to die.

It was here that J. P. Morgan & Company would put on the block the life's work of the Van Sweringens. At 3:30 PM, the collected assets of the Van Sweringen railroad empire would cease to exist as an entity unto itself. By five it would have transformed into something else.

Oris Van Sweringen straightened his tie in the mirror and prayed that it wouldn't be Midamerica that it transformed into. It was a sick thought, abandoning the careful structure that he and his brother had put together. Abandoning Midamerica was one of the hardest things that he had ever done. It had to be done, though. He had to get himself, his brother, and their railroads away from the shadowy Dietrich. The man wasn't to be trusted; even if his money had helped keep the Van Sweringens afloat through the depths of financial crisis, it was at a cost he doubted they could pay any longer. . . .

J.D. Rockefeller might be, in his way, as much a demon as Dietrich, but Oris knew the costs of dealing with the old oil man—and he doubted they were nearly as dear as the costs of dealing with Dietrich.

Even though all the arrangements were at the last minute. Even though he was walking into the auction only with an oral agreement that the Rockefeller interests would outbid Midamerica, he should have had some measure of confidence. He and Mantis had worked financial miracles on less firm a footing.

Somehow, though, the confidence that had been with him—*them,* both him and Mantis; lord, how he wished his brother was here with him—that confidence had abandoned him.

The Wall Street Journal was positive that Midamerica would win the day. In their eyes that meant that the Van Sweringens would again be in control of their empire. Oris had read the article several times. "They have weathered earlier storms," it said, "and had come through them seemingly none the worse off."

The praise and confidence of the *Journal* would have cheered him if it wasn't for the fact that Midamerica had become a sham, a puppet where it wasn't the Van Sweringens, but Dietrich, who was pulling the strings. The papers would have his name on them, but Oris knew who would triumph if Midamerica won the day. It wouldn't be them.

He paced the hotel room, and his mind kept fixating on the article as if it were some premonition of doom. It went beyond his usual unease about the press.

It was the word, "seemingly."

As if the *Journal* knew of the secret deals that had formed the unseen heart of what was to be Midamerica. As if it knew about a devil calling himself Eric Dietrich. As if the *Journal* knew that their survival would be only appearance.

As he paced the hotel room, waiting to depart for the auction, the phone rang.

Oris turned on the black device as if it were a viper coiled to strike him. He let it ring twice more before he was able to move and pick up the receiver. He knew who it was, could *feel* who it was, even before the connection was made.

Oris held the receiver to his ear a long time before he said anything. The line was unearthly silent, no sound, no breathing, only the static hum of the phone wires nearly too quiet to notice. Oris was tempted to hang up, at the very least let the other be the first to speak. To do either would be a meaningless victory, something that wouldn't mean anything, even to his own self-respect. His self-image was too much constructed around the gentlemanly forms. Rudeness was as foreign to him as a desire for fame.

He finally said, "Hello, this is Mr. Van Sweringen."

It was with a dull dread that he finally heard Mr. Dietrich's voice on the other end of the line. "Good day to you, Oris." Oris sank inwardly at the familiarity. It made him feel unclean.

"What can I do for you, Mr. Dietrich?"

"I have just concluded some business, and I thought you would be relieved to know that your representative—excuse me, *Midamerica's* representative—arrived safely."

Oris gripped the phone and realized that the receiver was shaking in his ear. "Why would I have doubted it?" *Why does he play with me like this. Midamerica is his now.*

"Oh, I suspect that you might have had some concern over Colonel Ayres' safety. I made a point of meeting his train, and I assure you that he is unharmed."

Oris felt his blood go to ice. What kind of devil was it that he was dealing with? He had never felt such an absolute implication of violence, even when he saw union agitators. Until he had met Dietrich, he had thought die-hard unionists were the most dangerous men he had ever seen.

"I also hear that your brother's health is stable."

"Thank you, Mr. Dietrich," Oris said quickly and slammed the phone down on its cradle. The mention of his brother had so chilled him that it felt as if the perspiration on his brow would freeze his skin down to the bone.

Does he know?

The unbidden question ran through Oris' head and would not leave. There was no way that Dietrich could know. The only people who had any inkling of Oris' renegotiation to have the Rockefellers shut out Midamerica was him, Mantis, John D. Rockefeller, and the Rockefeller lawyer. Everyone else should believe, with *The Wall Street Journal* that the Vans had thrown their lot in with Midamerica.

It was barely seconds before the phone rang again. Oris let it ring a half-dozen times before he dared touch it again. When he picked it up, the voice on the other end was, thankfully, not Dietrich's.

"Mr. Van Sweringen? Your car has arrived downstairs."

"Thank you," he said, hanging up.

*　　*　　*

Oris arrived at the offices of Adrian H. Muller & Son at around three, and the dingy yellow rooms were already filled with people. Of the mass of humanity, perhaps four-hundred strong, Oris could only identify a few others that mattered.

He saw the tall figure of George M. Whitney, the partner from J. P. Morgan. He wasn't here to bid, and he looked as if this whole transaction were beneath his notice, and that he wished to be elsewhere. The person who was actually here to bid for the Morgan interests was a tense look-ing lawyer from Davis, Polk, Wardwell—Oris felt slightly embarrassed when he realized he couldn't remember the list of names that went with the practice. Not that it mat-tered. The lawyer wasn't important for himself; he was important because he was the voice of the Morgan inter-ests, the interests that forced this auction.

If things went as originally planned, that lawyer would make a single prophylactic bid, and allow Midamerica's representative, Colonel Ayres to outbid and walk away with the lot. Oris walked up and talked to the Colonel for a few moments, but his mind was far away. He was watch-ing the room for the Rockefellers' lawyer.

The Rockefellers were going to outbid Ayres, and it would be enough of a surprise to generate the headlines that Oris detested. The last-minute plan was calculated to drive the price up just enough that the resources at Ayers' command wouldn't be able to outbid it. Oris' only worry at this point was that Dietrich himself might arrive to make a bid—Dietrich might be able to outbid everyone directly. Oris had no idea of the funds at Dietrich's command, but he knew they were considerable.

Oris slipped into an out-of-the way corner before the auction began, without seeing any sign of Dietrich or the Rockefellers. Dietrich's absence did little to calm Oris, be-cause occasionally his gaze would light on the Morgan law-yer. The man appeared so nervous that Oris suspected he had been talking to Dietrich.

At 3:30 the room was packed. In Oris' view, it was packed with people who had no business being here. It felt as if the crowd of strangers were invading something deeply personal. He put on his reading glasses and stared at some legal papers, but he was really staring through the page.

The auctioneer cleared his throat, silenced the room, and began reading what was for sale: Allegheny Corporation common stock; Cleveland Railway Company common stock; Cleveland Terminals Building Company second mortgage bonds; Higbee Company common stock. . . . It went on and on and on; it seemed forever to Oris. It felt as painful and degrading as having a public viewing of some intimate surgery.

The auctioneer rattled off numbers of common and preferred stock, gave values for notes and bonds in the millions of dollars, all in an antiseptic monotone that reminded Oris of Mr. Dietrich's dead voice. Alphabetically, he came to the most painful issues last.

122,000 shares of Van Sweringen Company common stock, 1.2 million shares Van Sweringen Corporation common stock—those, with the associated notes, made Oris' own name a repeated hammer blow into his skull. Six times the words "Van Sweringen" passed the auctioneer's lips, and each time felt like a violation.

Then came the bids.

The first bid came from the nervous Morgan lawyer. Somewhat shakily he called out, "Two million, eight hundred and two thousand, one hundred and one."

Colonel Ayers responded immediately to the auctioneer's call for higher bids. On behalf of Midamerica he placed a bid for two million, eight hundred and three thousand dollars.

Oris waited for the Rockefeller bid for three million.

It didn't come.

"Going once . . . Going twice . . ."

Oris stood up, the papers slipping through his fingers. Where were the Rockefellers? Where was the bid?

"Last call . . ."

He couldn't breathe while the auctioneer spoke. It was as if the universe was in abeyance, waiting.

But there were no other bids. Midamerica had won the auction.

Later, when crowds of people he didn't really know pressed too close to congratulate him, he began feeling as if he had crossed an impassable threshold. He was now tied to Dietrich, and there was nothing left for him to do but shake hands on Midamerica's behalf.

*   *   *

Oris was never able to talk to J. D. Rockefeller again. The man refused to talk to him, and his intermediaries refused to admit that there had ever been any deal between the Vans and the Rockefellers over the auction.

The New York Times would later call it the greatest auction of securities in Wall Street history, and an object lesson in what happens to such pyramidal financial empires. The *Plain Dealer* saw it as a net gain for Cleveland, that with the Van Sweringens retaining control, they would continue to bring the kind of economic development to Cleveland that they had in the past.

After the auction results were final, neither brother had more than fourteen months to live.

7

Stefan stood across the desk from Detective Inspector Cody, head of the Detective Bureau, and said, "I don't believe you're doing this to me."

Cody shook his head and looked over his glasses at Stefan. "It's not like you're being suspended. You aren't even being reprimanded."

"That's not what this feels like."

Cody took a smoldering cigar out of an ashtray on his desk and used it to point at Stefan. "I really don't care how it feels. You've been working nonstop almost since you joined the Homicide Squad, and I'm not the only one who thinks your judgment is starting to suffer."

"This is about the tramp, isn't it?"

Cody sighed and leaned back in his chair to the protest of springs and old wood. He puffed on the cigar and said finally, "Do you have to ask that?"

"I didn't do anything . . ."

Cody held up his hand, cigar clamped between two fingers. "This is just a vacation, Stefan. A rest. Take it."

"I don't need—"

"You don't? You're a good cop. Until recently you've had great instincts about what to pursue and what to leave alone. Now you're using up police time on a missing body that rightfully isn't even in the jurisdiction of the Homicide Squad. You're chasing suspects off-duty when you're one of a few cops that haven't had a part in the Kingsbury Run business. It's like you've started looking for trouble in your spare time. We don't need this. Starting Friday, you have a month off. Find a woman, have some fun."

"What about what he said, he knew Andrassy?"

"Stefan, have faith in the rest of the force. They have your report on this 'Iago.' What we *don't* need is yet another person working on one double murder."

Stefan nodded slowly.

"Starting Friday, you have four weeks off. Enjoy it."

Stefan left Inspector Cody's office, making an effort not to slam the door on the way out.

He stopped at his desk and picked up a stack of files. Nuri looked up just in time to see the pile of paperwork land in front of him.

"Hey, what are you doing?"

"Knock yourself out," Stefan said. "I'm going out for a drink." He picked up his hat and jacket from next to his desk and said, "See you in November."

"What?" Nuri asked.

Stefan didn't answer him as he left.

It was going to be a cold winter. Florence Polillo could feel it in the draft rattling the windows of her little flat. She sat in a rickety chair by the window and tried to remember what it was like to feel warm. Occasionally she would drink from the bottle she rested between her knees, but it didn't help.

She felt cold, and very, very old.

Eddie was dead.

The thought kept tumbling through her head, unwanted but irresistible. How could she go on with it all now . . . ?

She stood with the slow deliberateness of someone used to her own drunkenness. She rested the bottle on the table next to the paper. The story in the *Press* was about the identity of one of the decapitated bodies they had found in Kingsbury Run. One of them had been Edward Andrassy. The police had identified him by his fingerprints.

Eddie.

Of all the evil things to come home to after her mother's funeral. To find out that not only had Eddie been killed, but that someone had severed his head. Flo rubbed her own neck thinking, *That's how you kill them. . . .*

Flo tried to chide herself for caring. How many other men had left her for one reason or another? Men left her every goddamn night.

Somehow Eddie was different. Eddie was the only one

of the whole damned group that seemed to care beyond himself. Eddie had been the only one to question what was going on. He wanted out of this world as much as any of them. But he shared with Flo some questions about the cost, and more courage to voice them.

Flo wondered if that was what got him killed. She felt colder than ever.

The shades were drawn, but the sunset cut a molten line across the wall opposite the window. The line fell across the shelf holding her dolls. She turned to them and felt her eyes moisten. They stared back with eyes glassy and dead.

Flo loved the dolls. They were the one thing that followed her everywhere she moved. They were the only children she would ever have. But right now it seemed as if she shared her room with a dozen tiny corpses.

She sat at the table and watched the blind-carved sunlight cut molten-red stripes across the room. Everything was gray except the light. The room was colorless, emotionless, like every other room she'd rented by herself. She spent her life moving from place to place, wallowing in the ugliness. She liked to think that someday she would find someone or something that would make it better, lift her away from this endless numb grayness.

Melchior promised an escape from this dead world, and for a while she had believed him. But the grays were still gray, and the only promise of color was the sunlight washing her walls with the tint of blood.

If was all true, she would even lose that, the smoky-red sunlight that sometimes refused to warm her. She would be trading the sun for what might be grayness without end.

The sunlight faded, plunging her room into darkness. She lifted the bottle to her lips with a shaking hand, and another ice-cold hand touched her wrist. She froze at the touch, unable to move.

"Hello, Florence," the familiar whispery voice said from behind her. "You were missed." The cold hand traveled up her arm, and the only movement that Flo was capable of was an involuntary shudder.

She opened her mouth to explain, but fear and liquor

choked off her words leaving her stuttering, ". . . I . . . I . . . I . . ."

Another hand found her free hand, placing her in a cold embrace from behind. So cold, but in two places it was becoming very warm. Not the places a man usually became warm. His wrists, where they touched her skin, began pulsing with a warmth that throbbed deep within the vein.

Her visitor kept talking. "I know where you were, Florence. Your landlady, Mrs. Ford, drove you to Pierpont for your mother's funeral."

"H-h-how?" His wrists were like brands on her skin. A warm sensation spread beneath her skin, a feeling like the liquor, or like the first brush of sex before it became disappointing.

Lips brushed the back of her neck like the touch of a flame. She shuddered again and squeezed her legs together. "You are all a part of me now," he said. "Never forget that." His teeth lightly bit the back of her neck, drawing blood. A violent shudder shook her, and the bottle slipped out of her fingers.

She was no longer cold.

"I feel what any of you do." He licked the trickle of blood from her neck. "That was why Andrassy had to die with my enemy."

Flo was breathing hard now. Her body was filled with the warmth, the hunger, the need. Her world wasn't gray any longer, it was burning with reds and yellows. It was hard for her to speak. She wanted it so badly. But she managed to ask, "Why Eddie? Why that way?" Every word hung upon a shuddering breath.

"There are others like me, my enemies. Eddie betrayed me to them." He drew his tongue across the back of her neck. "All of you are too close to coming over to me now. A normal death might produce a crippled thrall. He had to die like one of us."

Flo was beyond speech now. She could smell the pulsing warmth in his wrists, his heart beating so slow it was agony. He released her hand and turned his wrist toward her. It felt like the sun shining on her face. He raised it to just below her mouth.

"You are leaving your world. Sever what ties you have left to it. When you join me, nothing and no one will follow you where you go." Below her, the skin slit itself along the vein. The long wound wept blood that seemed to glow with an inner light. It was impossible to refuse, even had she wanted to.

What was Eddie compared to this?

Flo descended on the offered arm and fed.

8

Friday, October 5

Stefan was at home, staring at a newspaper, but not really reading it, when the phone rang. He let it go a few times before he answered it. He was frustrated and didn't really want to talk to anybody.

When he answered the phone, it was Nuri's voice on the other end. "Hello, Stefan?"

"Yeah, what is it, Nuri?"

"I just called to see how you're doing."

Stefan shook his head. "I appreciate the concern, but how do you think I'm doing?"

"The vacation's got you out of joint, doesn't it?"

Stefan sighed into the receiver. "I just need to figure out what to do with myself."

"What are you going to do when you retire?"

"Let's change the subject. Are you calling from work? Is there a problem?"

"Yes," Nuri said. "It's not a problem, just something I thought you'd like to know."

"What?"

"Have you been following the Kingsbury Run murders?"

"I'm on vacation, remember?"

Nuri chuckled a little. "Well it's not like I'm doing any real investigating, but they need loads of people to tote that barge and lift that bale. They have me going through missing persons' records."

"So?"

"I'm looking at people who disappeared on or before September twenty-third, and while I've yet to find a match for our headless body, I did find someone you might be interested in."

Nuri paused and Stefan said, "Come on, spit it out."

"Apparently a colored woman lost her husband on September twenty-second, after a fight, last seen wearing overalls and walking in the direction of the railroad tracks around dusk."

Nuri was right, Stefan was interested. "Where, what tracks?"

"Would you believe East Forty-Ninth?"

"The Run?"

"The Run."

Stefan shook his head, "That has got to be the man I found—"

"Way ahead of you," Nuri said, "Get a piece of paper, I have her address."

Stefan quickly copied the name "Wilma Fairfax" and an address not too far away from the Run.

"If you're lucky," Nuri said, "the wife has a photograph of him, and you can put that case to bed."

"Thanks," Stefan said, shaking his head. He felt the return of some of the unease he'd felt when talking to Iago. Mrs. Fairfax's husband had been heading toward the Run at dusk. Hours later he'd been bleeding and screaming about the Devil.

Stefan wondered if the man had seen something.

He was quiet long enough for Nuri to ask, "Are you all right?"

Stefan nodded. "Yeah. I'm just wondering how I'm going to explain that the hospital lost her husband's body."

It was getting close on to nine o'clock when Stefan drove his car down the little brick dead-end street that Mr. and Mrs. Fairfax called home. The street was lined with apartment buildings that felt too large for such a narrow street. The bricks glittered, the street lights reflecting over broken glass.

As he rolled to a stop in front of the Fairfaxes' building, he thought he heard gunshots. He tensed and scrambled out of the car before he realized that the shots were from a radio, just someone playing the climax of "Death Valley Days" too loud. He straightened up, feeling somewhat embarrassed as the show drifted into a cigarette commercial.

He chided himself. There was an echo that made the

radio program sound deeper, and made the sound a little more realistic, but the error had to be mostly his own nerves. Something about this was making him uneasy, far more uneasy than the typical notification of the next of kin.

The Fairfaxes' building was a tired pile of brick that waved laundry out a few windows, but otherwise drew blinds against the neighborhood it found itself in. He walked up the front steps, trying to ignore the radio in the background. He could feel glass crunching under his feet all the way to the front door.

The halls inside the apartment were dark and narrow. They smelled of cooking and rusty plumbing. From behind the doors he could hear more radios, at a more decent volume, children playing, couples talking or arguing, and he passed one door that closed in the sounds of two people being very passionate with each other.

He stopped in front of the door to the Fairfaxes' rooms, and heard nothing beyond it. His unease increased.

Stefan rang the doorbell, and he could imagine the bell echoing in an empty apartment. There was no response. He rang again and called, "Mrs. Fairfax? Police. I need to talk to you."

Still no response.

He knocked and rang again. "It's about your husband."

With that, the door swung open into a spartan apartment. The person opening the door wasn't Mrs. Fairfax. Stefan stared dumbly at the man for a few minutes. For a few long moments Stefan was convinced he had gotten the address wrong.

But when the man said, "Detective Ryzard, fancy meeting you again," it began to sink in who this man was. Stefan wouldn't need any pictures to identify Mr. Fairfax. He was standing in front of him, the same man he had driven out of the Flats, the same man who had supposedly died at St. Vincent's Charity.

At least now he knew why the hospital had lost the body.

"Mr. Fairfax?" Stefan said. He tried to keep the shock out of his voice, but he couldn't help staring. It was the same man, the same face, clean of blood now. The same hair, graying at the temples. The same crazed eyes that seemed to be looking beyond everything.

"Yes, yes," Fairfax said, nodding. His eyes belied the

calmness of his voice, which was almost dead of emotion. His voice was a cold monotone, but his eyes were ablaze with something—anger, fear, hate, lust . . . Stefan couldn't tell, but it fed his own growing unease.

"Can I come in?" Stefan asked. "I think we need to talk."

"Of course," Fairfax said. "I apologize for any trouble we've caused you."

He opened the door on the little two-room apartment. The first thing that struck Stefan was the smell of burning wax. The main room was dim, lit only by a half-dozen candles. It took a moment for Stefan's eyes to adjust to the dimness enough for him to enter.

Fairfax walked over to a threadbare couch and sat next to an old woman that Stefan guessed was Wilma Fairfax. Now that the initial shock of seeing the man was receding, he noticed that the man was dressed differently. He wore a pinstripe suit that was tailored for him. It wasn't the height of luxury, but it was out of line for the apartment he lived in, as well as for the clothes Stefan had seen him in before.

"Mr. Fairfax—" Stefan began.

"You can call me Samson," he said, placing his hand on Wilma Fairfax's. Stefan noticed that she didn't move at the contact. She remained sitting, hands on her knees, staring at her lap. The woman didn't even look up to see the stranger enter her house. The posture worried him.

"Samson then. Just to reassure myself, you are the same Samson Fairfax that your wife reported missing? The same man I drove to St. Vincent's?"

Samson Fairfax nodded, much of his expression outside of his eyes invisible in the candlelight. "Isn't it obvious?" Stefan saw a hint of a smile that instantly vanished.

"Not if you believe the doctor at St. Vincent's."

Samson shrugged. "The doctor made a mistake, that's all. I have a sickness, gives me 'spells,' as my mother used to call them. I woke up on a cart with all these dead people, I got out of there fast."

Stefan nodded. "So why didn't you tell any doctors, or the police, when you recovered?"

"My family was more important. I had to take care of Wilma." Stefan noticed Samson squeeze Wilma's hand. The gesture looked less than tender. "You can understand that, can't you?"

Stefan nodded. Wilma's silence was beginning to disturb him. He turned to address his next question to her. "Why didn't you call us to tell us your husband had returned?"

"Why should she?" Samson said.

"She filed a missing person's report that's still open. That's how I found you."

"Oh," Samson said in a voice that seemed to grow even colder. "I did not know that." He turned to face his wife, and Stefan could almost see her wince. "I'm certain that it was just an oversight on her part. Wasn't it?"

Samson rubbed her knee, and Wilma gave a weak nod. She seemed to shrink in place. Stefan could almost feel what she was shrinking from. There was something present here, a weight behind Samson's eyes, steel in his voice, a hardness in his posture. None of it had been present the last time Stefan had seen the man.

Samson had been the same man who'd been crazed and near death in the Flats, but he wasn't. Stefan couldn't rationalize the feeling, but it felt as if the core of this man had been hollowed out and something ominous had been poured in to fill the empty space.

"Forgive my wife," said the man who looked so much like Samson Fairfax. "When I returned, she was quite ill. I've been doing what I can to tend to her."

He commanded attention away from his wife, as if she were mere furniture. Stefan felt the pull of his words and resented it. It was disquieting to realize that he disliked the man whose life he had saved.

"Are you a religious man, Mr. Fairfax?"

Samson responded with an iron stare. Stefan could feel the offense carried in the gaze. It wasn't the offense of a man whose faith was questioned.

"I'm asking," Stefan continued, "because of some of the things you said to me when I took you to the hospital. You talked about the Devil walking the tracks. You asked me to pray for you—"

"I do not need your prayers, Detective Ryzard."

"I just wondered what you had been referring to—"

"I was referring to nothing. It was deranged babble. There is no devil."

"Perhaps you saw something farther up the tracks. You've heard about the murders that happened in the Run the same night?"

Samson stood. "I think you should go. You are upsetting my wife."

Stephan stood, maintaining an uncomfortable eye contact with Samson. Something made him start to repeat the Twenty-third Psalm in his head. *I shall fear no evil,* Stefan thought as he asked, "Did you see anything on the tracks that night?"

"I was not in my mind then. I remember nothing of that evening."

Thy rod and thy staff, they comfort me. Stefan stared into Samson's eyes. "Then how is it that you know who I am?"

An ugly expression, near to hatred, broke across Samson's face like a wave cresting an insufficient breakwater. In his eyes, Stefan saw a fury that made him start reaching for a gun that wasn't there. He was off-duty. He shouldn't even be here.

I will dwell in the house of the Lord forever.

It was Samson who broke eye contact. "Get out of my house," he said. Stefan backed toward the door. He could hear the threat in Samson's voice, and he was in no position to test it. Maybe if he was here officially, he would have. Not now.

As he backed over the threshold, he could catch a glimpse of Wilma's eyes as she finally lifted her head to regard him. That glance frightened him, a glance from eyes that were as dull as those of a corpse.

"I did pray for you," Stefan whispered as Samson slammed the door on him.

Stefan stood before the door for a long time, but no noise emerged from the apartment beyond. Eventually he turned and walked away. As he left, his mind drifted back to Iago. There was no logic to the connection Stefan began making between the men. Nothing to link them but a similarity of presence.

And the murders in Kingsbury Run.

As Stefan walked to his car, his feet crunched across glass again. This time he looked more closely and saw fragments of a broken mirror.

9

Carlo Pasquale drove. That's all he did. There was more to what was going on, but he was involved in the Mayfield Road Mob through relatives, not through ambition. He had no desire to know. When Papa said drive, he drove, no questions.

As Carlo drove the long black V-12 Lincoln toward the docks, he thought he wasn't quite as ignorant as he wished to be. His passenger was going to a meeting with a man named Dietrich, and from the shotgun his passenger carried, it wasn't to shake hands. Carlo didn't want to know what Dietrich had done to anger Papa.

The Lincoln slid into fog coming off of the lake. The world turned gray outside. Carlo felt that the night had turned very cold, even though he was safely buttoned up in the car.

They were passing warehouses, and his passenger, till then mute, started giving him directions. In the fog, the car traced a maze that Carlo barely felt able to retrace, only from memorizing his passenger's directions, not from any visible landmarks.

Eventually Carlo heard the instruction, "Kill the lights and turn right into the next open bay."

Carlo did as instructed, turning the darkened Lincoln through a doorway already open to accommodate a large panel truck. Carlo pulled the Lincoln up next to the truck. The way into the vast darkened space was blocked by a concrete dock that rose to the level of the Lincoln's hood ornament. Carlo noticed that there weren't any men by the truck.

"Keep the engine running," his passenger said. "Be ready to pull out of here."

Carlo nodded. He knew his job. He wished it was all he knew.

As his passenger slipped out of the car, Carlo wondered if they would take the body or leave it here. He hoped they'd leave it here. He hated it when his passengers would ask him to help lug a newly dead corpse. Carlo wasn't particularly squeamish, but the idea of chauffeuring a dead man made him uneasy.

From the looks of things, it wouldn't come to that. The man with the shotgun would do his job and run. There would be other people here, and they wouldn't have the time to remove Dietrich.

Papa would be appalled at the thought, but Carlo hoped that whatever bodyguards Dietrich had would finish off his passenger as he shotgunned his target. It would make Carlo's job easier, give him a chance to stop for a drink on the way back.

Carlo's passenger was now just a shape slipping over the loading dock into the darkness. As Carlo's eyes adjusted he could see that the warehouse beyond wasn't completely dark. None of the lights inside the giant space were lit, but blue arcs from outside filtered through the fog and dirty windows to cast dim illumination across the floor in front of the loading area.

Carlo watched his passenger melt into the blackness edging the one irregular aisle of light. Then there was no sign of him anymore, his shadow inseparable from the vague mass of crates filing the void beyond Carlo's vision.

Carlo swallowed. His throat was dry, his palms slick against the steering wheel. The vibration from the Lincoln's idle didn't quite mask the fact that he was shaking. He felt his breath catch as if his throat were filled with broken glass.

Christ almighty, what's there to be scared of?

The terror made him want to cut out of there, cut out and keep driving until he'd put at least one state line between himself and this place. His hand even moved to shift the Lincoln into reverse.

Wherever the impulse came from, it came too late. Carlo saw something move in the aisle, and the sight transfixed him. The figure was a man, blond hair and pale skin cutting a shape in the darkness. When Carlo saw the figure walking in the dim blue light, he knew that he was looking at the source of his fear. There was nothing inherent in the sight of the blond man that should terrify Carlo, but Carlo froze, as if any movement at all would draw attention toward him.

Carlo was so focused on the figure of the man that when the shotgun went off, it caught him completely by surprise. A flash briefly tore through the darkness, silhouetting the blond man. The sound echoed through the empty space reverberating around the towering stacks of briefly-illuminated boxes.

On the boxes so briefly lit, Carlo thought he saw lettering in German gothic.

As the pale man collapsed, Carlo could move again. He began shifting, preparing to back out as soon as his passenger made it to the car. Carlo could see him running past the corpse, no tries at stealth now. The assassin's trenchcoat billowed behind him like a cape, and he held the shotgun before him as if warning the darkness out of his way.

Carlo revved the engine. He wanted out of here *now*.

The gunman made it nearly all the way back to the loading dock. Then, in response to something Carlo couldn't see, he turned around, raising his shotgun to bear on something behind him. There was no flash this time, but Carlo heard something snap as the shotgun flew away, thrown tumbling and broken into the darkness.

Carlo slammed the gas, backing the Lincoln out of there as fast as it could accelerate. Before he had made it halfway out of the loading bay, the gunman's back slammed into the windshield. Glass blew into the car, slicing at Carlo's face. The gunman fell all the way into the Lincoln, his head landing in Carlo's lap, bouncing on a neck too loose to be in one piece.

Carlo screamed obscenities at the dead gunman's face as he tried to keep the Lincoln from swerving out of control.

He looked up and saw, standing on the edge of the loading dock in front of the Lincoln, the pale man, Dietrich, the man who was supposed to be hit tonight. He stood impassively, arms extended in a Christlike gesture. Carlo could still see the ragged edges of the exit wound through the hole torn in his shirt. Carlo thought he could see the flesh moving.

In trying to maneuver the car back out on the street, the front fender clipped something as he attempted to turn. His hand slipped while trying to shift across the gunman's body, and he couldn't straighten out on the road. The back of the Lincoln slammed into the rear of a parked truck. The impact threw Carlo against the steering wheel, stunning him.

Carlo pushed himself away from the wheel and glanced behind him to see the damage. The Lincoln wasn't going to move again. The rear corner of the truck had crushed the back of the car past the rear axle. The back seat had buckled, and the metal of the truck had twisted to obscure his view out the rear. The inside of the car was filling with the smell of gas.

He pushed the body off of him and began forcing the driver's door open. He could only move it a few inches against the twisted frame, but it was enough for him to scramble out of the car. He fell on damp pavement, the spreading gas stinging the cuts in his hands. He forced himself up, fighting a throbbing dizziness that made him unsteady on his feet.

He stumbled away from the wreck in a direction that he hoped was away from the warehouse. Between the fog and the stinging in his eyes, he couldn't see where he was going. He tried to wipe the blood off of his face, but it only made things worse.

He almost stumbled into the pale man before he saw him. Carlo stopped when he could see the figure a few feet away, facing him. Carlo's throat was clogged by fear. He tried to reach out to steady himself, and his hand found nothing. He collapsed onto one knee in front of the man.

He felt his pulse in his neck, and in his temples. His breath was shallow and ragged, sounds muted under the rushing of his own heart. Before him, Dietrich stood, arms extended.

Carlo could see clearly now where the shotgun blast had torn away Dietrich's clothes. Underneath, Carlo could see the torn flesh in his chest and side. The edges of the massive wound seemed to knit together as he watched.

Carlo wanted to move, to run. He wanted to die, if that

was the only escape offered him. He looked up and couldn't tear his gaze away from Dietrich's eyes.

"The lords of this city will acknowledge me," Dietrich said. The voice was like a solid lump of ice lodged in Carlo's heart. "You shall become a vassal of my blood."

Carlo couldn't move, couldn't nod or shake his head. Speech was lost to him. Even if his throat could have formed words, language seemed stripped from him. The only words he could understand were those Dietrich spoke. The only meaning was in those words.

Dietrich's pale form was suddenly illuminated by a flickering orange light. A warm acrid wind blew by them, but Carlo was too far away from himself and the Lincoln to notice. His attention was focused in front of him.

Dietrich lowered his gaze, and Carlo's gaze followed as if he was looking with the same set of eyes.

Dietrich had begun to bleed. Until then, no blood had spread to stain his tattered clothes. But now a violent red began to seep from the closing lips of the wound. It almost seemed to glow in the flickering light, holding a warmth beyond anything that Carlo had ever experienced.

Even though Dietrich no longer spoke words, Carlo could feel his voice in his head. *Take of my blood. Take of my flesh.* It ran through his head, an obscene parody of the sacrament.

You've never held any power, Carlo. You've always lived in fear of those around you. You've always been an instrument of someone else's will. Take of me, and you will see those who have owned you bound to you in servitude. Or dead.

Carlo shuddered. Panic still raged in his body, but now other emotions raged alongside it. Anger led them. Carlo felt a burning rage at a family that thought so little of him that all they could see him as was a chauffeur for their hired assassins. Assassins they treated better than their own flesh and blood. The only respect he had belonged to Papa, and Papa had none for him. Carlo hadn't seen it until now, but all the talk of sending him away to college was simply an excuse to get rid of him.

With the anger came another emotion. A feeling even hotter against the growing coldness in his chest.

Grant me your fealty, bind yourself to me, and you will feast within my kingdom.

The feeling was hunger.

Carlo reached for the pale man, and the long arms embraced him as Carlo buried his face in the still-bleeding wound.

In the *Cleveland Press* the next day, the burned out Lincoln was mentioned alongside two other traffic fatalities. No one paid much attention to the accident, everyone knew how dangerous Cleveland traffic was. The only remarkable thing about it was the fact that the supposed driver was the only fatality.

10

Doctor McCutcheon led Stefan through a file room at St. Vincent's Charity. All the while the doctor shook his head and kept saying, "I don't know what to tell you, Detective Ryzard. The man was dead."

Each time, Stefan would nod and remain quiet. As far as he was concerned, he had seen Samson Fairfax alive and well, and he only had this doctor's word that he had ever been anywhere near death. He followed the doctor through narrow aisles of wood and paper. The single low-wattage bulb cast a yellow pall on the file room, drawing the brown rust stains on the walls, and some of the cabinets, into relief. The place smelled of steam heat and old paper.

"Here we are," said the doctor, stopping in front of a cabinet and smoothing his Errol Flynn mustache. He drew open a file drawer, which came free with a squeak of pained wood. The doctor began rummaging in the files.

"He claimed to have 'spells' that someone might take for death."

Doctor McCutcheon snorted. "A layman maybe. Sure, there are conditions that could produce a temporary coma-tose state. But the John Doe you brought me wasn't suffer-ing a fit, a trance, a fugue, a coma, or anything else—here we are." He drew out a slim folder that was labeled, "John Doe, September 23, 1935."

The doctor opened it. "Here are my notes. Respiration stopped at 2:30 AM. Despite efforts to revive him, we lost his pulse for ten minutes later. He never started breathing again. By 3:00 AM I declared him dead. It's all here if you want it—down to the names of the attending nurses."

Stefan took the folder and glanced at Doctor McCut-

cheon's notes. They told the story the doctor said they did.
Stefan shook his head. "I'm sorry to lean on you, Doctor.
I'm just trying to understand how I could see this man
again, alive and well, weeks after you declared him dead."

The doctor shook his head, "You couldn't have. There's
no way it could be the same man, no matter what he said."

Stefan sighed. "You don't think there might just be a
possibility—"

The doctor slammed the file cabinet shut. "The man I
tended died. Period. You have the file right in front of
you."

"If it weren't for the missing body—"

The doctor shook his head. "Talk to the guard who lost
the damn body. All I can tell you is that if the man you
saw was Samson Fairfax, the John Doe I treated was not."

Stefan learned from the hospital administration that Edward Mullen had been let go because of the incident. From
the sound of it, he had maintained throughout that someone from the coroner's office had picked up the body, despite the denials of Coroner Pearse and the absence of any
paperwork. It also sounded as if Mullen had been sacked
less for losing a body than for insisting on his own
innocence.

Mullen lived above a bar northeast of the intersection of
Euclid and East Fifty-Fifth. The building looked as if it
were a refugee from the other side of that intersection, a
refugee from its poverty-stricken and ill-kept peers in the
Third. It squatted on the corner of two unremarkable
streets, seeming to shrink from the working-class homes
surrounding it.

Evening was coming as Stefan pulled up in front of Mullen's building. The bar was open and getting a start on the
after-work crowd. The sky was a darkening pall above him,
and the folks on the street had to hunch themselves against
the wind.

Stefan checked the address twice before he got out of his
car. The only lights were from the bar, the small curtained
windows glowing out into the dusk, a small globe of light
carving out the doorway of the establishment, another lamp
picking out the name "Armand's" above the door.

The windows above the bar were dark. Half-height

wrought-iron fences tied themselves to the brick in front of the darkened windows, forming a faux balcony barely a foot wide beyond the sills of the windows. The one to the right had a window box that had bloomed once, sprouting flowering vines to wrap the iron rail. The plants' season was long gone, and the vines gripping the iron were brown and dead.

Stefan found the door to the upstairs hidden in the darkness along one of the side walls. The stairs and the hallway were lit only by two incandescent bulbs, and Stefan had to pick his way carefully up the stairs, half-wrapped in gloom.

Upstairs, from the sound, he might have been inside the bar itself. The sounds of clinking glasses, music, and loud conversation filtered through the black-and-white-checked linoleum. The sound carried so well that Stefan was worried about the strength of a floor that was thin enough to transmit sound so freely.

As if designed to capitalize on the fear, the floor of the hallway sagged in the center, a dip that followed the hallway along its short length across the building.

There were four apartments. Two doors on the right, toward the front of the building. Two on the left, toward the rear. Mullen lived in number four, the second door on the left.

Stefan walked up the hallway, away from the lights. The only thing that prevented Mullen's end of the hallway from being completely dark was the dim light filtering through the window here.

Stefan snorted. It smelled up here, of alcohol, urine, and food gone bad. He could hear flies tapping on the inside of the window, and on the sill was a strip of fly-paper that had fallen from the ceiling. The amber cellophane was almost completely covered by black insect corpses.

He pounded on the door. He heard nothing except the sounds of the bar below him, and renewed activity from the flies. The sluggish buzzing was just loud and close enough for him to hear above the noise downstairs.

Mullen, if he was home, didn't respond.

"Mullen, Edward Mullen! This is Detective Ryzard from the Cleveland Police Department. I want to talk to you!"

As he called out, a fly landed on the back of his hand. He had to shake his hand twice to get it off. He pounded the door again, and as his eyes adjusted to the dim light, he was beginning to see that a host of flies had settled on Edward Mullen's door. They were sluggish in the cold, and didn't fly away when he pounded on the door.

No one answered.

Stefan tried the door. It wasn't locked. He pushed it gently into an apartment that was shrouded in even deeper gloom than the hallway. The smell became much worse, the smell of something rotting. He gritted his teeth while pushing the door open with his foot.

He felt flies batter against his face and his arms, causing his skin to twitch.

It was still dark beyond. He couldn't see a foot beyond the doorway. All the shades in Mullen's apartment were drawn against the windows. The only light was what managed to leak past Stefan.

He already knew what he would see. He hoped differently. He prayed to God that he was wrong. But he knew he wasn't wrong. He reached inside the apartment, next to the door, fumbling for a light. When he found a switch, he hesitated for a few long moments.

For a little while he fantasized that he could just walk away.

He stood in the door, sensing—half imagining—that it was too warm. The smell of decay was a humid smell, making the air too fetid to breathe through his nose. Between the warmth, the dark, and the smell, he felt as if he'd been buried in a gangrenous wound.

Stefan turned on the lights.

It was as bad as he had feared. Flies were everywhere, dotting the walls, the ceiling, the couch against the wall.

Mostly, the flies covered Edward Mullen.

He was seated at a desk directly across from the door to the apartment. His back was to Stefan. He had collapsed across the desk, his head face-down on a stained blotter that was writhing with insect life. His right hand lay on the desk next to his head. It clutched a large revolver.

Automatically, Stefan's gaze followed the path of the phantom shot, to the wall left of the desk. The wall was alive with flies, almost a solid sheet covering the area where the contents of Mullen's skull had sprayed the wall.

Stefan's stomach tightened as he walked into the apartment, but he didn't let his mind dwell on it. He stepped up next to the corpse. Mullen had to have been dead, rotting up here, since he'd been fired from St. Vincent's. Stefan did as thorough an examination as he could without touching anything.

Mullen had written a note and weighted it down with the penholder in front of him. Gore had spotted the page, and old blood had spread beneath it, sticking the page to the desk, but Stefan could read what it said.

I cannot lie for the Devil, the only explanation that Mullen gave for taking his own life. Stefan looked up from the page, and noticed the crucifix hanging on the wall above the desk. The figure of Christ seemed to be looking down at Mullen with a grieving expression. The blood on the cross wasn't from the Savior.

Stefan left the apartment to call the scene in to the Central Station.

"What am I going to do with you, Stefan?" Inspector Cody asked. He had come, with a few more cops and the coroner's wagon, in response to Stefan's call. He stood next to Stefan's car, shaking his head at the spectacle of the body's removal. "What was it you were doing here?"

"I was trying to find out what happened to a body that disappeared from the morgue at St. Vincent's."

Cody sighed and looked up at the darkened apartments above the bar. "What did our suicide have to with it?"

"He was security when the body disappeared."

"And this body, it's part of a case you're working on?"

The silence stretched until Inspector Cody said, "Well?"

A wind came down the street, off the lake. It got under Stefan's overcoat and chilled him. Eventually he shook his head and said, "No, it isn't part of any official investigation."

Stefan could see his superior shake his head, as if in disappointment. "God, don't you have better things to do with your free time? Was the body a murder victim?"

"No—" Stefan said, then hesitated.

"What else?"

"—he may not even be dead, sir."

Detective Inspector Cody lowered his gaze to look into Stefan's eyes. "You'd better tell me the whole story here."

Stefan gave as complete an accounting as he could. Cody stayed silent through it, only moving to pull out a cigarette and light it. When it was over, he blew smoke toward the bar, as if trying to erase what was happening.

"Okay," he said finally, "I'm not going to reprimand you. It's just too much trouble when I'm retiring tomorrow." He looked up at the bar, "This and the Kingsbury Run business—what a note to leave on."

Cody shook his head, looked at Stefan, and said, "This isn't as your superior, it's just some advice from an old cop. Don't muddy the waters any further with extracurricular activities. What you have is a John Doe who didn't die, a doctor who couldn't admit his mistake, and a guard who lied to cover his own oversights and couldn't live with it when he lost his job. You try and read any more into it, my successors may not be as forgiving."

"But—" Stefan began. In his mind he saw the connection between Samson Fairfax and Edward Mullen. They had both seen the Devil, in some form or other. But as the thought formed, Stefan knew it bore little weight, no matter how certain it seemed to him. He was chasing a shadow that no one else could see.

"If you keep investigating anything off duty, beyond what's assigned to you, you risk getting canned. Do you understand that? I'd hate to see the department lose you."

Stefan nodded.

The doors slammed shut on the coroner's wagon. As it drove away, Stefan wondered what other lies Mullen might have told for the Devil.

11

Eliot Ness stood by the bar, martini in hand, and watched the powerful people mingle. He was here because someone in the Burton campaign invited him. Ness was a loyal party man and the invitation intrigued him, so he attended. He also attended the victory celebration because it was one of those high-profile parties where attendance could be a career move. Filling the ballroom around Ness were the most important and influential people in the city and, in a few cases, the whole country.

Ness sipped his martini and wondered who had invited him and why. There had been hints about openings in the incoming administration, but no one from the campaign staff had approached him. He certainly hadn't any opportunity to see the mayor-elect yet, much less talk to him. Burton was probably only going to show up to give a climactic, and boring, speech to the mass of high and mighty gathered in his honor.

Most of the guests were party officials and big donors. Ness was neither. He wasn't even local. The government he worked for was the Federal one. He lived in Bay Village, two suburbs west of the city, which meant that he hadn't even voted in the Cleveland mayoral election.

The explanation he'd come up with was the suspicion that someone invited him as part of the decor. The mayor had been elected in large part due to his platform of reform, law and order. Since the local police were as corrupt as anything Ness had seen outside Chicago, if the new mayor wanted law enforcement represented at his victory party, he probably wanted to go a little farther afield for those representatives.

"Mr. Ness? Mr. Eliot Ness?"

Ness turned to face the man calling his name. He was the one person in the ballroom younger than Ness. The man was in his late twenties and looked a little uncomfortable in black tie and tails. His hair was slicked back, not quite hiding its flaming red color.

"Yes?" Ness said, as he began to sense a familiarity. "You work for the *Press,* don't you?"

"The *News* now. Peter Napier." Napier extended his hand, and Ness was able to picture him in a rumpled suit and hat.

Ness shook the man's hand and said, "I never forget a reporter's face."

Napier chuckled. Ness' love for the press was no secret, and the press usually did its best to return the favor. "So, are you on some big case right now?"

Ness shook his head, "Not unless the Canadian whiskey stocking the bar missed passing through customs." Ness looked across the bar, and the bartender, an elderly man in a white jacket, shrank back a bit at Ness' glance. Ness sighed and said, "It's a *joke.*" The bartender smiled and laughed nervously. He returned to face Napier. "No big case. I'm just a guest here."

Napier nodded. "Well, I'm on duty here. Care to spare a few minutes?"

"Always," Ness said, draining the remainder of his martini.

"You were invited here— Were you involved in the Burton campaign at all?"

Ness chuckled. "If I'd been, you'd know, wouldn't you? No, I'm here as a private citizen to offer my congratulations to Mr. Burton."

Napier whipped out a notepad and jotted down a few words. "Do you think that inviting you here is intended to send a message to local gangs?"

"I can't speak for Mr. Burton, but I would like to think that it means that the new administration will have a cordial relationship with the Federal law enforcement agencies."

"Are you saying that Mayor Davis didn't have that kind of relationship?"

Ness shook his head, "Not at all. I simply think it is a

positive note that Mayor-elect Burton has shown signs that he fully intends to carry out the spirit of reform that his campaign promised."

"Would you consider an appointment within the new administration?"

The question took Ness aback somewhat. He was answering before it fully sank in, mostly because he had long ago trained himself never to fumble for words in front of the press. "Now that is a novel question. It would mean a big change. I've always worked for the Federal Government. Playing any role in a municipal administration would be a much different thing than anything I've done before."

"Does that mean that you wouldn't want the job?"

"Now that would depend on the job, wouldn't it? I've never been averse to a challenge, but the answer would have to depend on the exact situation. Right now it's all hypothetical." Ness looked around at the ballroom and finally whispered to Napier. "Off the record, where did that question come from?"

Napier smiled, "Off the record?"

Ness nodded.

"Friend of a friend who works for Burton. Someone close to the new mayor is going to suggest you for a job, a someone who's in love with the reputation you got in Chicago."

"No kidding?"

"Honest." Napier scribbled something on his notepad and looked up. "Now let me ask you about—" His expression changed. "Holy Mary, you must be pulling my leg."

"What?" Ness said, nonplussed.

Napier was looking over Ness' shoulder now, his eyes following something near the entrance of the ballroom. "I don't believe it."

"Believe what?" Ness turned to see what it was that was attracting Napier's attention. He saw people mingling, talking to each other. It took a moment before he recognized what it was that was attracting Napier's attention. A man was working his way toward a set of tables to the right of the main entrance. He wasn't dressed for the event, and what would normally be an impeccably cut three-piece suit stood out in the midst of the tuxedos.

Napier started moving to intercept the man, and Ness

followed. "Who is that?" he asked, managing to suppress a little irritation at having the interview interrupted.

"That's Van number one," Napier said. The comment did nothing to enlighten Ness. The man was obviously someone of some importance, otherwise someone would have stopped him before he had reached the party itself. Ness had the feeling that the man should be familiar to him, but his face held nothing that really distinguished him.

Meanwhile Napier was nodding, "Yes, it is. Oris Paxton Van Sweringen, by God. Someone left his ivory tower unlocked—"

The baroque name finally triggered Ness' memory, though the result was something less than concrete. He remembered a number of articles about the Van Sweringen brothers, all about trains, real estate, and financial pyramids.

"Didn't he just go bankrupt or something?" Ness asked. They were slipping through the high and the mighty, converging on the Van Sweringen brother. Ness could see where the man was heading, a table at the far corner of the ballroom, at which sat an ominous-looking blond man flanked by a pair of gentlemen whose type was all too familiar to Ness.

"Their corporate assets were auctioned off in the sweetheart deal of all time. They never lost control, despite all the lost and misinvested money." Napier shook his head. "The Vans almost never come out in public. They weren't even at the dedication of their Union Terminal Building. God only knows what Oris is doing here."

The two of them reached the table at the same time as Van Sweringen. Napier called to him as he had to Ness. "Mr. Van Sweringen?"

Once Napier spoke, drawing attention to himself, it seemed as if the world around the table slowed to a near stop. Van Sweringen and the blond man at the table turned their attention to Napier, while the two others turned their attention to Ness. Ness returned the attention.

"Yes, can I help you with something?" Van Sweringen's voice sounded strained. He kept glancing back to the table even as he spoke to Napier. Ness was unsure if it was the blond man, or his hoodlum bodyguards, that was making Van Sweringen so nervous.

"Peter Napier of the *News*," Napier said, holding out his hand. "If I could have a minute of your time?"

Van Sweringen left Napier's hand hanging in midair. "No." He shook his head. "I'm here to talk to Mr. Dietrich, not the press."

Napier wasn't put off that easily, "Perhaps I should introduce both of you to Mr. Eliot Ness?"

Ness stepped forward, saving most of his attention for Mr. Dietrich. All three of the table's occupants stood up, and Ness noticed that the bodyguard on the left looked a little uncomfortable at Napier's mention of his name.

Napier continued, "You might be familiar with his crime-fighting career back in Chicago."

"Mr. Van Sweringen." Ness gave his most disarming smile to the man as he took his hand. He noticed that the mention of law enforcement seemed to make everyone but Dietrich nervous. Van Sweringen's hand felt like a dead fish. He held out his hand for Dietrich, and it was taken in a much firmer grasp. "Mr. Dietrich."

Dietrich nodded and looked at Ness as if he was seeing much too deeply into him. Ness felt the man was measuring him for something. The man had more *presence* than anyone that Ness had ever met. There was a charisma there, a confidence that informed every movement Dietrich made. Looking into Dietrich's eyes, Ness could sense a will that had rarely been thwarted.

"Mr. Ness," Dietrich said in a richly accented voice. Even the European flavor to his voice added to the impression, as if Ness was in the presence of a peer of Stalin, or Mussolini. Ness kept eye contact, despite every impression that told him to defer to the man. Ness was proud, and he wasn't about to back down from anyone out of nervousness. If anything, nervousness made Ness more apt to stand his ground.

Ness smiled and let Dietrich let go first, even though it was a relief when the physical contact ended. "You are an uncommon man, Mr. Ness," Dietrich said with a small smile.

"You know me, then?" Ness asked.

"No, I do not." The smile became a little wider. "I am a recent immigrant to this country. All I know of you is what I see in your face. Iron overlaid by the appearance of youth. I am certain your opponents often underestimate you."

"He's the man who broke up the Capone gang in Chicago," Napier said. He was still watching Van Sweringen. Dietrich didn't seem to interest the reporter.

Van Sweringen seemed flustered by the attention and protested, "I'm here on private business with—"

Dietrich raised a hand, and Van Sweringen stilled his voice. "Just a moment," he said in a level voice. Ness was still trying to identify the accent. It seemed Central European, which was common enough in this city. "I am talking with Mr. Ness."

Dietrich seemed to take an interest in him. That was fine with Ness, the feeling was mutual. He should be aware of someone who flanked himself with Sicilian thugs and wore his own power like a tailored suit. "You're a recent immigrant, might I ask where from?"

"Recently I come from Budapest. Originally from some small country that you never heard of, which no longer exists."

Ness nodded. "Europe is an unfortunate place lately."

Dietrich laughed. "It has always been unfortunate, Mr. Ness. That is the nature of Europe." The two hoods didn't laugh. From the way they and Van Sweringen looked, he and Dietrich could have been holding each other at gunpoint, rather than making small talk. "But I see your next question, the current environment—especially around Germany—made it more reasonable to take my business here, to America."

"What is your business, Mr. Dietrich?"

"Investments," he said. "I took my capital out of Europe, and I am investing in this country's future."

"Ah," Ness looked around at the ballroom. "I assume one of your investments was supporting Burton's campaign."

"You are perceptive. I am a supporter of law and order."

Napier spoke up, sounding a little irritated at having been left out of the conversation. "I'm sure Van Sweringen can appreciate that, what with dismembered corpses being found on his rail line—"

Van Sweringen's face reddened. "How dare you connect that atrocity with me! That is no more related to me than— than—corpses washing up on the beach are related to the

Humphry Popcorn Company! One more statement like that and I'll have you brought in for slander! Leave—both of you—before I have you removed!" Van Sweringen's voice was steadily rising, and people were turning to look at them now. Ness suspected that if he continued shouting like that, it would be Van Sweringen they'd remove—on a stretcher after a heart attack.

Van Sweringen took a step forward to confront Napier physically, but Dietrich stopped him by placing a hand on his shoulder. Van Sweringen turned to face Dietrich, and they stared at each other.

For the first time, Ness could see anger in Dietrich's expression. Deep in his eyes was a consuming rage that focused on Van Sweringen. "That is enough, Oris," Dietrich hissed quietly. Ness would have expected Van Sweringen to start raging at Dietrich next, but instead he seemed to deflate under Dietrich's gaze. Without turning to face them, Dietrich said, "I'm sorry, Mr. Ness. Perhaps you and your friend should go now. Perhaps I will see you again."

Ness nodded, looking at the two thugs staring at him. "Perhaps," he said. Then he took Napier's arm and led him back toward the bar. They withdrew slowly enough for Ness to hear the start of a whispered argument between Dietrich and Van Sweringen. All he made out was Van Sweringen's voice saying something about his brother, and Dietrich saying, "How dare you talk so loosely—"

Ness wanted another drink.

Back at the bar he ordered a martini and asked Napier, "What was it you were taking about, that made Van Sweringen so furious?"

Napier ordered whiskey. "It wasn't like I was implying anything, Christ."

"What was it, though, 'dismembered corpses?' "

"Oh, well, there's this place, Kingsbury Run, where the trains cut through to the Union Terminal . . ."

Napier told Ness about the Kingsbury Run murders in all their gory detail. It only took a little while for the case to spark some familiarity. Ness had heard about it two months ago. Some paper had called it, "the most bizarre double murder in Cleveland history." He hadn't heard much about it since.

When Napier was done, Ness finished off the martini

and asked, "So what was his comment about the Humphry Popcorn Company supposed to mean?"

"God knows; I don't. Something about Euclid Beach Park, I guess."

"Know anything about Mr. Dietrich?"

Napier shook his head. "First time I ever met him."

"I thought the high and mighty was supposed to be your beat?"

Napier shrugged and swirled the Scotch in his glass. "Hey, I don't know the guy. Maybe he's new in town, maybe he isn't all that important. Either way he's low-enough profile that I haven't seen anything about the guy. Maybe 'Dietrich' is an alias?"

Ness nodded. "That would make sense."

Napier looked askance at him and said, "Why do you say that?"

"Did you see the goons with him?"

Napier nodded.

"Well, I think one of them is Carlo Pasquale, from the Mayfield Road Mob."

"Oh." Napier nodded sagely and drank his scotch.

Meanwhile, the lights dimmed and the mayor-elect began to speak. By the time the lights came back on, Dietrich, Van Sweringen, and Carlo Pasquale were all gone.

12

Friday, December 6

Florence Polillo waited until nightfall before she walked out of her flat. Sunlight was painful to her now, and she wouldn't face the day unless she had to. Shortly, the day would be lost to her forever. The bars were coming to life around her, and people she once knew occasionally shouted a greeting, or made a proposition. She ignored them all. She strode the sidewalk like a ghost. This world had been taken from her, and no one had yet given her one to replace it.

She didn't even feel that she belonged with Rose and the others. They, all but Rose, had been brought over already. She was the only other one left who hadn't. She and Rose were still human.

Still human, but with His blood in her veins, pressing His will into her own, opening every wrinkle of her mind to Him. She wanted Him, and she was terrified of Him. She wanted to join them in their eternity, but the necessary death scared her.

She had seen the death. The ceremony He underwent with His inner circle. They all had to see, and had to share the blood as it was all drained from the disciple from slashes in the neck, the arms, the legs. Only when it was completely gone would He replace it with his own.

Flo had seen it ten times now, and every time it seemed that more than blood was replaced. It was as if He filled the bodies with his own soul.

She shuddered at the memory and slid into a familiar tavern, a place where she had once spent time with poor Eddie.

The bartender recognized her when she pushed her way

through the crowd. "Hey, Flo," he said over the head of a patron, "long time no see."

Flo nodded and squeezed next to the bar. Before, she had been growing to hate these places—smoky, crowded, loud. Now it almost filled her with a painful nostalgia for a time before the blood, before the ache, before the death—

She gave the bartender a fiver and said, "Whatever that will buy me."

The bartender looked at her, looked at the five, and swapped a bottle of amber liquid for the money. He handed her a glass and she pushed away from the bar before he could say anything more.

She found a dark corner with a table all to herself and proceeded to get quietly drunk.

When she got to her third glass, an unfamiliar voice said, "Florence? Florence Polillo?"

She slowly looked up from the glass. She resented the speaker before she ever saw him. The liquor had barely had a chance to warm the December chill away, and when she saw him, the chill deepened, evaporating the grip of the booze.

The man wore overalls, clothing that was almost anonymous. His hair was black, except where his mustache met his goatee, where it had begun to gray. But what chilled Flo were his eyes, eyes as gray and hard as slate. For a moment, Flo thought He had finally come for her.

It wasn't Him, and that frightened her all the more.

He stood opposite the table and said, "Don't deny it. I can see who you are, what you are."

Flo finally spoke. "I don't know what you're talking about." She set down the glass because her hand was shaking.

The stranger shook his head and sat down opposite her. "You know Andrassy. You have the same master."

"I don't know—"

Her friend the bartender stepped up behind the stranger and placed a hand on the man's shoulders. *Not a man,* Flo thought.

"I think the lady wants to be alone, Mister." Flo was grateful for the interruption, and was simultaneously frightened for the bartender. He had no idea what he was interfering with.

The stranger turned to face the bartender, and Flo had a horrible fantasy of the stranger striking him down right there, tearing out his throat, of blood pooling on the stained barroom floor. But the stranger didn't attack. He stared at the bartender and said quietly, "I am bothering no one. I am not even here."

All the color drained out of the bartender's face as he nodded. The expression he wore was one of extreme terror, as if he had also seen Flo's gory fantasy and for a moment believed it might happen. He quickly slipped away, and once he was back behind the bar the stranger turned back around to regard her.

"Who are you?" Flo whispered.

"Call me Iago," the stranger said.

"What do you want?"

Iago's gaze bore into her skull. She felt as if her forehead was made of glass, and that those gray eyes could see every working of the mind underneath it. "I want you to name your master to me."

She felt as if her heart had stopped beating in her chest.

"One of the blood has thrown aside the Covenant, one of enough power that he threatens the Covenant itself."

Flo just shook her head.

"Do you think you and yours are the only ones of the blood? There is a society here, one your master could destroy. He has already killed one of us in addition to your friend; do you know how grievous an act that is?"

"I can't talk to you!" Flo said in a harsh whisper. Running through her mind was what He had done to Eddie. He had severed his head while he was still alive. He had mutilated the body . . . "Leave me alone."

"Unlike your master, I respect the Covenant. I shall not force you against your owner's will." Iago stood. "But I see your master's blood in you as I saw it in Andrassy. You and your master are part of the Covenant whether he holds to it or not."

Flo felt a shudder inside herself. She knew that she had to let Iago leave. She knew that it would mean her life, and her chance at something beyond life, if she opened her mouth.

Her hand shook as she whispered, "You knew Eddie?"

Iago stopped. "I knew the person your master slaughtered with Andrassy. I saw them both a few days before they were killed." He stepped back and returned to the chair. The crowd in the barroom seemed to recede from them, as if they'd been abandoned in a small corner of the world that no one could quite see. No one faced them, no one paid them any attention. Even the sound of their voices seemed to fade under Iago's, as if it came from a different reality.

"His name was Anacreon, and he was the oldest and wisest of the blood that I have known." He must have seen her expression, because he said, "No, not as old as the name. He was a scholar. He was my friend, he was once my master."

Flo shook her head, "But Eddie—"

Iago raised his hand, silencing her. "Anacreon took me long ago, initiated me into his circle, taught me the Covenant that has held our society together for nearly a millennium. That we do not slay those of the blood, allow those of the blood to be exposed, and take responsibility for those we bring into the blood. Without that law between us, all those of the blood would be slain—at our own hands or the hands of others."

"You told Eddie this?" This was not what He said. He said law belonged to the powerful, and that all those of His kind were His subjects or His enemy. He was the true lord of this world, and eventually all humanity would bow down to Him and His kind, and all of His kind would bow to Him. Anyone who opposed Him forfeited their lives.

All He had given the thirst thought His rule was a small price for the power, and the life, that He offered.

"Anacreon told Eddie this. I know that Anacreon had spent a year investigating something. An ancient who did not observe the Covenant. The last I saw him, he was with Andrassy, and Anacreon thought he knew who this ancient was. He did not tell me who, and within days they both had died." Iago leaned forward. "At the hands of your master."

Flo couldn't move, but she could feel Iago reading the agreement in her eyes. She wanted to tell him, scream everything, punish Him for taking Eddie. She couldn't. The price was too high. She could feel what He offered slipping away from her just for being in Iago's presence, and something inside her wanted desperately to hang on to what she had. All she had. The only thing she had.

"Anacreon was one of the great ones in this city. His loss, in this way, has panicked and confused those of the blood. My circle is devastated, nearly powerless without him. Without the information you can give me, I have no voice for the others. I need a name."

Flo felt the force of Iago's will pushing her, pulling the information. Even though He controlled her, body and soul, He wasn't here. Somewhere under Iago's gaze, her internal struggle transformed from her attempt to resist Iago to His influence trying to keep her from speaking.

"I found you," Iago said, his words pushing away everything but them and the table. She was alone, utterly alone with herself and Iago. Nothing could reach her here. "Others can find you," he said.

Flo felt she was falling into his gray eyes, losing herself. It was like giving herself up to Him, but without the pain.

"A name," Iago said.

Slowly, as if in a dream, Flo said, "He calls himself Eric Dietrich." Then, through the evening, Florence Polillo committed suicide with her words.

13

When Eliot Ness saw the reporters, he knew he was going to take the job the new Cleveland administration was offering him. He had only talked once on the phone with Mayor Burton, and since then he'd been wondering if the job of Safety Director was for him. Until now, his entire career in law enforcement had been within the Federal Government, and he'd always been on the front lines, not an administrator.

He came to City Hall to talk to the mayor, still a little unsure. Unsure until the press began to crowd around him. The third time a reporter asked, "Is it true you're going to be the chief lawman in this city?" he knew he'd take the job. It wasn't even lunchtime yet.

Ness was one of a crowd of people here to see the mayor, most probably here to see about jobs in the new reform-minded administration. Even so, he didn't have time to shuck his overcoat before he was ushered into the mayor's office.

The door shut, leaving him facing Mayor Burton. The politician stood behind his desk, leafing through papers as he talked to another man. His eyes glanced up at Ness once the door closed. "Thank you for coming, Mr. Ness. I'd like to introduce you to Joe Crowley, Assistant Law Director for the city."

Ness stepped up and shook hands with Crowley, then the mayor. "Thank you for inviting me. I was somewhat surprised at your phone call."

The mayor nodded. "I was surprised at how well-recommended you were. I'm afraid I did not know you beforehand," he glanced down at the pages in his hand, "though it seems I should have."

Ness felt irritated at the admission, but he didn't let it show in his face. He just nodded politely.

"Seems you were hell on bootleggers, and you helped put Al Capone away. Is that right?"

Ness nodded again.

The mayor put the papers on his desk and looked into Ness' eyes. "They tried to bribe you, and you threw them out. That's what impressed me the most. I need someone like you. The city's in a hell of a mess, and my predecessor practically abdicated while in office. I told the people that I was going to do something about crime, and the only way that's going to happen is if we clean up the police department. I need someone with an incorruptible reputation. If you're willing to take on the job, Joe here can swear you in right now."

Ness said he was willing.

Within moments he was holding up his right hand as Joseph Crowley swore him in before a crowd of reporters and city employees.

14

Oris Paxton Van Sweringen sat next to his brother's bed and tried to comfort him. Mantis James, normally light-complexioned, was even paler. His brow glistened under the single light in the private room, and his breathing was shallow and wracked with congestion. He had lost too much weight. His wrist was too bony under Oris' hand, and underneath the burning skin Mantis' pulse was much too fast.

The disease was in his heart, in his blood, and it had been made much worse by the influenza. Oris spent his time trying to think of some way out of this, some solution, better doctors, something. As usual, he was left empty, watching his brother, his companion, his best friend, being torn apart from the inside.

Tonight was another night that the doctors doubted Mantis would survive. His fever was too great, his blood pressure too high, his damaged heart working too hard to maintain a traitorous body. Oris tried to convince himself that he would rally again, as he had after the auction. But he hadn't been this bad off then.

There was a sour smell in the room, under the smell of fever and sweat. Oris tried to ignore it.

It was after midnight, early Friday morning, when Mantis opened his eyes and looked up at his brother. Quietly, he asked, "How goes the business, O. P.?"

Oris shook his head. "You were right about him."

His brother grasped Oris' hand. His grip felt hot, as if his skin was drawn tight over a boiler. "You did what we needed," he said.

"What we needed?" His own voice had weakened. "Is the business all we had? Is that all we ever had . . . ?"

"We have each other," Mantis said weakly. His eyelids drooped.

It shouldn't be you, Oris thought. He might have spoken, but if so, the words were too soft for Mantis to hear. *He put you here, because of me, to control me.*

"We have each other," Oris said so his brother could hear. Mantis' eyes remained closed.

Oris gripped his brother's hand tighter and realized that he was no longer feeling the flutter of Mantis' erratic pulse. "No," Oris whispered, "we have each other. We have to have each other."

He shook his brother with his other hand. His brother was so much dead weight. Still holding his hand, Oris called for the doctors, the nurses, someone to help. When the help came, Oris' throat was sore and the doctors had to pry his hand away from his brother's.

When they pulled his hand away, it was as if they were prying the heart out of his chest. He was pushed slowly away from the bedside as doctors and nurses crowded around. From their faces, Oris knew that there was nothing to be done.

"Why?" Oris asked. The question was silent, his voice had no breath to make a sound. The word stayed trapped in the hollowness inside him.

It was the devil Dietrich. He had taken away the two things that mattered most to Oris. And as he stood in the doorway, shaken and grieving, he thought of ways he could take revenge on the devil.

Two days into the job, Ness carried the last box of personal effects into his new office. The transition was going cleaner than he'd expected. He hadn't even had to miss his traditional handball game. Things were going well.

There was a paper lying on his desk telling him of all the meetings he had today, and the interviews he'd agreed to give. Next to that was a stack of file folders, personal histories he'd requested yesterday. By next week he expected to have a list of people within the department he'd be able to trust. He doubted that the majority of the cops in this city would appreciate him once he started in on his number one priority, cleaning up the corruption in the department.

It was about ten in the morning, the box put away, and he was halfway into the pile of folders when the intercom buzzed. Ness sighed.

"What is it?" he asked the box on the desk.

"Call for you, Mr. Ness," the secretary on the other end responded.

"Who?"

"The man won't give his name. He says he knows about a murder."

"Can you transfer that to a Homicide detective? I'm busy here."

"I tried. He says he'll only talk to you."

Ness looked at the folder in his hand and laid it on the desk in front of him, shaking his head. "Put the call through."

He picked up the phone with one hand, while saving his place in the folder with the other. "Hello, Eliot Ness here. What can I do for you?"

"Eliot Ness?" The caller was obviously trying to disguise his voice. It sounded as if he were at the bottom of a well.

"Yes, and you are?"

"Listen," the voice said. Ness could hear terror in the voice. The terror made him pay attention. Cranks aren't afraid. They don't sound as if they'll hang up if you do something unexpected.

"I'm listening," Ness said trying to sound authoritative. He was suddenly interested in the call.

"September fifth, last year, half a body washed up on Euclid Beach. A woman, killed by decapitation. Last September, two bodies were found by the tracks."

Ness had grabbed a pen and began taking notes on the cover of the file he'd been reading. *9/5/34, female, decapitated, Euclid Beach; 9/??/35, two men, tracks.* He was instantly reminded of the odd conversation he'd had at Mayor Burton's celebration.

"Yes, those were in the paper. What about them?"

"The same man is responsible for all the killings. He is a Hungarian named Eric Dietrich."

The blond man who'd been guarded by Carlo Pasquale. *Eric Dietrich, Mayfield Road Mob*, Ness wrote, then he added, *Van Sweringen?* Ness gripped the phone tighter as he wrote. "How do you know this?"

"I know Dietrich. You need to stop him. He's becoming more powerful."

Ness could hear the stress in the voice. There was something there, and he needed to draw it out. "I can't involve anyone in a murder investigation just on the basis of a phone call. You need to give me more."

"You have enough already. There will be more murders if you don't stop him. Murders and worse."

"Can you at least give me your name?"

"Good-bye, Mr. Ness." The line went dead as the caller hung up the phone. Ness held the phone for a moment, then hung it up, shaking his head.

In his brother's office in the Union Terminal Tower, Oris Paxton Van Sweringen hung up his brother's telephone and removed the handkerchief from the receiver. When he walked away, he left his brother's desk lamp on, leaving the desk as if Mantis James were just about to return to work.

As Oris left his brother's office, Eliot Ness was already ordering the immigration records for an expatriate Hungarian calling himself Eric Dietrich.

1936

15

Friday, January 24

The city was cold, the night air biting into Florence Polillo's face. It felt worse because it was after nightfall,
and she had been avoiding the sun for so long. Her coat
was too thin for the weather, and the cold she felt in her
veins made her feel like she was a moving pillar of ice.

She had been meeting with Iago, and he'd been telling
her of the society that existed in the night, beyond the
control of the creature that would be her master. Iago had
taught her a valuable lesson, even though His blood was in
her veins now, even though His domination was irresistible
in His presence, her mind was still bound more by fear
than by Eric Dietrich's will.

She was able to shut him out, keep the Master from her
own private thoughts. Enough will and she could become
her own . . . She had a chance to escape His notice, maybe
slip into that other world Iago was showing her. Slip into
a world without Him.

She maneuvered through dark, snowbound streets
toward the bar where she was to meet with Iago. For
once she was focused on the future with some optimism.
For once it felt as if the path she had chosen wasn't
irrevocable. For once it felt as if the ice inside her
might melt.

She cut through an alley between two tenements, and
she didn't see the shadow before it was upon her. A pall
dropped over her vision, turning the world black and
empty. Before she felt consciousness slip away, she heard
His voice say, "Florence."

His manner was that of a chastising parent, and it became
even colder before Flo lost her sense of the world.

*   *   *

Iago looked up from his drink. Nothing visible had changed in the bar, and until a few seconds ago, Flo had just been late. But he was aware enough to feel a shift. It was almost as if some of his blood rode in Florence Polillo now. She was close enough for him to feel something through it. Close enough to know that the worst had happened.

Iago stood up and left. No one stood in his way, or noticed him leave. He walked as if he had partially left the world. He walked as if the Devil himself was after him.

When Florence Polillo regained her consciousness, she was chained to a metal table in a long narrow room. Her mind was fogged, blurring her vision, turning the faces in her view into distorted monstrosities. She saw Him. He spoke to the assembly, those He had already brought over.

Most of the audience Flo had known for nearly a year. At the moment she couldn't recognize any of them. The speech He made was all about her betrayal, her unfitness for the new order, her ungratefulness, her rejection. . . .

She could feel the sense, even though the words were lost to her in the fog clouding her mind.

The ruddy light was dim, only revealing herself and those immediately next to her. She couldn't see to the end of the narrow room, and she could barely see to the ceiling.

They had stripped her, and the iron holding her was cold against her skin, almost as if her flesh had bound fast to the metal. Then He touched her, and what warmth she still felt inside her was drained away at His touch. The hand rested on her shoulder, and through the contact she could feel all the contempt, and the anger.

She could also feel the prod of His mind, trying to unfold hers. She resisted it. It would have been a final violation. In His touch she felt the frustration and the anger, and she knew she had managed to keep Iago's identity, if not her betrayal, to herself.

You will never be with us now.

He spoke, but she felt the words rather than heard them.

She could feel Him withdrawing His influence, taking back all His blood had given her. The isolation was devastating. When He finally drew the blade, she welcomed its bite into her neck.

16

Wind carved through the alleys around East Twentieth, slicing away any heat it found. As the morning dawned, little moved outside except that wind. Zero temperatures for a second week kept everyone inside, near some source of heat. Some never even left their beds. Many churches stood empty.

As dawn broke, a dog began howling over the wind. The howls were almost painful, as if the cold were killing it. It howled, straining at its leash as if to break it. Its claws scraped for purchase on the ice-covered ground, and it would occasionally leap, to have its lunge snapped short by the chain that held it captive.

The dog's tongue lolled, and occasionally only the whites of its eyes would show. Where the collar bit into its neck, there were flecks of frozen blood marring its black coat. It appeared as if the cold had driven it mad.

It hadn't.

The animal's straining, its howls, its abortive lunges, all had the same object at their focus. A few yards away from the extent of the leash, across the alley, a bushel basket lay against a factory wall. Across the top of the basket was a burlap sack, its weave slowly turning white with frost. Slightly visible underneath the burlap sack was part of a human hand.

Stefan and Nuri were one of the first homicide teams to visit the scene. The call had been put in by a local butcher who thought the basket had been filled with hams stolen from his shop, at least until he had a decent look at its contents.

When he and Nuri arrived, Stefan thought that the scene was more appropriate to a Hieronymus Bosch depiction of Hell than of a police investigation. A man held a howling dog back from the police clustered in the alley. A photographer was taking pictures while the detectives and the coroner's people took an inventory of the basket's contents.

Stefan watched the inventory as if in a dream; right arm, both thighs, the lower half of a female torso. All were neatly dismembered, the cuts too clean to seem real. It was as if the victim were little more than a disassembled mannequin.

Stefan couldn't help but remember the time on Euclid Beach, finding the body that had been so insulted that it ceased to be perceived as a body. The feeling was reinforced when the police spread out to search for more remains.

He, Nuri, and the other detectives questioned the local residents, but the bitter cold had kept them all inside. The most anyone had heard was the dog. As the Sunday progressed, Stefan felt more and more that something evil had fallen over the city.

The cold continued as the police tried to reconstruct the life of the victim. Her identity was quickly discovered through the fingerprints of the one arm. Florence Polillo had a six-year-old record in Cleveland for soliciting and occupying rooms for immoral purposes.

Stefan and Nuri were part of the investigation, questioning Flo's associates, acquaintances, visiting the bars she frequented in the Third Precinct. Little clearly emerged about her past. She wasn't someone that people *knew*.

They found three possible marriages, but only one of the husbands was found. They found no trace of the first. Andrew Polillo was her second husband, but he'd been abandoned by Flo six years ago, and hadn't even known where she'd been staying. The third called himself Harry Martin, a tall blond man she had apparently brought back from Washington, D.C. The most solid sign of Mr. Martin was a hotel manager who said he'd given rooms to Flo and her husband, and that her husband seemed to be rough on her. Harry Martin himself, couldn't be found.

Added to that was a rat's nest of tangled lovers, aliases,

jobs, and arrest records out of which nothing concrete emerged.

A week into the murder investigation, Stefan heard of another ephemeral lead, but one that disturbed him. It disturbed him all the more because there was nothing he could do to follow up on it.

There were literally dozens of people that the detectives wanted to find; old madams who had employed Flo, people who provided her with drugs, a long list of Italians who had associated with her, a seaman who had visited her, a black woman who had visited her in jail, a gambler, several black men who might have been her lovers—and one gentleman, possibly Italian, who matched the description of someone who had been seen with Edward Andrassy.

It was the last that disturbed Stefan, because the description of this man also matched that of Iago.

By Thursday the seventh, more of Flo's body was found, preserved by the cold, close by to where the basket had been found. The new pieces included Flo's upper torso, which was enough for the coroner to pronounce decapitation as the cause of death.

Despite this, and a possible link to Andrassy, the newly appointed head of Homicide, Detective Sergeant James T. Hogan, told the press that the Flo Polillo murder was to be treated as totally unrelated to the Andrassy case.

Stefan wasn't the only one who didn't believe Detective Hogan's pronouncement.

17

Stefan and Nuri left the Central Station at eleven in the morning. The day was as cold as any yet. Their breath fogged in the car, even with the heater going.

"What a day," Nuri said in a puff of fog. He rubbed his hands together. "Do we have to go out in this?"

Stefan pumped the brakes to stop his Ford at the corner, allowing some of the insane Cleveland drivers to barrel past the intersection in front of him. He looked at Nuri. "We're supposed to follow up this call."

"Another anonymous call— Am I the only one who thinks the Polillo case isn't going anywhere?"

Stefan shook his head as he watched a Lincoln shoot by in front of him. Watching it, he thought that Clevelanders drove as if their cars were weapons. The light changed, and Stefan paused to make sure that the cross traffic had actually stopped.

During that pause, the rear passenger-side door opened, letting in howling wind and snow. Stefan turned with Nuri to see what had happened. Behind them, someone's horn blared at them.

A young man pulled himself into the back seat of Stefan's Ford, pulling the door shut behind him. Stefan reached for his gun and began to ask, "What the hell do you—"

"What the—" Nuri said, apparently achieving recognition about the same time that Stefan did.

The horn blared again, as Eliot Ness shook snow out of his hair.

Ness looked at both of them from the back seat and said, "I think you better start moving again."

Stefan turned away from the chief law enforcement officer in the city, and pumped the gas. The V-8 sprang through the intersection, tires squealing.

"Detectives Ryzard, Lapidos," Ness said.

"Yes," Nuri responded. "Sir, what are you doing here?" Nuri echoed Stefan's thought.

"I'm not here," Ness said. "And you can forget the tip, it won't pan out."

"You know that?" Stefan asked.

"Yes. I made the call."

Stefan squeezed the wheel and felt his knuckles pop. "What the hell are you doing, meddling in a murder investigation?" Stefan looked at Ness in the rearview mirror. He looked younger than Nuri, with a face that belonged on a college campus, not a police force. This was the man the papers made such a fuss about, the man who was going to clean up this city. Stefan didn't like him.

"I want you to drive to City Hall—"

"Am I a chauffeur now?" Stefan said.

Stefan saw Ness frown in the rear-view mirror. He didn't care. He'd never liked what he'd seen of the Safety Director's grandstanding, and his first meeting with the man wasn't improving the impression.

"What are you doing here, sir?" Nuri repeated. His voice carried the tone of someone stepping between two men throwing punches at each other, carrying equal parts reassurance and fear at being drawn into the melee.

"I'm here because you two are being assigned to something that can't be dealt with through normal channels." He stared at Stefan through the mirror. "I need an investigation that won't ripple the political waters."

Timid attitude for the centurion who's supposed to deliver the city from the barbarians.

"What investigation?" Nuri asked.

"The same one you're on now, the Polillo murder—"

"Everyone and their brother is on that already," Stefan said.

Ness nodded and began pulling folders from a briefcase he carried, leaving them on the seat next to him. "You two are no longer on the official list of investigators. You're now reporting directly to me." He patted the folders next to him. "No one else is to know about your investigation."

Stefan started to say something, but a burning feeling in his gut stopped him.

"Why?" Nuri asked.

"Your investigation will include powerful men that the rest of the force don't even know are part of the investigation. The evidence is too slim to make this public even inside the administration—"

"There's a connection," Stefan said. "Hogan's denying it, but there's a connection to the Andrassy murder."

Ness nodded. "I've ordered that there be no official connection between those murders. That's what you're going to do. Connect them, Polillo, Andrassy and his John Doe companion, and the Jane Doe that washed up on Euclid Beach in September '34."

They were pulling up on City Hall. "Why the secrecy?" Stefan asked.

"I've left you some notes on it. There're also some numbers that you'll report to. Go back to the station and type out a report about how this lead never panned out. You'll find orders reassigning you. I have to go now, I'm meeting the press upstairs."

Ness left the rear of the car, slipping up the snowbound steps of City Hall. "I'll bet," Stefan muttered.

In the rear seat were a pile of papers. Stefan looked at Nuri as he turned back to the road. "Get those, would you?"

Nuri pulled the stack of folders on to his lap. He opened the top folder. "It seems to be the immigration records for someone named Eric Dietrich."

Stefan led Nuri up to his apartment. Nuri followed him up the stairs, carrying the pile of folders Ness had left them. Stefan had decided that, with the secrecy involved, it would be better to go over everything somewhere private. He distrusted the publicity-minded Ness, but he was also drawn to the assignment, the same way he'd been drawn to the nondeath of Samson Fairfax.

Behind him on the stairs, Nuri said, "I keep wondering, why us two? Wouldn't Musil and May make more sense?"

Stefan shook his head, "Not if there's supposed to be a secret investigation." He stopped in front of his door and pulled out his keys. "Whatever Detective Sergeant Hogan says is 'official,' everyone is making a connection between Andrassy and Polillo. If Musil and May were suddenly reassigned off of both cases, someone would notice. You and me, we're only part of the Polillo case."

The door swung open into Stefan's sparse apartment. A sense of social unease struck him. Stefan couldn't remember the last time he had invited someone into his apartment. He was suddenly conscious of how empty it seemed.

Blinds cut off the rest of the world, and as Stefan turned the switch, the living room seemed to shrink under the light. The only furniture here were a few cane-backed chairs and a table. There wasn't even a carpet to moderate the sound of their footsteps.

Nuri walked in and unloaded his burden on the table as Stefan took away a coffee cup and plate left over from breakfast. Thankfully, Nuri made no comments about his apartment. Though he did glance up at a crucifix, the only decoration on the wall.

"What is this about a Jane Doe?" Nuri called to him as Stefan put the dishes in the sink.

"Two years ago, part of a body washed up on Euclid Beach. I was there."

"Part of a body?"

Stefan started putting a coffeepot together. "Yes, the lower part of a female torso. We found the upper part later on. Cause of death was probably decapitation."

Nuri whistled. "That makes all of them, then," he rustled through the files, "All killed by decapitation. Something of a signature."

Stefan made coffee while Nuri perused the files. When Stefan returned with two cups, Nuri said, "I don't see any connection to this Eric Dietrich, other than that he seems to have arrived in the country the April before Jane Doe washed up."

Stefan took the other chair. "As far as I'm concerned, we're investigating the murders, not Dietrich—"

"But—"

"Eric Dietrich is just a hunch on Ness' part," Stefan sipped his coffee. "First, I want to look at all four of these deaths and see everything that ties them together."

Outside, the winter wind rattled the windows. A radiator

issed in the corner. Nuri cradled the mug as if using the coffee to warm his hands. "Other than the decapitation?"

"What else?"

The folders for four murders were spread on the table. "They were all moved. None were killed where they were found. All the blood ended up somewhere else." He tapped on the file for Andrassy and his John Doe companion. "These bodies were actually cleaned off."

"Think there's any question that we're dealing with a maniac?"

Nuri nodded. "It looks like that, though . . ."

"Though what?"

"I get an odd feeling looking at these bodies." He picked up a picture of the basket where Polillo's remains were found. "Don't you get the sense that there's some ritual involved?"

"Doesn't mean we're not dealing with someone's private madness."

"I guess not."

Stefan looked at Nuri, whose expression was cast down at the files before them. "But you think differently?"

"What if we're dealing with a group here?"

The idea made Stefan shudder. "Let's concentrate on what we have, what we know. We can speculate later."

Nuri nodded and added, "Have you noticed the really odd thing?"

"This whole case is odd."

"No, I mean it might be coincidence, but according to this, both unidentified bodies were preserved in some sort of chemical. The body that washed up on Euclid Beach, and the body next to Andrassy, both had some odd chemical reaction with the skin."

Stefan nodded, "Okay, so our killer stores the bodies somewhere. He probably is a madman—"

"But why not Andrassy and Polillo? The only real difference is that we've identified them."

18

Iago stood before a long table. The table had chairs for twelve, but only ten elders faced him. Deaths had emptied the last two seats. Despite that present evidence of danger, the audience was both the most impassive and the most hostile he had ever performed before. Out the windows beyond them, the gray-black skyline—night-dark and wrapped in smoke from the Flats—was more attentive, and more welcoming.

He had come here to warn them, the greatest in each circle that ruled Cleveland and the surrounding state. None wanted to hear what he had come to know; about the being calling himself Eric Dietrich; about the humans Polillo and Andrassy; or about the deaths that had emptied the chairs at this high table.

When Iago had finished, the room fell silent. For a while the only sound in the boardroom was the soft moan of the waning winter wind outside. Inside, under stares from the soft-lit portraits on the wood-paneled walls, Iago waited for a response.

Lucian, first among all that were here, was first to talk, as always. "Iago, your information serves you and those of the blood well." Lucian leaned back, narrowing his ebony eyes, taking away half of what he had given, "But I do not hold such a high regard for your *opinions*."

That was it, Iago felt. He faced the most senior and powerful of their kind that were in the region. Lucian had known Moses Cleaveland when he'd stepped off at settler's landing in 1796, the two women here had been in the Indian communities here before then. Every one of the faces looking at Iago were of the blood before the Civil War—

when he was still a human actor drafted into the Union Army.

They were old enough to be too conservative. To be too blind.

Byron, second to Lucian, but a power in his own right, spoke, echoing the elder's words. "The two humans, as you say, may have been in the process of coming over to the blood. Their deaths, so entwined with our peers Laila and Anacreon, speak to that. And, what that loss has meant to your circle has not escaped us." Byron shook his head. "But to accept the word of a human prostitute that her master is *Melchior*? That creature was destroyed long before any here was born."

Not before Laila, Iago thought. *She would have been the only one of you to know him for what he was.* He did not speak. He could not interrupt the elders. If he did, the impropriety would prevent any of them from hearing what he said.

Byron continued. "Again, while there may be a grave violation of the Covenant here, and the humans' master is likely responsible, there is little evidence that that master is, in fact, the man Eric Dietrich. That man has been photographed abroad in the daylight, and none here or abroad claims him as one of the blood."

To do both would be too powerful for you to credit, Iago thought. If they couldn't accept that Dietrich was the ancient Melchior, then of course they couldn't accept him abroad in daylight. The chief vulnerability they had, aside from the thirst, was the light from the sun. In all of history, there had been only half a dozen of the blood who had achieved enough of a level of power and self-control to walk under the sun without turning into so much dead flesh.

Believing Iago was wrong was much easier than accepting that there might be a hostile presence here, millennia old, and more powerful than any who sat in this room.

Raphael, several seats down from Byron and Lucian, looked at Iago with what might have been sympathy. "The Covenant has been broken, even if not by whom Iago suspects."

One of the women, Jana, asked, "Has that ever been established?"

"It would be wise to treat it so," said someone else.

"That means that someone is attacking the Council directly," said another.

Iago noticed Raphael looking across at Byron and Lucian as he said, "That's not necessarily so. There were the two humans who had nothing to do with us." That seemed to head off the scent of panic that the question had begun to spread through the room. Iago frowned. He thought that these old fools could use a little panic. At this point, some more fear would be constructive.

It seemed wrong. He remembered the panic through his own circle. Centered around Anacreon the circle had been chaotic, but powerful. If Anacreon had still lived, it would have been him to speak after Lucian, not that smarmy Byron. And from what Iago saw, Byron was little better than a thrall to Lucian. Byron led a circle which seemed little more than an extension of Lucian's own power.

Iago didn't listen to much of the debate, after it began. Debate was a kind word. It was little more than a war of assertions, each gaining weight with the seniority of the proposer. None contradicted the root assertions by Lucian and Byron, that Iago was wrong, and that Melchior was so much ash scattered on the hills of Bavaria.

Iago left the building lost in disappointment. The leaders of his kind would treat this as a simple matter of murder, not as the threat it was. He slogged along the sidewalk downtown, wondering what was going to happen to his people.

He kept walking until he felt a tap on his shoulder. He turned to see Raphael standing behind him. He hadn't sensed him approach. That made Iago even more nervous. Raphael came from an era of ships and whaling a hundred years before Iago lived. If Raphael hid himself so well from Iago, what hope did any of the elders have against a being that was millennia old?

"Iago," Raphael said.

Iago nodded. "Sir." The word tasted sour in his mouth.

"Eric Dietrich is doing too much good for many of the Council to move against him."

It wasn't what he was expecting to hear, so Iago didn't respond for a moment. He just stood, staring at Raphael's face, wondering what the other was thinking.

"Whoever he is," Raphael continued, "he is warring with human forces that some of our own would like to see diminished. As long as Dietrich is an enemy to certain criminal elements in this city, parts of our Council will not move against him."

Iago nodded. "I see."

"There is worse," Raphael said. He reached out his hand. "But I need a pledge of fealty from you before we talk further."

Iago looked at the hand. "Why?"

"Because otherwise I cannot say what I need to say. Because you have no friends on the other side of the table. Because Anacreon's circle is disintegrating without him."

Iago looked at Raphael and said, "What about my loyalty?"

"To Anacreon? He is no more. Your only loyalty is to help avenge him."

After a long time, Iago took Raphael's hand and said, "By the name I've chosen between us, I so pledge." In his heart he apologized to Anacreon.

The event was small in ceremony, but it hung heavy with power. It felt as if the center of gravity shifted between them.

After their hands separated, Raphael said, "Perhaps you know that there are those who are not grieving for the loss of either Laila or Anacreon. . . ."

19

A month into the Safety Director's special assignment, Stefan's apartment was papered with notes, charts, and copies of police photographs. His spartan apartment had become a shrine to the murders. The investigation was the last thing he saw when he went to bed, the first thing he saw when he woke up in the morning.

He and Nuri would spend hours poring over the papers, looking for common threads binding the murders together. They also reinterviewed dozens of people the initial investigation had talked to. Stefan managed to confirm to his own satisfaction that the man who called himself Iago was seen in the company of both Andrassy and Polillo, but little else new surfaced.

The only connection between Andrassy and Polillo seemed to be their sordid pasts. Both frequented the Roaring Third, Precinct, a morass of tenements, bars, flophouses, and pool halls. Polillo was a prostitute, and Andrassy had been involved in pimping men and women.

It seemed likely that they met, might have even known each other, but there was nothing to confirm it. Stefan, however, was growing convinced that when Iago had said, "Andrassy's whore," he was referring to Polillo.

Because they were covering so much ground, on four murders, by themselves, it wasn't until a month into it that Stefan drove his Ford up Walnut Street and pulled in front of a run-down hotel. "Here we are."

"This is it?" Nuri asked.

The building was in sad shape. Most of the windows were gray, except where yellowed newspaper covered a break in a pane. The brick walls were black with grime. On the stoop, under the rusted sign, two old men were sharing a bottle between them.

Stefan opened the door and stepped out. "Time to check out Polillo's last known husband."

Nuri got out of the car and lit a cigarette. He shook his head. And said a phrase that he'd started chanting before every one of the past dozen interviews, "This is not going to be another vanishing lead."

Stefan walked around the car and patted Nuri on the back. "Come on."

The manager had a little fly-specked office off of the lobby. There was barely enough room for him to sit, so Nuri and Stefan were left to crowd the doorway. After the man had made the obligatory noises about already telling the police everything, they got down to questioning about Polillo's past.

"She came back from Washington, D.C., with a new husband?" Stefan asked.

"Don't know where she been," the manager said, "but she called the guy her husband."

"Harry Martin," Nuri prompted.

The manager nodded. "That's the name he gave. Queer, that guy. Didn't like him. Misused her, I think."

"Misused her?" Stefan asked. "How?"

"She got too damn pale." The manager tapped under his eye. "Shadows like bruises. Seemed hurt a lot. Then there was screaming from the room." The manager looked up at both of them. "Don't look at me like that. I don't mess with my tenants' business."

"This was through the end of 1934?" Nuri asked.

The manager nodded.

"Can you describe the Harry Martin gentleman?" Stefan asked. From the files, the police had yet to find the man.

"Yeah, sure. Hard to forget. Tall, blond, hair too long. Foreign-like. Gave me the willies just by hanging around—"

Nuri surprised Stefan by pulling out a photograph and handing it to the man. "Is this him?" Nuri asked.

The manager took the picture, his eyes widened. He began nodding vigorously, "Yeah, yeah. That's the guy right there. Never forget those eyes."

The manager handed the picture back to Nuri, and Nuri handed the picture to Stefan. Stefan looked at it.

It was the picture of Eric Dietrich from the immigration record.

Back in the car Stefan said, "I guess Ness is on to something." He didn't want to admit it. The crowded morass of the Roaring Third slid by the Ford. For a while they both sat in silence. Eventually Nuri said, "You really don't like Ness, do you?"

Stefan snorted. "He's a glory hound, in it for the press coverage."

"Come on," Nuri said, "He strikes me as one of the most honest cops in this town. The force could certainly be cleaned up. You told me that yourself."

"Maybe I'm wrong," Stefan said, "But I think he's too in love with his own image. The gangbuster from Chicago."

Nuri shrugged. "Well, we have a connection with Dietrich now."

Stefan nodded. The car slid past a pawnshop, the window was crowded with misplaced objects. One of the objects was a golden crucifix that reflected sun into Stefan's eyes as they passed. "We can't question him directly," Stefan said. "Not if we're to maintain this secrecy."

"What should we do next?"

"The obvious thing is to get missing persons records from Washington, D.C. If that was where Polillo met 'Harry Martin,' there's a chance that's where 'Martin' met the other victims, if he's involved. And since Dietrich is a businessman, we should uncover any business he had in D.C." Stefan shook his head. "What do we know about this fella anyway?"

"He's an immigrant from Hungary, he's wealthy. We don't have a lot else."

"Is he a Nazi?"

Nuri shrugged.

"The Nazis are into rituals. Think that may have something to do with what's going on?"

Nuri shook his head. "From what I've heard about the Nazi Party, I wouldn't be surprised."

"That's worth following up. His political affiliations. How

he arrived in the country . . . Do we know how he arrived in the country?"

Nuri nodded, "He had his own ship. The *Ragnarok,* a small freighter, German registry. From the information I have, it's in port here."

"You don't say?"

Night was falling as Stefan drove the Ford toward the docks. He pulled to a stop a few blocks short of the warehouse they were interested in. Beyond, the lake was visible. On it, the bulk of the cargo ships nearly dwarfed the small form of the *Ragnarok*. The small freighter that Dietrich owned was marked by the red and black German flag. People moved over the docks, and lights blazed through the night. Except on the *Ragnarok* and the warehouse.

"Doesn't seem to be a lot of activity around Dietrich's property," Stefan said. "Are you sure that he's still using it?"

"According to the shipping records," Nuri said while shuffling a stack of all the papers that the two of them were able to liberate without a warrant. "This warehouse and the ship have been seeing constant activity back and forth from Europe ever since Dietrich emigrated."

"Does it say where in Europe?"

"Spain."

"Figures." Stefan opened the door and looked toward the darkened warehouse. "Shall we go take a look?"

"Without a warrant?"

Stefan shrugged. "I don't think we'd be able to get one and maintain Mr. Ness' secrecy." He shut the door behind him. The wind off the lake carried the smell of rotting fish and diesel fumes. It chilled his skin. "Besides, whatever connection we have between him and Polillo, this is still a fishing expedition." He walked around to the rear of the car, opened the trunk and removed a flashlight.

Nuri got out of the car as Stefan slammed the trunk shut. "Let's see what Mr. Dietrich is bringing into the country."

"Who says he's bringing stuff *into* the country?" Stefan asked.

Nuri shrugged.

The two of them walked down the darkening aisle between the waterfront buildings. The temperature dropped, and a light dusting of snow drifted past the lights around them, a swirl of pallid motes against the darkling sky. The noise of the docks, the sound of engines and of foremen shouting orders, all seemed muted the closer they came to the darkened warehouse.

They stopped in front of the massive double doors closing the loading dock. Low and to the right was a more human-sized door, dwarfed by its neighbor. The building carried no markings identifying it, the entrances plain and whitewashed. Stefan tried the knob on the smaller door, and found it locked.

He stepped back. "Are you sure this is Dietrich's warehouse?"

Nuri nodded. "I did some work on Dietrich's background. I unearthed as much of his business holdings as I could without drawing attention to myself."

Stefan looked at Nuri, "You were doing this in your spare time?"

"You didn't like him as a suspect, but I had the feeling he was going to turn up." Nuri turned to face Stefan. "I hope you don't think I was going behind your back."

"No. No." Stefan shook his head. He felt uneasy again. He hoped that it wasn't his distaste for Ness that kept him from following up on Dietrich sooner. "So this is it?" He looked back at the massive locked portal. "It looks abandoned."

"Dietrich owns it."

"Does he use it, I wonder." Stefan edged around the side of the building. There were windows on ground-level, but they'd been whitewashed, too. Stefan's unease heightened. Something was being hidden in here. For a moment he wondered if it would be a good thing to know what it was.

He kept edging down the alley between this warehouse and the next, the only light filtering through the frosted windows of Dietrich's neighbor.

Halfway down the alley, the way was blocked by a new fence, about eight feet high. Stefan could see, through the boards of the fence, a metal ladder bolted to the side of Dietrich's warehouse. He looked back at Nuri, who was following, and pointed above the fence with the end of the flashlight. There the ladder was visible, hugging the wall all the way to the roof. Then he handed the flashlight to Nuri, grabbed the damp wood of the fence, and began climbing.

His body protested the exertion. His joints were too old to take these kind of athletics with good grace. However, he managed to reach the top of the fence. Straddling it he could see into the fenced-off alley beyond. Another fence blocked off the other side of the alley from the ladder. Next to the ladder, a side door led back into Dietrich's warehouse.

Stefan looked down and waved Nuri up. Then he dropped down on the other side. He heard a ripping sound and felt a sharp pain as a nail caught his pants leg. He fell to the ground and stumbled, trying to keep his balance.

Nuri dropped down afterward. "Are you all right?"

Stefan nodded as he looked at his left leg. The pants were torn up to the knee, and a narrow gash followed the line of the tear up his leg. It bled badly, but Stefan could feel that the wound was shallow. "Not bad, just a scrape."

Nuri pulled the flashlight from his belt, where he had shoved it. He walked up to the side entrance and tried the door. "Locked here, too."

"Let's go up and take a look around." Stefan walked up to the ladder and started pulling himself up.

"Are you sure you're up to that?" Nuri was staring at his leg.

"I'm fine," Stefan said. He tried not to wince when he put weight on his injured leg. "Come on."

After he pulled himself up a few feet, Nuri followed.

The roof was a treacherous slope of corrugated steel. The troughs were slick with ice, and parts were buried under a foot of snow. The roof angled up to a wall where Stefan could see windows, windows that weren't whitewashed.

There was a narrow wooden catwalk laid on the roof. It led from the ladder to where another catwalk hugged the wall ahead of them. It was snowless, and the only place on the roof where he could step without being certain of breaking his neck.

Stefan walked nervously onto the narrow strip of wood. Even though it was covered with tar to help traction, it was as icy as the roof around it, and it had no guardrail.

"Be careful," Stefan said to Nuri as his partner cleared

the edge of the roof. Slowly he began ascending the slope
to the wall ahead of them.

Nuri joined him on the roof, his breath coming out in an
even fog. "What are we doing here, Stefan?"

Stefan edged up on the wall. The wind was sharper up
here; the cold cut into the skin of his face, his hand, and
especially his wounded leg. He looked back at Nuri, who
was edging gingerly to follow him. "Anything more concrete than we have," Stefan answered him. "A connection
to Andrassy. Some indication of who the other victims are.
Maybe the killing ground."

Nuri lurched up to the wall and hugged it. "Killing
ground?"

"Our killer has someplace private he can do his work.
Where he kills, mutilates the bodies, drains them, cleans
them off, stores them."

Nuri looked around and nodded. "He could do it here.
It's private enough."

Stefan nodded. "I'm wondering why the windows downstairs were whitewashed." He edged along the wall until he
found a window that had been damaged by the ice. It sat
crooked in its frame, and after he'd kicked the ice and
snow away from it, it opened freely.

He peeked through the window, into the darkened warehouse. He saw no sign of movement. The floor was a mass
of darkness marked only by the blocky shadows of shipping
crates. Below the window, Stefan could see a catwalk following the length of the warehouse. He looked over at Nuri
and waved him forward. "Looks like no one's home," he
whispered. "Give me the flashlight."

Nuri handed it to him, and Stefan slipped in through the
window, dangled a moment, and dropped onto the catwalk.
He listened for a moment for any movement in the warehouse, and all he heard was the echo of his own steps. He
waited until he was certain that no one was walking around
in the warehouse before he turned on the flashlight.

He shone it down the catwalk toward the front of the
building. A ladder led down from that end.

Stefan inched away from under the open window and
waved Nuri through. After a moment there was a grunt,
then a loud crash as Nuri dropped onto the catwalk. The

sound seemed to echo forever in the open space of the warehouse.

"Could you try to be a little more quiet?" Stefan whispered.

"Sorry, it's icy up there. Lost my grip." Nuri wiped his hands off on his jacket, then pulled out his gun.

Stefan waited until they'd both reached the floor of the warehouse to pull his. The longer he was in this place, the more dead it seemed. The air hung still, musty and cold. Nothing moved in the darkness as Stefan shone his flashlight around. Even the rats seemed to have abandoned this place.

Nuri walked up beside him as Stefan shone the light on the crates stacked on the floor of the warehouse. There were dozens of them, oblong crates eight feet long, stacked like bricks. Black German Gothic was painted on the sides of the crates.

"Coming or going?" Stefan wondered aloud.

"Coming," Nuri said, placing his hand on top of the flashlight so the beam moved down a few inches. It now illuminated more writing in the side of one crate, this time in Spanish.

Stefan moved down an aisle between the crates, sweeping the flashlight over them. "Any sign what's in these?"

"Nothing in English."

Stefan looked over the crates, dozens of them, all the same size, the same proportions. He felt the unease attack him again. The subliminal wrongness striking him full force.

"We have to open one of these," Stefan said.

Nuri stepped in front of the flashlight. "Are you sure?"

"Look at the crates, look at the proportions. We're looking for a killing ground."

Nuri looked around. For a moment he didn't seem to know what Stefan was talking about. Then recognition seemed to strike him. "My God. They're just like coffins."

"Slightly bigger," Stefan said. "We should check this out." He stepped up to a lone box near the edge of the main piles. It lay by itself on a wooden pallet, the top coming up to a little less than waist height. "See anything we can pry this open with?"

"There's a fire ax on the wall over there." Nuri pointed at the near wall. Stefan swung the flashlight over to illuminate an ax and a fire bucket hanging on the wall. He handed the flashlight to Nuri and walked over to retrieve the ax. Freed from the hooks holding it to the wall, the ax was heavy, handle cold and damp to the touch.

He stepped up next to Nuri. Stefan wondered how close he came, at that moment, to feeling like the murderer—weapon in hand, the burning feeling of fear in his gut, the tension.

Nuri swept the flashlight so the beam illuminated the crate. The wooden lid was nailed shut and held fast by two thin metal bands. The edges were splintered and chipped. The surface was stained by oil and grease. The crate had been on a long journey.

Stefan hefted the ax, and brought it down on the side, where the top met the rest of the crate, over one of the thin bands. The band snapped and whipped away from the ax with an eerie vibrating sound. It echoed through the warehouse long after the sound of the ax's impact had died. When the band stopped moving, Stefan took the ax to the remaining one. That one snapped just as easily.

Stefan then wedged the blade in under the lid of the crate and began prying it open. The nails slid free with a screech of the damned. He had to move around, prying at every edge. When he'd opened it an inch or so, he had to adjust his grip on the ax and open it with the flat of the blade.

Eventually the lid was free, and he could slide it off the edge.

Nuri stepped up to the box and shone the flashlight in. All that was visible at first was a layer of straw packing. Stefan reached in with the ax and pushed the straw aside with the flat. Underneath was a polished wood surface, slightly curved, dark, reflecting the flashlight.

"My God," Nuri whispered as Stefan reached in with his hand, scooping the packing away from the object buried inside the crate. "It *is* a coffin."

Stefan stared at the head of the coffin. It was relatively plain, dark wood with little embellishment. But there was no mistaking what it was. He told himself that this was beyond what he expected, but somehow it wasn't. The fear and unease were growing in his stomach. He wanted noth-

ing more than to leave now, have his questions safely
unanswered.

Instead, he looked across the coffin at Nuri and said,
"We have to open it."

"This is macabre," Nuri said. But he nodded.

Stefan cleared all the packing off of the top of the coffin.
He walked around to Nuri's side, the side that opened.
There, he saw something that his knotted fears didn't
expect.

Centered in the flashlight beam was a latch and a padlock. "Who locks a coffin?" Nuri asked.

Stefan didn't know. But now they had to know what
Dietrich was shipping inside this box. Stefan brought the
ax down on the padlock. He had to do it three times before
the lock gave, springing open, falling into the packing
around the side of the coffin.

The two of them stood there for a long time, making no
more moves toward the coffin. Stefan told himself that he
was just waiting to hear if all the noise they'd made had
alerted anyone else in the warehouse. The warehouse was
silent as ever—the air heavy, cold, and unmoving.

Again, he felt the impulse to abandon the coffin uno-
pened. There was a feeling he didn't want to know what
was going on here.

Stefan leaned the ax against the crate and wiped his
palms against his legs. Despite the cold, a drop of sweat
stung the cut on his leg like a bee sting. He looked at Nuri,
who held the flashlight and his gun.

"Here goes," he told Nuri. As he leaned over the coffin,
he said, "Cover me."

Stefan was glad that Nuri didn't ask, "From what?" Stefan didn't have a ready answer for that question.

Stefan took hold of the lid, expecting resistance from
fused hinges, expecting the sound of protesting metal. Instead, the lid flew up silently, as if the coffin had been made
the day before.

The smell hit him first, making his eyes water, obscuring
his view of the occupant. There was a heavy perfume that
almost burned, and underneath a festering corruption that
matched any corpse he had ever come across. He had to
back away from the coffin.

"This is incredible," Nuri said. He held the flashlight

trained inside the coffin. His gun was pointed at its tenant as if it might suddenly start moving.

Stefan blinked his eyes clear. The body inside the coffin was an old man. He was bald and had a long white beard and mustache. The flesh had sunken on his face and the hands folded on his chest. The skin on the skeletal body was white and papery. The funeral suit he wore was loose and baggy. The satin on which the corpse lay was marred by dark stains.

Nuri raised the flashlight to point at the rest of the warehouse. "Dozens," he whispered. They had found evidence, beyond what Stefan had ever expected.

"Why ship corpses into the country?" Stefan asked.

"Maybe he is a maniac," Nuri said. "This is insane."

Stefan nodded. "But we have something now. We can box this body back up, call in Ness, and get everything cleaned u . . ."

Stefan trailed off, because a sound had intruded into the silent warehouse. A rustling noise, very close by. Then a voice, barely above a whisper—

"Du bist nicht der Meister."

Nuri swung the flashlight back to the coffin. The corpse was gone. He kept swinging until the light landed on the dead old man, standing next to the coffin.

"God save us all," Stefan whispered.

"Es war schon so lange . . . Ich kann das Leben riechen." The thing spoke, grimacing. Its face distorted, the jaw shifting, the teeth growing longer. Its nostrils flared as it stared at Stefan. Stefan wanted to move, but his gaze was locked on the thing's cloudy gray eyes. Despite the core of panic that raced through him, igniting every nerve in his body, he was unable to move.

The thing had become bestial, the face twisted almost into a canine form. Nuri shouted something at it, but Stefan couldn't hear it through the blood pulsing in his ears.

It leaped at him.

In the moment eye contact was severed, Stefan could move. He only had time to stumble backward, away from the thing. It wasn't enough. Clawed hands, smelling of perfume and decay, seized his legs, toppling him.

It sank its teeth into his left leg, above the wound. Its

teeth were like a brand searing his flesh. He might have yelled in pain, but he didn't hear himself over the gunshots.

Nuri fired at the thing as soon as it had leaped, and he kept firing until the gun was empty. Stefan saw the shots hit. He saw blood splatter from the thing's chest. He saw the thing lurch with the impact. He saw tattered flesh hanging from the exit wounds.

It remained on his leg. Stefan was starting to feel cold and fatigue. As if all the warmth in his body, all the life, was draining out the wound.

Stefan grabbed the thing's head. He tried to pry it away. His fingers tore at the thing's flesh, digging long bloody grooves in the sides of its face, but Stefan couldn't move it.

"Stefan, move!" Nuri's voice shouted from above him.

Stefan let go and collapsed. He felt as if all the solid matter in his body had liquefied. He was losing the feeling in his hands and feet. He looked up with a darkening vision and saw Nuri, partially illuminated by a flashlight that had fallen somewhere, facing the three of them. Nuri was raising the fire ax.

Nuri brought the ax down on the back of the thing's neck.

It did more than every gunshot, and all of Stefan's struggles put together. Its back arched, tearing away part of Stefan's flesh as its face pulled away. Stefan used the last of his strength to pull away from the thing. He pushed away with his arms, sliding on a slick of his own blood.

The thing made a sound, a screech that tore through Stefan's chest as if one of its putrescent claws was wrapped around his heart. It tried to turn to face Nuri, but Nuri pulled the ax free and brought it down again. Its body stopped moving as its head was turned on a half-severed neck at an impossible angle.

A final blow separated the head completely from the body.

Stefan tried to push himself upright, even though he felt consciousness slipping from him. Nuri dropped the ax. He was shaking his head, looking at the thing that was a corpse again. Not only had it stopped moving, it had returned to being the same skeletal old man that had lain in the coffin. The hands were just hands. The face was human again. If not for the blood covering the thing's lower face, it looked as if they had just removed a body from the coffin to mutilate it.

Nuri grabbed the flashlight from the ground and walked over to Stefan, shining it at his leg. Stefan wished he hadn't. His lower leg looked like a piece of raw hamburger. It was still bleeding, and Stefan felt as if all the heat in his body was spilling out the wound.

"We have to get you to a hospital." Nuri set down the flashlight, stripped his jacket and tie, and tore off his shirt to wrap up his wounded leg. The white shirt turned red instantly.

"Call in," Stefan said, his voice coming out in a hoarse whisper. "Ness was right."

"Yeah," Nuri said. "After we get you to—" He looked up from the makeshift bandage. "What's that?"

A sound filled the empty air of the warehouse. It was soft, almost subliminal. It wouldn't have been noticeable if it wasn't for the silence that had greeted them here. The sound was a scratching, almost ratlike.

Nuri picked up the flashlight and swept the beam around, searching for the source of the sound. It illuminated nothing that wasn't there before. Meanwhile, the sound grew louder. It grew louder until Stefan could tell where it was coming from.

"God save us," Stefan whispered. "The crates . . ."

Even in the dark, behind the flashlight beam, Stefan could see the color drain out of Nuri's face. There were dozens of crates, and the sounds were coming from inside, as if in each one, something had awakened.

Nuri got on Stefan's left side and slipped an arm under him. Nuri was only in an undershirt now, and where his skin touched him, it felt hot where his own was cold and clammy. Nuri pulled him upright fast enough to make him dizzy.

They stumbled together, as around them the scraping turned into pounding. They were accompanied by mumbled voices. Incomprehensible whispers. Stefan could feel the things in the crates now. More horrors like the old man thing. All half-dead, but animate. Animate and hungry.

Their progress toward the front was too slow. The noises increased in volume the closer they got to the entrance.

Stefan felt panic that one of the crates might explode open, and that one of these things would look upon him.

Stefan feared that if he fell under that stare he wouldn't be able to move.

Nuri managed to drag him all the way to the front door. Stefan leaned against the doorframe as Nuri fumbled with the latches holding the human-sized door shut. "What *is* this?" he said as he pulled at the bolt locking the door.

Behind him, the warehouse was dark without the flashlight. But the silence was only a distant memory. The scraping and pounding had stopped, but now the warehouse was filled with the sound of dozens of voices whispering to each other in several languages.

Stefan clutched his wounded leg, but blood still spilled from between his fingers. His awareness of everything other than the voices was fading. He seemed to be falling into a dark, whispering void. When Nuri pulled him through the door, Stefan fell into darkness.

20

Stefan woke up in a hospital bed. He knew it from the smells and sounds before he had opened his eyes. When he did open his eyes, and saw the face of the public safety director, he immediately wanted to close them again.

"How do you feel?" Ness asked him.

Stefan almost responded by asking, *Where are the reporters?* But, instead, he told Ness, "I feel like my leg's been torn open."

There was a ghost of a smile on a face that looked younger than Nuri. "I suppose so. You lost a lot of blood. You've been unconscious for nearly forty-eight hours."

Stefan leaned back and groaned. After a few minutes he said, "Did you get him, at least?"

"Who?"

"Dietrich. Who else? We connected him to Polillo and his warehouse is filled with—"

"No, we don't have him." Ness turned away. "Your partner's crazy story aside, by the time he got you to the hospital and called in this whole mess, the warehouse was empty."

"But the connection to Polillo?"

Ness nodded. "Hotel manager's gone missing, too."

Stefan closed his eyes. It was almost as if he could still hear the polyglot babble from the crates in Dietrich's warehouse.

"—until I could talk to you."

"What?" Stefan asked, opening his eyes.

"I said I've put Detective Lapidos on leave. I need to talk to you about what happened in the warehouse."

Stefan shook his head. "I'm not sure I believe it."

"Whatever happened put one of my men in the hospital, and I want to hear it."

Stefan looked at his boss and wondered if it was a good idea to tell everything. He decided it wasn't, but he told Ness everything anyway. He retraced their steps from the hotel manager's office until the point where he'd lost consciousness.

When he was done, Ness was wearing an incredulous expression. "Well, it matches your partner's story."

"But?"

"But *what*?" Ness looked at Stefan with a penetrating stare. "Do you need to be told that it's so much bushwa? Have you been listening to yourself?"

"It's what happened."

"I don't know what happened, but it didn't involve animate corpses." Ness shook his head. "If it weren't for some witnesses, I'd have trouble believing you were there at all."

"What?" Stefan sat up. He didn't expect any part of the story to be believed. He would have expected Ness to assume that he and Nuri were just two more dirty cops who'd conspired on a crazy story to cover something up. That's what he'd think in Ness' position.

Ness pulled a chair up to the side of the bed and sat down. "A longshoreman saw some men empty out the warehouse. They were the crates you describe." Ness shook his head slowly. "You and Nuri spooked somebody."

"But you don't believe what we saw?"

"What do you think?" Ness looked down at Stefan's leg. "The doctor confirmed that's a bite wound. But in his words, 'probably from a large dog.'" Ness looked up into Stefan's eyes. "I would never abide my people lying to me. If not for your record, I'd fire you right now. As it is, I'm sure you told me things as you remember them."

"What about Nuri?"

"He's new to the department. I hoped that the corruption hadn't gotten to him yet." Ness looked thoughtful for a moment. "You two stumbled onto *something*. It was dark and confused . . ."

"But what *happened* in there?" Stefan asked, mostly to himself.

Ness stood up. "I don't know." He walked toward the door and turned. "I'm spread thin with the department investigation, so I'm keeping you two on Dietrich, for now. Despite all this."

"Yes sir," Stefan whispered. He closed his eyes and tried to forget the voices.

"But I don't want to hear another thing about walking corpses."

Even after two days, the smell was rank to Iago. It hung in the air around the docks, over the smells of the lake and industry. Iago squatted across the street from the unmarked warehouse, sensing the smell of death, like old smoke around a dead bonfire. The smell was little more than the psychic vapors of one of the blood, the remnants of the emotion as the spirit was torn from the flesh.

Iago crouched on the roof across the street and watched the warehouse. He knew it was empty now. He had come here two nights ago, when he had first sensed the death within. He had arrived in time to see the trucks loading their cargo. He had felt the presence of the others within, agitated inside their boxes, death fresh in their senses as it had been in Iago's.

He had followed the thrall convoy as far as he could into the city, but he had been on foot. That plus caution had made him lose them within the city.

Now all that was left was the scene of death here, and the sense of blood. Iago contemplated the blood-smell for a long time. He was not as good at reading as some, but he could tell that it was a thrall's blood, someone bound to Melchior—someone bound to the same being that had been binding Florence Polillo—another of Melchior's followers, purged for betrayal.

What worried Iago more than the death was the presence of all those crates. Melchior wasn't just collecting thralls here, he was bringing them over from wherever he had been hiding the past millennia. A single vampire as old as Melchior flouting the Covenant was frightening. The possibility of him having a whole circle of followers, all raised outside the Covenant, made Iago's heart cold with terror. There might not be enough of the blood within the Covenant here to stop him.

After a long time of watching, Iago felt the warehouse was truly empty. He jumped off the roof and darted across to the entrance next to the loading bays. The door hung open on its hinges, the doorjamb splintered. He paused to examine the door. It had not been like this when the thralls left with their cargo. Someone had broken the door in.

Iago slipped through the damaged entrance and paused.

Who had broken in? Not Melchior's thralls, nor anyone in a circle known to him. That left the humans. If so, it wasn't thievery. The break-in was too blatant for the docks, which never truly slept. Also who would steal what had been contained within?

No, Iago thought as he ran a finger along the edge of the splintered wood, where the lock had gone. *Police or the Mafia* . . .

Iago shook his head. He suspected that if it had been the Mafia that had struck this place, it would no longer be standing. It had been the police. Fortunately for those officers, they had arrived after the thralls had left.

There would be nothing inside now, Iago knew. However Melchior flouted the Covenant, Iago knew he would leave nothing of importance for the humans to uncover.

Even so, to come this close to having human law enforcement discover the nature of those of the blood, that was itself an egregious violation that demanded punishment, if not execution—if the council could ever admit it had happened.

Iago's hand tightened into a fist. He was tired of being powerless. He was tired of the blindness of those more powerful than he. All of them, everyone who sat on that council, had been created by the Covenant, were protected by it. The threat was aimed at their own hearts, and they would not see it.

Laila would have seen it. Anacreon had been about to.

Raphael was the one left who might . . .

Iago stepped into the warehouse. His footsteps echoed through a space that was large and completely empty. The thralls had taken everything but the smell of blood and death.

He walked to the center of the floor, under the high ceiling, and stood under a shaft of blue moonlight that filtered from the unpainted windows far above him. He closed his eyes, spread his arms, and took a deep breath.

The impression slammed into him: a hideous hunger; the smell of fresh blood; hammer-blows to the chest; still moving toward the blood; the taste of it fills his mouth as the final blow slams into his neck. The vision, the sensation slammed into Iago like an ice pick to the brain. He dropped to his knees.

The dead one. He'd been feeding.

Iago shook off the remnants of the dead soul, and pushed himself shaking to his feet. It hadn't been ritual. It hadn't been retribution. It hadn't been Melchior at all. It was the first time that Iago had considered that the death inside the warehouse might not have been like that of Andrassy, or Polillo. He had assumed that Melchior had disposed of another of his chosen.

He'd been wrong. It was in the ghost-taste on his lips, and the phantom ache of bullet holes in his chest. Humans had killed one of Melchior's thralls.

Humans.

That explained why the cops had broken in, and why Melchior had abandoned this place. Iago had been wrong. He had thought Melchior had avoided revealing those of the blood.

Humans had seen, had felt, and had lived to tell others. Human policemen.

As the blood-taste faded from his tongue, Iago realized that the taste-smell was familiar. He knew at least one of the policemen who had been here.

What remained for him was to decide what to do about it.

"Wake up, policeman."

Stefan was pulled out of a drugged slumber by a cold presence. He felt it in a paralyzing panic that gripped him—a panic, like drowning in quicksand, leaving him unable to move.

A familiar panic.

"Wake up, policeman." The voice came from outside but Stefan could feel an echo that seemed to come from the depths of his chest, as if he was hearing half the voice from inside himself.

A familiar voice. It took all of Stefan's willpower to open his eyes and look at the speaker.

It was the man he remembered: Iago of the train tracks. He wore the same overalls, the same pointed beard, the same cold gray eyes. He wore a different porkpie hat, but otherwise he was the same anonymous figure he'd been before. There was still nothing in his appearance that could account for the racing of Stefan's heart.

"What are you doing here?"

"You ask a troubling question." Iago paced around the foot of Stefan's bed. His dull clothing seemed to fade into the shadows, emphasizing his pale face and hands. Iago seemed ghostly, almost insubstantial. "I came here before I knew myself what I would do with you."

Stefan struggled to sit up, against his injury, and against the weight of his fear. He wished he had his gun, even if he was unsure what good it would do him. He was beginning to recognize the cold presence that Iago had in common with the thing in the box, especially in the eyes.

Especially in the eyes.

"God help us all," Stefan whispered.

Iago took a step back and smiled. "Hold on to your faith, my dear policeman. It may be the only thing you have that is worth anything."

For some reason that comment wounded Stefan more than the fear. His memory locked on to his wife and still-born son.

Faith? What Faith?

"What are you—"

Stefan's question was interrupted when Iago made an inhuman leap, landing on the bed as lightly as a cat, feet to either side of Stefan's torso. Iago squatted above him, laying a finger on Stefan's lips. "Shh, be quiet. Ask no questions I cannot answer, policeman."

Iago looked into Stefan's eyes, and Stefan felt as if his soul was under assault by the stare. "We have a common enemy. I know you were in his storehouse. I know what you found there."

"What?" The question forced itself through Stefan's lips.

"I shall not tell you what you already know. Prepare yourself, policeman. Polillo and Andrassy are incidental to what's going on. Dietrich must be stopped."

Iago leaped off the bed.

"I will help you if I can, policeman."

Stefan tried to ask a question, but his visitor had alread
slipped back into the shadows, disappearing. All that re
mained was the sense of anxiety he left behind him.

21

Somehow, Stefan's wound began healing without becoming septic. The hospital sent him home with a pair of crutches. It would be weeks before he'd be fully healed, so he stayed at his apartment while Nuri kept an eye on Dietrich.

All though the warming days of April, Stefan's apartment became a repository of information on Dietrich. Nuri would take photographs, research, bring documents, and Stefan would spend the days studying them.

Dietrich wasn't the only thing Stefan investigated. Every few days Stefan would send Nuri afield to a number of university libraries to find books on the occult, demonology, and finally—almost reluctantly—vampirism.

Nuri had seen the same things that Stefan had, but he had the same reaction as Ness—the "Dracula stuff" was so much bushwa.

Stefan was less sure, and he carried on his house-bound investigation on two parallel tracks; Dietrich—and the creatures of the night.

Dietrich was nominally in the import-export business. The most specific record anywhere about what he actually handled was from customs, and all that said was "European antiquities." The customs officers who had signed off on the paperwork, clearing a half dozen loads of "antiquities" into the country, all had the ominous characteristic of no longer working at customs. None of the officers were reachable by the time Nuri traced the paperwork. They were gone, and the hotel manager was gone—it was too reminiscent of Edward Mullen, the suicide.

After the confrontation in the warehouse, Stefan had some idea of what those "European antiquities" might be.

There had been six loads of them since April, 1934.

The first arrival of the *Ragnarok,* five months before part of a human torso washed up on Euclid Beach, seemed now more than a coincidence. The victim could have easily been thrown overboard, floating for months before the current let the pieces drift ashore.

Other records, from the State Department, confirmed the fact that Florence Polillo could have met Eric Dietrich in Washington, D.C., that same year. Dietrich went there shortly after first coming to this country, demanding and receiving political asylum.

If he was a Nazi, he was an out-of-favor one. The German government wanted his deportation. Dietrich was wanted by the SS for crimes of vague and unspecified nature. Apparently, someone in the State Department thought Dietrich enough of an asset to the United States for it to thumb its nose at the Germans and allow Dietrich to stay in this country.

It was about the time Dietrich cleared his way through the State Department when Florence Polillo returned from D.C. with her new "husband," the one the missing hotel manager had identified as Dietrich.

After that point, around the end of 1934, the paper trail began to vanish. Dietrich had formed a corporation around himself, but little of that corporation's transactions made it into the public record. The warehouse, the *Ragnarok,* and the dusty old mansion on Euclid were all the concrete assets that could be traced to Dietrich's corporation.

But there was little question that Dietrich's corporation was something major. He'd been seen with the likes of the Rockefellers, the Morgans, the Van Sweringens. Aside from a handful of political donations, Dietrich's business dealings were invisible.

Dietrich, fortunately, wasn't. Only a few days into the investigation, Nuri had managed to compile an extensive photo album on their quarry. One of the first things that Stefan picked up on was the driver of Dietrich's limousine. He recognized the man as Carlo Pasquale, a small-time member of the Mayfield Road Mob. At first it seemed that Dietrich might be working with the local Mafia.

One of the pictures changed that assumption. Nuri had caught Dietrich visiting the scene of a warehouse fire. The fire was long over, and Dietrich looked over the ruins with an ugly expression. Nuri explained that the warehouse was apparently one of Dietrich's holdings, two or three companies removed from him. The fire was apparently arson.

Dietrich was at odds with the local mob, perhaps even at war.

Other photographs seemed to suggest the range of Dietrich's interests. He was at the Union Terminal downtown. He was at the East Ohio Gas Company. He showed up at banks and at factories. Nuri could follow him all the way across town in a single day.

Stefan's research on vampires was just as earnest, if less informative. All the traditional folktales were different and, in some cases, contradictory. The only common theme seemed to be a dead thing that fed on the blood of the living. There wasn't even any common thread that agreed on how a vampire was created. The folk causes ranged from being born with a caul, to having a cat jump over the grave.

However, most accounts agreed that decapitation was an element in the destruction of a vampire. That made Stefan think about the unknown victims again. Decapitated, mutilated, and drained of blood. In both cases, the flesh had undergone some chemical process. It had possibly been a preservative, but what if it had been something else?

That didn't explain why Andrassy and Polillo suffered the same fate. As far as Stefan could tell, they'd only been creatures of the night in the mundane sense.

Then there was Iago, who might be the unknown Italian that had been seen with both Andrassy and Polillo. Someone who spoke of a Covenant that the deaths broke, who spoke as if some Sicilian *omerta* was at stake. Someone who knew what happened at the warehouse, and who believed Dietrich was involved in the murders. It was as if Dietrich and Iago were on opposite sides of a gang war.

Was Iago an undead thing, like the creature in the warehouse? Stefan thought he could feel it in Iago's eyes, in the way his psyche seemed to press against his own.

What foiled all his wild speculations about Eric Dietrich was the fact that almost all the pictures Nuri brought him were of Dietrich abroad in daylight. That seemed to argue against such thoughts.

Near the end of Stefan's convalescence, Nuri brought in a picture that Stefan hadn't expected. In retrospect, though, it made a perverse sort of sense. It was a nighttime picture of Dietrich walking with a Negro. Stefan recognized the man. He was Samson Fairfax, the man he had found bloody and crazed the night Andrassy's body had been dumped. The man who had been declared dead.

The memory came back, the last time he had seen him. The feeling of an evil presence, and the fragments of a shattered mirror outside his tenement building. Samson Fairfax *had* seen the devil on the tracks that night. Stefan wondered if it had been Dietrich.

Edward Mullen, who had allowed Samson's body to escape, had lied for the devil, according to his suicide note.

They needed to talk to Samson Fairfax.

Stefan still limped as the two of them stepped out into the tenement-lined brick dead-end where the Fairfaxes lived. They stepped out of the car in broad daylight. People watched them suspiciously from the stoops, and from a few open windows. Children yelled at each other across the street.

Nuri looked at their destination and said, "You know, you're making me nervous with this supernatural crap."

Stefan fingered a rosary he held in his pocket and said, "If you forget about all that, Samson Fairfax is the best bet for a witness we have."

Nuri nodded, but his expression showed that he was still uncomfortable with Stefan's thinking about the undead. Stefan couldn't understand it. Nuri had been at the warehouse, too. He had killed the thing.

They both entered the building, which had stayed just as Stefan remembered it. It was as dark in the narrow hallways as it had been the night he had first come here. They passed a few open doors, and occasionally a face would look out from the crack in the door and ease it shut as they passed.

When they reached the door to the Fairfaxes' apartment, Stefan knocked. Nuri stood next to the door, hand on the butt of his revolver.

There was no answer. Stefan hadn't expected any, not at this time of day. He knocked again, as his other hand fingered the rosary.

"Police, open up."

Again, there was no answer. Stefan looked across at Nuri, and tried the door. It came open, unlocked. He felt a strange sense of déjà vu as the door opened on a darkened apartment. It was the sound of the flies, and the smell of sour meat, long gone bad.

The light didn't work, and Stefan was forced to walk across the room and open the shade on the window. The shade was fastened so securely that Stefan had to tear it in half to let light into the apartment.

Behind him he heard Nuri say, "Good Lord."

Stefan slowly turned to face the room behind him. It was the same as he'd seen it before, peeling wallpaper, candles long ago guttered out. The threadbare couch.

Wilma Fairfax.

Stefan identified her because she still sat in the place where he had left her, slumped slightly against the arm of the couch. Otherwise, she was unidentifiable. She had been here long enough for the flesh to recede, for the soft tissues to shrink away. She sat, nearly mummified, just as Stefan had left her six months ago.

Nuri shook his head as Stefan hobbled to the couch.

"He's not coming back here," Nuri said.

Stefan nodded, wondering if he'd been responsible for her death, leaving her with her husband back then.

"You'd think someone would have called this in before," Nuri said. "At least complain to the landlord about the smell."

Stefan turned to look at Nuri, "We'd better call this in."

"Do we bring up the connection to Mr. Dietrich?"

Stefan shook his head, "Leave that to Mr. Ness. Right now it's just a suspicious death, and we want Mr. Fairfax for questioning."

22

Monday, May 4

Iago stood outside the Union Terminal and stared off at the Soldiers and Sailors Monument. The monument took over a quarter of Public Square, its lone eagle-topped pillar reaching toward a dark, starless sky. It was a concrete memoir of the Civil War, and Iago was drawn to it, to the bronze statues at its base, the men trapped eternally in the throes of death.

Sometimes that was how he felt, a being trapped eternally at the precipice of death, suspended over the abyss, never to fall.

He was waiting for a disreputable man.

The night-life crowds had thinned, leaving the area dark and lonely. It also made Angelo's approach all that more obvious. He tried to appear subtle, but there was no doubt where the dark hulking figure was walking, even though he didn't make eye contact with Iago. He stopped on the sidewalk about four feet from him, facing the terminal, looking over the facade as if his stopping next to the lone figure of Iago was a coincidence.

Iago didn't care. It was Angelo who should be worried if their conversation was seen. Iago handed the man a fat envelope, and Angelo took it.

"It's like this," Angelo said, as he slipped the envelope into his pocket. "I ain't seen these guys so twitchy since before the last Porrello brother was hit. The guy's racket is moving stuff into the country, moving it all over the place. But he don't act like he knows who runs this town. You get it?"

"What kind of stuff?" Iago asked.

"Who the fuck knows other than he jimmied Customs to

get it in? Even if you're legit you gotta pay us respect, right? This guy ain't legit. He's gotten warnings. Big Al is pissed."

Iago nodded.

"More pissed since his people turn up dead, and no one can get a finger on this Dietrich's people. It's like they're all ghosts, no one sees them."

"They've tried to take him out?"

"Hell, of course. Big Al sends his best guns up against this guy. They don't come back. Worse, Carlo—like a son to him—ends up this Dietrich's driver. Six months, five hits, all balls-up—and on top of everything there's this Ness guy . . ."

"Listen, Angelo," Iago said. "Fire's your only chance against Dietrich."

"Don't worry, we'll get the bastard. People don't get away with this shit with us."

"You don't know what you're dealing with."

"Like I said, don't worry. Big Al's collected more hardware than Mussolini took into Ethiopia. Dietrich's going to come down *hard*." Angelo made a point of looking at the clock above the Union Terminal entrance and said, "Got go now." He patted the breast pocket where he had stashed Iago's envelope. "Nice talking to you."

He walked away, leaving Iago with a hollow feeling. How could he warn him, warn *anyone*, without breaking the Covenant?

23

Sunday, May 10

At three in the morning, a quartet of dark sedans drove down Euclid, heading west. Each sedan carried five heavily-armed men and a driver. They drove past all but one of the remaining decayed mansions of Euclid Avenue. At the last one, a sandstone structure out of the last century, the cars pulled onto the lawn and began disgorging gunmen.

Stefan Ryzard saw the assassins approach from his station overlooking the Dietrich house. He was on the roof of a neighboring warehouse where he could watch the whole grounds of the black sandstone mansion. When he saw the first sedan drive up, he had some idea what was happening. He dropped his field glasses and began running down to his car, and the radio.

As Stefan ran, dark-suited men ran around the house, covering every entrance. Half carried shotguns, the other half carried Thomson submachine guns. The small army coordinated their activity, all of them kicking in doors at the same time.

There'd been lights on in the Dietrich house. When the doors splintered open, they all went out. The gunmen rushed the mansion, and shortly afterward, the gunfire began, flashing light across the narrow windows.

Stefan reached his car and called in what was happening. As he did, he heard the first scream. It was high-pitched, more like a dog's yelp than a human voice. The sound tore into Stefan. He dropped the microphone and drew his revolver.

He still limped on his barely-healed leg as he ran across the street. He took the long way around, crossing far enough down Euclid that the drivers wouldn't notice him. Fortunately for him, the drivers' attention was riveted on the mansion.

It sounded like a war zone inside there. The rapid fire hammer-blows of the Thomsons occasionally punctuated by the sledgehammer of a shotgun blast. In the few lulls in the gunfire, Stefan heard breaking wood and glass.

He circled around a small neighboring office building, so he could approach the property from the rear. Even as he was doing so, he was thinking of how insane this was. He was closing on a mob of over a dozen gunmen without any backup. He was trying to get himself killed.

As he crossed the property line, emerging into underbrush that used to be a formal garden, he heard more screams. For a moment it sounded as if, somewhere inside the dark Victorian manse, the gates of hell had been opened up and Stefan could hear the damned.

Despite the death that certainly awaited him, Stefan was pulled forward. Something in there drew him and wouldn't let him go. He pushed his way through the overgrown garden, toward the gunfire, toward the screams.

As the noise reached its apex, Stefan was almost at the edge of the undergrowth. As he pushed forward the final few yards, he tripped on a small ivy-covered statue. He fell on the ground, face-to-face with a stone cherub with a broken arm. It took him a few frantic moments to catch his breath before he pushed himself upright.

When he got to his feet, there were no more screams, no more gunfire. The dark edifice was mute.

Stefan slowly approached the rear porch where the gunmen had kicked in the door. The only sound now was the wind through the wild garden behind him. He held his revolver before him as he climbed the stone steps before the entrance. He could see little beyond, the door had swung mostly shut behind the gunmen.

He reached the door and pushed it in, slowly, with his foot, bracing his gun to follow the transit of the door. The air was thick with the smell of gunfire.

Once the door was open, Stefan stood in the doorway, allowing his eyes to adjust to the gloom. He looked beyond a short hall, into a sitting room that had served as a battlefield. An antique table had been splintered, garish

nineteenth-century wallpaper was torn through with bullet
holes, chairs were overturned, and broken glass glittered in
the moonlight that filtered past the torn drapery.

In the middle of the floor, on an Oriental carpet, was a
Thomson amidst its scattered cartridges. The only sign of
the man who had carried the weapon was a crushed fedora
pinned to the ground under the remains of a Tiffany lamp.

Stefan inched into the mansion, feeling the pull combined
with a growing anxiety bordering on panic. What was he
doing here? Patrol cars should be arriving any minute. . . .

He pushed through a doorway into a main hall domi-
nated by a curving staircase. Like the sitting room, the walls
were marred by gunfire, and the air was thick with smoke.
Two more weapons lay scattered on the ground at the base
of the stairs, about thirty feet from the broken front door.

As Stefan stood in the empty hall, he heard a noise. It
was the thump-thump-thump of something solid hitting the
floor repeatedly. It took him a moment to realize what the
sound was. When he did, he ran to the foot of the stairs
and brought his gun to bear on the grand staircase.

He did it just in time to see the source of the noise
before it disappeared. Someone had dragged a body up the
stairs, and Stefan had turned just in time to see the feet of
the corpse disappear around a corner.

Stefan ran up the stairs, but the pain in his leg delayed
him long enough so that when he reached the head of the
stairs, there was no sign of his quarry. He stood there, in
the darkness, listening. What he heard was the faint sound
of something ripping, as if something was being torn apart
in some remote part of the mansion.

He slowly walked down the corridor. His pulse was in
his throat, and he felt the acid sensation of near-panic in
his gut. He was too aware of his own breathing and heartbeat. Again, he asked himself what he was doing here.

However, he continued to follow the sound. It was nearer
than it first appeared. A door stood closed at the end of
the hallway. From beyond it came the sounds, and a ferric
smell. Eventually the tearing sound was replaced by a wet
sucking.

When Stefan reached the door, he found himself unable
to move. His hand froze on the doorknob, and he couldn't
force himself to open it.

In the distance, he heard the engines of several cars rev up and retreat, accompanied by a squeal of tires. His grip tightened on the knob, and he slowly began turning.

In response, the sound from beyond the door ceased. Stefan sucked in a breath and began pushing the door open.

He felt a hand on his shoulder. It was as cold as a block of ice.

Stefan whipped around, bringing his gun to bear on the tall pale form of Eric Dietrich. The man was unarmed, but Stefan felt such a wave of unmistakable menace that his first impulse was to fire his revolver, and continue firing. But his hand was frozen, unable to pull the trigger.

"Detective Ryzard," Dietrich said. He barely spoke above a whisper, but the words throbbed in Stefan's ears. His hand still rested on his shoulder, and the touch seemed to suck all the heat, all the will, out of Stefan's body. Dietrich's eyes were holes of deep black, portals to something invisible and terrifying, something that wouldn't let Stefan turn away.

"Put down the gun, Detective. The assassins are gone." There was a smile on Dietrich's pale face. His expression was condescending, as if finding amusement at a crippled man.

Stefan didn't want to lower his gun, but his arm acted on its own, obeying Dietrich's words.

"They've escaped, Detective. I suspect your job is elsewhere now." Dietrich released his hand, and Stefan said a silent prayer of thanks. Stefan moved his head slightly in the direction of the door behind him.

Dietrich's expression darkened. The change in Dietrich's manner froze Stefan with a force as if Dietrich had reached into his chest and squeezed shut his heart.

"You wish to *see*?" he said. Anger thickened Dietrich's accent. He grabbed Stefan's shoulder again. The force let Stefan know that Dietrich could snap his collarbone if he wanted to. Dietrich spun him around to face the massive oak door. The wood was black in the darkness, and Stefan felt as if he was about to be cast into the abyss.

"Open the door," Dietrich said from behind him. Stefan could feel Dietrich's breath on his neck. It wasn't warm. It was dry and cool and smelled of carrion. Stefan understood now, in his gut, the devil that Samson Fairfax had met on the tracks.

Again, his arm, unbidden by him, reached for the doorknob. Stefan tried to lower his arm, pull it away. His will crashed against Dietrich's words like the lake before a breakwater.

Stefan's hand, almost alien to him now, grasped the doorknob and began to turn.

With all his will, Stefan tried to keep himself from opening the door. Sweat blurred his vision, and his pulse hammered at his temples. He pushed against his arm, but he couldn't even slow the movement.

The door opened.

Dietrich pushed him forward, into an empty room. Stefan stood, dumbstruck for a few moments. There was no sign of the things he thought he had heard. The windowless room was bare of anything but a dusty, threadbare carpet. There was only the one door.

"Here is what you wished to see," Dietrich told him, the accent receding. "An empty room. Those rooms here I don't yet use are equally empty."

Stefan asked God for the strength to speak, and somehow he found it. "Where are the others? Servants, bodyguards . . ." He trailed off before he said *undead.*

"There is no one else here," Dietrich said.

There was an arrogance to the lie, as if Dietrich didn't care if Stefan believed it or not. Standing in the empty room, Stefan believed if any others were here, he wouldn't find them—nor would he find any bodies.

He turned to face Dietrich. He put his free hand into his pocket and found a rosary. It comforted him more than the revolver that he still held limply in his right hand. He looked at Dietrich and tried to fathom where the sense of menace originated. Dietrich didn't look menacing; the only truly unusual aspects of his appearance were his overlong, feminine hair and the depth of his eyes.

The eyes . . .

That gaze was like hell staring into him. Stefan gripped the shreds of his faith together and asked, "What happened here, Mr. Dietrich?" He didn't even expect an answer, but the questions gave him a feeling of being afloat in a situation that was out of his depth.

Dietrich did answer him. "A number of gunmen stormed my house, destroying furniture, shooting holes in the walls. They are gone now."

"You survived." Stefan squeezed the rosary. To ask anything, to act at all, took a supreme effort. He was suddenly convinced that the questioning was a test of his faith, and if he stopped his questioning he would be damned forever.

"They never shot me."

"Never shot you," Stefan repeated involuntarily. He felt his will slipping and he forced out, "What were they doing here, then?"

"A warning," Dietrich said, "from people whose protection my company has refused to pay."

"Who?" Stefan asked. The air seemed thicker, making it hard for him to breathe.

"That is your job to find out. I have no further interest in the matter."

In the distance, Stefan heard sirens. The backup he called for was finally arriving. Dietrich cocked his head slightly at the sound. To Stefan, it felt like the sound of salvation. It became easier for him to think, to talk, to act.

"Why did the gunmen drop their weapons everywhere?"

"I think you are mistaken," Dietrich said. "If you look again, I believe that you'll see that they left nothing behind."

The missing servants probably cleaned that part up.

"We're going to have to search this house," Stefan said.

"Of course you are." The assertion was followed by the same condescending smile. "And you will find nothing."

The sirens closed and Stefan slipped out from under Dietrich's hand.

"We should meet them," Dietrich said, motioning Stefan back down the hall. Stefan walked ahead of him, feeling as if he had just avoided damnation.

He walked outside, down the great stone steps at the entrance of the old Victorian house. Ugly-colored police cars, their lights ablaze, were there to meet him. He walked across the lawn as if in a dream. Somewhere along the way he had holstered his gun and pulled out his badge.

When he approached the first officer, he told him what had happened. Or, more exactly, what Eric Dietrich said had happened. He wanted to say something of the menace he felt in that house, of the things he'd heard, perhaps almost seen—but the words wouldn't form.

All that was left of what happened was the gunmen, attacking and then disappearing.

With some trepidation he assigned officers to guard the site while more patrols and detectives arrived. As he waved the men toward the house, he saw Eric Dietrich standing in an elaborately arched doorway. In the doorway he seemed taller and more pale. The wind tore at his long blond hair; that and his evil smile gave him the aspect of an angel of destruction.

After giving the officers their orders, he walked back to where his own car was parked. When he'd turned the corner, out of sight of the old house, he became aware of how his left hand ached. He pulled it out of his pocket, and found his fist still clenched around his rosary.

He eased his hand open. When he did, a few drops of blood fell to stain the ground. The crucifix was embedded in his flesh, its bloody imprint now carved into his palm.

Stefan repeated Our Fathers until he reached his car.

24

Friday, May 15

St. John's was a small whitewashed box of a church hidden in the midst of the working-class homes and shops in Stefan's old neighborhood. It was wrapped inside a wrought-iron fence. Flowers grew in small plots behind the fence, taking up most of the tiny yard that served the church. The sky was overcast, and the splash of blues and yellows seemed the only color to a monochrome scene. Stefan stared at the building for a long time before he stepped through the gate.

He thought it would mark some transition when he walked back here. He feared it wouldn't.

Stefan walked the slate walkway, past the subdued statue of Mary, past the sign naming the place. Father Gerwazek was still pastor here, like he'd been all of Stefan's life. He stopped and wondered how close Gerwazek might be to retirement; the man had to be nearing seventy. They'd probably close the church down then. St. John's was a small, redundant parish. Too close to St. Vitus. The congregation was never very large, mostly eastern European immigrants that weren't of Slovenian descent like the rest of the community around Fifty-Fifth and St. Clair.

He quietly slipped through the doors in the front of the church, where Mass was already in progress. He did his best to be unobtrusive as he took off his hat and crossed himself and faded to one of the back pews. Gerwazek was in the middle of a Latin prayer, but Stefan couldn't help but think he noticed his arrival.

Stefan sat through Communion this time, but he didn't walk up to take the host. He hadn't taken confession in

years. In a way, that, not the Mass, was what he was here
for.

"What brings you here, son?" Father Gerwazek sat behind the desk in his little office and looked Stefan up and
down.

Stefan wished he could tell if the look was disapproving
or not. He had an urge to leave right then, to forget about
it all. None of this, none of his past was going to help him.
He wasn't even sure what kind of help he needed.

He sat down and shook his head. "I don't know, Father.
I think I'm trying to find my faith again."

"You haven't been here for a long time, have you,
Stefan?"

Long enough that Stefan was surprised that Gerwazek
remembered his name. "Not since I buried Mary, and our
son."

"I remember." The sympathy in Piotr Gerwazek's eyes
was difficult to look at.

Stefan waited for the trite words that usually followed,
about how tragic to lose his wife in childbirth. Tragic to
lose his only son as well. How hard it must be. Must have
been. Stefan waited, but Gerwazek said nothing more.
None of the phony words of comfort that Stefan heard so
much of whenever someone learned of his past.

Just *I remember.*

Somehow Gerwazek knew that was enough.

Stefan felt his eyes burn as if the loss was still fresh. "I
know I shouldn't," Stefan said. "But I feel abandoned, as
if my beliefs counted for nothing."

"You still grieve," Gerwazek said. "He grieves with
you."

Stefan stared at his hands. "Everything around me, everything since, is so corrupt, so base— What if He had
abandoned us? What if this is all there is?"

Gerwazek stood and walked around the desk. He placed
a hand on Stefan's shoulder. "We all feel abandoned at
times. It's our faith that draws us through those times
whole. You're here because of that. You know."

"I don't want to be lost, Father."

"You aren't, my son." Piotr Gerwazek squeezed his
shoulder. "You aren't."

25

Every circle had its meeting place, and the place Raphael chose for his befit his past as a seaman. To Iago, little distinguished the *Janus* from any of the other vessels docked at the marina. As yachts went, it was of average size, smaller than many. It was outshone by those representing ostentatious wealth that survived the Depression.

Iago had a membership card, given to him by Raphael. But it was deep night, and he had to use the keys Raphael had presented him. He had to pass two gates before he even stepped onto the pier where the *Janus* was docked.

It appeared that he was one of the last to arrive. The *Janus* was lit in a subdued manner, and he could feel the presence of others. As he walked up, a guard slipped out of the shadows to confront him. He wore a tuxedo, but he carried a tommy gun loosely in his hands.

The guard represented fear, and Iago didn't like it. The guard wasn't even one of the blood, just a human servant—perhaps bound, maybe only an employee.

Iago shook his head and said, "I am a guest of Raphael."

"Why are you here?"

"To take in the night air."

The guard nodded at the correct responses and stepped aside, back into the shadow from which he'd emerged. Iago walked up the gangplank, around the deck, and stepped down, through a door, and into the meeting room.

Raphael stood at the far corner of the room, arms folded. Everyone else, about a dozen, were seated on couches, facing him. Raphael was in the middle of a speech.

". . . members of the Council have interests in direct opposition to the Mayfield gang, and will not act while Die-

trich is diminishing them. Other members might take the
threat seriously, but are afraid to act. Worse are those
members who see this as an opportunity to advance themselves among us, those who'd use Melchior's own methods
if the Covenant did not bind them—" Raphael paused as
he saw Iago enter the room. "News?" He directed the
question at Iago.

Iago shook his head. "The Mayfield gang isn't going to
risk anything more on Dietrich. They've lost too much already." Iago had spoken to Angelo several times, and each
time the local gang seemed less eager to confront Dietrich.
Every time they had tried to "teach him a lesson," they
lost more men.

Raphael shook his head. "It is time for us to act," he
said.

"Without the Council?" asked one of the younger ones.

"What about the Covenant?" asked another.

Raphael looked over all of them and said, "The Council
will not defend the Covenant. The duty of protecting it falls
to those willing to do so. It is either that, and slip the
balance of power toward us, or bring in outside forces and
cede our heritage here to them." Raphael looked at each
of them in turn. "We will fight this invader."

"What about the thralls he has brought into the country?" Iago asked. "His force may already outnumber our
circle."

Raphael shook his head and paced in front of the cabin's
bar. "Numbers should not worry us. Our target is the master, not his blood-bound slaves. What are they without
him? A loose collection of rogues, easily dealt with."

Iago didn't feel as optimistic, but he kept his mouth shut
about it. He was still the newest member of this circle,
little better than a thrall himself. His connection with the
underworld, the information he brought, that gave him a
seat here—little more than that.

It was galling, after being Anacreon's right hand. That
was, unfortunately, how it worked. One's status rose and
fell with those above. When Anacreon met his death, most
of Iago's voice in the community died with him. Joining
with Raphael at least gave him back something, even if
Raphael seemed to be after Dietrich-Melchior for the status

it would bring him and his circle more than protecting the Covenant, or even avenging Anacreon.

Iago didn't care; at least Raphael was doing something. Those who moved the Council were paralyzed by fear or the thought of gaining power.

Raphael talked on about his plan to destroy Melchior. The options were limited because of Melchior's age and power. He had enough control of the flesh to go out in sunlight. It was possible that even decapitation and removal of the heart might not bring the true death. Then there was the problem of the dozens of thralls under his command. Avoiding them would be difficult, and dealing with them after their master's death would be more so.

Raphael went over all of that and came to the conclusion that Iago had tried to impress on Angelo—as far as he could without breaking the Covenant. "To be certain of Melchior's destruction, he must be trapped in a conflagration. No ordinary fire that he might escape, but a thing intense enough to consume the flesh before he has the time to react. If this happened where a number of his thralls are, so much the better." Raphael smiled. "Fortunately, I see a simple way through to this."

Iago sat up, suddenly more attentive. He thought that any trap involving Melchior would be terribly elaborate.

"I have some of my own contacts," Raphael said, "And I've learned where he is keeping many of his thralls. Melchior has hidden them among the immigrant population of this city. Much of this city is of the same European descent as his thralls, and they find comfort with the Slavs, the Poles, the Czechs—the neighborhood that he has chosen is perfect for our purpose. In the midst of this neighborhood is the device of his own destruction. He has even visited there already. Melchior may not yet be enough of this century to realize . . ." Raphael trailed off.

Iago sensed it, too. Something was wrong. There was a sudden deep tension in the air, and something that could have been fear. Everyone in the cabin stood at the same time, all sensing the same thing.

"All of you, get out of here," Raphael shouted. His head was cocked as if he were seeing something other than the cabin around him. His smile was gone, replaced by a stony expression. "This place is no longer secure."

Iago backed toward the door he had just entered. As he did, he heard something thump onto the deck. He pushed his way through the door and was swamped by the smells of blood and petroleum. He was the first to reach the head of the stairs.

Someone stepped out in front of the stairway, leveling a machine gun down toward the cabin. Iago didn't have time to think. He dove as the man began firing down the stairs. Iago felt two or three shots slam into his chest and abdomen as he hit the deck by the gunman's feet. He could feel the pull of his flesh as his skin tore apart and reknit around the wounds. It felt as if the muscles tore free of the bone.

A wave of heat and orange light washed over the end of the yacht in front of him. He ignored it for the moment as he pushed himself upright next to the gunman. The man was ignoring him, firing down the stairway, emptying his Thomson.

Iago grabbed his neck from the side and pulled him back like a rag doll. He could tell by touch and smell that this one was just a bound human, which meant he didn't hesitate when he tore open the gunman's throat.

He tossed the body aside, and it landed next to another. Iago saw the broken corpse of one of Raphael's guards. Iago turned back toward the stairway. He had just barely formed a thought of helping the others . . .

The other end of the boat was an inferno. Orange flames rippled across the deck, in his direction. Before Iago had taken a step, he heard glass shatter at his feet. The gasoline wiped out any other odor. He felt it on his skin.

He only had one choice. He raced the fire to the edge of the boat and dived over the railing. He hit the water like a rock, flames already tearing at his legs. The black water grabbed him and pulled him under.

The sense of death followed him into the water. He could feel the life being torn away from those on the boat. He sank, unbreathing, to the bottom.

26

Stefan was at the Central Station, sifting through files he'd amassed on Dietrich, when he heard the news. All morning, like the whole week before, talk had been on the upcoming Republican National Convention. It would open on the eighth, and a good proportion of the police force, including Ness, was involved with the security.

Stefan wasn't. He sat behind his desk and tried to make sense of the information they'd gathered on Dietrich. Occasionally he would tell Nuri about his speculations, but for the most part, he kept them to himself. There was still little direct connection between Dietrich and the bodies.

But late on Friday, the conversation slipped away from Republicans and began to dwell on murder. Stefan was poring through a typed list of Dietrich's known business associates when he overheard Detective Orly May saying to someone, "They found another one."

The way he said it prompted Stefan to get up and walk over to him. "Another what?" Stefan asked. He suspected what the answer would be, since May had been on both the Andrassy and Polillo murders.

He turned around, and the answer wasn't a surprise. "Two kids found a head by the railroad tracks, wrapped in a pair of trousers."

"Which tracks?"

"A little west of the Kinsman Road Bridge, by the rapid-transit."

That was less than a mile from where they found Andrassy in the Run. Trains again . . .

*   *   *

Stefan drove out to where Nuri was supposed to be staking out Dietrich. He found him at the same warehouse overlooking the Dietrich mansion. When he walked up, Nuri turned around and said, "You're early. I thought you weren't going to be here until eight."

"Change of plans; we have a meeting."

Nuri looked back in the direction of the mansion. "But he hasn't left the mansion. If we're supposed to keep an eye—"

"We've missed it." Stefan walked to the edge of the roof and leaned against the wall overlooking the mansion. The clay tile was warm under his hands. "There was another murder. We missed it. We were watching him, and we missed it."

"Is it connected to—"

"A severed head, found by the Kinsman Bridge over the Run. I'd think so."

He looked down at Dietrich's residence. In the light it seemed out of place, a chimera of the prior century. "Hard to believe," Stefan muttered, "that thirty years ago all of Euclid was like that. . . ."

"Where'd he slip by?" Nuri asked.

Stefan kept staring at the building. Looking at the blackened sandstone for signs of life. "He knew," he said finally. "He knew we were watching him. He probably knew from before we started." He turned to Nuri. "Somehow we have to get ahead of him."

"So what's this meeting? How do we get ahead?"

"We're going to talk to someone about Dietrich."

A half hour later, the two of them were walking into the Union Terminal downtown. When they entered the lobby, the last of the commuters were being replaced by the first of those coming into town for the nightlife.

"I've seen Dietrich coming here often enough," Nuri said as they pushed their way through to the elevators.

Stefan nodded. "Something about trains. And we're standing at the heart of the largest rail empire in the country."

The elevator doors slid open and the two of them slipped inside.

"Do you really think Van Sweringen is involved?"

"I'm not sure, but Dietrich has been seen with him, and the bodies are collecting on the rapid-transit property."

They rode the rest of the way up in silence.

There was a sense of foreboding as they left the car and walked to the offices of the Van Sweringen Company. Stefan tried the door and found it unlocked. When they entered the offices, though they were lighted reasonably well, the sense Stefan felt was of an empty darkness, a sense of void.

There was a desk for a secretary, but no one was manning it.

"Now what?" Nuri asked.

"We see if Mr. Van Sweringen is in." Stefan led Nuri down a hallway past rows of empty offices. The sense of emptiness became oppressive. Near the end of the hallway, close to the corner of the tower, they passed an open office whose door read, "Mantis James Van Sweringen."

Nuri stopped at the door and whispered. "Do I remember wrong, or did the papers say this one died?"

Stefan nodded without saying anything. The office of Mantis James was eerie. The desk lamp was on, illuminating a neatly kept desk. A small stack of papers rested on one side of the desk, as if waiting for someone to return and read them. Everything was clean and dusted, as if the occupant was just about to return. The only sign of how long it had been since Mantis James had been here was a Christmas card peeking out from the stack of papers.

Stefan pulled Nuri away, feeling as if they had just desecrated a tomb.

Oris Paxton, the surviving Van Sweringen, kept an office a little farther down. It was the only one that was occupied. Stefan stopped in front of the half-open door and pushed it open with one hand. The office was a mirror of Mantis James'. Sitting behind the desk was an average-looking man in his late fifties. He was dressed plainly, and the clothing contributed to the subdued impression the man gave.

He was shaking his head at the papers in front of him, the expression on his face grave. He didn't look in their direction when he said, "William? I thought I told you to go home. . . ."

"Mr. Van Sweringen?" Stefan said.

Oris Van Sweringen turned to face them with a bit of a

start. "Who are you?" There was a challenge to the words, but Stefan thought he could hear a little fear in his voice.

"My name is Detective Ryzard, and this is Detective Lapidos. We would like to ask you some questions about a business associate of yours."

The fear left, replaced by an expression somewhere between disgust and contempt. "The ICC just can't leave a businessman alone, can it? We almost tottered over the edge, and you won't be happy until you push us over, will you? At this rate," he tossed the papers he'd been reading down on the desk. They scattered in a fan across his blotter. "At this rate, everything will go bankrupt in four months. You can talk to our council—"

"We aren't from the Interstate Commerce Commission," Nuri said.

Oris Van Sweringen stood and looked at both of them again. His eyes narrowed. "Who are you from, then?"

Stefan pulled out his badge and showed it to him. "Cleveland Police. We want to ask you about a gentleman named Eric Dietrich. We believe you may have had business dealings with him."

He looked from the badge to Stefan's face, and Stefan could tell that the fear was back. The man had some self-control, since it only showed in his eyes and in a twitch at the corner of his mouth. It took him a long time to say anything. He eased himself back into his seat and said quietly, "I have had informal dealings with the man. I know nothing about him except that he came from Europe, escaping the Nazis."

"What kind of informal dealings?" Stefan asked.

"I don't think I have to answer that."

Nuri stepped forward. "This *is* a murder investigation, Mr. Van Sweringen. We would appreciate your cooperation."

Oris Van Sweringen glared at Nuri, but as he did so, the color drained from his face, and his knuckles whitened where he gripped the desk, but his voice was clear and steady. "I would appreciate it if you would talk to my lawyer."

"If—" Stefan began.

"Would you gentlemen please leave my offices?"

Nuri looked across at Stefan. Stefan nodded and took a

step back. "I'm sorry you don't want to talk to us, Mr. Van Sweringen."

As the two of them backed out, Oris Van Sweringen said quietly after them, "Is this Ness' doing?" It sounded less like an accusation than a genuinely worried question.

They didn't answer him.

On the way to the elevator, Nuri said, "We're on to something here."

Stefan nodded. At the moment he was thinking less about the connection between Dietrich and Van Sweringen than about his final question about Eliot Ness. There was no way that he should know that the two of them were working directly for Ness. There was no way for him to know that this was nothing other than a normal investigation. Ness wasn't even publicly involved in the murders, much less Dietrich.

Either something had leaked—or Oris Van Sweringen had some reason to think that Eliot Ness might be interested in him. As they walked to the elevator, he asked Nuri, "If you were going to keep an eye on Mr. Van Sweringen, where would you camp out?"

Nuri stopped walking and turned to face him. "What are you thinking?"

"Maybe Dietrich isn't the only man Ness has staked out."

Nuri looked thoughtful. "I'd want some place in this building. There's nothing overlooking it. Maybe on this floor, or a floor above or below." Nuri looked up and down the hallway. "Rented under some sort of front, since Van Sweringen's company owns this place, doesn't it?"

"One of his companies." Stefan said. "And you'd probably want to tail him as he left."

"What do you want to do?"

Stefan walked back toward the elevators. "We're going to tail Mr. Van Sweringen ourselves and see who turns up."

Saturday, the papers all reported the discovery of the body. As the coroner was matching the head with the body, Eliot Ness was working—nominally—on security arrangements for the Republican National Convention.

At ten-thirty in the morning, Detective Stefan Ryzard, disheveled and sleepless, burst in on the Safety Director and demanded, "What do you think you're doing with this investigation?"

Ness looked up from the desk. In contrast to how Stefan looked, he was neat, eyes clear, hair combed back. To Stefan however, he still looked like a college student. "Detective Ryzard?" he said.

Stefan leaned forward on the desk and said, "Why weren't we told about the surveillance on Van Sweringen?"

Ness put down the files he was working on. "What are you talking about?"

"I'm talking about the two boys you had attached to him from the Union Terminal all the way back to Hunting Valley." Stefan glared at Ness. "We're supposed to be investigating Dietrich and his connection to these murders. Another one shows up yesterday, and I find out now that we're operating on incomplete information."

Ness shook his head. "You have all the information on Dietrich we have."

"Do we? Why weren't we told of the surveillance on Van Sweringen? What has *that* turned up?"

Ness leaned back in his chair. "If there is such an operation, you wouldn't be told for the same reason they couldn't be told of yours. We're dealing with powerful people, people who could interfere with the investigation. The less exposure the elements have with each other, the less likely the entire operation will be exposed—"

Stefan made a disgusted noise and turned around. "We're policemen, not spies."

"Right now you're both."

There was a long pause before Stefan said, "Do you want my badge?"

From behind him he heard Ness say, "What?"

Stefan studied a corner of the frosted glass window on the door. It was like peering into a depthless gray fog. He swallowed and said, "If I can't have all the information on this investigation, I'm resigning."

Stefan heard Ness stand. "You can be reassigned."

Stefan spun around, looking into Ness' eyes. The contact gave him uneasy memories of looking into the eyes of the undead thing in the warehouse. But behind Ness' eyes there was life, and a soul. "You don't understand. I've lived and breathed this investigation for too long. I have a hunk missing from my leg. You gave me the assignment because you said I could be trusted. If I can't have full information after what I've been through, I want no more part of this department."

They looked at each other. Ness glanced down at the files on his desk and said, finally, "I don't want to lose you. Not now." He glanced up and his eyes were hard. "I take threats as badly as I do bribery. If you had given your ultimatum at any other time, I would have shown you the door myself. Remember that."

Stefan wondered what was so special about this particular moment.

"What do you want?" Ness continued.

"I want to know why you're watching Van Sweringen, how long you've been watching, and anything substantial you've found out."

"Sit down," Ness said, motioning to a chair. When Stefan sat, Ness began, "It started with two events. First, I overheard a conversation between Dietrich and Van Sweringen. Then there was an anonymous phone call I received last December thirteenth. Does that date recall anything to you?"

At first Stefan tried to connect it with one of the murders, but after a moment it came to him. "That's when Van Sweringen's brother died . . ."

"That call began this investigation." Ness stood up, walked to a filing cabinet and took a key out of his pocket. "That call connected Dietrich to the Andrassy murders, and with the body that washed up on Euclid Beach in September '34." He opened the cabinet and withdrew a thick file. "From what I overheard months earlier, I had a strong immediate suspicion that Oris Van Sweringen made that call. Maybe prompted by the death of his brother."

Ness handed the file to Stefan, "That is the accumulated information gathered by the detectives watching Van Sweringen. Take notes, but the file isn't leaving this room."

Stefan nodded.

"You're the only one other than myself that knows this." Ness sat down and looked at Stefan deeply. "If I'm right, if Van Sweringen made that call and his accusations were right, then it has to stay that way or Van Sweringen is in danger."

Stefan leafed through the file. "What about this conversation you overheard. What was it about?"

"It was at a victory party for the Burton campaign—"

Carlo Pasquale could barely remember his previous life. So much had changed within him that he felt like another person. He no longer even thought of Papa, or his family, or his former job, in anything but the most abstract sense. He was part of the Master now, an extension of the Master's will, and his body.

The pain and blood of that conversion was so distant it was no longer even a memory. In the parts of his mind that still moved freely, Carlo thought of himself as a machine wound by the Master. A human machine that would eventually cease being human.

But Carlo Pasquale still drove.

This Monday it was a limousine owned by Eric Dietrich, and it stopped at several hotels to receive the Master's guests. He stopped to pick up half a dozen men, all in Cleveland for the convention. Three were senators, three were congressmen, all held seats on important committees. All were invited to dine with Mr. Dietrich, who had become a very important contributor in the past three years.

Carlo Pasquale listened to them talk among themselves. They talked about the growing crisis in Europe, about the economy at home, about their fears about FDR's executive power. Carlo was still human, but his thoughts and concerns had drifted so far from humanity that the conversation was little more than an alien language to him.

He drove the party down Euclid as the sun set. He knew that these six men would have the Master's blood forced upon them, that they would become as much a human machine as Carlo was. Carlo still had enough of himself left to realize that he should feel some emotion at that fact, but the only thing he felt was a detached sense of irony that the most powerful would be brought to slavery.

Like Carlo.

And Carlo Pasquale drove.

Book Two

July 1936—February 1937

The Phantom of Kingsbury Run

1

Iago stood in one of the darkened exhibition halls of the Great Lakes Exposition. It had taken him a long time to recover from his injuries. Even when he fed three times as much—which meant four or five people if he wished to stay short of killing—it had taken weeks for the burns on his legs to heal.

Even so, he was lucky.

He stood in the long echoing hall, alone. He stared at the glass case in front of him. It was unlit, the Exposition was long past closing this evening, but Iago's sensitive eyes could focus the dim light enough to see by.

Behind the glass, behind the ghost of his own reflection, was a display that wasn't part of the planned exhibits. This one was more makeshift. Room for it had been made at the last minute.

Resting behind the glass was a death-mask, along with a small placard asking if anyone could identify the man. Iago could. In the dark, Raphael's face hung, almost floating in the darkness behind the glass. His expression was peaceful, almost one of sleep—not the slack inactivity that plagued his kind in the daytime, but a true mortal sleep.

For Raphael, the long endless hunt was over.

His head and body had been found by the railroad tracks, like Polillo, Andrassy, and Anacreon. . . .

Anacreon, and now Raphael. Iago had known two communities, two homes, since he had walked into the night. Melchior had destroyed both of them.

"What use is a Covenant that only I keep?" Iago whispered, placing his fingers on the glass above Raphael's face. The glass was cold. Iago felt as if Melchior had torn out a

piece of his soul. Anacreon was one thing; he had lost his mentor, his friend, and the master of his circle—but there was still a community out there. His world still had rules, and he still had a place within it.

Now it seemed as if that had crumbled, leaving him adrift.

What use is a Covenant that only I keep?

The thought itself was self-destructive heresy. Simply questioning the Covenant was a dangerous thing to do. It was supposed to protect those of the blood, fashioned at a time of their near-extinction. But if one as powerful as Melchior flouted the Covenant, what point was there to it? Especially if those who were supposed to be first among those of the blood enforced nothing. . . .

Now Iago suspected that it was beyond enforcement. He had tried to contact members on the Council, but he had not found them. He suspected that those who had not suffered Raphael's fate had fled.

Once he had pictured his kind as having a certain dark nobility, a dignity granted by a centuries-old culture. It was a fraud. They were all little more than brute animals, savage and cowardly at the same time.

What use is a Covenant that only I keep?

The answer was, no use at all.

Melchior had to be stopped at any cost, and if Iago stood by and obeyed his own Covenant, he would soon be fighting alone. And there wasn't any way he could defeat Melchior alone. To someone that ancient, his own blood would betray him. Melchior would sense him long before he was able to do any good.

"What was your plan, Raphael?" he asked the glass. "What conflagration? What is it that Melchior is not enough of this century to realize?"

Iago had tried in vain to uncover some evidence of Raphael's plan, some sign that might tell him. But Raphael had been too smart for that. He had left no evidence that could be uncovered. Nothing had been left behind him. All Iago knew was that it had to do with the location where Melchior had placed his thralls. Somewhere in the Slovak community.

Once he knew where, he would know how.

2

He called himself Byron. He had been the second most powerful member of the Council that ruled the night in his city. Now he was dressed in rags and bound inside a wooden box. His mind reeled with the hunger. He hadn't fed in days. The only sensation he had, aside from the hunger, was a rhythmic rattling sensation, and the maddening smell of blood.

He had tried to escape what was happening. He and his circle had abandoned Cleveland when he saw that the power games he had fallen into with Lucian were wildly unbalanced. The Council might have been moved to act with the death of Raphael, but Byron had known it was already too late.

He had made it all the way to Chicago, and had begun talking to others of the blood, trying to find someone with the power or inclination to intervene. But before he had gotten anywhere, he had been taken.

Through the darkness he heard a screech of metal, and the rattling rhythm stopped. It had happened before, and like the prior times, the sudden change is his environment cut through the haze of his hunger, and he began fighting his imprisonment.

The aching lack inside him had yet to eat away all of his strength, or all of his mind. In his manic kicking and pulling, he focused his mind upon the smell of blood outside. His feet slammed the inside walls of the box containing him, his hands struggled with his bonds.

This time, after days of motion and stillness, dazed hunger and manic rage, something gave. His foot broke through one of the sides of the crate. The smell of blood was intense now, overwhelming. He scrambled for the hole like a madman. The force of the smell gave him the strength to break his bonds and push apart the crate around the hole his foot had made.

Driving him was a hunger frozen deep in the core of his body, a void inside him that could only be filled by the essence of the living. The drive was primal, and almost absolute. It was powerful enough for him to take two steps away from the crate that had been his prison before he realized exactly what he saw.

He stood inside a long rectangular chamber. The wooden walls had gaps between the boards that allowed moonlight to slice the interior into strips of narrow light alternating with wide bands of darkness. The smell of blood was rank within the car, as was the smell of overripe meat. Outside was the sound of chirping insects, but in here was only the buzz of flies.

Near his feet was a head, severed from its body. Moonlight slashed across it, revealing an eye and a swath of skin that had already begun to discolor. A fly walked across its cheek as Byron watched. He knew the face.

It had been one of his circle, one of the trusted ones he had taken to Chicago with him. He raised his eyes, and, for once, the hunger was forgotten.

They were everywhere, the bodies of his chosen. A dozen souls who had pledged fealty to him lay in this car, mutilated, their essence staining the straw bedding their corpses sprawled upon. Heads, their staring eyes accusing him.

Fear had completely replaced hunger.

There were giant sliding doors on either side of him. He dove to the right and began pulling madly at the latch. The door had been secured from the outside, but that hardly mattered to him. He pulled, and eventually the latch snapped. He spilled out over the moonlit railroad tracks.

Byron pushed himself upright and moved with a terror that he had not felt for over a century, not since he was human. He stumbled, running, through the weeds by the tracks. He had no idea where he was; all he wanted to do was get away from the massacre behind him.

He had not gotten far before he heard a voice say, "Do you think you can escape *me* so easily?" It was as much in his head as in his ears. He knew then, felt in his core, that it was the ancient Melchior bringing this evil.

Byron spun around to find the source of the voice. Melchior was not that simply found. He saw the tracks, the woods bordering them, and a motionless boxcar, alone on a siding.

Byron screamed at the sky, "Why?"

"You are weak," came the shuddering reply. It slammed into his brain like a hot iron, dropping him to his knees.

"You hide from yourselves and the cattle that should serve us."

Byron looked around wildly, but his gaze could not find the speaker. The area felt abandoned, far from any artificial lights. The long grass rustled around him as he tried to gather his courage in the face of the thing threatening him. He spoke, his words sounded small and hollow on the wind. "*We* follow the Covenant."

"Empty words." The voice slammed into his head. "You knew me, what I did. If you loved those chains of the Covenant so much, you would have moved against me. But you did nothing, and when that no longer served you, you tried to flee." A shadow moved in the long grass in front of Byron. "Your kind disgusts me. A member of my proud race, nothing more than a scared animal."

Byron tried to stand, to move, but his body was still locked in the grip of his fear. That and the force of the being talking to him held him fast to the spot. As he tried to move, the shadow before him unfolded itself, became a dark figure emerging from the grass.

Facing him was Melchior, the ancient one. The first vampire ever to be punished under the Covenant, his corpse supposedly reduced to ashes. "What do you want?" he whispered.

The shadow stepped closer, parts of it resolving into pale skin and hair. "I want to take back everything that was lost to us with that blasphemous Covenant. I want us to rule again. I want the heads of my enemies on pikes in front of my palace. I want the cattle to worship my name."

Melchior reached out and touched him. Byron felt the touch like a brand that seared his flesh down to the bone, bone that felt frozen. "You were to be honored, like the others. Their blood fed my power, my service. Their essence will be part of my reign." Melchior shook his head slowly as he looked down at Byron. Byron could feel a wave of emotion that was too much like pity. "Not now. Your coward's blood will soak useless into the ground."

Byron heard the slide of metal, and managed to turn just in time to see the blade descending.

3

Friday, July 22

It had gotten to the point where the investigators began numbering the bodies. The newest one, decapitated and left by the B&O tracks in Brooklyn Township on the West Side, was labeled Number Five. It was Five because there was still no official connection to the corpse that washed up on Euclid Beach back in 1934. Officially, Andrassy and his still-unidentified companion were the first two of these murders.

Number Five was different because it was obvious that the man had met his death on the spot where the body was found. Unlike the others, he lay in the blood spilled by his death. To most everyone in the department, the recurring theme of the railroad tracks made it certain that the murderer was preying on transients that rode the rails. It seemed an obvious conclusion.

Stefan Ryzard felt it meant something else.

"As far as I can tell, he hasn't left his hotel room," Nuri said. His voice was thin and rattled at the other end of the phone.

Stefan shook his head. Nuri had followed their quarry to his business meeting in Chicago. He had watched him for nearly a week, reporting back nothing more sinister than meetings with a few congressmen—

That was sinister enough when Stefan thought about it.

"Something's rotten here." Stefan massaged the part of his leg that still ached.

"Yes," Nuri said, "but we've been watching him for months. We've yet to catch him doing anything."

Something rotten. "Are you certain he hasn't left?"

"I've been watching the room—"

"Dietrich knows he's being watched. Maybe he slipped out unobserved."

There was a pause, and then Nuri said, "You don't think I'm doing my job?"

Stefan tapped the desk with his fingers. "No, that's not it. But can you get a look inside his hotel room?"

"Yes, but wouldn't that be tipping our hand? You know he could order what's going on from anywhere."

Stefan nodded. "I want to know for sure that he's there. Otherwise I don't think we have a hand to tip." Stefan stared at his desk. On the blotter were fountain-pen doodles of fangs and crosses, the words "vampire" and "blood" heavily embellished. "One thing, though," Stefan added.

"What?"

"Go in during daylight."

"You want me to break into a hotel room in broad daylight?"

"It's safer."

Stefan could hear Nuri sigh. "This is more vampire stuff, isn't it."

Damn it, you were there, Stefan thought. *You saw everything I did.* He wanted to say it, but instead he said, "Just do it that way."

"If you say so."

"I do."

Nuri hung up the phone and wondered what he was getting into. The Chicago cops didn't know he was here, and if he got caught breaking into someone's hotel room, especially someone as wealthy as Eric Dietrich, there would be a lot of explanations to go through.

Nuri didn't know how Dietrich could have gotten past him. He had a room on the same floor, positioned where he could watch the exits downstairs, and the door to Dietrich's room. There were windows, but they were fifteen stories up.

Nuri checked his gun and slipped out into the hallway.

He felt oddly out of place here, disconnected from the rest of the world. He walked through a hall emblazoned with garish wallpaper, over deep red carpeting. It was a hallway into another era.

Dietrich's door was at the end of the hallway, with the

most expensive suites. When Nuri reached it, he knocked just below the gilded numbers. He wanted to be sure that no one was home before he blithely popped the lock. A long minute passed without an answer. Nuri knocked again.

Again, no answer.

Maybe Stefan was right, and Dietrich managed to slip out from under him. That worried Nuri. If this time he missed him, how many other times? How long had he thought he'd been watching Dietrich, when he wasn't?

He knocked for a third time, and when he received no answer, he began working on the lock. In a few moments, the door swung open on a darkened room. The smell was musty for a hotel room, and it took him a few minutes for his eyes to adjust to the gloom beyond.

It was a huge suite, and Nuri faced the living area. Two large windows would have looked out over Chicago and to Lake Michigan beyond, but the drapes were closed on them. It even looked as if additional drapes had been added over the hotel's own, so not even a glimmer of the late evening sun leaked through.

Nuri had been trying to ignore Stefan's superstitious fears. Vampires were creatures of myth. But alone, facing these windows, shut against the day, it was hard to deny Stefan his myths. . . .

Which made no sense, since Nuri himself had seen Dietrich walking abroad in daylight.

Whatever the case, he didn't hear or see signs of anyone present. He let the door close behind him as he fumbled for the light switch. The lights came on, but feebly, half the bulbs dead or removed. They gave a weak illumination that was thick with shadows.

Something was disturbing about this room, something that Nuri couldn't quite identify. After standing by the door a long time, Nuri thought it could be something in the smell. It was rusty and didn't belong in a hotel room.

Nuri slowly walked into the living area, looking over the furniture, the end tables, the additional curtains on the windows. He could see signs that the room had been used; no maid had been here to clean up after the visiting congressmen. The ashtray was dirty and held the stubs of two cigars, and a few crystal glasses sat here and there on the tables.

Nuri bent over and took a whiff of one of the glasses.

There was a strong smell of whiskey, but it wasn't the odor he was looking for.

He moved around toward a short hall that led to the bedroom, and across from it, the bathroom. As he stepped into the hall, the smell was worse. He identified it now.

Blood.

Nuri swallowed and drew his gun. The smell was stronger near the bathroom, so he slowly opened the door, using the jamb for cover. The smell of blood became more intense as he swept his revolver to cover the small darkened room. The smell was becoming sickening, so Nuri tried to breathe through his mouth as he fumbled for the light switch.

Above the sink, a light came on.

There was a mirror above the sink, but it had been covered with a layer of butcher paper. As Nuri's gaze traveled down it, he saw a few red-brown dots sprinkled across its lower surface. Then he looked at the sink itself.

The porcelain was covered in blood. From the looks of it, it had once filled the sink. It had dried in patches, but a thick blackish-red liquid still filled the bottom about half an inch deep. On the counter, next to the sink, sat a crystal glass, twin to the whiskey glasses the congressmen had drank from.

The inside of the glass was also coated in gore. One side of the rim was smeared with it, inside and outside, as if someone had drunk from it.

The sight made Nuri ill.

Nuri pulled out a handkerchief and held it over his nose. He had seen dead bodies before. Most were bloody to one extent or another. This was somehow different. It wasn't the sight, or even the smell that sickened—it was the thought of what had been done here.

Nuri stood a long time in the otherwise empty bathroom, staring at the sink. What *had* happened here?

Nuri had little chance to reflect, because the door opposite the bathroom flew open. Nuri turned in time to see a shadow fly out of the darkened room beyond. It came straight at him, and he barely had a chance to dive out of its way through the bathroom door.

He rolled onto his back in the hallway to the living area. The shadow dove on him, and Nuri fired. In the dim light he saw the bullet slam into the gut of Samson Fairfax. The bullet tore through the expensive suite he wore, spattering t with flecks of gore. The wound didn't bleed.

Fairfax dove on top of him, his face distorting as fangs seemed to grow from his jaw. Fairfax grabbed his gun hand n a grip like an iron band, and Nuri could feel the bones n the hand shifting and each finger became a clawed talon.

Nuri struggled under Fairfax, trying to break free, but all he accomplished was to inch the fight deeper into the room. Fairfax straddled him, his face turning into something demonic, taloned hands drawing blood from Nuri's wrists.

It opened its mouth and began leaning its face toward him. The breath was fetid, stinking of carrion. But worse than the smell was the fact that it was cold. Fairfax's breath held nothing of the heat of life in it.

Nuri whipped his head around in a panic, but he couldn't move. He was pinned to the ground. The thing held his wrists so he couldn't turn his gun—

His gun.

Nuri was panicked beyond his disbelief, and he was ready to try anything. His gun was pointing toward the over-draped windows. It was the only chance he had.

As he felt Fairfax's lips on his neck, Nuri struggled to aim his revolver, and fired. Four times he shot at the upper-right of the window, where the curtain was anchored. The fourth shot hit something.

With the crashing of glass, the curtains fell away as their weight tore the rod from the wall. Suddenly, the whole room was washed in the rose light of sunset. The light washed Fairfax and Nuri.

Fairfax pulled away, and Nuri could see the muscles trying to tear themselves back into human form. He moved fast, faster than Nuri could credit, but he didn't see where he was going. His eyes were squeezed shut, as if the light was too painful to see.

Nuri scrambled away, backing toward the center of the light. He stopped and held a gun on Fairfax. It wasn't necessary. Fairfax was paying little attention to him right now.

Fairfax had stumbled backward quickly, seeming to attempt a retreat into the safety of the darkened bedroom. But, with his eyes closed, he had slammed into a wall instead. He staggered, as if numb or disoriented, each step seemed more unsteady than the last. All expression was gone from his face, the skin a slack mask, the eyelids no longer bunched up, but drooping over half closed eyes. He waved his hands as if blind, but his arms hit furniture and lamps without his notice.

The spectacle was even worse than the demonic transformation when he had tried to kill Nuri. In less than a few seconds he seemed to have become little more than an animate corpse, stumbling around blindly.

Nuri slowly pushed himself to his feet.

Fairfax stumbled into the room, like an exaggerated silent movie drunk. That was the most disturbing, the silence. Fairfax said nothing, didn't even seem to breathe. The only sound was from the furniture he toppled. Every step now, he seemed on the verge of falling.

Nuri was over the panic now. He knew he had to get this man out of the light, somehow the sunlight was killing him. Nuri needed a witness, someone who had seen what was going on.

Nuri ran up into the center of the room. He held his gun level, and reached out with the other. "You need to come with me, Mr. Fairfax."

Fairfax didn't seem to hear him, and he stumbled blindly into his arm. Nuri tried to grab him, but as soon as Fairfax seemed to notice the resistance to his forward movement, he stumbled backward—straight into the window.

Nuri tried to grab him again, but he was moving too fast, and bullet holes and the wreck of the draperies had weakened the windows already. When Fairfax's weight fell on it, the windows gave way, spilling Fairfax into the sky.

Nuri saw him fall the fifteen stories to the street below. The body slammed into a parked sedan with an explosion of glass. He seemed to stop moving long before he hit.

Nuri watched as a crowd began to circle the car, a few looking up toward him.

Nuri was certain that this time Samson Fairfax was dead.

Now all he had to do was figure out how to explain this to the Chicago cops.

4

Stefan stood in the corner of Ness' office. "We're getting Detective Lapidos back," Ness told him as he hung up the phone on his desk. "We're lucky that they weren't too ornery about it."

Stefan exhaled a little in relief. He'd been worried that the Chicago DA might make a stink over Nuri's presence here.

"What were you thinking, telling Nuri to break in here?"

Stefan looked at Ness. Staring at his young boss made him feel that much older. "Another body turned up, and I wanted to be sure that Dietrich was there."

"And he wasn't," Ness pointed out. "I let you get away with the warehouse, but this is completely out of our jurisdiction. We're both lucky I know people in Chicago that could smooth over this mess."

"But we have him now," Stefan said. "The blood, the attack on Nuri—"

"What we have—more precisely, what the Chicago Police have—is Samson Fairfax, already wanted in connection with his wife's death."

"Aren't they even going to talk to Dietrich?"

Ness nodded. "Of course they are. But Dietrich wasn't there, and Fairfax was. Without a witness tying him to anything illegal, the DA won't lift a finger when he's got a corpse to hang everything on."

Stefan balled his hands into fists and muttered, "How many bodies is it going to take?"

Ness narrowed his eyes and said, "That's quite enough. Don't push things." He leaned back in his chair. "I know that ever since the warehouse, you've had some odd ideas about Dietrich, and I've let them by because it'd be hard to replace you." He glanced at a stack of files piled on the corner of his desk. "But I'm beginning to wonder about your judgment."

Stefan had unpleasant memories of Inspector Cody telling him the same thing.

"I'm thinking about putting you and Nuri back on regular duty."

"But what about the Dietrich investigation?"

"I can put a pair of fresh eyes on it," Ness said.

Stefan felt himself sinking. How could he explain Dietrich in a sane manner? How could he tell Ness that no one that replaced him would understand the evil? Stefan tried. "No one else is going to understand what they're dealing with."

"And you do, Stefan? You know everything?" Ness shook his head. "That's just what I mean. You're too close to this investigation. Your reports come close to being hysterical. Sometimes they read as if you believe something supernatural is going on here."

Stefan swallowed. Something supernatural *was* going on here, something demonic. What he said was, "I've kept myself to what I've seen, and what I've gotten from witnesses . . ."

"Maybe new eyes will see something else." He reached over and began shuffling through the files on his desk. "Anyway, I need to do something about this Chicago business. I've been trying to deal discipline to the whole department, so I can't just let it by. You and Detective Lapidos are going on two week's leave, then you're being reassigned."

"But—"

"This may only be temporary. But I want you getting some distance from your work. You can't fly off the handle every time a body shows up."

Stefan nodded, "Yes, sir." His stomach was tied up into a knot of bile; he needed to leave. "Can I go now?"

Ness nodded, his face already turning toward a file he had pulled off of his desk.

Stefan really began to hate him. The only reason he saw for being removed from the case was he had come too close

o breaking Ness' precious secrecy. With Nuri's conflict in
he hotel, there was almost certainly some press attention.
Press that Ness didn't orchestrate.

God forbid that the press might say something unpleas-
nt about Ness and his department. Stefan felt cynical
nough as he left that for a while he believed that Ness'
whole departmental cleanup was a public relations gag.

Stefan was back at his desk putting things away when
Nuri called. Stefan picked up the phone, and the first words
he heard were, "Stefan, I've talked to the coroner, some-
hing strange—"

"Nuri, you better get back here," Stefan said. "Ness
pulled us off the case."

"What? Why?"

"I guess he didn't like how we were handling it."

There was a long pause and Stefan could almost hear
Nuri thinking, *you mean how you were handling it.*

"Does he know about this?" Nuri asked, finally.

"Know about what?"

"The autopsy on Samson Fairfax."

Stefan shook his head, "I thought he fell out a window
after you shot him."

Nuri sucked in a breath and said, "That's what I thought,
oo. But the coroner insists he's been dead at least a couple
of weeks, and that the gunshot and the fall occurred
afterwards."

Stefan held the phone, unable to say anything.

"He says there seems to be some sort of chemical preser-
vative contaminating the body. Just like Andrassy's friend."
Nuri waited for a response, and after a few moments said,
"Stefan, are you there?"

Stefan nodded, as if Nuri could see him. "I'm here, come
back. I said we're off this case."

"Okay. Are you sure that you don't want this followed
up? I'd hate to think I've gone through all this grilling for
nothing. I can probably get a copy of the coroner's report."

"It's over, Nuri," Stefan said, his voice heavy.

"If you say so. I'll get on the first train back."

Stefan was about to say good-bye, but instead he told
Nuri, "But get a copy of that report before you go. Just
n case."

"Like I said, if you say so."

"Godspeed, Nuri."

"Are you all right?" Nuri asked.

No. "Yes, I'm fine."

"See you tomorrow, then," Nuri said. The line died as he hung up.

Stefan slowly rested the handset back into the cradle and resumed cleaning his desk. There were notes and speculations he didn't wish to leave in the office while he was gone.

5

FDR was in town to visit the Great Lakes Exposition. As usual, the president was followed into town by dozens of aides, officials, and other political types. As usual, when such people came to town, Carlo Pasquale waited in a limousine. A few of FDR's entourage would be meeting the Master tonight.

Despite accusations of being a class traitor, members of FDR's administration weren't adverse to meeting with wealthy businessmen. Carlo thought it was almost amusing.

He waited outside the Exposition, far back from the rear of the motorcade. He watched the uniformed police controlling the swelling crowds and waited for his guests. Cops used to make him nervous. Even before, when he was working for the Mayfield Road Gang and two-thirds of the cops were bought off, cops had made him nervous.

Not since he started serving the Master. The Master's protection went far beyond anything his old bosses could manage. No one could mess with him; he was invulnerable. The Master saw what he saw, and those who saw Carlo saw a piece of the Master. Carlo saw it in the way people turned away when he looked at them.

His old employer had tried to bump him off several times. Each time the Master had seen it, and the assassins were as dead as those who tried to kill the Master—except for those the Master chose to serve Him, as Carlo did. The Master was very persuasive.

Carlo watched the evening sky and wondered how many more sunsets he would see.

Carlo pushed away the thought. The Master needed service in the daylight as well as at night. It was his honor to

remain human. If the Master would grant him eternal life
He would in his own time. It was best for him not to think
about that.

Carlo turned and studied a sign for the Aquacade a
the exposition.

It was after dark when Carlo Pasquale delivered his passengers to the Union Terminal Tower. They were going to
meet the Master in one of the offices he held in the building. The Master had just come from Chicago. Carlo heard
that He had dealt with a legal problem.

Carlo smiled. He knew that all the Master needed to
solve any legal problem was talk to the DA. Money didn't
even have to change hands. The Master could *convince*.

Carlo waited outside, leaning against the fender of the
limo, taking drags on a cigarette. He felt good, as if he had
found his purpose in life.

Behind him, through Public Square, transit cars rattled
by. Carlo listened to the sound of the electric trolleys as
he watched his smoke curl up into the darkened sky. He
was watching the smoke spread in the windless air when
he felt something stab him in the back of his neck.

He tensed up and dropped the cigarette, more in surprise
than in pain. It fell against his leg, burning a hole in his
trousers and searing his leg. He sprang away from the car,
slapping at his burned leg and simultaneously turning to
see what had stabbed him.

His move was way too awkward, and as he turned, his
leg slipped from under him. He slammed into the sidewalk,
but he didn't really feel it. His body felt wrapped in cotton.
His vision blurred as he tried to look up. All he could make
out was a darkened shadow leaning over him.

His last thought, as he lost consciousness was, *Master . . .*

Carlo Pasquale woke up hearing a babbling chorus of
shrieks and smelling the rankest odor he had ever encoun-
tered. The sound was like the entrance to the gates of hell.
The smell was old blood that had gone sour. He had
smelled it before, and for a few panicked moments he
thought that he had offended the Master and was to be
executed like an enemy.

Then he opened his eyes and faced a light shining down

n him. It was too bright for him to see anything except
what was immediately next to him. He was on a concrete
floor, stained and tacky with blood. Also, Carlo noticed
with a sense of disorientation, the floor was dotted with
feathers. After blinking a few times, he noticed cages just
outside his field of vision. Tiny cages, coated with feathers
and manure.

The horrid sound was the cackling of chickens, thousands
of them outside the area he could see.

He tried to sit up, but he couldn't move. He was
weighted and bound with chains, too much for him even to
lift, much less escape.

Beyond the light, a voice spoke above the sound of the
imprisoned birds. "Are you awake, Carlo Pasquale?"

Carlo yelled at the voice, "You're making a hell of a
mistake. I got protection."

"I know. That is why you're here."

"Mr. Dietrich is going to find you—"

"No, he isn't." The voice was much too calm. "Your
master can't save you."

Carlo was about to shout something more, but he
stopped when he realized that the voice had said "master."
That was a secret. No one was supposed to know that he
had fed from the Master. No one should know that He was
the Master.

The voice moved in a circle around him, but he couldn't
see the speaker, or hear the footsteps over the din. "Your
master is bound through you, can see what you see, but
what do you see? What do you hear? What do you smell?
This place is so rank with sensation that even someone as
powerful as Melchior will not be able to pick you out of it
before I've had what I want."

When the voice said "Melchior," Carlo shuddered. Others weren't supposed to know the Master's true name. He
struggled and began to feel the first stirrings of fear, the
first sense that he might not be fully protected.

"You can't do this," Carlo yelled. "He won't permit it."

The voice laughed. "I'd admire your faith, if it wasn't
Melchior's blood talking through you. You're less than a
thrall, less than human even, a debased thing, a
perversion."

"I work for Dietrich, and he'll—"

Something splashed across his legs from the shadows. The smell of gasoline watered his eyes. His voice caught in his throat, choking on the fumes. The cacophony of poultry redoubled in volume. Carlo began a renewed struggle against his bonds.

The voice spoke again, as another splash of liquid fell against Carlo's chest.

"Melchior fed you just enough of his blood to bind your will to his. Not even enough to pull you into our world had you died."

"I don't know what you're talking about."

More gasoline splashed into his face, burning his eyes and searing his lips. He maniacally shook his head from side to side, fighting the pain. He had to hold his breath against the smell.

"Melchior is one of the blood, Carlo. A demon out of your mythology. A vampire. His blood contains the seed of his nature, his will. A little, and you become a willing extension of his will. Enough will pull you across the threshold of death, make you a thrall, an extension of his body, of his unlife, bound to him until his destruction." The voice stopped circling, stopping at Carlo's head. The speaker bent forward. Carlo strained to see the man's face, but even when he leaned into the light, Carlo's burning eyes couldn't make out more than a blur.

He wanted to call out, deny what the man was saying, but something held him silent—more than the choking fumes that kept his breath from him. Something in the core of his being was frozen at the presence of this anonymous being. Something fearful that bound his will like a vise. It was terrifyingly similar to what he felt in the presence of his Master. . . .

"Those of the blood have few weaknesses, Carlo. Sunlight can kill the flesh of all but the most powerful. Dismemberment is Melchior's favored method of assassination. Then there's immolation of the flesh." Carlo felt a hand brush his cheek. He felt a leather glove leave a trail on his wet cheek. The touch felt like a brand against icelike skin. Carlo began shivering. Inside, his body felt frozen. It had been several long minutes, and he still wasn't breathing.

What's happened to me?

"Your master promised you life after death. . . ."

Somehow his voice managed to find itself. "No," he whispered, tasting gasoline along with his own stale breath. Even through the fumes, Carlo began to realize that the smell of blood came from him as much as anywhere else. His breath was like cold carrion, and tasted like sour iron through the gasoline.

"I needed you to talk, Carlo. To talk against the creature that bound you. The only way to do that was to take you as my own. You're mine as much as his now. My thrall. My flesh."

"But what . . ."

"Look at me!"

Carlo could do nothing but obey the command. His eyes opened, despite the burning. Despite the streaming tears. He looked up into a golden mask. The mask was twisted and frowning, covering the whole face except for the eyes. Those eyes stared into his own with a burning pressure that made him forget the sting of gasoline.

The other gloved hand laid itself on Carlo's other cheek. Both hands clamped down with a pressure as heavy as the chains across his chest and legs. His head was held immobile.

"I see into you, Carlo Pasquale. You will remember everything of Melchior that you saw or heard. His actions, his plans, where he keeps his allies. You will remember, and you will speak them to me."

Carlo felt Melchior draining away inside him in the presence of this new Master. He opened his mouth and spoke, despite the part of him that was terrified of doing so. He spoke, and he couldn't tell if he used more his voice or his mind. It seemed days he spoke, everything falling up into that frowning golden mask.

After he had said everything, the hands let go, and his head fell exhausted to the ground. It was over. Carlo began to recover a little. It was just another change of bosses, after all. He had gone through it once, he could go through it again. Hell, this guy, mister anonymous, had pulled him all the way over. Which was more than Melchior did.

He really was invulnerable now, he couldn't die. . . .

Carlo screwed up his courage and said, "Okay, you've got everything, boss. Can you let me go now?"

Carlo realized that he could sense, somewhat, what his

boss was feeling. The emotion seemed to roll off of him like an invisible cloud-bank. The feeling Carlo got wasn't reassuring. It seemed like pity.

The masked man stood and reached into the pocket of his dark overalls. "You don't understand," he said. "I cannot allow Melchior to discover my blood within you. If he finds that, he can find me."

"Look, I won't roll over on you," Carlo's voice took on a pleading tone. "Hell I don't even know who you are."

"I'm afraid you never will." The masked man pulled out a book of matches.

Carlo Pasquale burned.

When Carlo's burning corpse stopped trying to move, Iago removed the mask of Tragedy and tossed it into the fire, followed by his gloves. The air was rank, with thick tarlike smoke, and the surrounding poultry were deafening with their objections.

Iago couldn't breathe comfortably, but he stayed to watch Carlo reduced to ash. He didn't watch with any enjoyment. If it had been possible for Carlo to live, as thrall or as owner of his own blood, Iago would have preferred it.

But Melchior had claimed this one as his own, and that meant that Melchior would find him, eventually. It would be simple for Melchior to sense an elder's blood in another, and sense whose. It would be simple even if Carlo had been slain in a less complete manner. Iago could not leave any trace of himself behind, otherwise there would be little chance for him. The fate of the Council told him that much.

All Iago had was anonymity. Even if Melchior sensed what happened to his puppet, all he would have was a forest of impressions impossible to pin down, a masked figure draining Carlo of his secrets.

Iago stared at the charred black flesh as the flames died down. He wished Carlo had known more for the price he paid. For the price Iago paid. The slaughter he had just committed, taking what another had claimed, and bringing him over only to kill him. It savaged the Covenant as badly as Melchior did.

Those of the blood do not kill those of the blood. . . .

6

Stefan Ryzard stared at the ceiling of his apartment, trying to sleep. Moonlight washed through the bedroom, giving everything a pale blue glow. In the shadows, barely visible, pictures still clung to the walls. Stefan had not taken down any of the remnants of his long investigation into Dietrich. The walls were still covered by papers, surveillance photos, and forensic details of the mutilated corpses.

His part was over. It was no longer his problem. He kept telling himself that. Despite that, he didn't take the papers off of his wall. He couldn't stop thinking of Dietrich.

The fact that Dietrich existed was an ache inside him. The more Stefan thought about him, the more he became convinced that Dietrich was the devil that Samson Fairfax had told him about, the devil that Edward Mullen couldn't lie for anymore.

Whoever investigated Dietrich, Stefan knew that they'd find little more than he had. No direct connection to the murders. Perhaps they'd see signs of the supernatural that no one else would credit. Surveillance would be useless, and Stefan expected anyone who got too close to Dietrich would disappear like those mob assassins.

He lay naked on sweat-stained sheets, trying not to think of what was happening out there. It wasn't his business anymore. . . .

A shadow passed over his bedroom window, wiping away the moonlight, plunging the room into darkness. Stefan bolted upright, his heart racing. Before he could make out what had passed in front of his window, it was gone.

Still, Stefan sat up on his bed, the copper taste of fear searing his mouth. The window was open to the night air, and next to the window a picture of Edward Andrassy's decapitated body fluttered in the breeze.

In a few minutes, his breathing and his pulse returned to normal. He slipped off the bed and walked over to the window. He closed it, throwing the latch.

Even with the window closed, there was still a chill in the room.

"Greetings, Detective Ryzard."

The voice came from behind him, and Stefan spun around to face it. Standing in his bedroom, in front of the only door, stood Iago. His overalls were black in the moonlight. He looked paler, gaunter than he had seemed the last time Stefan had seen him.

"What do you want?" Stefan whispered. He didn't ask how he had gotten in. If Iago was the same kind of being as Dietrich, it seemed that they had a talent for not being seen when they didn't want to be seen.

"I want an end to Eric Dietrich."

Stefan shook his head. "You're too late, I'm off that case."

"Look at your own walls," Iago said, his eyes boring into him.

Stefan couldn't answer that. He wasn't actively investigating Dietrich, or the murders. He didn't interview anyone. He didn't watch the suspects. . . .

But the case still obsessed him. Dietrich still gripped his thoughts. Stefan still felt the cold overpowering presence of the devil named Eric Dietrich. It was as if, having touched him, Stefan had tainted his own soul.

"Why are you here?" Stefan said. His breath was dry and tasted like copper.

"I need an ally, policeman."

Stefan felt the force of Iago's will spilling over, overwhelming his own. He prayed to God for strength, and found enough to take a step backward. "Why should I help you?" his voice came out in a hoarse whisper. "Why should I help any of your kind?"

Iago took a step forward. The moonlight splashed across his face, carving shadows across his pale skin, making him look like a marble bust of the Devil himself. He ran his hand over his beard. "You know me so well that you know what I am?"

Stefan backed to the wall, the wall that bore a crucifix. "An undead thing," Stefan said. "A damned soul. A creature of Satan."

Iago laughed, but he stopped advancing. "You've decided, then, haven't you? We're Vampyr, Nosferatu, Dwellers of the Darkness." Iago released his beard and bowed with a flourish. His eyes, however, remained on Stefan's own.

"I won't help any servant of evil," Stefan said. He wanted to cower, he felt his knees wanting to bend, but he held his back straight to the wall. Thumbtacks dug into his backside, where he had posted pages on Dietrich and the murders. He didn't move. He held his spot under the cross, fearing that any more movement might lead to collapse.

"Am I evil, then?" Iago said. "This your Bible says?"

"You feast on the living."

"Didn't your savior say to drink of his blood? Eat of his flesh?"

Stefan's stomach tightened at the blasphemy. He straightened and said, "In the name of God and Jesus Christ, I command you to leave me."

Iago actually took a step back. "You should listen to me, policeman."

The retreat emboldened Stefan. He stepped away from the wall and reached for the crucifix. "In the name of the Lord—"

Iago hissed at him. His face retreated into shadow, but Stefan thought he could see parts of it, bone and skin, move and distort. Iago's voice lowered from the cultured tone it usually took, and became closer to a growl. "What Christian charity is this?"

Stefan took a step forward, holding the crucifix.

Iago slunk backward. He spat like a cat, his body hunched over and twisted, completely in shadow now. He pointed at Stefan, his finger reached into the moonlight. It had changed, becoming a twisted thing that was almost a talon. "You make a mistake." The voice was harsh now, barely human. "You might pain me, but your faith in that stick will be as nothing to Melchior. He is your enemy."

"Begone, fiend of Satan, in the name of the Lord, Jesus Christ." Stefan took another step forward.

Iago shrieked and leaped. Stefan stumbled backward, but the leap didn't carry Iago toward him. Instead, Iago leaped at the bedroom window. The manic dive carried him back into the moonlight, and gave Stefan a single terrified glimpse of what he'd become before he slammed through the window.

The window shattered, the frame exploding outward, as Iago sailed out into the night— If what Stefan saw was still Iago. He had only a glimpse as it had sprung by him, but what Stefan had seen resembled a twisted bat-winged gargoyle, skin like horn, and a mouth with pointed jaws and teeth longer than its clawed fingers. It had crashed naked through the window, tearing most of it away from the wall. He heard the wreckage crash onto the ground below before he stepped up to the window.

A chill wind blew in, rocking pieces of the window frame back and forth. Around him. Pieces of wood now pointed out into the night, while below him, broken glass glittered on the street. The only sign that Stefan saw of Iago was a shadow moving, almost too quick to see, on the roof of the apartment across the street, three floors above him.

Stefan stepped back from the windows and saw, on the floor, the remnants of a pair of black overalls. The seams had burst open. Stefan crossed himself and prayed for his own soul.

An elder named Abraham began the last twenty-four hours of his three hundred years of existence in the Union Terminal Station. He had traveled from Chicago in a private car, and upon his arrival there was little of the night left. This didn't disturb him. He wasn't hurried. After three centuries, he was never hurried.

He walked out to the street, ignoring the humans around him, and because he wished it, the humans ignored him. None would remember seeing him pass.

Once he passed through the foot of the Terminal Tower, and faced Public Square, he stood in the middle of the night-empty street and breathed in the air.

Even here, far removed from everything that had happened, he could smell the corruption. Something ugly was at play here. For the first time, Abraham felt his confidence shaken. He knew that there was a slaughter going on here.

The circles in Chicago knew that there were circles here being devastated, their leaders being killed and left for dead.

For years, those outside the demesne of Cleveland saw it as an internal problem. A circle, however large, was loath to interfere with the internal problems of another circle.

It wasn't until those outside lost all contact with the Council in this city that they even considered sending one of their own to investigate. Even then, the debate took months, while the only contact with the community in Cleveland were confused individuals escaping the collapse of their society—some little more than thralls freed too soon by the death of their master.

Until now, Abraham had theorized that the destruction had been wrought by a member of the Council itself, someone whose ambition for control finally outstripped his loyalty to the Covenant. The other likely suspect was someone in the society who had lost his mind. Though, when one of the blood went mad, the madness rarely persisted this long before the offender was disciplined.

Abraham now felt that both possibilities were wrong. There was an oppressive psychic pall over the city. Something dark and powerful was in control of the city now. Abraham could almost feel it become aware of him.

In the past century, nothing had been able to frighten him. The emotion was so old and ill-used that it took a few moments for Abraham to realize that fear was what he was feeling right now. A cold hand gripped his chest, and for a few long minutes he stopped breathing and his heart stopped beating.

He had an impulse to walk back into the Union Terminal, reboard his velvet-curtained train car, and leave this place. For moments he considered accepting the disgrace of abandoning his job here, rather than stepping forward and confronting what had taken this city.

Abraham only considered it, and the fear was only fleeting. He was, after all, one of the oldest and most powerful beings in this country. He walked off into the night, to find the remnants left by those of the blood, and of the creature that had slain them.

*   *   *

Abraham stepped into their meeting place, a long table before a set of tall windows. From here he could see into the seething industrial valley of the city. He stepped up to the table and placed a hand upon it. It disturbed a layer of dust.

Twelve chairs were behind the table, five were overturned.

Abraham looked at the chairs and spoke quietly to himself, "Laila, Anacreon, Raphael, Byron . . ." Abraham looked at the last chair, lying on its back on the floor. "Who?" he asked.

The being responsible had been in this room. Abraham could feel the presence. It had sunk into the walls like an evil smell, a spiritual rot. He could almost see the man walking into this private chamber, and methodically tipping over the chairs of his victims.

Like disposing of the bodies in public, it showed an almost incomprehensible arrogance.

The air changed. It became heavy, weighted with the darkness around him. He could smell, sense, one of the blood enter the room. Abraham should have noticed another's presence long before it was this close. As he turned to face the visitor, he had a disturbing thought—he was only perceiving the other because the other permitted it.

The darkness seemed to deepen near the doorway where the visitor stood, but Abraham could still see him clearly. His most notable feature was blond hair too long for this age. The spirit behind his eyes flared brighter than any Abraham had ever seen before. Behind most eyes Abraham saw a candle he could make dance or dim at his whim. Abraham knew that he could no more influence what was behind these eyes than an eyedropper could influence a bonfire.

The visitor leaned forward on a cane, and looked Abraham up and down. There was a half-smile on his face, as if he saw something amusing. "Are you looking for something here, my friend?"

Abraham didn't lie. His purpose was evident. "There's been a violation of the Covenant here. The local elders have failed to deal with it—"

The other laughed. When he did, whatever heat and light

were left in the room seemed to drain away. "The elders are gone."

"Four, yes—"

"All." The visitor walked forward. His presence seemed to radiate cold, sucking the heat off of Abraham's skin. "All of them have left, one way or another."

Abraham couldn't look away from his eyes; the power there, the age, the infinitely cold arrogance wouldn't allow him to. "It is you," Abraham said. This was the creature he had been sent here to stop.

Abraham moved in a flash. Before he had even allowed his conscious mind to think, talons had extended from his hands and he was bringing them down on the visitor. Both hands aimed overhand, across the chest, toward the heart. Removal of that organ would be as fatal as decapitation.

Abraham's victim didn't move as his talons came down, slicing into the chest cavity. He tore through clothes, flesh, and bone too easily. It was almost as if the flesh gave way before he reached it. Then his hands jerked with an impact that almost dislocated his shoulders.

The cane clattered to the ground.

The visitor held each of Abraham's wrists. Abraham's hands were buried deep into holes in the visitor's chest, just below the pectorals. The visitor's suit was shredded, and Abraham's arms were spattered with tarlike blood up to his elbows. Light glinted off of the torn flesh, as if it were moving.

The visitor showed little sign of pain, or even discomfort. That was when the fear came back. Abraham could feel the lungs shredded beneath his hands. Such an injury would have taken Abraham to the ground at the very least. This thing before him barely noticed.

Abraham tried to remove his hands, but the visitor was stronger. Much stronger. He was held fast.

The laugh was worse this time, worse because he felt it in his hands more than heard it. It was nearly silent, and it was accompanied by blood dripping from the visitor's lips.

"This is your Covenant?" The voice was below a whisper, its breath sucked in through the holes in his chest. "Strike down any with the will, the power, to take what is due him? Hobble our race? Keep us silent and cowering in the shadows? That is your creed?"

Abraham tried to pull his hands away. His muscles tore from bone and reknit themselves into more efficient patterns, but it was no use. And while he struggled, the flesh around the wounds began pulling together, the gore flowing into itself, fusing under new skin.

"So terrified of death, of discovery, that a handful of bodies can paralyze you. The fact I am here is proof enough that I am necessary."

Abraham struggled as the stranger's flesh wrapped itself around his hands. As he struggled, the tarlike blood that coated his arms began to flow upwards. He could feel it under his jacket advancing along his upper arms, toward his neck. Feeling that, the fear turned into panic.

The blood was everything to his kind. Mind, soul, and flesh were all one with the blood. In all of them the flesh shifted with the will, but it was near the apotheosis of power for the blood to act as an extension of the body, moving to its own will. Abraham had never seen it, and had never met anyone who had. It was something a millennial ancient might aspire to.

The blood tightened around his arms like a serpent. He felt his own skin tear and give way as the burning tendrils sank into his own flesh. When the blood seared down to the bone, he felt the flesh binding him give way. He was thrown backward, slamming up against the unused meeting table.

He slid to the ground, unable to move. A burning alien presence slid beneath the skin, traveling from his arms, to his neck, his head. While Abraham felt the presence burn into his mind, he felt something else. The blood carried a name, an old name.

"Melchior," he whispered, a last conscious act of his own will.

Melchior stepped forward, the tatters of his suit bloodstained and hanging over a naked, unblemished chest. "I can read you now," he said, standing over him. "I read you, Abraham, as easily as you could once read a witless thrall. I smelled your presence the moment you entered my demesne." He knelt down next to Abraham and cupped his chin. "It *is* mine now, no one left here to challenge my authority. I already own countless human puppets, and thralls beyond your own petty imagining. I see through all their eyes, as I see through yours now."

He stood up, pulling Abraham upright by the chin. Abraham's legs followed through with the motion against his will. He felt the complete domination of Melchior. He couldn't act now except as Melchior willed.

Abraham kept thinking, over and over, that Melchior had died centuries ago.

"You came to see," Melchior said. "See you shall. I shall take you to Lucian; you will bear witness to my kingdom." He passed his hand over Abraham's eyes and the world became a black void.

When Abraham was called awake, he had recovered some of his will. Enough to move, to turn his head, to think. All of it was too late to do him any good. Melchior had overwhelmed him for long enough to bring him into the heart of his new kingdom. Long enough for him to be chained.

The room was long and dimly lit. He was at one end, and a mass of pale faces filled the other end, spreading back into the darkness. Melchior stood between him and the crowd of spectators. The watchers were of many races, and wore the battered clothing of the unemployed, the drifters, the homeless. Their faces were worn and dirty, and all wore the same expression. They all looked upon Melchior with a beatific expression of faith.

Melchior held a golden cup in front of him, and gave it to the crowd. When he handed the cup to someone, he would say, "Drink of my blood," and they would drink. It was a dark mass, and it disgusted and horrified Abraham at the same time. The bond between master and thrall was personal, sacred. To spread one's own blood so widely was something close to pure evil. Melchior's kingdom was a megalomaniac's attempt to control as many beings as possible.

Abraham saw the cup pass from mouth to mouth, and he saw in those eyes a worship. These dregs saw Melchior as a god. Trash that no one of the blood would lower themselves to call their own, these Melchior took.

It sickened Abraham.

As the ceremony continued, he tried to free himself. He

struggled, but while he normally would have the strength to part his chains, his confrontation with Melchior had drained him too deeply. Melchior's blood, the blood that bound the slaves in front of him, had burned too long within him. Abraham's body and spirit had exhausted itself just to fight free from those internal chains.

If only he could feed, himself, regain his strength.

After what seemed an eternity of struggle, Melchior turned with the cup in his hand.

"Welcome to my kingdom, Abraham," Melchior said. "These, and countless others like them, they call me Lord." Abraham strained against his chains and Melchior smiled at his struggles. "You're the pinnacle of what our race has become. Weak. Without even the strengths of your dubious Covenant." Melchior held up the golden chalice, the inside stained with red. It glittered in the candlelight, the odor powerful, seductive. The liquid pulled at him, tearing at the emptiness inside him.

"You want to take it," Melchior said. "Take it, partake in *my* Covenant." Abraham's soul was at such a low ebb, the weakness and the hunger so strong, that he wanted to take it. Abraham was close to pledging fealty to this dark lord if it meant to end to the burning void inside him.

Then disgust overwhelmed Abraham. He was of free blood. He took his own blood, untainted by any others of his kind. What had flowed through Melchior's veins wasn't blood, it was liquid slavery. If he partook willingly, he would become Melchior's, little more than the rabble worshiping him.

From somewhere, he found the strength to say, "Go to hell."

Melchior frowned and upturned the cup next to him. Blackish liquid spilled on the straw-covered floor. He dropped the cup and took a step toward Abraham. As he moved forward, his followers surged forward to fall on their knees before the spilled blood.

"This *is* hell," Melchior said, "and I am its lord and master."

Melchior walked close enough that Abraham felt his breath on his cheek. It was cold against his skin.

"Poor choice, my friend." Abraham heard the scrape of metal. "You will become part of my body one way or anther." Abraham saw the shine of a blade in Melchior's hand. "If my blood does not flow in your veins, your blood shall flow in mine."

The last thing Abraham saw was the circle of Melchior's thralls sucking his blood off of the floor.

Then the world went dark for good.

7

"Something has to be done about these bodies that keep showing up," Mayor Burton said. Sweat sheened on his face as he looked across the court at Ness. They stood in a handball court at the Cleveland Athletic Club. Ness was holding his own against the older man. His matches with the mayor almost inevitably turned toward business. Ness suspected half the time it was to throw off his game.

"I wanted a crime-fighting administration," Burton gave the ball a savage return. "This is making it look bad."

Ness scrambled for the return and said, "Which bodies?" Ness suspected "which bodies;" he read the same papers that Mayor Burton did. What had been a deep, almost subliminal, unease about the decapitated corpses turning up in the Run and elsewhere seemed to have erupted into full-fledged panic. The papers were beginning to scream now.

This was the first time that the mayor had brought up the subject.

Burton made it to the ball, and in a breathless voice told him, "The Kingsbury Run murders, Ness."

Ness let the ball pass by him and turned to face Mayor Burton. "I have investigations ongoing—"

"I'm sure you do." Burton nodded and wiped sweat from his forehead. "That's not the point. I'm sure you're doing your job. You've done good work cleaning the graft from the police department, and in everything else from organized crime to traffic safety."

"But?"

Burton turned and looked at him, "*But* people are raving

at there's a maniac loose in the city and the police aren't
oing anything to catch him."

Ness nodded. "Making public any suspects might sabo-
ge the investigation."

"I need something public, Ness. Your greatest strength
making yourself look good in the press. I need you to
o that. I need public demonstration of the department's
ill in this matter." Burton walked over to a bench,
rabbed a towel, and flung it over his shoulders. "I want
e public to know we're after this guy. I want every spare
an on it. You understand me?"

"Yes, sir, I think I do."

The meeting was on a Monday. A month and a half after
eing taken off his secret investigation of Dietrich, he was
alled in with a lot of other cops into a briefing on what
as being called the "Torso Murders." He was there, with
e other detectives, under orders to behave as if every-
hing was new to him.

He noticed some press on the way to the meeting, and
e couldn't help thinking of it as some sort of publicity
tunt. Stefan didn't know if he really wanted to be here, so
e took a seat way in back of the room, far away from the
lackboard, the tacked-up pictures, and the coroner.

Ness was here, as well as Emil Musil and Orly May, the
etectives in charge of the public investigation. Nuri wasn't,
ut Stefan didn't think too much about that. Their partner-
hip had ended when he was removed from the Dietrich
ssignment, and he hadn't seen much of his former part-
er since.

The room was cramped as more of the Homicide squad
led in. Eventually no seats were left and people began
ning up in back. By then the room was filled with thirty
r forty people. The air was stale and thick with cigarette
moke, and the crowd added a claustrophobic pressure to
he room.

Ness spoke first. "We all want this madman caught.
very new body is cause for growing panic. We're here to
o over what we have, to try and get a picture of the man,
omething concrete we can give to the press."

That confirmed Stefan's opinion that this was all a grand-
tand play for the reporters. As Ness kept talking, Stefan

scanned the room, reporters and policemen, sweating in the stifling heat of this enclosed room. No windows, or even a fan.

Even so, as the coroner and the county pathologist got up and began reviewing each individual murder, Stefan felt cold wash over his body. They explained the deaths by decapitation, the emasculation of three of the bodies, the locations they were found.

Every single one of the deaths had been by decapitation. Some were dismembered, some not, but that was the singular fact of all the murders.

As other detectives added details of their own investigation, Stefan remained silent. Every one of them told of leads that went nowhere, crank calls, and bogus confessions, but none of them came close to the land where Stefan had trod.

They all talked of homosexual madmen, sexual perversion, insanity, even Jack the Ripper. None came close to discussing Eric Dietrich; none, it seemed, had come near the man Ness had set him to investigate. Ness himself didn't add Dietrich's name to the mix. It was as if his whole investigation had meant nothing, had never happened.

They were all looking for a human madman. Even Ness, who had heard everything that Stefan had seen. Even when they mentioned the lack of blood in and around most of the corpses, they didn't see. Maybe they *couldn't* see.

They were looking for something darker than a sexual pervert.

One of the doctors present was talking about the hypothetical profile of their murderer, "He commits the murders in a private place. He has to be middle class or above—have his own house or a large apartment where he can dismember the bodies and clean them off."

"That," someone said, "or access to someplace private professionally. A warehouse, a storeroom . . ."

A train, Stefan thought.

He was here just as a member of the Homicide unit. But as the talk went on around him, he was back on the case again, and thinking of Dietrich's business dealings with Van Sweringen, and all those pictures of Dietrich at the Union Terminal Downtown.

8

Nuri Lapidos stood at the edge of a fetid swamp and watched the Pennsylvania authorities drag bodies from it. One of the New Castle cops was explaining to one of the Cleveland detectives that this swamp was a dumping spot for crime gangs, that there'd been half a dozen bodies found here over the years.

The latest one lay next to the shore waiting for the coroner's van. It was dark with slime, swollen by decomposition, and emitted a smell that was beyond Nuri's experience. The black midges that seemed to coat the surface of the swamp also coated the body like a second skin.

Nuri held a handkerchief over his face and tried to be unobtrusive. His, now solo, investigation of Dietrich was still secret, even if the murder investigation was becoming more high profile. This was the first time that any of the detectives tried to connect the murders in Cleveland with anything out of state.

There was one obvious connection. The corpse was missing a head.

How many more bodies have we missed because they weren't dropped somewhere obvious?

The question disturbed him. The corpse that washed up on Euclid Beach, how many others might be still in Lake Erie? How many more might be in this swamp?

The search for other bodies dragged on into the night. Nuri left the scene after it became too dark to see anything. He had seen enough, anyway. He had added the new bodies to the "torso killer's" tally. The body was far enough gone that Nuri doubted that it would be identified. Anonymous, like five others.

He waited by the one Cleveland police car and lit a cigarette, waiting for the other detectives. He took long drags on his smoke, trying to empty his lungs of the smell the corpse had left there.

Somehow it felt ominous that there were bodies this far afield. It gave the impression that the high-profile investigation only covered a small element of what was going on here.

Nuri watched the flashlights shining through the woods between him and the swamp. The beams were fragmented, seeming more to cast shadow than illuminate anything. The dark seemed to sink into Nuri, down to the bone.

"Nuri Lapidos," a voice called from the darkness.

The voice startled him. He dropped his cigarette; it tumbled off his clothing, throwing embers into the night. He turned to face the speaker, who stood on the other side of the dirt road, away from the police lights. "Who's there?" Nuri asked quietly, his hand drifting toward his holster.

The man stepped out of the darkness. He was dressed anonymously, his overalls and porkpie hat matching thousands of unemployed workmen who drifted from city to city. His face was different, pale skin, black goatee, and riveting eyes—all were more extraordinary.

"Good evening, Detective," he said.

"Who are you?" Nuri asked. "How do you know me?"

"I've seen who you are. You watch a creature calling himself Dietrich. You play your detective's games as if he were a mortal open to human forms of prosecution."

Nuri stepped back. His hand was on his gun now. "Who are you, one of Dietrich's men?"

The man laughed. "You fight an arrogance which sees you as less than a threat. Human authority can never touch him within your law." The man looked into Nuri's eyes, and he felt something deep within those eyes pressing down on him, preventing him from moving. He tried to draw his gun, but his hand refused to move. He tried to speak, but his mouth wouldn't move.

The man stepped up to him, close enough that the weight of his presence was like a pressure in Nuri's chest. "Say nothing," he said to Nuri. "An army of police, playing your police games, would not bring down the thing called Melchior. Melchior must be destroyed."

"Wh—" Nuri barely managed to choke out a word before the man reached out and grabbed his throat. It was barely a touch, but it crushed the breath from his voice.

"I said, do not speak." The man's voice lowered to a whisper. "I want only one thing from you. You will convince Detective Stefan Ryzard to meet with me."

Nuri tried to say something, but all he managed was a strangled breath.

"You will tell him to meet with Iago when he calls. Every passing day, Melchior increases his temporal power. His tendrils already reach to the farthest points of this country and beyond. Eric Dietrich must be destroyed before he becomes unassailable."

Iago lowered his hand from Nuri's throat. Nuri bent over, gasping for breath.

"You will tell your partner this, and he will meet me."

Nuri raised his head and drew his gun.

It was too late. Iago had retreated into the darkness from which he had emerged.

"He could have killed me!" Nuri yelled at Stefan. He stood in the center of Stefan's spartan living room, turning, staring through the papers that were still tacked up on the walls. Stefan stood by the entrance to the kitchen, two cups of coffee cooling in his hands.

"Calm down, Nuri." Stefan tried to sound reassuring, but even in his own ears he sounded condescending.

"Calm down?" Nuri stepped up to a wall and tore a page off of it. "What *is* this?" He tore off another sheet and waved the crumpled pages in front of him. "What the fuck is this? You're off this case."

Stefan nodded. He was. He kept telling himself that. But he had no ready explanation why these pages still collected on his walls—some of them added as recently as this morning.

"Why does he want *you*? Of anyone, why you—and why go through me to get you?" Nuri stared at him as if Stefan was the one threatening him.

Stefan walked over to the lone table and pushed a pile

of papers out of the way with the cups as he set them down. A few years of recently-acquired train schedules slid to the ground to scatter over the bare wood floor. Stefan didn't move to pick them up.

"Sit down," Stefan said.

Nuri dropped the documents he'd torn from the wall and walked up to the table. He leaned on it and stared into Stefan's eyes. "What's going on? Why you?"

"Maybe I'm the only one who believes."

"More vampire crap? With what I've seen, I almost believe it myself—at least we have some nut group that really makes an effort—"

Stefan shook his head. "No, Nuri. I am talking true evil, supernatural, blood-drinking demons walking upon the earth."

There was a long silence before Nuri said, "No, I don't buy spirits, seances, mediums, or supernatural beings. If there are such things, there's reason behind it, a disease or some sort of infection—"

Stefan's voice became grave. "Sit down."

This time Nuri did as he asked.

"Iago came here before he confronted you." Nuri looked surprised, but he stayed quiet. "He is one of these dark things. He cringed before the crucifix, and when I called on the Lord, he became a bat-winged demon and escaped."

Nuri stared at him, his expression told Stefan that his former partner thought he had cracked.

Stefan waved toward the bedroom door. "The window hasn't been fixed yet. You can see the wood covering the hole. And I still have the overalls that tore away when he changed."

The silence stretched a long time before Nuri reached for the coffee. He looked at the cup as if he wished it was something stronger. "I wish I had more trouble believing you. But I've seen bodies that soaked up bullets and kept moving." He drained the cup. After a while he said, "All we need is Boris Karloff."

"Bela Lugosi," Stefan said.

"What?"

"Lugosi. Karloff played Frankenstein's Monster."

"Oh." He kept sipping his coffee. "I suppose you've gotten holy water and all that other good Catholic stuff."

Stefan nodded.

"I want to know what a Jew is supposed to do with a vampire."

Neither of them laughed.

9

It was a couple of weeks before Iago made himself known. This time he called and specified a meeting place. Stefan agreed, and took Nuri with him. The place was on Short Vincent, in one of the smaller nightclubs vying for space in the narrow alley. The crowd was thick with Friday night partygoers. The area was noisy and garishly lit.

To Stefan the whole area seemed a manic attempt to frighten away the evil spirits of the night. Not far beyond a caveman chanting around a feeble campfire. The club they were meeting in was hidden between two other, more impressive, facades. The entrance was little more than a narrow doorway. It would have been easily missed if they hadn't known where they were going.

Stefan led Nuri inside, and immediately the character of the night changed. Outside, the bars of Short Vincent tried to push away the night. Here, inside, the club seemed to embrace the darkness. The lighting was dim enough that Stefan had to wait for his eyes to adjust before he could distinguish anything about his surroundings.

The windowless main room was several steps down into the ground. The decor was a decadent combination of brass and red velvet. Stefan noticed that the place had no windows, and no mirrors. As they stepped into the room, Stefan noticed a few faces among the patrons turn to look at them. The stares continued until a rail-thin waiter came to them and said, "Gentlemen, you are expected."

He extended an overlong arm toward the rear of the room, and began to lead them into the depths of the club. Stefan and Nuri followed through the unusually quiet crowd. Near the back stood a line of velvet curtains hiding individual private booths. Their guide led them to one and drew aside the curtain.

Iago sat on one side of the table. Stefan slid in on the other, followed by Nuri. The curtain slid shut, leaving them alone with the demon. Stefan felt in his pocket where he kept a rosary and a vial of holy water.

Iago's long hands cupped a glass in front of him. Stefan couldn't see what he was drinking, and he didn't want to. He still wore overalls, though they didn't make him seem as out of place as they should have. The aura of darkness he carried with him seemed to match this place.

"We're here," Nuri said. "Speak your piece." There was an edge of confrontation in Nuri's voice. More than Stefan would have liked. He let Nuri go on. His nerves had been frayed ever since Iago had confronted him.

Iago rotated the cup under his hand. The glass fractured the light from an electric candle that was the sole illumination in the booth. "I'm fighting a war, gentlemen."

"With Eric Dietrich," Nuri said.

"His name is Melchior, and he is older than you can imagine. He was near a myth among my own kind. Among yours he was forgotten entirely."

"Your kind . . ." Stefan whispered, letting the words hang in the air.

A small smile drifted across Iago's lips. "Ah, you still maintain that we're the incarnation of evil. Believe what you will. You will still help me. I have stepped too far beyond the bounds of my own Covenant to allow you not to."

"What Covenant?" Stefan asked.

"We shall be civil, then?" Iago's gaze drifted downward and back, almost as if he could see the holy items in Stefan's pocket. He looked from Stefan to Nuri and back again. "Believe me, I do not like using threats. I could have taken you, either of you, into the fold—you would have done all that I wished then, willingly. But that is counter to my purpose. My hope is that, hearing me out, you will see what the real evil is." He took a sip from the glass. "I am evil in your eyes solely because your mythology tells you so. Melchior's evil is much more tangible, much more threatening to both of us."

"We know he's killing people—" Nuri started to say.
Iago held up a hand, silencing him.

"You know little or nothing," Iago said. "It all begins
and ends with the Covenant, a Covenant that has crumbled
around me until I've come this far. Respect the sacrifice I
am making by enlisting your aid, respect it by hearing me
out without interruption." There was a tangible force of
will behind the statement, originating in his depthless eyes.
Stefan felt as if he couldn't interrupt even if he wanted to.

"As long as there has been man, there have been those
of the blood. Because we were ageless, lived in the night,
and mostly because we fed on man, we've been hunted to
near extinction countless times. Even as we chose humans
to bring across into our own world, even as the rare human
would rise to us on his own account, our numbers were
always small. The last time we were brought that close to
annihilation, those of the blood formed the Covenant."
Iago leaned forward. "That was close to a millennium ago.
The Covenant was a simple law, designed to preserve us
from man, and from ourselves. We do not slay those of the
blood. Any act by one in thrall to us is taken as an act of
ourselves. And we never reveal those of the blood to those
outside the blood. . . ."

Iago allowed the sentence to trail off, allowing its significance to sink in.

"My life would be forfeit for saying this much to you, if
my society still existed here. However, in this demesne the
Covenant now means as little as human law did a few years
ago." Iago frowned, and Stefan could feel the aura of hate,
anger, and perhaps fear emanating from the being sitting
across from him. He fingered the rosary.

"There was, at the time of the Covenant, an old one.
Melchior may have been thousands of years old by then.
He ruled his own kingdom, safe from the purges mankind
laid upon his own kind. He was ruthless in his rape of his
people and his land, he amassed riches, and was unashamed
in public displays of his nature. He would execute his rivals,
human and vampire alike, beheading them, dismembering
them, emasculating them."

Iago took another sip from his glass. "He slaughtered
until the only ones of the blood under his rule were those
under direct thrall to him. When the Covenant was made,

he was the first one of us to be condemned by it. He was to be burned on a pyre of his own followers.

"Somehow, he survived."

Iago paused, and Stefan felt the hold on his tongue loosen. He let the question rise to his lips. "How? Doesn't fire kill your kind?"

"As well as any of you. It wasn't Melchior on the flames." Iago lifted his hand, and while Stefan and Nuri watched, the flesh began to flow like melted wax. The fingers lengthened, nails grew into black talons, the skin became thick and leathery. Stefan squeezed his rosary as the hand before him turned demonic.

"Our will," Iago said, flexing the transformed hand, "Our soul, everything within us is bound within the blood. Our blood controls the flesh, moving it to our will. Wounds are nothing to us unless they destroy flesh and blood, dismember us, or destroy the brain or the heart." He clenched the demon hand and the transformed flesh spilled back into itself, becoming nothing more than a hand again. "Melchior avoided the flames, by allowing another to be burned in his stead, a mere thrall."

Iago looked into Stefan's eyes, and Stefan felt as if those disturbing eyes were seeing too deeply. In his head, Stefan began to recite Our Fathers until Iago's gaze shifted to Nuri.

"Those fulfilling the then-new Covenant believed that they had taken Melchior. What they saw was a corpse with Melchior's face, and Melchior's blood in its veins. They didn't realize the extent of Melchior's power, even then."

Iago held out his hand. "The power of my blood ends at my skin. I could make of you thralls bound to my blood, have my blood run through your veins, and you would be mine, but only in that your will would become mine. Melchior's thralls not only become his will, but his flesh as well, his eyes, his ears." Iago balled his fist. "My will can change my flesh. Melchior's can change any of his thralls'."

The realization began to sink into Stefan. They never had a hope with the surveillance, not when Dietrich could change himself to appear as anything. He had probably walked by both of them, under their noses, countless times.

"His power is such that he can walk abroad in full daylight without the sun driving the spirit from his flesh. He might even be able to survive the kind of dismemberment he issues his victims. Total, complete destruction of the body is the only certain way to kill him before he becomes unapproachable."

There was a long pause. Stefan could feel that Iago was leaving it to be filled with questions. It was Nuri who asked, talking for the first time since Iago entered his monologue.

"You said we didn't know what is going on. What is going on?"

"Melchior wishes to reclaim his temporal kingdom. He believes that our race should rule, and that he should rule our race. He has begun with subtlety, binding humans to him, sometimes with money, sometimes with blood. He already has a secret hand in all the affairs of this city, and his influence extends across this continent."

Stefan shook his head. "Why are you talking to us? You have this Covenant, there should be others of your kind to help you—"

"You don't understand," Iago said. "The bodies you've been finding, headless, dismembered, they are the leaders of our race. Melchior has been systematically exterminating those of any power and influence that could be in his way. Those not yet executed are paralyzed by fear. We know, you see. He leaves the bodies to inspire terror, while our own Covenant prevents any from revealing what is going on."

"Except you," Nuri said.

"It is my survival," Iago said. "Carried to its limits, Melchior's plan will be the extermination of every one of us who is not of his own blood." He looked at Stefan, and again he felt the sensation of Iago seeing too much of him. "You I chose because I need untainted humans to aid me. Melchior would sense one of the blood if any approached. He would know me, because his thralls have tasted my blood. Humans would be a cipher to him. No human organization—not the police, not the crime mobs, not the FBI—can close on him, because he has ears in every corner of those groups. But individually you can act without his knowledge. He is not omniscient."

"Beyond your threats," Nuri said, "why should we help you?"

Iago looked at Nuri. His expression was grave. "Didn't

you hear what I said? Melchior plans the extermination of everyone who is not of his own blood. Humans who enslave themselves to him will have the privilege of being the cattle for his empire. Those who don't . . ."

Iago didn't finish the statement, but Stefan could feel the implications in his gut. For all he believed this thing across from him to be evil, there wasn't any way he could walk away from this now.

10

Detective Simon Aristaeus stood in an unobtrusive corner of the Union Terminal Building, leaning against a bank of phone booths. He held a copy of the *Cleveland Press* in his hands, but his eyes weren't focused on the paper. With his head lowered, and the brim of his hat shading his eyes, he watched the crowds coming and going through to the train station. He was watching for one man in particular.

He wondered what Van Sweringen would make of the police surveillance of him in his own building. Detective Aristaeus didn't quite know what to make of it himself. He was reporting to Ness, not his supervisor, or even the Chief. That, with the vagueness of his orders, and the cover of secrecy, gave this the feeling of a fishing expedition. He knew he wasn't the first cop to be given this duty, and the way things were going, he wouldn't be the last.

He listened to footsteps echo off marble and wondered if he was ever going to see Van Sweringen. He was supposed to be making a business trip to New York, but there were a lot of ways down to the tracks, and one of the other cops down here could have already seen him and called it in. He wondered if anyone would have the courtesy to tell him if Van Sweringen had already left in his private passenger car, or if they'd just leave him here, forgotten, waiting.

It was late evening when he finally saw his quarry. Van Sweringen walked through the station with near anonymity. As he watched, Detective Aristaeus doubted any of the crowd realized that the man walking in their midst was the titular head of one of the largest railroad empires in the country, and the man responsible for the construction of the building they walked through.

Detective Aristaeus didn't move his head, but his gaze followed Van Sweringen, picking out the people accompanying him. He noted Wenneman, Van Sweringen's secretary. He also noted two others following the pair—

Detective Aristaeus was taken by surprise when he recognized one of the two men following Van Sweringen. He knew Detective Ryzard; he was part of the homicide unit. What was he doing here?

He didn't spend much time worrying about it. Once Van Sweringen passed him on the way to the trains, he casually folded his newspaper and slid into one of the phone booths. He called into the station and made a perfunctory report to one of Ness' secretaries. Ness himself probably wasn't even working on a Sunday.

Detective Aristaeus hung up the phone, hesitated a moment, then made another call. He made a report similar to the one he had just given, but this time he added the detail of Detective Ryzard's presence. After he had spoken, he listened for several minutes. Then he nodded and said, "I shall do as you will me to."

Detective Aristaeus hung up the phone, left the paper, and walked into the terminal, following Ryzard and Van Sweringen.

Stefan and Nuri boarded the train about three cars up from the private car carrying Oris Paxton Van Sweringen. Stefan was still wondering how they were going to confront Van Sweringen. The last time they hadn't gotten very far, and now they had to press it. Stefan needed to know which trains were running under Dietrich's—Melchior's—control.

They sat in the car, waiting for the train to begin moving. Next to him, Nuri muttered, "I don't believe we're going through with this." He was looking out at the platform.

"You've seen what Melchior is doing."

Nuri shook his head. "I've seen odd things, but nothing that convinces me Iago is telling us the truth."

Stefan frowned. That was one of his own fears. How could he trust a monster from the same race as the being they were charged to destroy? Evil was evil, and by merely listening to Iago, he felt that they were being ensnared in the darkness.

"We're just gathering information right now. We'll do nothing until we're sure of where we stand."

The words sounded empty even to Stefan. By boarding the train they had stepped outside their roles as policemen. Ness had warned them off of Van Sweringen, and being here would be grounds for a suspension or a transfer. If, as Stefan suspected, there was any strongarming to get what they needed to know, they could be very easily dismissed from the force.

What they were doing was very close to the edge, and their motives were completely beyond the pale. They were gathering information to help them target Melchior. They were engaged in conspiracy to murder.

"Just planning," Nuri whispered.

The underground platform of the Union Terminal slid by them and the train pulled itself along the tracks. Soon the motion fell into a rhythm as they slid out the east side of downtown. Behind them, the lights of the Terminal Tower cut a hole in the night the shape of a thin gravestone.

"Just planning," Stefan said. That's all they were doing. Planning the death of a man named Eric Dietrich, who was supposedly a thing named Melchior.

On one level, they were just marking time until they found a way to deal with Iago and his threats. On another, they were really going through with it.

Stefan had decided early that the worst place to attack Melchior would be his residence. He had seen an attempted hit by a score of assassins. He was too well defended there. No, the best place, in Stefan's mind, to attack Melchior would be in transit. Stefan knew that Melchior controlled trains somewhere, even if there was no official records of the fact. Stefan was almost certain that there was some private agreement with Van Sweringen, and that parts of their rail line were under Melchior's control.

If they discovered the lines that Melchior used, they'd have a better chance of isolating his movement. If Iago was right, he wouldn't be aware of surveillance originating outside of the police department. With only the two of them, there would be no spies to warn him.

Once they knew the cars Melchior used, it would just be matter of planting some explosives.

Stefan shuddered at the thought. He still wasn't used to ne idea, even if he'd been partly aware of the implications ver since he'd known what Dietrich-Melchior was. He had nown that the presence of a vampire required it to be lain.

He just wished there was another way. Iago maintained here wasn't. Melchior was so powerful that only complete nd instant destruction of the body would kill him.

"When do we go?" Nuri asked.

"After everyone's asleep. You might as well catch a ap yourself."

Nuri nodded, but didn't close his eyes. Instead he stared ut the window at the darkened world.

Detective Aristaeus sat in first class, the only conscious erson in the private cabin. Across from him, three people vere crumpled in a heap on the seat. He paid no attention o them; once they had fallen unconscious they no longer nattered to his plans.

The shades were drawn on all the windows, and he sat lluminated only by a single weak electric lamp. The light nade the world slightly jaundiced.

His revolver lay on the seat next to him. In his hands he ield two bottles of liquid so red and thick that it was almost olack. His hand shook as he set down one, opened the other, and drank.

They were into Pennsylvania before Stefan decided to nove. It was nearly three-thirty in the morning, and the rain had gone silent except for the rattle of its passage across the tracks. Most of their fellow passengers were isleep.

Stefan grabbed Nuri's arm and they made their way back hrough the car. Neither of them spoke. They passed :hrough three cars before they reached the end of the pas-senger cars. They stood on the platform before Van Swern-gen's private car.

The entrance was locked, but the lock was a simple one to jimmy, even with the motion of the train and the wind whistling between the cars. Nuri muttered something about feeling like a hit man. Stefan didn't comment. In a way that was exactly what they were.

They slipped into the car, which resembled one of the first class passenger cars, only with two cabins and richer decoration that Stefan could barely see in the darkness. All he could really notice was the brocade of the carpet.

The two of them slid along the darkened aisle to the rear, where Van Sweringen's room was. Again the door was locked and Stefan found himself forcing it. Behind him Nuri had taken out his revolver and was watching back the way they had come.

In a few minutes he popped the door open.

The two of them slipped into the darkened chamber. The half of the cabin they entered had chairs and a table, and a window watching the darkened Pennsylvania wilderness pass by under an overcast sky. Half of the cabin was shut out by a heavy curtain that rippled gray and black in the darkness.

The curtain was moving.

Stefan and Nuri exchanged glances and looked again at the curtain. Stefan felt a wrongness here, almost as if he was in the presence of Iago, or another minion of darkness. With one hand he pulled out a rosary, and with the other he withdrew his revolver.

He motioned Nuri to one side of the curtain, and he stationed himself on the other. Once they were set on both sides, Stefan motioned for Nuri to pull back the curtain.

The curtain drew aside, revealing Oris Paxton Van Sweringen lying on his bed, and another man leaning over him. When the curtain drew aside, the man dropped something from his hand, something he'd been holding to Van Sweringen's mouth.

He turned, holding a revolver, but Stefan saw the man's face, and recognition made him hesitate. The man was Simon Aristaeus, a fellow detective in the Cleveland Police Department. The shock of seeing him gave Aristaeus enough time to turn fully around. Nuri had his gun leveled at Aristaeus and was shouting, "Drop it!"

For a moment the tableau held, the three of them unmoving, guns pointed at each other. The silence was filled with the rhythmic clatter of the rails. From the slowing of the car, and the shadows outside, they were entering a rail

ard. It lasted until Van Sweringen stirred, groaned, and
at up. Stefan had just enough time to see that his mouth
vas dark with blood before hell broke loose.

Aristaeus used the distraction to move, and there were
wo gunshots in rapid succession, neither from Stefan's gun.
Aristaeus kept moving to the side of the car, while Nuri
olded over and fell against the wall. Van Sweringen yelled
omething incomprehensible as Stefan turned to cover
Aristaeus.

This time he didn't hesitate firing. He couldn't tell if he'd
it him or not. Whatever happened, Aristaeus fell upon the
emergency brake cord and everything shuddered against
he sudden lack of motion. Stefan fell over and Van Swer-
ngen tumbled out of his bed.

Aristaeus remained upright and scrambled out the front
door in all the confusion.

Almost immediately, there was another jerk as something
outside collided with the car. Then there was silence.

"What the blazes is going on here?" Van Sweringen said
as he pushed himself off of the floor. Stefan ignored him
and went to Nuri. Nuri was clutching his right shoulder; he
ooked up at Stefan and groaned a bit.

"We need to get you to a hospital—"

"No," Nuri said through gritted teeth, "This will keep.
Get after that bastard."

Stefan hesitated a moment, then nodded and ran out the
door. The door between cars was already swinging shut
behind Aristaeus. In the distance, came the sounds of people roused by the sudden stop. Stefan ducked through the
door, and had to duck back as a gunshot whistled past him.

Aristaeus was outside, and Stefan's few quick glances saw
him running away across the tracks. When he was sure
Aristaeus wasn't taking aim at the cars, Stefan dove out
after him. He stumbled. The area between the cars was
broken and uneven. Van Sweringen's car had been pushed
up in a collision with its neighbor, buckling the space between cars.

Stefan fell out to the side, and pushed himself up as a
bullet kicked up a divot of gravel near his hands. This time
he had a chance to steady himself and return fire.

Aristaeus was about fifty yards off, and showed no sign
of being hit. Stefan fired again, and Aristaeus dove behind

a stationary boxcar. Stefan began running across the gravel chasing him. He ran, following the tracks through the sparsely lit railyard.

Aristaeus was ducking behind lone boxcars parked on a siding at one edge of the yard. Stefan just reached the first in the series of cars when another shot splintered the wood about a foot from his shoulder.

He could hear Aristaeus moving out there, and Stefan suspected that if he moved from the cover of the boxcar the next shot would find its mark.

He holstered his gun and swung himself up on the rusty iron rungs set in the side of the car. He pulled himself up toward the roof of the boxcar. Once on top, it gave him a view of the other boxcars on this side of the railyard.

He knew that Aristaeus was behind one of the cars, so he waited for him to make a move. Aristaeus did—he ducked around a car about twenty yards away, at the edge of the tracks, and put another shot into the side of the boxcar Stefan was on top of. Then he began running into the long grass lining the rails.

Stefan yelled at him, "Stop, drop the gun!"

Aristaeus responded by beginning to turn back toward him. Stefan didn't wait, he fired two shots. Aristaeus buckled, the gun going off wildly. He dropped and disappeared into the grass.

Stefan stood there, on top of the boxcar, watching for more threatening movement. There wasn't any. It was as if Aristaeus had fallen through a hole in the earth. Stefan couldn't see where he had fallen, the dark grass had swallowed him up.

Behind him came the sounds of machinery, trains, and the babble of people. Stefan could also hear the voices and footsteps of three or four people—probably rail police—running toward him.

Around him and the boxcars, everything was suddenly silent. The only movement in his field of vision was the twisting fog from his breath, and the distant motes of campfires just outside the boundaries of the yard.

Stefan holstered his weapon and let himself down. He headed toward the edge of the tracks, where Aristaeus had run off into the grass. He had just reached the edge, spotting the barely visible signs where Aristaeus had torn up

he grass in his scramble to escape, when behind him came
a voice, "Hold it right there!" Stefan's shadow sprang up
in front of him transfixed in the center of a flashlight beam.

He turned around, squinting in the light, to face three
railroad policemen. "I'm the police," he called out to them,
reaching slowly for his badge. "Detective Ryzard." He held
out the badge so it glinted in the flashlight beam. He ne-
glected to name the city, because, wherever in Pennsylvania
they were, they were far out of his jurisdiction.

"The man out there just shot my partner," he added.

One of the railroad bulls edged up to see Stefan's badge,
then he waved at the one with the flashlight. The beam left
Stefan and began sweeping over the grass.

"Sorry, Detective," said the one next to him. "We have
this accident on the Nickel Plate Line, and then all the
gunshots . . ."

Stefan nodded. He wondered if the man knew how defer-
ential he was sounding now. Stefan supposed when your
job was predominantly rousting hobos off the tracks, you
might get over-respectful for a "real" policeman.

Stefan ended up leading the three railroad cops into the
grass, following Aristaeus' broken trail. At this point Stefan
was glad for the backup, even though it seemed that Aristaeus had dropped like a rock. With what he was involved
in, Stefan wasn't going to take anything at face value.

They made their way deeper into the grass, closing on
where Aristaeus had dropped. Stefan noticed that they had
gained a quiet audience off in the distance. The hobos and
tramps had abandoned their fires for the moment and had
closed in to watch the commotion. They were far away, too
far to make out individuals, and apparently too far for the
railroad cops to care, but they gave the whole scene the
feeling of a performance, as if Stefan was an actor in some
medieval morality play.

The four of them reached the place where Aristaeus had
dropped. The place was marked by flattened grass and
splatters of blood. To one side lay Aristaeus' revolver.

There was no body.

"What the hell?" said the railroad cop who'd checked
Stefan's badge.

"Ain't no way he could've run off without us seeing
something," said the one with the flashlight. Even so, he

panned his light across the edges of the grass, looking for signs of where Aristaeus might have retreated. The grass waved back, undisturbed.

Aristaeus was gone.

Nuri lay slumped against the wall, his hand clutching the hole just below the shoulder. He tried to keep pressure on the wound, but blood kept leaking through his fingers. His other arm lay useless at his side, warm and slick with blood. The wound, and the entire upper quarter of his chest throbbed with every beat of his pulse, as if a giant hand was squeezing the life out of him with every heartbeat.

"Good lord, what's happening here?" Oris Paxton Van Sweringen bent over him. The man was gathering up a bedsheet and bent over Nuri to press it to his wound.

Before Nuri had a chance to speak, the door burst open a man stepped into the car. Nuri recognized Van Sweringen's secretary. He looked as if he'd just fallen out of bed.

"Are you all right, sir—" The man stopped when his gaze landed on Nuri. The carpet had already soaked up a pool of blood that nearly reached his feet.

"I'm fine," Van Sweringen said, wiping blood off of his mouth with the back of his hand. "This man needs to get to a hospital. Get an ambulance, and for heaven's sake keep it out of the papers."

"Yes, sir." The man turned on his heels and left.

Van Sweringen shook his head as he tried to keep pressure on the wound. "Why are you here?" he whispered, half to himself.

"Dietrich," Nuri said. His voice was weak and tasted of blood.

Van Sweringen showed no sign of surprise. In fact, he nodded. "He's finished with me, isn't he? Just like he was finished with Mantis." His face took on a longing expression, and he shook his head a few times as if to clear it. "He was an assassin, wasn't he? The man who shot you."

"Need to know—" Nuri started to say, but he began coughing up blood.

"I know who you are. You walked into my office a few months ago. I chased you away." He shifted the sheet over the wound and Nuri groaned. "It was fear. It kept me from doing more than I did. Even when I lost Mantis, all I could do was call in secret. . . ."

"What—" Nuri tried to form a question, but the pain and the blood wouldn't let him. He felt as if he had started tumbling through empty space, and Van Sweringen's face seemed impossibly far away.

"I think you were too late," Van Sweringen said. "I can taste my own death coming. Nothing left to be afraid of." With his free hand he reached around his neck and removed a chain. Hanging from it was a large, plain cross. Van Sweringen dropped it over Nuri's head.

In his mind, Nuri tried to explain he was Jewish, but by then his brain seemed to have lost any connection with the rest of his body. He wondered if Van Sweringen was wrong about whose death he was probably tasting.

Van Sweringen leaned forward, as if to kiss his cheek, and Nuri distinctly heard the words, "Cleveland Trust."

Then, as the world began fading away into a dull gray void, Van Sweringen's secretary ran in saying help was coming. Van Sweringen nodded, and said, "Arrange for a new car to New York."

"Yes, sir," the man said, and vanished.

Van Sweringen said other things, but Nuri was past hearing them.

11

Wednesday, December 2—Friday, December 4

Nuri spent days in a drugged stupor, long enough for a dusting of snow to collect on the ledge of the window next to his bed. His arm was in a cast up past his collarbone, held upright by weights. Tubes entered and left his body, and the upper right quarter of his chest was home to an intolerable itching.

Becoming conscious of his surroundings seemed an interminable process. It seemed an eternity before he could even focus on Stefan's presence.

"What . . ." Nuri whispered when he finally managed to find the power to speak. It was as if he were trying to finish the question he had been asking Van Sweringen.

Stefan leaned over and touched his good shoulder. "Rest."

Nuri turned and tried to focus on Stefan's face. His memory was a feverish jumble of images. He knew he'd been here for a long time, and he knew that Stefan had been here at times, but the images and the memories never settled down into a coherent whole. It was frustrating, like trying to remember a dream as it slipped away.

"Rest," Stefan repeated. "You've been fighting an infection."

Nuri closed his eyes and rested.

Later on he woke up and asked, "How long have I been here?"

Stefan was still there, or he was there again. "Ten days."

Nuri looked sideways at Stefan, "What happened?"

"How are you doing?" he asked. Stefan looked ragged,

as if he hadn't showered or shaved in days. "The doctors say you'll be able to go home in a few days."

"What happened to Aristaeus? Van Sweringen?"

"Aristaeus got away." Stefan pulled his chair closer to the bed. "Van Sweringen's dead."

Something sick filled Nuri's chest as he heard that. "Dead?" he whispered. He kept thinking of the man saying he tasted death. . . .

"Heart attack on the way to New York," Stefan said. He ran both hands through his hair and said, "We were too late."

"You don't think it was a heart attack?"

"I'm sure it was. Didn't you see what Aristaeus was doing?" Stefan pulled a small bag out of his jacket pocket. It was wax paper, and Nuri could see brown stains inside of it. "He dropped this in Van Sweringen's car."

"What is it?"

"A vial of blood. Half empty. He was pouring it into Van Sweringen's mouth when we showed up." Stefan looked at it. "You listened to Iago, didn't you? Melchior's blood."

Nuri looked at the bag in Stefan's hand, and looked at Stefan. "You think Van Sweringen was killed. With that?"

Stefan nodded.

Nuri didn't know what to say. What Stefan was saying smacked of voodoo, of magic. Nuri had seen things were close to the supernatural, but he still clung to the belief that there had to be a rational explanation for what was going on.

"Did he say anything to you?" Stefan asked, putting the envelope and its vial back into his pocket.

"He said he tasted his own death." He reached up to his neck and felt under his hospital gown. The cross was still there. Clumsily, he lifted the chain up over his head and gave it to Stefan one-handed.

Stefan took it.

"He gave it to me. You can have it."

Stefan held the cross up to the light. "Did he say anything about it?" He seemed to be studying it, turning it on edge.

Nuri searched his memory and remembered the words. "Cleveland Trust," he said.

"Ah-hah," Stefan said as he pulled the oversized cross apart. The cross split apart into two separate crosses hinged at the base. Sandwiched between them, glinting in the light, was a key.

12

Downtown Cleveland was covered by a fresh dusting of snow. Christmas lights decorated the outsides of the department stores, and windows were draped with ribbons of red and green. As Stefan walked down Euclid, he heard carolers in the distance singing "Silent Night."

The season didn't move him. He walked with his head lowered, seeing mostly the gray slush that covered the sidewalk. He held his trenchcoat close to him, holding his hat against the cold. In one hand he clutched the key that Van Sweringen had passed on.

Stefan wished Nuri was with him. He felt isolated, alone. He walked past the holiday decorations and felt as if he was the only one who saw the darkness under the surface.

He stopped at East Ninth, and looked across at the Cleveland Trust Building. It squatted at the opposite corner of the street, a neoclassical building with a domed roof. Even this staid building had a few wreaths in deference to the season.

To Stefan, the way the late afternoon shadows had darkened every portal of the building, it resembled a massive tomb, the wreaths from some recent funeral.

Stefan crossed the street and entered the edifice. Once inside, the small decorations, a ribbon here, a bough there, did little to dismiss the somber character of the bank. Stefan swallowed and walked toward the manager's desk.

It took some convincing, and the flash of his badge—which meant little since he and Nuri had been suspended—but the manager eventually allowed him down to the deposit vault to use the key.

Stefan carried the box to a cubicle, wondering what Van

Sweringen saw fit to hide here. The account wasn't even in
Van Sweringen's name, which meant that the lawyers handling the Van Sweringen estate, and the lawyers handling
its creditors, didn't know this box existed.

Alone, in a stall, Stefan lifted the lid of the safety deposit box.

It finally felt a little like Christmas. On top was a copy
of an agreement between the Van Sweringens and Eric
Dietrich. It dated from September '35, but seemed to carry
hints of an agreement several years back.

Stefan rifled through the other papers. There was docu-
mentation of European investment in the Van Sweringens'
pyramid of corporations. Stefan wasn't an accountant, but
the papers listed numbers that, to Stefan, seemed to have
kept the whole Van Sweringen pyramid afloat much longer
than it should have.

Stefan suspected that without Dietrich's money—the con-
text made it clear who the money came from even if the
benefactor was never named—the whole system of inter-
laced companies would have tumbled apart as early as '31.

By September 30, '35, Eric Dietrich had become a full-
fledged silent partner. It went far beyond what Stefan had
expected. From the papers that he held, it seemed possible
that Dietrich was in control of the largest rail empire in
the country.

Stefan had thought that, at the most, Dietrich had control
of a few lines through his relationship to Van Sweringen.
Stefan felt cold as he realized that the thing calling itself
Dietrich had access, control of, lines from the Missouri Pa-
cific to the Chesapeake & Ohio.

He had planned to find Dietrich's private car and use
that as a point of attack. That target now seemed much
more remote.

13

"**Y**ou're delaying," Iago said.

Stefan didn't look at him; he knew what he would see in those eyes. Instead, he looked out over the frozen lake, toward the breakwater. The night was cold and quiet, Lake Erie black as onyx, refusing to reflect the feeble stars. "I don't want any innocent bystanders caught in this."

"Do you know what we're dealing with?" Iago said. "We cannot afford to be gentle."

"What is the point in fighting an evil if we ourselves become evil in the process?"

Stefan could hear Iago pacing behind him. "You are quite clear in your belief that I am myself an evil worthy of damnation."

"I'll move when I am certain that I can destroy Melchior without harming anyone else."

"The point is destroying him before he becomes unapproachable, if he isn't already—"

Stefan shook his head. "We're dealing with explosives here. I won't set off a bomb in the middle of the city."

Iago made a disgusted noise. "A train, then," Iago said. "Which one?"

"I need you to find that out for me."

There was a silence. "Do you know what you're asking?"

"I don't want to know," Stefan said, staring out at the black horizon. "What I need to know is a train he'll be on, and when. One of the trains he's using for his own purposes."

"This is all you need?"

Stefan nodded, turning away from the darkness to face the lights of the city. "Yes," he said.

Iago was facing away from him, toward the city himself. "I'll give you this. Stay by the phone the next three nights, be ready to act when I call."

Two nights later Iago wore the mask of Tragedy again. He carried the chained body of a person who in life was a prostitute named Rose Wallace. He had wanted one of Melchior's human thralls, the ones who had yet to turn and had less of a bond to their master, but time was too short to be picky.

He carried her into the darkness of another slaughter-house, awash with the smell of chickens and blood. It was a different place than where he'd talked to Carlo Pasquale, but it hardly mattered. The place was the same concrete darkness filled with animal shrieks and the smell of blood.

He dropped Rose Wallace on the ground and pulled out a hypodermic needle. In the darkness, the steel needle, twisted handle, its glass shaft, all seemed to be some obscure torture device.

Iago slid the needle into the flesh of his wrist, the gap between glove and sleeve where a small strip of skin was visible. The needle sank in to the base, and Iago withdrew the plunger, allowing the glass tube to fill with his own black-rose-colored blood.

Iago withdrew the needle and knelt next to Rose Wallace. He slid the needle into a vein in her neck. Her body jerked as he injected the blood into her system. He watched the blood push from the tube, knowing that it was now a matter of his survival or Rose's. Once his blood was taken into her body, he couldn't allow her to leave. Melchior could not be allowed to taste Iago's blood on one of his thralls.

Knowing that he would have to destroy Rose, whatever she managed to reveal to him, made him feel that Stefan Ryzard was right. His kind *was* evil.

He could feel the pull toward Rose as his blood sank into her system. He didn't hope to displace Melchior's influence as completely as he did with Carlo, but he hoped that he connected deeply enough to have Rose answer his few questions.

He knelt over her and watched as Rose Wallace's eyes

opened. In them Iago saw a maelstrom of terror and betrayal. Iago began asking his questions.

The phone tore Stefan from sleep. He ran and grabbed the receiver.

"There's a special run of the Nickel Plate, February fifteenth. It leaves the Union Terminal at three in the morning. He will be on it, the last car."

"Iago?" Stefan asked. Something sounded odd about Iago's voice. It had always sounded diabolically confident, superior. Something had drained out of it.

"I must go. You won't hear from me until it's done."

Stefan opened his mouth to ask a question, but the line was already dead. His hand shook as he laid the receiver back in the cradle.

This was it. He had the information he wanted. Now he just had to go through with it.

That Sunday, Stefan saw Father Gerwazek before Mass.

He had been going more regularly since all this had started happening, trying to rebuild some relationship with God. He was unsure if it was working. He still felt as if the divine was impossible to reach from where he was. Yet, he went to the confessional, like he had when he was a child, like he had before his own wife and child had died.

He knelt in the booth, and for a time it was completely dark. He could feel a surge of claustrophobia. Then the door on the other side of the screen slid aside, letting in light and dappled shadow.

Before anything else was said, he asked, "Do you believe in the supernatural, Father?" The question came out of him in a rush. He had never talked to Gerwazek about the things he'd been experiencing, about Dietrich, about Iago's kind. His confessions had been about more mundane matters.

There was a pause, as if Gerwazek was gathering his thoughts after the break in form. "I believe in the supernatural," he said. "I believe in God. I believe that the host becomes the flesh of Christ. I believe in the possibility of divine intervention in worldly affairs."

"And Satan? Tangible physical evil?"

"That, too, is part of my faith." Gerwazek paused. "What troubles you?"

"I believe that I am fighting a supernatural evil."

There was a longer pause, then, slowly, Gerwazek told him, "You must pray, my son. There is only one good in the realm of the supernatural, and that is what comes from God. If what you fight is not worldly, then your only aid can come from Him."

Stefan opened his mouth to say more, but something inside him felt as if he had said enough. It was time to purge himself of his burdens. Slowly, Stefan began to tell Gerwazek of his sins.

Afterward, he took Mass.

14

Stefan waited in the darkness and prayed. He stood in a concrete alcove deep under the Union Terminal Tower. Beyond the track in front of him the darkness was subdivided into a forest of girders. There were a few lights, red and green and sodium yellow. None seemed to reach very far. The smell was damp and musty, heavy with soil and grease.

Stefan cupped a flashlight with his hand and shone it so it only illuminated the watch on his wrist. His train had ten minutes to arrive. His breath was short and burned the back of his throat with the taste of copper.

At his feet was a satchel, pushed far back against the concrete wall. It was heavy, and carried enough dynamite to reduce a railroad car to kindling. It also contained the blasting caps, wire, several rolls of cloth tape, a pair of wire cutters, and a small hand-held plunger.

Stefan had wanted a timer, but he was lucky he could get his hands on what he did. What it meant was that he was going to be on the train when Melchior's car detonated. He would just have to hope he was far enough away.

It was noisy down here, even at this time of the morning, with the trains coming and going through the underground passageways. So Stefan felt the oncoming train before he realized he heard it. It was early.

He pressed himself back into the protection of the alcove and extinguished his flashlight. The train screeched by him, a moving wall close enough to touch. It was already slowing to a stop. The air resonated with the screeching of its brakes.

The train was short, only a few passenger cars long, and

it passed from in front of him as quickly as it had appeared.
As soon as the last car slid by Stefan grabbed the satchel
and stepped out on the tracks. The train was receding down
the tunnel, slowly coming to a stop. Stefan ran after the
train.

He caught up with the rear car just before the train came
to a complete stop. He grabbed a rung on the rear of the
car, pulling himself up as he flung the satchel over his
shoulder. When the train had stopped completely, Stefan
was laying flat on the roof of the rear car.

Stefan buried his face into the roof, praying that his dark
clothes helped him blend into the gloom in the top of the
tunnel. The concrete ceiling of the tunnel lay flat above
him, pressing down. Below him, he heard motion on the
platform. People moved down there, oddly silent.

Carefully, Stefan turned his face to look down on the
lighted platform. It was almost a shock to actually see him,
Melchior, Eric Dietrich, standing on the platform. Melchior
stood oddly still as others moved bags around him. He
stood, hands wrapped around a long cane, long pale face
framed by a mane of too-long blond hair, his shoulders
covered by an ankle-length fur-lined coat that seemed more
appropriate for a prior century.

He radiated power. Just standing there, Stefan could feel
that he was the axis on which everything in his field of
vision was turning. He could feel that, even though Melchior didn't move, didn't speak, didn't even turn his gaze
away from the middle distance where he was staring. He
didn't do a thing, but still, when Stefan saw him, he had
an urge to turn and run, to abandon what he was doing, to
leave the whole city and whatever else to Melchior.

He closed his eyes and prayed for himself, and for his
actions. He hoped to God what he was doing was right. If
the creature down there was merely a man, what he was
going to do was no more than murder . . .

He told himself that Melchior, at best, was a murderer.
And what Stefan had seen made him much darker.

As he prayed, he felt a burning awareness cross over the
side of his body. He carefully looked back to the platform,
and for a horrified moment he thought Melchior was looking directly at him.

The moment passed as Melchior's head kept moving. He adn't seen Stefan. Still, it was a few long moments before e was comfortable breathing.

He lay there for what seemed like hours before the train vas loaded and began moving. It slowly pulled out, through he tunnels under the terminal. The car slid through the choing darkness, slowly at first. Concrete passed over his ead, much too close. Stefan hugged the roof of the car ven closer.

Even though it couldn't be more than a few minutes, it eemed an eternity before the train left its underground varren, before the concrete ceiling opened up into a cold vinter sky. All Stefan could think of was getting this lone as quickly as possible, before someone discovered im.

Stefan pushed himself to his knees, icy wind searing his ace. He had to turn his face to blink away the tears the vind burned into his eyes. He tied his satchel to the roof f the car and reached inside, taking out sticks of dynamite nd the cloth tape.

Stefan crawled to the four corners of the car, anchoring he explosives, setting blasting caps, and wiring the deadly lements together.

As the darkened cliffs of Kingsbury Run slid by him, tefan made a dangerous climb down the side of the moving car. He planted dynamite at the base of the car as he eld on to the side one-handed. He scrambled up just as he train began reaching the lights of the East Fifty-Fifth ailyard.

He'd been making good time. He had a lot of the car vired in just a few minutes. But as he pulled himself up nto the roof of the car, he had a sick realization.

The train was slowing down.

This wasn't in his plan. The train was supposed to leave he city limits. It was supposed to be on some tracks hrough some abandoned countryside when he pulled the witch—

But the train was going into the yard, not past it. He was osing his chance. Not only was the light enough that someone would see him up here, but there was no telling what vould happen to Melchior when the train stopped. He ould leave the car, change trains. . . .

He wasn't fully set up, but it was now or never.

Stefan maniacally connected the last two wires to a spool, grabbed the hand-held plunger out of the satchel, and began moving, trailing wire, toward the front of the train. He stood upright and ran, the wind dying as the train slowed. He jumped the gap between cars twice before he lowered himself on a ladder between a pair of cars.

It might be too close, but he was out of time. They were in the yard, and the train was maneuvering itself into a siding. Stefan stood between cars and fumbled with the end of the spool, attaching wires to the plunger.

He only had one wire attached when the door between the cars opened.

In front of Stefan, caught in the cadaver glow of one of the yard's arc lights, was the face of Detective Simon Aristaeus. He saw Stefan and grinned. Stefan dropped the plunger, letting it dangle from one attached wire, and went for his gun.

His hand never reached it.

Aristaeus' arm shot out, faster than Stefan could fully react. He grabbed for Stefan's neck, and Stefan tried to dodge. It wasn't enough. Aristaeus grabbed hold of his shoulder with enough force that Stefan could feel his collarbone snap.

Aristaeus pulled him back through the half-open door. Stefan felt wood slam into his side, and he heard glass shattering. Then he was in the air, flying through the aisle between banks of empty seats. He landed on his wounded shoulder, and he felt the end of his collarbone tear through the skin. He shuddered with pain as the warmth of his blood spread across his chest.

"Detective Ryzard," Aristaeus said, walking slowly up the aisle. He shook his head, tsking.

He stopped to stand over him. "Aren't you a pain in the ass?" He laughed. "You think you can fight this? You think you can do anything to stop what is going on?"

He knelt and grabbed Stefan by the hair, pulling his head up to face him. Stefan groaned as the fractured bone in his shoulder withdrew.

"You killed me," Aristaeus said. "You know that? Stone dead, through the heart." He grinned, and the grin was

redatory. Aristaeus' nostrils flared, and Stefan realized
that the strongest smell in here was his own blood.

"Killed me, but there was enough of the Master in me
that it didn't even slow me down. You didn't save the old
man, and now I'm stronger than ever. You're a sap if you
think you can fight something like this."

Aristaeus' face was twisting. Stefan could hear the skin
protest as his jaw distended and the skull began twisting
into a muzzlelike form.

Stefan pulled the rosary out of his pocket and called on
the name of the Lord.

God must have been with him, because Aristaeus backed
up as if he had been struck. Even in the distorted face,
Stefan could see signs of shock and surprise.

"Yea, though I walk through the valley of the shadow
of death," Stefan said, holding the small crucifix out before
Aristaeus. Aristaeus let go and Stefan fell to the ground,
unable to break his fall with his bad arm. With the good
arm he held up the rosary as he pushed himself past Aristaeus, toward the door, using only his legs.

"I will fear no evil: for thou *art* with me;"

He made it to the door, and he strained, his back to
the door-frame, to push himself upright using only his legs.
Aristaeus watched him, and Stefan kept the rosary between them.

"Thy rod and thy staff they comfort me— ugh"

He made it upright. He was standing next to the ladder,
the plunger still dangled from its single wire. All it needed
was for him to finish the connection.

He couldn't lower the crucifix.

"Thou preparest a table before me in the presence of
mine enemies;"

As he spoke the words, he raised his right arm, feeling
the broken bones dig inside his shoulder. His eyes watered
with every movement, and his face had broken into a sweat
in the winter air.

"Thou anointest my head with oil;"

His hand found the other wire, and with trembling fingers
he managed to hook it over the unused terminal in the
plunger.

"My cup runneth over."

He spun the wing-nut tight. But there was no way to activate the dangling switch one handed. He had to drop the crucifix. He looked at Aristaeus, who had become a slavering fiend, with a razor-toothed muzzle and claws dangling to his knees.

It was his only chance.

"Surely goodness and mercy shall follow me all the days of my life: and I will dwell in the house of the Lord forever."

Stefan dropped the rosary and grabbed the plunger. Aristaeus began moving instantly, but this time Stefan managed to move faster. He clutched the plunger to his chest, shuddering with the pain of his wounded arm, and twisted the switch home.

Nothing happened.

Somehow, before Aristaeus descended on him, he managed to try it again. Nothing.

Stefan looked up, and Aristaeus was just standing there in front of him. In the distance, down the car, Stefan heard someone clapping. Aristaeus stepped aside, and there, at the other end of the car, stood Melchior.

Standing next to him was a Negro woman holding in her hands two lengths of severed wire.

Stefan dropped the plunger, but Aristaeus grabbed him before he could make any move at escape. Stefan didn't even try.

Melchior looked at him with bottomless eyes that seemed to grab his soul and tear it from his body. Stefan prayed to himself as Aristaeus reached into his bloodied jacket and pulled his revolver from his holster. Then, with his foot, Aristaeus kicked the rosary off of the side of the train.

"You've done something impressive," Melchior said, ceasing his applause. His face was hawklike, more predatory in its human form than the distorted mask that Aristaeus' face had become. His mane of blond hair seemed to blow around his shoulders wildly, even though there was no wind inside the car. "You've attracted my attention."

He stepped next to the Negro woman who held the wires. She didn't move, even to breathe, as if she was a statue.

tefan wanted to run, to escape, but Aristaeus held him
ast.

"You see, *I* decide who among the herd is important to
ny purpose. *I* pick those who will be in thrall to me. Of
he countless, pointless millions, a handful are worthy of
ny touch, my direct control." Melchior drew a hand across
he woman's shoulder. "Fewer come into my fold."

He nodded to Aristaeus, who pushed Stefan down to his
nees. Stefan felt dizzy from blood loss and the pain in
is shoulder.

"You're at the beginning of a new age, Stefan Ryzard.
oon the human trash will be burned from the face of the
and. When the foundations of your civilization are stripped
way, what's left of the cattle will call me Lord."

Stefan closed his eyes and shook his head. He felt as if
e were in the train car with Satan himself.

"You think not?" Melchior's voice was soft, seductive.
"The work you've seen was part of my plans before your
ncestors decided to accept the middle-eastern cult you
old so dear. I knew when those of my own great race
leposed me, nearly a millennia ago, that I would eventually
educe Europe to ashes. Within a decade, this land's troops
vill march from Paris to Moscow. I will follow that army,
o rule those occupied lands."

He's insane. It was too much for Stefan to credit. Arisaeus grabbed Stefan's jaw and pulled his face upright. Ste-
an looked into Melchior's eyes, and his doubt dropped
way.

Melchior nodded at him, still standing behind the
woman. "My world is come. You cannot fight it. Those of
ny own race are impotent. Those such as you are less than
nothing. And despite that, you interest me."

The train jerked, and Stefan heard the cars jostling
against each other. Melchior waved to Aristaeus, and Stefan felt two inhuman hands clamp down on his shoulders.

"I've decided that I want you."

Stefan's heart shuddered and struggled against Aristaeus'
grip. In response to his futile struggles, Aristaeus increased
his grip, driving sharp daggers of pain into his broken
shoulder. Stefan groaned. "God!"

Melchior shook his head. "Such misplaced faith."

Suddenly, and without warning, Melchior struck out at

the woman before him. Stefan saw the flash of a silve
blade reaching over the woman's shoulder. It slid throug
her neck without slowing. Stefan couldn't close his eyes o
turn away, and watched horrified as the woman's head tum
bled down the front of her body.

Blood didn't spray. It simply oozed weakly as the head
less body dropped to its knees and fell forward, the morta
wound facing Stefan. Melchior stood over the corpse an
stared at Stefan. "An act as simple as that is beyond you
omnipotent God. Thousands have called upon Him t
strike me down, and I still walk the earth."

Stefan stared at the body, lying in a small pool of thic
blackish blood. He couldn't help thinking of the other bod
ies he had seen.

"You wonder why I killed her? My own thrall?" Mel
chior stepped over the body and began walking toward Ste
fan. "She had been corrupted by the blood of another. No
enough to displace my will within her, but enough to mak
her offensive to me. She suffered the fate of all those wh
offend me." He knelt down in front of Stefan, close enoug
that Stefan could feel his breath in his face. His breath wa
cold. "I offer immortality to all those who serve me b
taking of my blood. I offer it, and I can take it away. I ca
give you more in this world than the empty promise o
your tortured savior."

"Lord protect me," Stefan whispered.

He felt Aristaeus back away from him, but Melchior only
smiled. "You think your lord intervenes? You think H
causes those of the blood to shy away from you or you
cross?" Melchior shook his head. "It is nothing more tha
you, Stefan Ryzard. Your faith is unpleasant for some, ar
annoying itch. They can see the devotion in your eyes an
it drives the weak ones away."

"Hail Mary, full of grace, blessed art thou—"

Aristaeus let go of him, but Stefan never had a chance
to react, because Melchior's left hand grabbed his shoulder
"Look at me, Stefan Ryzard. I am not weak."

Stefan's gaze fell into Melchior's eyes, pulling his soul
after it. He fell into a void, surrounded on all sides by
Melchior's irresistible presence. Melchior's will pushed
against him like a tidal wave, swamping Stefan's feeble re-

sistance. Every effort Stefan made to resist seemed to suck him deeper into Melchior's twisted soul.

With one set of eyes, Stefan was sinking into the depths of hell. With another, he could see Melchior before him, waving Aristaeus to the side. When Melchior raised his hand, Stefan was unrestrained, yet he couldn't move. It was as if his mind had been totally severed from his body. Even the pain of his injury seemed remote now.

Stefan tried to call for help, at least in his mind. But under the force of the mental undertow, he couldn't remember his prayers.

"Bare your chest to me," Melchior said.

Far away, Stefan felt his hands raise to tear open his clothes. It was hard to concentrate. It was becoming less clear to Stefan where he was, and what was happening to him. Even the basic knowledge of who he was seemed weak and eroded.

It would be very easy to forget, to give up. Somewhere inside his mind, that thought inspired a mortal terror. He couldn't give up his soul. What was left of Stefan didn't give up, it retreated. Everything he was, everything that trembled at Melchior's presence, drew back as far into his mind as it could. Stefan's identity shrank under the flood of Melchior's will and disappeared somewhere far from his conscious mind. Melchior's mind filled the spaces it left behind.

"Many give themselves to me willingly." Melchior raised his arm before the shell that had been Stefan Ryzard. He held his hand before him, and the skin split apart along the lines of the palm. Blood pooled in Melchior's cupped hand, spilling over the edges. "It pleases me to take from you."

With those words, Melchior took the blade in his other hand and brought it down across Stefan's chest. Even when the sword separated the rib cage, opening Stefan's heart to the air, his body didn't topple. Melchior's will was like a physical force holding the body immobile.

After the sword fell, before Stefan's blood had time to pool at his feet, Melchior's bloody hand entered the wound. The hand grabbed Stefan's still-beating heart, coating it with Melchior's own blood.

Melchior held him like that for an eon, Stefan's blood drenching the floor of the car below them. Stefan's heart slowed to a stop, and with it, the bleeding. Stefan's body never moved, and his eyes never closed. His gaze remained locked upon Melchior.

Eventually, Melchior smiled and withdrew his hand. It came out of the wound, soaked with gore, but as he held it in front of himself, the blood moved with a life of its own, drawing back into his palm, sinking into the raw meat of the palm before Melchior's skin pulled itself over the wounds in his hand.

As if an imperfect imitation of Melchior's hand, the edges of the massive wound in Stefan's chest began to pull themselves together. Now Stefan's body moved, collapsing to the floor, shuddering as the flesh and bones of his chest reformed themselves. Even the bone that pierced the flesh of his shoulder withdrew as the skin pulled itself over the wound.

In moments, Stefan lay on the floor, curled in a fetal position, eyes blankly staring. He lay in a pool of his own blood, but his body showed no sign of any injury. He breathed, and his heart beat, but both so shallowly that there was little sign of life. His clothes now hung upon him as if he had lost forty pounds.

"Rise up," Melchior said.

Stefan's face gave no sign of understanding the words, but his body obeyed. He got unsteadily to his feet. His eyes still stared blankly ahead.

"Accompany me," Melchior said, and Stefan did so, following Melchior and Aristaeus through the train. He didn't spare a look right or left, or even for the body of the woman that still lay across their path.

They passed through the length of two more empty cars. Past the one on which Stefan had planted his explosives, into a car that hadn't been on the train when Stefan had boarded. It appeared as a normal boxcar, misplaced at the end of a passenger train. And the trio of them had to step off of the unmoving train and walk to the side of the boxcar.

The door slid open on a dark empty space. A few candles flickered in one end of the car. Melchior led them up into the car, Stefan following, silent, staring and unaware.

Chained at the rear of the car was Iago.

Melchior looked upon him and said, "I wanted you to

see your ally before you die. I wanted you to see how deeply you failed."

Iago looked up with a pale, wasted face. "You'll fail, Melchior. And destroy all of us with you."

Melchior laughed.

"The Covenant was to protect us. If humanity believes in what you are, they'll do anything to destroy you and all like you."

"The voice of fear and weakness." Melchior walked up to Iago. As he did so, he gestured to Aristaeus to close the door. "Our noble race is meant to rule this mongrel cattle. Fear of them is a perversion that has poisoned our race since the inception of your Covenant."

Iago spat, carefully avoiding Melchior's gaze. "And you are meant to rule our noble race?"

"Who else of us remains unfettered by your perverted Covenant?"

"You are the perversion," Iago said.

Melchior took a hand and ran it along the side of Iago's face. "Take a look at what it is you fear." Melchior pointed his blade at Stefan, who stood, face blank, empty and staring. "Without your Covenant any of our race could have ruled, but you've preferred to cringe in the shadows."

"Your time was over a millennium ago."

Melchior shook his head. "No. Look across the ocean and see the rulers the cattle choose for themselves. Stalin, Hitler, Mussolini . . . The cattle beg to be controlled. If I only offer my hand, they will willingly wrap it around their own throats. My time is just beginning." He took the blade and brought it up to Iago's neck. "It is your time that is over."

Iago finally looked up into Melchior's eyes and said, "Because of you, the time of our race will be over."

Melchior raised the blade and sliced through Iago's neck. The body fell against its bonds as Iago's head toppled from his shoulders. The body twitched a few times, spraying the wall behind it with tarlike blood.

Melchior stepped back, shaking his head as if in disgust. He turned away from the corpse and faced Aristaeus. "Take another of my servants and dispose of the bodies."

Aristaeus' countenance had nearly returned to human

form. "What about him, Master?" He nodded slightly at Stefan.

"Detective Ryzard is nothing but an empty shell now. Forget about him."

Aristaeus nodded and left to fetch another thrall to help him dispose of Iago and Rose Wallace.

15

Nuri Lapidos had come off of suspension only a day
before someone found the body of "Number Seven,"
an unidentified woman. The tension in the rest of the city
had filtered down into the squad-room. Everyone talked
about "The Phantom of Kingsbury Run."

When he heard the talk around him, the bogus confessions, the innumerable tips and leads that went nowhere,
the inability to identify the body, he could almost sense
the presence of the unnatural. He could almost hear the
superstition in the other detective's voices.

Nuri was still on probation, sitting behind a desk filling
out paperwork, ignoring the ache of his barely-healed chest.
He tried not to think about what was going on around him.
He tried not to think of Iago. . . .

What could he do? Stefan had disappeared, presumably
to act upon Iago's direction. Iago had disappeared, too.
And yet another corpse turned up. Nuri couldn't help but
think that it would be Iago and Stefan who would be turning up next.

No one was going to stop Eric Dietrich.

Book Three

―⚬⚬⚬―

June 1937—August 1939

THE WAGES
OF SIN

1

Aristaeus disposed of the bodies in different places. It was months before the body of the woman was found, after it had been reduced to little more than a dismembered skeleton. It would be years before Iago's bones would be discovered in a Youngstown dump.

In one sense, Stefan was aware of this. His memory was still intact, and he was aware of what went on around him. In another sense Stefan wasn't even conscious. What thoughts crossed his conscious mind weren't his own.

Information from the outside world fell on his ears, as Dietrich's thralls talked around him. And while he heard the words, the ideas attached sank into his memory without a trace. Those words weren't commands by the Master, and therefore they weren't important.

But he heard and saw, even though his thoughts were a blank void.

He was in the basement of a house that stood somewhere in a Slovenian neighborhood around East Fifty-Fifth, near the St. Clair area where he had grown up. Down here with him, sitting around a card table, was Simon Aristaeus. Two others sat across from him, both former members of the Mayfield Road Mob.

"So that body was yours, eh?" said the one on the right. Aristaeus called him Dante. As he spoke, he tossed a few red chips into a pile in the center of the table.

"Nah," Aristaeus said, tossing a like number of chips into the pile. "Call." He looked at the other two and added, "Raise you five." He tossed in a blue chip.

The Italian on the left, who Aristaeus had called Tito,

shook his head and folded his cards on the table. "I thought you took the knife to her?"

"See you," Dante said, tossing in his own blue chip. "Isn't that what you said?"

"Aces over tens," Aristaeus said, spreading his cards on the table. Dante said "Fuck," dropping his hand, as Aristaeus pulled the pot over to his side of the table. "No, I just dropped off the body. I saw the Master Himself separate her neck. Anything I did was just to make it easy to move the dead bitch around."

Dante gathered the cards, shuffled, and began dealing. "Does that ever worry you?"

"What?" Aristaeus said, picking up his cards, one at a time.

"That He kills His own like that?" Dante said, finishing the deal and picking up his cards.

Aristaeus snorted, shaking his head and tossing a red chip into the pot. The others followed suit. "Two," he said, tossing a pair of cards in front of him. "Why should it worry me? I serve Him, that's what matters."

"Three," Tito said. "Didn't she also? She was the one who brought Iago to Him, wasn't she?"

"Dealer takes one," Dante said.

"She allowed herself to become contaminated with another's blood. She wasn't purely the Master's any more." Aristaeus glanced across at the dealer and tossed in a white chip. "Ten."

"Shit," Dante muttered.

"Here," Tito tossed in his own white chip and leaned over the table. "Now wait a minute. How many effing times have we watched Him take apart one of his rivals, and feed us the poor bastard's blood?"

"That's different," Aristaeus said. He looked across at Dante who was still looking at his cards. "Well?" he said.

"Give me a minute," Dante said.

"How the hell is it different?"

"First off, the bastard's dead when He offers us his blood. Second, He always takes first, it *becomes* his blood . . ."

"Okay, see you and raise ten," Dante said.

Aristaeus tossed in another white chip without comment.

"Then why don't it become *ours*—" Tito looked across at Dante. "What, you think I'm crazy? Fold."

Dante smiled, "Jacks over kings. There."

Aristaeus shook his head, "Four threes."

"Fuck," Dante said.

Aristaeus turned to Tito and said, "It don't become *ours* because we aren't a thousand years older and more powerful than anything we drink from, got it?" He pulled the pot in toward himself. "It's about power."

"So if we drank from the White Zombie over there," Tito pointed at Stefan, "we'd be all right?"

Aristaeus laughed as he took the cards. "You'd be in no danger of handing your soul over, but I'd still think you'd piss off the Master." He shuffled and said, "Change of pace, five card stud."

Dante sighed.

As Aristaeus dealt out the first two cards, Tito kept looking in Stefan's direction, as if he'd just noticed him standing in the corner of the basement. "What's the zombie's story?" Tito asked. "Don't he ever talk?"

"He's the Master's pet, and no, he don't ever talk. Now ante up, you got the king."

Chips flew into the center of the table.

"He was a cop, right?" Dante asked.

Aristaeus nodded. "And he tried to blow the Master up."

As the third card was dealt out, Tito looked over at Stefan and said, "Sometimes I don't understand our boss."

"King-ten bets," Aristaeus said.

Tito tossed in a chip. "Why's He kill one of His own, and bring over someone who tried to kill Him?"

"Don't ask questions like that," Dante said. "You were supposed to be in on a hit on Him, remember?"

Tito shrugged, "I'm entitled to wonder, ain't I?"

"You want to know why?" Aristaeus said as he dealt out another card. "Because it amuses Him." Aristaeus tilted his head toward Stefan. "That fella especially."

"Why him?" Tito asked, tossing his bet.

Dante looked at Tito's hand and said, "Fuck," again. He flipped his cards over and said, "Fold."

"I think because he was a Catholic." Aristaeus tossed in his bet and dealt out another card.

"So, *I'm* a Catholic." Tito tossed in a chip, "What's that got to do with anything?"

"I ain't fighting your pair of tens with this crap." Aristaeus folded his hand. Tito drew in the pot and Dante said "Finally, someone else wins a hand."

"So?" Tito said.

"This guy here had some faith, Tito," Aristaeus said "Enough so when he held up a cross, it was painful. He was the kind who think we're spawn of the devil, sold our souls."

Tito looked over at Stefan again and said, "No wonder he don't talk much."

Dante looked up at a clock on the wall and said, "I think it's time."

"What? Can't we go another hand now I'm finally winning?"

"Dante's right," Aristaeus said.

Tito dropped the cards and cursed.

"Let's get the zombie and go," Dante said. "I've lost enough here."

The trio, Tito somewhat reluctantly, walked over and led Stefan out of the basement and to a waiting car.

The summer night wrapped itself around the dark sedan as it slid through the empty dark streets of the east side It drove south toward the train tracks. Their final destination was a warehouse that stood near the tracks a short distance from the East Fifty-Fifth railyard, also a short distance from the now-infamous Kingsbury Run.

The warehouse appeared dark and empty, but there was a lot next to it that was hidden from view by a twelve-foot fence plastered with old cryptic posters. They drove around through a large gate that slid aside for them at the last minute.

On the other side, the sedan found a space for itself in a crowd of similar cars. Dozens of people walked through the lot, between the cars, toward the gaping maw of the loading bays. In the back of Stefan's mind burned a memory of a different warehouse, a smaller one near the docks. But the memory didn't burn enough to make it to the front part of his mind.

He followed Dante, Tito, and Aristaeus through the pale

ush of people. Memory tried to assert itself whenever he assed a face that bore some familiarity, this one a reporter or the *News*, this other man a member of the city council, e third another detective, this fourth a local thug into the rotection racket. Just passing them he could feel, in his ut, in the air he breathed, the difference between those ho still wore a human form and those who had become amned completely, like him.

Somewhere he feared—not for the walking dead that accompanied him to the warehouse, gone already—a small iece of him feared for those that still lived. He feared for e ones who had not yet tumbled off the precipice into e abyss of the damned.

He feared, but he could not pray.

The maw of the loading bays took in the advancing rowd twelve abreast. The procession advanced in silence. he silence was out of reverence for, and fear of, the dark essiah they had come here to worship. They filled the arkened chamber, hundreds strong.

The only noise was a repetitive moaning that came, not om the silent throng, but from men and women who were hained to the support beams evenly spaced through the rowd. There were easily a dozen of these captives in place round Stefan, naked, heads covered by sacks, four to a ost, facing each point of the compass, arms drawn back o far around the girder that the joints must be broken.

Stefan had been present, with the others, waiting, for fteen minutes or so before he heard the doors behind hem rattle shut. The faithful were all here.

For a few moments the warehouse was completely dark, he only sounds those of the moaning captives. Then a oice came from the darkness, a deep, instantly recognizble voice.

"Welcome, flesh of my flesh, blood of my blood."

A light shone upon a raised platform in front of the rowd. And there stood Melchior, arms outstretched as if blessing. Even the moans seemed to cease in deference o the timbre of Melchior's voice.

"Welcome, those bound to my service." Melchoir lowred his arms. He was tall, and his hair hung loose around is shoulders. He wore a crimson robe that hung around im like a bishop's garb. On a small table before him was a long blade and a goblet. He took the goblet in one hand and held the other over it. The skin of that hand split apart and blood wept from the wound into it.

"This is my blood, which has granted you eternal life. Drink it in my service."

Melchior held the cup aloft and lights came on, illuminating the pillars with the twisted, captive bodies chained upon them. Stefan could feel the edge of madness cut into the room, under Melchoir's bidding. In himself he felt the perverse hunger grow.

"This is my flesh," Melchoir said. "It is time to renew our communion. Feed, my children, and be sated."

At those words, it was as if someone had opened the gates of hell within that warehouse. The whole crowd descended upon the pillars as one. Stefan found himself within the horrid mob, tearing tooth and claw into the flesh of the chained captives, letting the bright, burning, living blood spill over his hands, his face, his mouth. Melchior's children climbed over themselves to reach the human victims, to sink their teeth into some yet-unmolested piece of flesh.

Even those who still lived, who didn't need the living blood to survive, joined the frenzy, tearing into the flesh with their bare hands.

Stefan fell away from the girder as soon as the gnawing hunger was no longer a force within him. Falling back he could see his victim. The frenzied crowd still undulated at the base of the pillar like some crimson multiheaded beast. Rising above it, where there had been a human being, was now just a bloody skeleton held together with strips of sinew.

Even through the empty, dead chambers of his mind, Stefan could feel the disgust and self-loathing coming from the small part of him that was still himself.

In front of the platform, a select group of Melchior's faithful had gathered to drink from his goblet. A dozen of the new and the favored were able to feed from the master himself.

As the frenzy faded, and the crowd withdrew from their feeding, Melchior again drew attention toward the platform. A light illuminated the back of the platform, an area that had been in darkness until now.

A body hung upside-down, dangling from a chain anchored in the ceiling. Melchior raised His knife and announced, "Here is a traitor to the blood. A keeper of a false Covenant."

The Master cataloged the multitude of sins committed by the creature chained behind Him. All amounted to being a vampire outside Melchior's fealty. Stefan saw the Master raise His blade and remove the creature's head. But by the time the head fell on the platform, and Melchior took the victim's blood, Stefan had withdrawn in himself past the point where the scene held any significance.

2

Monday, June 7

"No chance it could be Stefan Ryzard?" Nuri asked Sam Gerber, the coroner. Gerber had been elected successor to Pearse, and Nuri suspected it was because the small man looked at home in a morgue.

Nuri had come down here after hearing that they had found a number eight.

On the table before him Gerber had laid out an incomplete set of skeletal remains. His gloved hands touched the skull, briefly making him resemble a twisted Hamlet. He shook his head, looking at Nuri through thick glasses. "No. This was a woman, shorter, and a Negro."

"But she belongs on the list?"

"If you want, you can see the marks on the vertebrae where the knife—"

"No, thanks," Nuri said, turning away. "I should go."

Gerber continued to talk about when his final report would be ready. Nuri just nodded his head as he left, not really listening.

He had come down here expecting to find Stefan. He didn't know why he felt Stefan would end up on the list. It seemed that the decapitation was saved for special categories of Eric Dietrich's victims, and from his expedition to the swamp, Nuri knew that they weren't finding all of the bodies.

Still he expected the next headless corpse to be Stefan.

In a way he almost hoped so. The uncertainty of having his ex-partner missing, with no sign of his fate, was gnawing at him. Stefan had stepped into something dark, and what might have happened to him could be worse than a death by decapitation.

Nuri walked back from the morgue, returning to the mundane world of police work, unenlightened and fearful.

3

Tuesday, July 6

It was the summer that some of the worst parts of Europe came to visit the city. Striking workers mixing with Communists verged near to riot enough times that the National Guard had been called in to keep the peace. By the start of July the downtown area, especially around the Flats by the river, looked as if it was under martial law.

Carl Selig had never been to Cleveland before, and he felt out of his depth. He stood on a road overlooking some train tracks, feeling intolerably hot in his uniform, wondering what would happen if he got in a situation where he had to shoot somebody. He had his Springfield ready, as he was ordered to, but the thought of firing it made him weak in the knees.

Fortunately, today he had a quiet spot to observe. No demonstrators waving red-and-black flags, no one throwing stones or bricks, no hired thugs trying to club the workers into submission. Standing here, overlooking the quiet rails, Carl could try to believe that the presence of the guardsmen was quieting things down.

He could believe it if it wasn't for the rumors that found their way to him. He heard about shots being fired, of looting downtown, and one grotesque story about a human body, or parts of one, seen floating in the river.

Thinking of those things made him wish he was back in Oberlin.

At least he had a quiet spot to tend to. There was little here to watch but the occasional train passing by, and a small village of tin shacks where about half a dozen tramps made their home. The lack of anything else to draw his attention made him more aware of how hot he was, and how the sweat was gathering under his helmet. The tramps had a fire going, and the smell of it made the heat feel worse.

At least the sun was going down.

Night came, and though Carl was still a few hours short of relief, he began to feel a little easier about the riots. Nothing was going to happen in front of him today. He should have been able to relax a little.

Instead, he kept thinking of the body—or what the private telling him insisted, the *pieces* of it—found floating in the Cuyahoga. It was a gruesome idea, and Carl's mind had trouble letting go of it. Even more gruesome was the story that there was some maniac who had chopped up eight other people before this one. Every one killed by cutting off their head.

It would have been another stupid scare story if it wasn't for the fact that Carl had heard about the murders in Cleveland long before he ever came into the National Guard.

Carl decided that a maniac he could shoot. He had doubts about a striker or a Communist, but a full-fledged madman he figured he could shoot. Though as darkness fell across the tracks and the little shantytown, Carl hoped his theory wouldn't be tested.

Near the end of his watch, he heard a train. That wasn't unusual. What caught his ear was the sound of it, the odd lengthening note that made it seem as if the train was slowing down. The appearance of the eastbound train bore that out. As the engine's lights swept across first him, then the hill below him, then the tramps' shanties, then the hills beyond, Carl could see that the train was screeching to a stop just below him.

There was no sense to it that he could see. There was no station, no siding, no landmark to speak of outside of the little collection of rough shacks below. The tramps themselves gave witness to the remarkable event. They made their lives on the tracks, and certainly knew more arcana of the rails than Carl, but they stood and stared at the slowing beast as if they, too, were dumbfounded as to the reason it was stopping.

The train came to a complete stop, the engine somewhat distant now, and before the little tramp village sat a line of black boxcars. For a long time there was no sound but a soft hissing from the direction of the engine.

The tramps, out of curiosity, or out of a sudden wander-lust brought on by the proximity of transportation, began to approach the cars. The light was dim, only from the fire by the tramps' camp, but Carl counted seven of them.

Carl felt a sudden unease, a prickling at the back of his neck. Everything seemed suddenly so wrong, as if the normal world had just fallen away from him, leaving him naked in some netherworld. The scene below him was nearly a hundred yards away, but he still took a step back.

As if triggered by his evil thoughts, the doors on the dark boxcars slid open in front of the tramps. There was a sudden flurry of motion that Carl could barely make sense of. He had a brief impression of grasping hands from the darkness, some barely human. He thought some of the tramps tried to turn, perhaps even run. It seemed only a second before he saw the tramps' kicking feet retreat into the darkness of the boxcars and the doors slide shut.

Carl stood in stunned silence for the space of a heartbeat . . .

. . . and another . . .

When he heard a scream from below him, he broke from his paralysis and began running down the slope. He stumbled madly, brush tearing at his uniform, roots twisting his ankles, but somehow he remained upright even as he lost his helmet. He called out, "Stop," and the word was little more than an inarticulate bellow that seared his lungs.

The scream continued, merging with the sound of the engine firing up to move again.

Carl raised his Springfield in some vain hope to stop the train, and it was then that the brush finally caught his feet, sending him tumbling face-first into the ground. He lost the Springfield in the fall, but it didn't go off.

Carl pushed himself up to see the train moving past him, accelerating. As he watched, he was certain that he heard, under the sound of the screeching engine, the scream abruptly cease.

By the time Carl had reached his feet, the boxcars were long past him and the train was moving by as if it had never stopped. Cars slid by him, clattering along the tracks. There was no sign of what, if anything, had happened.

Carl had no idea what to do. None of his standing orders covered this situation. He stood and watched the train pass by. Too soon, it seemed, the last car passed him. He was left in the darkness by the tracks, the only light the remains of the tramps' fire, the only sound the receding noise of the train's passage.

Slowly, Carl backed away from the tracks, climbing the hill, gathering his gun and his helmet. He began to wonder if what he had seen had actually happened.

1938

4

Monday, March 21

"Four of these in the past year," Mayor Burton said. He stood with Ness on the handball court, but neither of them were playing. "The last one floating down the Cuyahoga."

Ness nodded. There didn't seem to be much to say. With the press becoming less than supportive, Ness was hoping that the body in the river would be the last and that he'd hear no more of this madman. There had been a barrage of criticism after the last body, and the Democrats had used the failure of the Torso Murder investigation against Ness and Burton in the last election. During the campaign the Democrats said that they didn't need a "G-man from Chicago;" they needed a local lawman who wasn't more concerned about witch-hunts in the police department than he was dead Clevelanders.

"Something has got to be done to ease the public mind," Burton said.

Ness could only smile weakly at that. Every few months, the mayor would fixate on the one problem of the killer. Ness didn't have that luxury. He had to deal with problems as far-ranging as corruption in the department, to union racketeering, to traffic safety. Somehow, whenever anyone talked about these murders, they lost sight of all the progress Ness had made in these areas. It was annoying.

"Can't we do a dragnet, a house-to-house search—"

Ness shook his head. "You know what kind of resources that would take? We can't even be sure he's in the area. He hasn't left us any signs for nearly eight months."

"You could find his butcher hall, the place he dismembers his victims."

"It's an extreme reaction, sir. I don't know if it is warranted."

Mayor Burton leaned against the wall of the court and wiped a little sweat he had left over from the game. "Maybe. Have there been any leads in the case?"

"Too many." Ness waved over the hardwood floor of the court and said, "I could fill this court ten feet deep with transcripts of every tip we've gotten, every interview we've done, and every false confession we've received. Everyone from taxi drivers to National Guardsmen have seen something suspicious in the Run." He shook his head and said, "The publicity on this case makes people crawl out of the woodwork."

Burton gave him a look as if he couldn't believe Ness bad-mouthing publicity of any sort. "Well, I just want you to remember that a house-to-house is always an option."

"It's not even certain that our man's in the Roaring Third."

Mayor Burton shook his head. "The three victims you've identified were all from the area—"

"The identification of Rose Wallace was tentative, not official—the remains were skeletal."

Mayor Burton waved his hand as if it wasn't an important enough detail to be bothered with. "And you wouldn't get long odds that all these unidentified bodies weren't tramps and transients."

Ness nodded, Mayor Burton was just repeating the most popular theory, that this maniac was some homosexual predator, preying on the underbelly of Cleveland's population. Though the last one, in the river, had a manicure that was at odds with him being a tramp.

Ness would have felt better if one of the "tramp" victims had been invited. "We are investigating that angle. Every night now we have some detectives undercover in the shantytowns around the flats, and up toward the Run."

"*That* I'm glad to hear." Mayor Burton picked up a towel from a bench by the door and wiped the back of his neck. "Well, I have to get back to the office, I have meetings to attend to. I suppose you have work to get to."

Ness nodded.

As Mayor Burton left he turned to face Ness one last time, "Remember, it's always an option."

"I know," Ness said as the mayor left.

When Mayor Burton entered his office, Eric Dietrich was waiting for him. The man was seated across from his desk. Mayor Burton hung up his overcoat and said, "I've been expecting you."

Dietrich nodded, "I like to hear news of your administration from you. The newspapers can distort things." He twisted his cane in his hand so the handle spun in front of him.

"That's true," Mayor Burton said as he moved around behind his desk. He didn't extend his hand or make eye contact. He knew that Dietrich didn't mind; he seemed to be aware of how his touch, and his gaze, disturbed others. Dietrich remained seated at an angle, turning his cane, looking off into the corner of Mayor Burton's office.

"I do want to reassure myself that my recommendations for the next Republican administration reflect well on me."

"I understand." Mayor Burton did understand. Dietrich was very active behind the scenes in the Republican Party, and it seemed clear, ever since he'd become mayor, that Dietrich had some voice in the cabinet makeup of the next Republican president. Originally Burton's ambitions had never extended much beyond the cleaning up of his own city. But Dietrich represented opportunities he could neither refuse nor ignore.

"The mutilation killings, those still worry you. No progress?" Dietrich kept twirling the cane.

The mayor nodded. That seemed Dietrich's personal fixation. Rarely would the businessman ask him questions about taxes or how he managed to get the city coffers to pay deferred salaries of city workers. Always crime. Always the murders and how he planned to deal with them.

"Yes, but it's been months since we've had one. Maybe we've been lucky, and the monster died, moved, or was imprisoned for something else."

"And perhaps you just haven't found his latest."

Mayor Burton didn't like the way Dietrich said that. "I've talked to Ness about stepping up the investigation. We're already using every resource at our disposal."

"Not quite," Dietrich said, and he stopped twirling his cane. "If you wish to be sure to drive a dangerous wolf from the forest, drive away the deer. Perhaps even burn the forest."

Dietrich's voice sounded grave, and Burton leaned forward. "What, exactly, are you saying?"

"You know where he draws his victims. I've heard you say it often enough. The nameless tramps and hobos that line the tracks of this city."

"Drive the tramps away?" Mayor Burton asked. "How?"

5

Thursday, April 7

Detective Nuri Lapidos was doing his turn in purgatory. He was dressed in old ragged clothes that itched and refused to fit right. The rain and mud weren't helping. He slogged along the tracks under the glare of the rail-yard lights, but more often in the darkness. The only things he carried that were at odds with the tramp outfit were a badge and a revolver, both well hidden.

The badge was for the railroad cops, the revolver was to be for the murderer that was supposed to prowl these rails. He doubted that the revolver would help if they met. He also doubted that they would meet down here by the train tracks.

Still, Nuri followed his assignment, slogging through the mud, stopping at the small temporary communities the rootless unemployed had thrown up around the flats. He would stop here and there, and try and dry himself by someone's fire.

Through the night he would try to talk to the people he met, talk about the stories they had formed about the predators in the darkness along the tracks. Between these talks he would walk along the tracks, looking like a potential victim for those predators.

Few of the stories he collected would be fit for the homicide squad. Even so, they made Nuri uneasy.

He heard stories about a pale man, or sometimes a woman, interrupted while drinking the blood of a sleeping man. Sometimes these nocturnal creatures would run, and sometimes they would turn demonic and attack the witness. The stories were always accompanied by nervous laughter—though whenever someone claimed to be that witness, they didn't join in the laughter.

It was late now, past midnight, and Nuri was slogging along to find a fourth group of tramps tonight. He pulled his ragged overcoat around him, more against the darkness than against the rain, which had already soaked him to the skin.

He stumbled forward, leaving the tracks, making for a blurry spot of light that seemed to hover underneath a drawbridge that extended over the Cuyahoga. He was halfway to it before he saw that the glow was more than a simple campfire. Some of the small makeshift buildings were burning.

Nuri started running. The night air in the river basin played games with sound. One moment he heard nothing but the rush of rain, and the next he was certain he could hear laughter. Under the laughter there could have been screams, inhuman screams, like an animal caught in the flames.

Nuri, still running, drew his gun.

Shadows ran out of the darkness toward him, faster than anything had a right to move. The shapes were only vaguely human as they loped by him. Nuri raised his gun, but the shadowy figures passed by him as if they didn't even see him, or didn't care.

Nuri had only the briefest impression of claws, leathery skin, and a loping stride. Then they were gone, and all that was left was an odd keening sound coming from between Nuri and the fire.

He didn't want to advance any further, but those things might have left people there, in the fire. Nuri looked back after the things, but the darkness had swallowed them. Then he advanced toward the fire.

The keening became louder.

The smell of things burning, flesh and hair, began to reach him through the rain. It became stronger as Nuri approached something that lay on the ground between him and the fire. The thing steamed in the rain, and Nuri was almost upon it before he could see what it was. When he did see it, he stopped.

Before him was a corpse burned across most of its body. It was twisted, the flesh charred and black. Steam rose from it in the rain. The shape was only vaguely human, and not only because of the destruction wrought upon its flesh. Like the shapes that had passed him in the darkness, this thing's limbs were misproportioned, its back was arched, and its skull was twisted into a muzzle that had too many teeth.

Empty eye sockets stared at him from a face of blackened flesh.

Nuri looked up. The fire was dying away. He could still hear laughter, and a pair of voices. The voices weren't close enough to make anything out yet. Nuri started edging toward the fire again.

Something grabbed his ankle.

Nuri pitched forward, and his revolver went flying into the darkness. He sucked in a breath and got a mouthful of sour mud.

Something clung to his leg. Nuri scrambled to flip himself over to look at what was grabbing at him, and in a flash of lightning, saw the corpse clutching at him.

As he watched, the charred form moved. The flesh was burned enough that he could hear it rustle. The corpse made another sound, something like breaking bone, as it turned toward him.

Nuri sat up and tried frantically to pry the charred hand from his leg. The thing moved slowly, but it was advancing on him, pulling itself by the one arm. Fluid leaked from cracks in its black skin as it moved. The face had changed, the muzzle retreating, so what closed on him was a naked human skull covered with a few remnants of crumbling black flesh.

It was keening at him.

Nuri tore at the hand gripping him until his fingernails were bloody. Its grip was like an iron band on his ankle. He tore at the exposed tendons on the back of it, and in response, the grip briefly loosened. Nuri tore his foot away, leaving the thing with his shoe.

The thing opened its black jaw and keened at him. The sound was filled with an unnatural pain. Nuri could hear the hunger in the sound. He couldn't separate the noise into words; he suspected the thing had no tongue, but he could almost understand what it was saying.

Let me feed.

Nuri scrambled backward, away from the thing.

It tried to follow, but it moved slowly, pulling itself along the ground with the single arm. The other arm hung loose at its side, little more than blackened bone. Nuri outdistanced the thing and reached his gun. He kept backing into the darkness and kept the gun trained on the thing.

Nuri managed to get a dozen yards away, and the thing stopped moving. It began keening again, louder than ever. It seemed to have lost track of him.

Nuri was about to stand up, as soon as his heart stopped racing, when the voices approached. Nuri looked toward the dying fire, and saw four silhouettes walking toward the corpse through the rain. The one in the lead carried an ax.

Instead of standing up, Nuri lowered himself flush with the mud, hiding in the ditch where he found himself. He watched the quartet approach the still-keening corpse. Even though the thing still moved, splashing around itself with its single arm, none of the four showed any reaction. They walked on, businesslike, as if an animate corpse was no big deal for them.

In another flash of lightning, Nuri could see the face of the lead man, with the ax. It was Simon Aristaeus, the man who had shot him in Van Sweringen's train car. He led three other men whose faces he still couldn't make out in the darkness.

"What a frigging mess," he heard one of the anonymous ones say as they closed on the still-moving body. "We lost, what, four?"

Aristaeus shook his head and said, "And we got five. Six counting him." Aristaeus waved the ax in the direction of the corpse. "Not a bad night's work."

Another one of Aristaeus' followers said, "And at this rate we'll never get them all. And burning everything is damn messy. What if the cops see us?"

"Then we have to kill some cops," Aristaeus said, walking around so he was behind the thrashing creature. The thing had become even more animated, as if it knew what was coming. Unfortunately for it, the more frantic its movement, the less effective it was. It seemed to have lost not only its one arm, but most of its legs. It couldn't move more than a foot before Aristaeus stepped up behind it and placed his foot in the center of its back. The weight pushed the blackened skull into the mud, muffling the thing's cries.

"Besides," Aristaeus said, as he handed the ax to one of the others, took off his jacket, and rolled up his sleeves, "if the Master has his way, soon the cops will be emptying these hoovervilles for us." He traded the jacket for the ax.

"Why would the cops do that?" one of the others asked.

"They're looking for a maniac who's lopping off people's heads, don't you read the papers?" With that, Aristaeus swung the ax in a wide arc down toward the corpse. Nunn couldn't tear his gaze away as the blade descended on the pinned thing's neck. The ax came down with such force that the creature's neck barely slowed its progress, its momentum continuing its arc on the other side of the body.

Aristaeus rested the ax on his shoulder, and stepped forward to kick the head away from the body. It rolled a few feet before stopping, its eyeless sockets pointed at the sky.

The corpse was now only a corpse; it neither cried nor moved.

"So why would they roust the hobos around here?"

Aristaeus walked over to the head and crouched by it. "They can't identify any of the bodies, and the ones they could are from the Roaring Third. They're sure that their maniac takes his victims from the worthless garbage around here. If they don't find their maniac, and they panic enough, they'll end up rousting them. Incidentally rousting the last hiding place for the Master's enemies."

"Almost ironic," one of the ones in the dark said.

"Tito," Aristaeus said, "I didn't picture you as one for such big words."

"Fuck yourself," came the response.

"This is one less bloodsucker who's catching a train out of town." Aristaeus bent over and picked up the head. It was now completely inert and more skull-like than ever. He turned it so it faced the others. "Fire," Aristaeus said, "the great equalizer."

"I still think it's a frigging mess."

Aristaeus stood up and handed the skull to the speaker. "That might have belonged to someone over two centuries old. You think we could have taken him without torching everything?"

"*If* he was old and powerful," said the man now holding

he skull. "For all we know he could have been turned esterday."

Aristaeus laughed and took back his jacket from the one e called Tito. "Well if he'd been turned yesterday, I doubt e'd be moving after we torched him. Besides, that's what n equalizer means; we don't have to care about things like ge and power—now let the zombie get the body." Arisaeus craned his neck so he looked past his first two companions at the one who hadn't spoken. "Come over here."

The last member of the quartet walked forward, reached lown, and grabbed the body by the shoulders. In another lash of lightning, Nuri saw his face.

It was Stefan.

Nuri sucked in a gasp and tried to push himself flatter nto the mud. Pale and drawn, wearing a blank expression, ut it was Stefan. Somehow they hadn't killed him, they ad *taken* him. Nuri wanted to do something, to intervene, ut fear rooted him to the spot. In his gut he knew he wasn't looking at a normal set of hoodlums. His gun would e useless against them.

He stayed motionless until they had carried the body away.

After giving them enough time to leave, Nuri stood up nd walked back to where the fire had been. All that was eft was smoldering ash. He looked for bodies, but they were gone, and any signs of blood or flesh had been washed way with the rain.

6

"I don't believe you," Ness said, "and I don't believe this."

Nuri stood there, in Ness' office, unable to say anything coherent in defense of his report.

"You sound less lucid than the tramps you're supposed to be taking stories from." Ness paced around his office, circling Nuri. "I don't know what went on back there, but it wasn't what you wrote down in this report."

"It's what I saw—" Nuri started.

Ness sighed, "And that's supposed to make this better? I expect stories like this when a witness walks off the street or I talk to a drunk who's lived under a bridge and in a bottle for the past five years. Even Ryzard, after he started cracking, had a superstitious immigrant background." Ness stopped pacing and faced Nuri. "I expected more of you. You went to college, you're supposed to be smarter than this."

"Sir—"

Ness held up his hand. "I don't want to hear it. It was a shame that you were teamed with a man right before he went around the bend. It couldn't have been easy. But I expected you to straighten out. You're convincing me otherwise."

He picked up thin folder from his desk and waved it at Nuri. "You know what this says to me?" Ness said, "It says that you listened too well to the tramps' ghost stories and probably drank something you shouldn't have."

Ness walked around and sat down behind his desk.

"The ashes are there, you can see where everything burned."

Ness nodded. "No doubt. Like I said, you might have seen something, but not this. At least I hope not, because I don't want to believe that one of my detectives, when seeing someone dismembering a body, would cower and hide. According to your own report, you had your gun drawn and they were armed only with an ax."

"It was Aristaeus and he was . . ." Nuri couldn't finish the sentence because it would have sounded absurd in the light of day.

Ness nodded, completing the unfinished sentence, "Undead? Do you know how ridiculous that sounds? I allowed Ryzard some slack because of seniority. He was an old hand and, unlike half the cops I found in this department, he was clean. I made a mistake. I won't repeat it. I will not have a detective who refuses to confront suspects because he thinks they might be the bogeyman."

Nuri felt his gut shrink inside him, but all he could do was nod. Ness was right.

"Aristaeus may have gone dirty, and he might have even shot you—though I have to say that when I heard about that debacle, I was half-convinced that Ryzard was the one who shot you—but that doesn't justify your behavior." Ness opened up the file and said, "If you strip away the eyewash about a moving corpse, what you have here is a report of two bent cops and a pair of Sicilian hoods chopping up a body—presumably killed by them—and carting away the evidence. While you sat by and watched."

Ness closed the file. He looked up at him with piercing eyes, and, for some reason, Nuri thought the Safety Director looked older now. "Do you realize that I have another victim of this maniac, a woman's leg floating down the river? And out of half a dozen officers I had in the field last night, you're the only one who saw anything—and it's all garbage."

Ness tossed the file back on the desk. "I'd transfer you to the traffic division if I wasn't trying to clean that department up." He folded his hands. "As it stands, you're going to be doing paperwork for a while, a *long* while, and maybe you should think about your choice of career."

Nuri didn't have an adequate response. Even though he thought he didn't have a choice at the time, somehow, in retrospect, he had screwed up.

Nuri turned to leave the office, and Ness added, "The only reason you're still on the force, Nuri, is because you're honest. For all my work, it still seems a rarity."

Nuri nodded and mumbled, "Thank you," as he left.

7

"So what were their names?"

The gentleman drinking across from Nuri hemmed and hawed until Nuri slid another few bills to his side of the table. The two of them sat in the back of a small bar a few blocks away from East One-Ten and Woodland, the Bloody Corner where so many of the Porrello family had been killed.

The gentlemen taking the money was part of a more recent, and more violent organization. An organization that seemed to have very tenuous ties back to Eric Dietrich.

Nuri sat back and waited, sipping his drink. He felt something like an outlaw himself, even if he wasn't doing anything illegal, yet. He was still officially desk-bound, but over the past two months he had been conducting his own private investigation, trying to track down Aristaeus and the goons who he'd seen with him. Eventually, he hoped to find Stefan.

He still didn't know what he'd do if he found any of them.

"Yeah," his dinner companion said, "Tito and Dante Marcello—Them the ones I saw with the Greek—"

"Aristaeus?"

"Whatever the fuck his name was."

Nuri nodded, "So you know where I can find these brothers?"

"They used to hang down on Mayfield, though as far as I know, they don't hang anywhere anymore."

"You know where they're likely to show up."

The man drank from his glass, and looked nervously

around himself. "You know that people who get in the way of these people tend to disappear or . . ."

"Or what?"

"Or they become these people." He polished off his glass. "I don't want to know what happens. Tito and Dante were supposed to hit Eric Dietrich. Now they work for him—though work for might be too weak a word for it."

"Where can I find them?"

"You might see Tito driving a sedan around St. Clair after dark." He pushed the glass away. "That's all I'm going to tell you. The stories I've heard about these guys make me sick and nervous, and I've blinded deadbeats with an icepick." He picked up his hat from the seat next him and put it on, casting shadow across his face. "If you fear the Devil, stay away from these people."

He left Nuri sitting there. After a while Nuri emptied his own glass.

8

It was fetid day, and flies were alive all through the trash heaps along Shore Drive. The wind off the lake did little to mitigate the heat of the day. Men in ragged clothes poked through the rubbish looking for something salvageable.

One man waving away the flies from one section of trash stopped still for a long time. He stood still long enough to draw the attention of his anonymous fellows. A few walked up to where the man stood, staring, no longer waving the flies away. Some held their hands up to their mouths even though they were used to the smell of the garbage and the sour lake smell that covered the area like a blanket.

One turned away and vomited.

In front of them, covered by flies, laying in the detritus like just another piece of garbage, was a human torso, blackening with decay.

Some ran to get the police. Even as they did so, a crowd gathered like a storm. The news broke from the shoreline like a sour wave off the lake. When the police cars sped up to the scene, there was a waiting mass of spectators, and a few photographers still taking pictures.

The scene transformed. The men there were no longer the ragged scavengers, but uniformed police, detectives in cheap suits, and the mass of the public from the offices downtown. The police tried to keep the crowd back from the scene, clearing the rubbish for hundreds of feet in either direction.

It wasn't far enough. To one side, within the mass of the crowd that stood amidst the rubbish to watch the police's ghoulish work, came a disturbance. A ragged circle formed in its midst like an air-bubble on the surface of dirty water. The men on the edges of that circle wore suits and hats, but wore expressions not too distant from the sick faces of the scavengers. They held their hands to their mouths, holding handkerchiefs to their noses.

Police converged on the spot within minutes, hoping to find the missing pieces of the corpse. What they found was a new corpse entirely.

The bodies were number eleven and twelve before the coroner even looked at them. The story had flowed through the city flooding bar after bar, office after office, until the evening papers could only provide a footnote to the ocean of rumor.

The next day, Mayor Burton stood in front of Ness' desk and said, "This has got to stop."

He said it flatly, with little emotion. All the impact in his words came from the fact that he stood in Ness's office when he said it. Having the mayor stand there was unusual enough to emphasize everything he said.

Ness stood as well, out of deference, and motioned to a chair, "Why don't you have a seat?"

Mayor Burton didn't seem to hear. The door was still closing behind him as he dropped a copy of the *News* on the desk between them. The torso killings were front page news. *Fingerprint is Lone Torso Murder Clew,* though Ness knew they would be extremely lucky if they could line up a match for the victim's print.

"We've had to clear people out of the morgue," Burton fumed. "Over a hundred people today trying to get to see Gerber's autopsy. This is becoming a ghoulish circus act." He paced a few times in front of Ness's desk and repeated, "This has to be stopped."

"We're expending every effort—"

Mayor Burton shook his head. "Not *every* effort. I told you after the last victim how I wanted this handled. You're going to handle it now."

"Do you know what you're asking?"

Mayor Burton nodded. "I am asking for every single policeman, every single detective, I am asking you to raze his hunting ground and to do a house-to-house search of the

THE FLESH, THE BLOOD, AND THE FIRE

Third. You'll either find him, or put such a fear of God into this demon that he'll quit this city forever."

Ness glanced down at the paper, and wondered how the mayor's orders would be reported. He looked up at Mayor Burton and asked, "Are you sure you want this?"

"I was elected because I wanted to end the crime and corruption that's marred this city since Prohibition. This is the ultimate corruption, Ness. I'm thinking how the future is going to judge us over this case. You're young yet, you have a reputation and a future. Think of where you want to be after this, and think of how it would be if you had this—" Mayor Burton waved at the newspaper, "—as an unsolved albatross around your neck."

Ness looked down at the paper and nodded. At least this way the papers could point at something to say that there were things being done.

Judgment had fallen on Sodom.

That was the thought that kept running through Nuri's mind. Wagons of police, firefighters, and detectives drove down into the flats, followed by carloads of reporters. Everyone, it seemed, carried an ax, a sledgehammer or a crowbar. Nuri had no clear idea how many there were, but it felt like an army.

It didn't seem a modern army though, nothing like a scene from the war in Europe; this was more like a force contemporary with the pharaohs, a Judgment writ in wood and steel.

Nuri rode in the back of one of the open trucks, seated on a wooden bench at the head of a line of uniformed officers. There was an awful anticipation in the faces of the police. Some laughed and joked to each other, but to Nuri it all seemed hollow.

They were anticipated. Even before the officers stepped out of the lead trucks with their megaphones, dirty men in ragged clothes had stepped out of their rough-built hovels to stare at them with clouded eyes.

Several officers with megaphones called out that everyone was under arrest, and there was to be an orderly file to the waiting wagons. There was little reaction at first. The ragged men stared at the new invaders to their realm as if they didn't quite believe they were there. Then the lead

officers waved at the open trucks, and the policemen began
to dismount off the rear.

That was when the chaos started. The sight of the ranks
of police and firemen, all armed with clubs, pickaxes,
sledgehammers, prybars ignited something in the spectating
crowd. Some advanced on the waiting wagons, as they had
been told. But many looked at the forming line of police,
and fear filled their eyes.

Those ran.

The police descended.

The light seemed to fade from the sky as the world
around Nuri seemed to erupt into anarchy. He followed
the officers; his duty was to somehow note any suspects or
leads as they passed through this little shantytown. Thrust
into the midst of this riot his duty seemed laughable. The
line of officers descended on the small army of transients
and hobos, with a viciousness as if it was the fault of these
that the torso killer had descended on Cleveland.

The police fell upon them with clubs, the handles of axes
and sledgehammers. They pulled them down by the arms,
the legs, by their hair. Following the police, the firemen
brought the city's wrath down upon the little shacks that
these people had made their homes.

Tarpaper shredded, wood snapped, and tin whined in
agony as the firemen attacked the flimsy structures.

Then they burned.

Suitcases and trunks were trampled in the melee. The
storm raged around and past Nuri, and as it passed him, it
left little in its wake. Nuri stood on a trampled plain as the
violence passed him by. There was nothing left that could
be called a shelter. Broken wood and clothing littered the
ground with no discernible pattern. Smoke rose from pyres
that used to be people's homes.

Near Nuri's feet lay a small silver frame, broken in half,
glass ground to powder by a fireman's boot. Torn and wa-
terlogged with mud was a picture of a little girl, her face
obliterated by the footprint.

Nuri looked away from the picture. It made him feel sick.

He looked upward and saw the sun about to set.

9

While darkness fell over the city, a dark-paneled truck followed in the wake of the police. It drove slowly, two men in dark suits hanging off the sides, watching the remains of the shantytowns they passed.

Stefan sat in the cab with the driver, Aristaeus. He stared ahead at the road, a river of black. The truck's lights were out. Occasionally the truck would hit a bump and the weight in the back would shift. When that happened, Stefan winced, but not greatly enough for the driver to notice.

"There," called out either Tito or Dante, riding the sides in back.

Aristaeus slowed the truck to a stop, silent except for the crunch of gravel. He opened the door and stepped out, and he pulled Stefan after him. Stefan moved without resisting.

Tito and Dante had already dismounted. One carried a shovel, the other a pickax. Stefan could sense dimly what the others felt, the presence of one of the blood, somewhere near here. Aristaeus grinned and waved the two over to the debris-covered field that used to house a few dozen homeless men, and maybe one or two of the fugitive undead.

Tito and Dante walked straight to a pile of charred and splintered wood near the center of the flattened shantytown. Tito began moving the ashes aside with his shovel, and Dante stood aside with his pickax raised. Within minutes, Tito had uncovered a mound of loose dirt.

Aristaeus walked up to the scene. Stefan followed because it was expected of him. This wasn't the first time he had witnessed this tonight, and it wouldn't be the last. Not

until the back of the truck they rode was filled. They we
finishing off some of the last of the Master's enemies
this town. They were uncovering the few who were tryi
to hop a train unseen from the shanties along the track
The Master had choked off most of the other routes o
of town.

Aristaeus nodded, and Dante let the pickax fall on tl
mound, the point of its blade sinking its full length into tl
soft earth. In response, the earth screamed. It was a sour
torturous and brief, more felt than heard. It tore out
chunk of what was left of Stefan's soul.

Around where the pickax had fallen, a trickle of blac
tarlike blood emerged from the ground.

Tito began clearing away the earth, revealing the crea
ture that had buried itself to protect itself from the su
The face was revealed first, eyes staring, mouth packed wit
dirt. He was unremarkable, the face almost anonymous e
cept for the contortion of pain left on it.

Tito cleared off all the dirt from around the body, revea
ing Dante's pickax embedded deep in the chest. While th
was going on, Aristaeus had been staring at his watch.
little after all the dirt was gone, Aristaeus nodded at Dan
and said, "Ten minutes, long enough. He won't get u
again."

Dante pulled out the pickax, slowly and with difficult
The body raised a few inches with the blade before it bega
sliding free from the wound. When the body let it go, f
nally, with a wet sound, it thudded back into the dea
earth.

"Okay," Aristaeus said to Stefan.

Stefan had been here enough times that he didn't nee
elaboration. He reached down, grabbed the corpse by th
shoulders, and began dragging it back toward the truck.

Meanwhile, the trio moved on to another mound c
debris.

The process seemed endless. When it seemed that the
had finally come upon the last transient village, there wa
another to be razed. Events seemed more and more de
tached from reality the deeper into the night it progresse
News of what was happening spread, and occasionally the
would come to a collection of shacks that had been aban

oned earlier in the evening. Even so, things progressed
the same way. The officer with the megaphone would an-
nounce that everyone was under arrest, and then the police
would descend on the empty shantytown, and the firemen
would burn the place down to the ground.

It was one of those near-empty towns where Nuri was
ambushed. He was in the lead, with a collection of officers,
kicking open doors, checking for anyone hiding from the
advance of the police. Not for the first time Nuri was feeling like an officer in the German SS, checking a village
for undesirables.

Then, suddenly, the police were set upon by twice as
many dirty men. The attack caught all of them off guard.
One moment they were walking in the midst of a forest of
empty tar-paper hovels, the next they were surrounded by
angry hobos armed with bricks and broken planks of wood.

The two groups fell on each other as if they were both
in the middle of a war. An officer fell by Nuri's feet, blood
streaming from his temple, and Nuri reached for his gun.

Before he reached it, he felt something slam across the
back of his head. The impact was blinding, and he stumbled
forward. Even the sounds around him seemed blurred as
the world turned to a dark mush around him.

By the time he recovered from the stunning blow, he was
on his knees in the mud, retching. Nuri waited for the dizziness to pass before he opened his eyes and looked around.

There was no sign of the melee around him. He had the
disorienting realization that he didn't know where he was.
From his memory, he had only stumbled a few feet from
where he'd been struck, but from a look around at the
unfamiliar ground, and at how much darker the night was,
he must have been wandering for much longer.

He pushed himself upright from the sour pool by his
knees and tried not to collapse from the sudden wave of
vertigo. After swaying a few moments, he checked himself out.

His hat and his jacket were both gone, but his gun still
sat in its holster. The back of his head was a sore bloody
mess, but his hair was matted. The blood had had time
to clot.

When he took a few steps, he realized that he had lost

one of his shoes in the mud. He cursed and took off th other one so he could walk.

As he made his way to the road, he could see signs the war that Eliot Ness was waging on Cleveland's transien population. Beside him, he could see the remains of raze dwellings where he had passed earlier in the night. Bot sides of the battle were gone. The police gone toward th next collection of hovels, the inhabitants fled or in polic custody.

It was empty, and almost silent.

Almost.

Nuri walked, listening to noises that seemed to com from around a bend in the road. His stockinged feet sli silently on the bricks in the road as he made his way towar an area darker than the rest of the night. Around the benc the road ran under one of the dozens of bridges tha crossed the Cuyahoga. The bridge was a railroad trestle and its girders were a dark spider-web against an overcas sky.

Coming from the darkness beyond, the source hidden b the corner of an abandoned warehouse, were the sound of shoveling earth and shifting debris. Nuri also heard th sound of whispered voices, too low to make out individua words. When he reached the corner of the building h heard a soft, solid thud followed by a brief agonizin scream that abruptly cut off.

The sound seared through Nuri, causing him to close hi eyes so tightly that color shot through his field of vision The sound didn't even last half a second, but Nuri's heac throbbed with it.

He drew his gun, already knowing what was around th corner from him. The darkness beyond was more than jus the shadow of the bridge. His face and hands were slick with sweat, and his breath came in slow shuddering gasps He wanted to run, to abandon this place. But he kept think ing of the time he had seen Stefan and had done nothing but hide.

He eased his way around the corner of the building, hold ing his gun before him. The first thing he saw was a dark silhouette of a panel truck, similar in size to the one he'c been riding. The back was covered, so he couldn't see what the truck carried.

Beyond the dark truck, he could see figures standing in
the midst of one of the ruined shantytowns. He could see
the edge of a shovel and the end of a pickax. As he
watched, one of the figures drew the pickax out of the
ground.

Nuri walked slowly to the side of the truck opposite the
figures. Every step was an effort against a building well of
fear. He knew what he faced. He could almost smell it.
And he didn't have anything that could fight them. He had
the gun, but he had seen the uselessness of it twice now.
A bullet couldn't stop them. . . .

Nuri reached the other side of the cab and looked around
the front of the vehicle. He saw another figure dragging
what could only be a body from where the figures had
congregated. The others walked away from the hole they
had made.

They can die, Nuri told himself. He had seen them dead
by fire, by sunlight, and by decapitation. He had no fire,
and sunlight was hours away, but he dwelled on decapitation. These things still had brains, and they couldn't func-
tion without them. . . .

Nuri took a few deep breaths and began a crouched run
from the front of the truck, around the debris, circling upon
the three shadowy figures. The terrain tore at his feet, but
he kept running, closing on them.

He was only a few dozens yards away when his foot
slipped on a broken piece of wood. The three of them
stopped and turned. Nuri could recognize Aristaeus immediately, even in the darkness.

Aristaeus held out a hand, as if to silence his two companions. The one carrying the pickax looked directly at
Nuri with a stare that froze the blood in his veins.

Nuri swallowed his fear and braced his gun with both
hands.

Aristaeus waved his hand, wearing an expression near a
smile. Nuri was sure he saw him, and recognized him.

In response to Aristaeus' small wave, the other two ran
for him. Nuri felt the impulse to flee, to run as fast as he
could, get away even if there was no way to outrun them
at the speed they were going.

Instead he brought the gun up to point at the face of the

one with the pickax. As that one brought the pickax bear against Nuri, Nuri fired, twice.

When Nuri fired they were only separated by about fiv yards. The shot was impossible to miss. The pickax fell t the ground as its bearer's head snapped back with tw holes erupting in its face. The whole back of the sku seemed to have evaporated. The body dropped to th ground.

Before the body hit the ground, Nuri could see a shove swinging at him. He dropped and rolled out of its way barely fast enough. The blade grazed his head, hard enoug that he almost blacked out.

Nuri rolled, pointing his revolver upward, toward his a tacker. The shovel was coming downward as his gun fired One shot missed, throwing sparks as it glanced off the blad of the shovel, the other shot found its home in his attack er's forehead.

The shovel still came down, but slowly enough for Nu to dodge it. The blade buried itself into the ground next t Nuri's right shoulder. The body followed, face-first into th ground next to the shovel, the back of the skull a sof dark mess.

Nuri pushed himself away from the body, scrambling up ward to face the last of them, Aristaeus.

He turned on Aristaeus and saw a gun pointed at him Aristaeus hadn't moved from where he stood, and he wa much too far away for a sure head shot. Nuri saw all thi in a moment and dived behind a pile of broken wood.

He dove just in time, because he heard Aristaeus' gu fire, and he could swear he felt the breeze as the bulle passed between his neck and his shoulder.

He landed on a pile of shredded tar paper, nails tearin into his legs and his left arm.

Aristaeus called out to him, "Good job, Lapidos. Thos two will be out for a few minutes, at least. Probably neve get their minds back, such as they were. But that's just a almost. What do you think your chances are now? I ca see out here like it was full daylight, I can smell your bloo now, and my reflexes are twice yours." Nuri could hear th crunch of Aristaeus' footsteps as he closed on his hidin place.

"I know exactly where you are," he kept talking. "If yo

ove, I can put three bullets into you before you aim. But
ll make you an offer. Toss out your gun, offer me your
lood, and you might have a new life."

Nuri swallowed. His throat felt dry.

"I've wanted both of you since the train, Lapidos. I
dn't have to miss just then."

The gun in front of him was shaking. Blood was soaking
to his clothes from the wounds tearing into his arms and
gs, blood also dripped from his head, blurring his vision.
uri's breaths were beginning to sear his throat.

He was going to have to dive out there and try to shoot
ristaeus. He didn't have a choice.

He tightened his grip on the revolver, and prepared to
pring out from his limited cover. Then he heard some-
ing.

Aristaeus was still talking, but beneath the sound of his
oice was something else, a rustling sound, as if the ground
ere shifting. At first Nuri thought it was Aristaeus, but as
he sound became louder, Aristaeus stopped talking, as if
e'd just noticed the sound.

Whatever the distraction was, Nuri took the opportunity
o spring from his cover and level his gun at Aristaeus. But
vhen he saw Aristaeus, he didn't fire.

Aristaeus was only ten feet away from him, but he had
urned away from him. Aristaeus was facing something that
vas rising from the ground, clawing its way from a mound
f earth. He wasn't talking to Nuri anymore.

As Nuri watched, Aristaeus fired four shots into the
hadow clawing its way out of the earth. The thing showed
o sign of being hit. It pulled itself upright in front of Arisaeus, dirt crumbling off of its shoulders. From the mid-
hest up to its head, half of it was frozen. Half its face, and
he right side of its chest was a twisted, pale representation
f a human body, milk-white and frozen in a contortion
f agony.

The other half was out of a nightmare, fanged like a
lemon, one arm as long as Aristaeus' body and ending in
taloned claw. It stared at Aristaeus with a face that was
half a human corpse, and half a gargoyle. The human eye
vas pale and clouded, staring at nothing, the other eye was
ed, and as deep as hell itself, and stared directly at
ristaeus.

Aristaeus' gun shook and he pulled the trigger again. The gun clicked home on an empty chamber.

The thing's arm swung up toward Aristaeus and clampe home on his neck. Aristaeus dropped the gun and his bod began changing. Nuri could hear the sound of stresse bone, and the sound of flesh tearing like canvas. But wha ever was happening to Aristaeus was happening too late t do him any good.

The demonic arm lifted Aristaeus off of the ground, an Nuri could see blood flowing from where the taloned fir gers were crushing Aristaeus windpipe. Aristaeus clawed the arm, kicked at the open air, and made strangled blood noises. In a few moments he wasn't moving and the bod had regained a semblance of humanity.

Nuri didn't move.

The half-thing drew Aristaeus' body toward itself an turned its monstrous face so its half-muzzle could smell th corpse. Its face wrinkled, and it tossed the body aside as disgusted by it.

Then it turned its attention to Nuri. Nuri raised his gu to level on the animate half of the thing's face, but its on living eye held him in an iron grip impossible to break Nuri fell into that one blood-red eye as if he was fallin into a sea of fire.

Its taloned hand grabbed its opposite shoulder, the on that was human flesh, from which hung a dead human arm It grumbled something, almost unintelligible through hal of a nonhuman mouth.

In the grip of that thing's stare, Nuri could understan the words.

"Useless," it said. "Dead already."

It drew closer, and the smell of rot almost dropped Nur to his knees. It looked down at Nuri, its body rearrangin with the sound of breaking bone and tearing skin. Fang and talons withdrew. As its arm came away from its shoul der Nuri saw that the dead human part of its body wa pockmarked with sores that wept a fluid that smelled o rotting meat.

"Too far gone," it said as it grabbed Nuri's shoulder wit the arm that had killed Aristaeus. The arm was huma now, and the face that was within inches of Nuri's own wa now fully human, half trapped in a putrefying death-agony the other half twisted in a expression of frustration and despair.

"I cannot drink with half a mouth," it whispered, and closed its one demonic eye. When the stare left him, Nuri was able to move again. He backed quickly away, the thing releasing its grip on him.

It collapsed before him. "Too shallow," it whispered.

Nuri backed away from the thing that now was only a naked human corpse. He had only taken a few steps when he felt something grab his shoulder. He spun around and fired.

Nuri had a brief glimpse of his face as the bullet tore into Stefan's throat. He scrambled backward as Stefan grabbed the injury and fell to his knees. Blood spread from Stefan's mouth and from both sides of the wound. He swayed on his knees, and for a moment Nuri was certain that he had killed him.

Then he saw the edges of the exposed wound pulling together, as if the flesh was so much bleeding clay. He backed away from Stefan, and glanced back toward where the first two lay. The first one, the one who held a pickax, was still face down, but now his head was intact, and his limbs were beginning to vibrate as if he was having a seizure.

The wounded Stefan still knelt in front of him, but the wound was almost gone. He was hissing, and his face was distorting.

Nuri had one bullet left. He wanted to run, but he couldn't abandon Stefan again. Nuri looked into Stefan's face, and saw eyes that seemed a well of pain slicing into his mind. Nuri stepped to the side as Stefan lowered his lengthening hands from the wound in his neck. The only sign of the damage now was the blood. He reached a clawed hand toward Nuri as Nuri edged around him.

Nuri brought the butt of his gun down across the back of Stefan's skull. Stefan's eyes widened as a clawed hand grabbed Nuri's leg. Nuri brought the gun down again.

Stefan's eyes rolled and he fell forward.

Nuri looked at his friend's body and sucked in copper breaths as he looked for signs of life. The body didn't seem to breathe. Nuri was almost certain Stefan was dead, until he looked closely at the gash where his gun had landed.

Even in the dark he could see the edges of the wound knitting together.

Close by he heard moaning coming from the two he had shot in the head. The sound was mindless and chilling. He had to get out of here.

This time he wasn't going to leave Stefan.

He holstered his gun, grabbed Stefan by the shoulders, and began dragging him back toward the dark truck that was still parked by the road. The ground cut into his feet as he made his way backwards toward the road.

The moaning began to sound like an animal growl. He couldn't see any of the bodies any more. They had been lost in the darkness. Nuri's heart raced as the growls deepened, and seemed to move.

They seemed to come from all directions, echoing beneath the bridge, getting louder.

Nuri backed into the door of the truck, and he scrambled to get the door open and drag Stefan's unconscious body inside. Nuri was halfway across the seat, Stefan only half in the truck, when something leaped at the cab. Part of the roof caved inward, and the glass in the front window shattered, spraying shards across Nuri and Stefan.

Nuri was only half in the driver's seat, and he tried to run the clutch and the gas with one foot as he hit the starter. The engine made evil grinding noises as he shifted, but it lurched forward.

Nuri was driving and trying to pull Stefan all the way into the door when something else hit the truck hard enough to make it swerve slightly.

Nuri drove the truck as fast as he could push it, rocketing through the uneven roads of the Flats. As the truck shook across the broken pavement, something landed on top of the hood of the truck. It had jumped off of the top of the cab and it smashed the hood inward. The thing was wolflike, its face a naked slavering muzzle filled with dagger teeth. Across its leathery torso, it wore the bloody remnants of a cheap suit.

Nuri swerved the truck madly, trying to shake this thing off the front. It hung on tenaciously, talons piercing the truck's hood, twisting the metal into handholds for it.

It gibbered madly at him, nonsense syllables combined with an animal growling. It leaned into the driver's side, opening its jaws to tear at him. Nuri jerked the wheel to the left, trying to evade the creature's bite.

The truck jumped the curb and slammed head-on into a low brick wall. Nuri was thrown against the wheel with a force enough to crack his ribs. The thing on the hood tumbled backwards into the remains of the wall.

Nuri tried a few futile times to get the truck moving again, but the engine just whined at him. Something was moving in the back, and Nuri smelled gas. He reached over Stefan and tried to open the passenger door. When it didn't give, Nuri raised his foot and kicked it open. The door sprang open and Stefan fell out into the street.

Nuri scrambled out of the cab.

Even though the creature on the hood was buried under a pile of bricks, it still moved. Nuri heard the grinding sound of bricks rubbing together.

As he grabbed Stefan's collar and began dragging his unconscious form across the street, something began tearing at the canvas cover over the rear of the truck—tearing from the inside. Nuri could see the claws sticking out of the canvas as it shredded the cover.

Nuri allowed one hand for Stefan and pulled out his gun with the other. He hesitated, because the smell of gas was everywhere, even his stocking feet felt newly wet. Back by the truck, the ground glistened. Nuri kept backing away, saving his shot.

But he had little chance. In a moment the thing in the back had torn itself free of the canvas. It was even larger and more feral-looking than the one that had landed on the hood. And it still carried the pickax.

The other one had freed itself from the tumbled masonry, and it stood on the cab, turning toward Nuri.

Nuri fired.

The shot was wild, with him firing one-handed. It sparked off the brick street in front of the truck. As Nuri had feared, the glistening street erupted into a sheet of fire.

Nuri dropped the gun and grabbed Stefan with his other hand. He had dragged Stefan through the puddle of gasoline, and he was soaked with it. Nuri pulled him backward as fast as he could, as flames enveloped the broken truck.

He made it to the other side of the street, to a small ditch filled with stagnant water. He rolled Stefan into it and followed, more concerned with the fire than any demonic pursuit.

It wasn't until he was standing ankle-deep in the drainage ditch that he thought of the two creatures by the truck. He looked back.

In a few seconds the truck had become little more than shadow in a rolling sheet of fire. From the fire came a high breathless wail that Nuri knew didn't come from the flames. On either side of the truck were two humanoid figures, themselves little more than shadows wrapped in fire. They were moving away from the burning vehicle, but even as they stepped out of the radius of fire, the fire accompanied them. Neither made it more than ten feet before collapsing on the street.

On the street in front of Nuri, he could see his own footsteps blaze and gutter out.

10

The burning of Cleveland's shantytowns was only the prelude. Police descended on the Roaring Third in a house-to-house search for the murderer. Even as police kicked in doors and crawled through every room in the precinct, looking for signs of the killing ground, the papers were beginning to sound sour notes about Ness.

The press couldn't stop what had become the largest manhunt in the city's, and perhaps the nation's, history. The house-to-house search found prostitutes and pimps, gambling halls and numbers runners, conmen, thieves, and hustlers . . .

But no killing ground.

The priest's office was crowded by bookshelves and files. Papers towered over Nuri. The man behind the desk, Father Gerwazek, was older than Nuri expected, his hair snow-white, his hands liver-spotted. Aside from that, the man gave a reassuring impression of solidity.

The priest pushed his thick glasses back on his nose and looked at Nuri, "But you won't tell me this man's name?"

Nuri shook his head. "I've told you all I can."

"But you want me to agree to come with you and retain your confidence?" Gerwazek shook his head. "You're asking a lot from an old man."

"My friend needs a priest," Nuri felt odd saying that.

Nuri had already seen his own rabbi, for the first time in years. While he never had the courage to explain fully what had happened, Rabbi Schimmel had heard enough from Nuri to realize that they'd been talking about a Catholic man in some sort of spiritual crisis. "If this man was a

Jew," he'd said, "would you take him a priest? It's his faith
not yours." Nuri had still almost taken his friend to temple
while he was still unconscious. In the end he had thought
better, and followed Rabbi Schimmel's advice. It wasn't his
belief that mattered, it was Stefan's, and the beliefs of those
things in the darkness.

Nuri shook his head. "I've done what I can for him, and
it isn't enough."

"And you won't tell me where he is?"

"It's better if you don't know."

Gerwazek seemed to debate with himself for a moment
and then asked, "What made you decide to come to me?"

"I think my friend used to be part of your parish."

After a while Father Gerwazek sighed and said, "I won't
turn away a request for aid, even if the secrecy makes me
uncomfortable."

"Thank you," Nuri said, standing and offering his hand.
"If it makes you feel better, think of this as a confession."

Nuri drove Gerwazek in a borrowed unmarked car. The
priest made few comments as Nuri drove, aside from asking
him once if he was Catholic. More than once Nuri wondered if he was doing the right thing. He was at the end
of his rope. He couldn't think of anything else to do. Stefan
needed help, and the help he needed seemed way beyond
anything he could provide.

Eventually he drove through the Euclid entrance to
Lakeview Cemetery.

"Here?" Gerwazek asked, voice uncertain.

Nuri nodded. "I needed a special place. I suppose a
church would be better." Nuri maneuvered the car through
twisting roads until he had passed a few hills into a quiet
part of the cemetery. Behind them the sky was a flaming
red beyond the imposing mass of the Garfield Monument.

When Nuri parked the car, Gerwazek put a hand on his
arm. "Where is your friend?"

Nuri nodded up the hill, toward a large tomb set up on
the hillside. "There's a small chapel in there."

"He's in there?" Gerwazek stared at him for a long time,
his eyes distorted by his thick glasses. "Mr. Lapidos," he
asked, "is your friend alive?"

Nuri let the silence stretch for a long time.

Gerwazek squeezed his arm and said, "Mr. Lapidos?"

"I don't know how to answer that question."

The priest just stared at him, and Nuri could almost feel his own foreboding rubbing off on the priest. Nuri turned and said, "We have to wait until sunset."

"I'm not sure this is a good idea," Gerwazek muttered, more to himself than to Nuri.

"I can take you back," Nuri said. He wasn't going to force anyone's involvement in this. There would be other priests—

"No, no," Gerwazek waved his hand, dismissing the thought. He was now staring up at the tomb on the hill. "Are you going to tell me now what is going on?"

"I think it'd be best to wait until you see him." Nuri turned to watch what of the sunset he could see behind the Garfield Monument. The color slowly drained out of the sky, the monument darkening until it was only a squat silhouette. He turned to the priest and said. "I should warn you though, I've had to restrain him."

Gerwazek didn't respond; he just continued to stare up at the tomb.

Nuri didn't let them leave the car until the last of the daylight had leaked from the sky. The place where they'd parked was in enough shadow that Nuri grabbed a flashlight so they could see their way to the tomb. Nuri went slowly, in deference to Gerwazek's age, but the priest seemed to take the climb better than he did.

"Why here?" Gerwazek asked as they reached the wrought-iron gate barring the door to the tomb.

"Because of the chapel," Nuri said. "A church would have been better, but I couldn't take him to one without too many questions." Nuri opened the gate; it was unlocked. "There are dark things connected to him now, things that are probably searching for him. I'm hoping that blessed ground might protect both of us."

Inside the tomb, there was a soft groaning. The sound was quiet, but it cut through the walls as if the stone was paper.

Gerwazek stared at the closed door.

"He's awake," Nuri told him. He could see the first signs of what might have been fear cross the priest's face.

Nuri pushed the inner door open on the darkened chamber, and took Gerwazek's arm. "Come on. He needs our help."

They took a few steps inside, and Nuri swept the flashlight until it landed on Stefan.

"Christ preserve us." Gerwazek crossed himself.

Stefan lay on the floor, under the flashlight beam. His clothes were filthy, torn, and covered with blood. The faint smell of gasoline still hung around him.

His arms and legs were tied, and he was cowering in a corner as if trying to escape the cross on the wall above him.

He turned to face Nuri and Gerwazek, his face sunken and pale, too close to the face of a corpse. "Let me return to Him," he said in a whispery voice that was little louder than the wind outside. Even so, the words cut into Nuri's ears as if they'd been shouted at him.

Nuri responded, "I brought you a priest."

"More torture," Stefan turned to look at Gerwazek. His eyes were dead, empty, black, though when Nuri looked into them, he thought something moved inside that darkness.

Gerwazek must have seen it, too, because he crossed himself again.

"I know you," Stefan said to Gerwazek.

Gerwazek nodded, staring at him. "What happened to you, Stefan?"

Stefan laughed. The sound was weak, almost silent. "Can't you smell it, Father? I've been damned. I've been dragged so far into the abyss that your presence is painful to me." Stefan turned away to face the wall. "Tell him to let me go, Father. Let me return to the darkness where I belong."

Gerwazek turned toward Nuri, "What have you done to him?"

"I had to restrain him, for his protection as well as mine—"

Gerwazek looked up toward the ceiling whose shroud of darkness wasn't pierced by the flashlight. "But here? He should be in a hospital."

Nuri shook his head. "Anywhere else, and he would die

ith the morning light. Anywhere else, and I'm sure his
master would come for him."

"His master?" Gerwazek said. He looked down at Stefan, who had withdrawn into a silent immobility. He walked
toward Stefan, his shadow falling across Stefan's body. "Mr.
Lapidos," he said as he knelt over Stefan's body, "you have
to explain all this if you don't want me to report what's
going on to the police."

Nuri walked up next to Gerwazek and said, "I am the
police."

"Do your superiors know that you're keeping prisoners
in a cemetery?"

Nuri shook his head.

Gerwazek reached out a hand and felt Stefan's neck.
"He's cold as ice."

"Be careful—"

"He's *dead*."

"No, he isn't."

Gerwazek turned to face Nuri and said, "There's no
pulse at all. You've killed him."

"Watch out," Nuri said. Gerwazek turned, but a bit too
late. Stefan had already turned his head and sank suddenly
long teeth into the meat of Gerwazek's hand. Gerwazek
gasped.

"Damn it," Nuri said. He raised his flashlight and
brought it down across Stefan's face. The light went out
momentarily. When the flashlight flickered on again, Nuri
saw that it had been enough of a distraction for Gerwazek
to pull his hand free.

Gerwazek held his bleeding hand and stared at Stefan.
Nuri stared as well. As they watched, Stefan's nose,
smashed by the flashlight, reordered itself, straightening,
shrinking, healing itself. The fangs also withdrew. In a few
moments all that was left of the incident was the smeared
blood on Stefan's face.

"What is this?" Gerwazek said quietly.

"Do you believe in vampires, Father?"

11

Stefan wondered how long they could keep him like this. They had shut him up in a small room. Stefan suspected it was underneath Father Gerwazek's church, St. John's. He had not fed for days, and most of the time he was too weak to get off of the small cot in the room.

He wondered if it was possible for him to die of the hunger that gnawed inside him.

Most of the time he just lay on the cot, eyes shut, feeling the void eat away inside him, only noting the passage of the day by the crushing fatigue that tried to claim him. Despite that, he never truly slept, not even the non-sleep that normally claimed him in the daylight hours.

Worst of all, every night, Father Gerwazek would come in and talk to him. The man's faith was a burning presence, uncomfortable to be near, and the smell of his blood was an agony—an agony that was never sated since Father Gerwazek would always stay behind the door to the room, too wary to enter after Stefan's first taste of his blood.

This night was like every other night so far. Gerwazek was at the door, the smell of his blood permeated the room, igniting Stefan's painful thirst. He talked to Stefan, saying, "God has not abandoned you."

Stefan's voice didn't rise above a whisper. He stared at the ceiling as he said, "I was taken from God's sight."

"No one has that power, Stefan."

"You know nothing of what happened to me." Stefan's whisper became harsh with anger. Father Gerwazek should smell Satan within him, the same way Stefan could smell the priest's untainted blood. He should see Stefan with the

athing and fear that Stefan felt burn into him every time
e saw that ember of faith burning behind Gerwazek's eyes.

"Our savior died for the wickedness of the world. That
edemption is open to anyone who will take it. The only
ne who can deny that to you is yourself."

Stefan sprang at the door and screamed, "You know
othing of what happened to me." On the other side of
ie door, he could hear Gerwazek stumble backward.

"He ripped away any connection I had with your God
hen He damned me with His communion. I can't look
pon your blessed icons without pain; if I mouth the words
f your faith, my tongue cracks and bleeds. My presence
ere, in a place you deem holy, is a painful fire within me.
Iy soul is destroyed, all your salvation offers me now is
ie destruction of my body." Stefan slammed the stone wall
ext to the door with his hand. The impact was hard
nough to resonate the wooden door and splatter blood
cross his arm.

He pulled his hand away from the wall, the skin flayed
ver the knuckles. As Stefan watched, the skin pulled itself
ack over the wounds with a tearing sensation that was
ore painful than the impact.

"You cannot save me," Stefan said as he watched his
and restructure itself.

"You aren't dead—" Gerwazek said from the other side
f the door.

"Yes, I am," Stefan said. "Yes, I am."

"You still walk the Earth," the priest said. "That means
ou are still open to Christ's redemption."

"I was killed, my soul damned, and my body cursed to
alk the Earth. Don't you understand? Every legend casts
ie beyond the pale—"

"I know, I know. But you aren't dead, Stefan. You may
ave been infected with a dread affliction. But that cannot
estroy your soul."

"But—"

"Those legends were propagated by people who believed
aat any disease was either a curse from Satan or a judg-
ient for your sins."

"You don't know what you're talking about."

"Perhaps you don't know either," Gerwazek said. "What
know is that, while your affliction is novel to my experi-

ence, the idea that God has abandoned you is all too com
mon." Gerwazek paused before he finished. "Every time
I've seen that, it has been the person who's abandone
God, not the reverse."

"Do you think I chose this?" Stefan screamed at th
door. *"You think I wanted this to happen?"*

He heard Gerwazek move away from the door. "Perhap
I should go now."

"This was taken from me," Stefan said, collapsing agains
the door. The smell of blood, the hunger, was all forgotten
All Stefan felt was a deeper and even more painful void
"He took this all from me."

Gerwazek had left him, and all Stefan could do was lea
against the door and weep.

12

Nuri came to Gerwazek's church regularly now. He never felt completely at ease there, but he needed to see Stefan. In an odd sort of way it was beginning to have an effect on his own faith. He was going to temple more, and beginning to pay a little more attention to the sabbath.

It was as if he was fighting off the visits to the church, trying to purge the Christian iconography that struck him every time he came here.

Each time he came, he told himself that Stefan might have improved. Each time he was disappointed. Nuri was coming close to giving up, even if Father Gerwazek wasn't.

He reached the church just when the day was dying. It was a small, unpretentious building in the middle of the Slovenian neighborhood near St. Clair and East Fifty-Fifth. It was an old wood-frame building that offered no competition to the stone cathedrals that congregated downtown, or even to the much closer St. Vitus, which served most of the surrounding community. This place predated the erection of St. Vitus by several decades, but looked as redundant as Nuri guessed it was.

The Civil War-era building was marked as Catholic only by a small sign and an unobtrusive statue of Mary standing next to the front stairs.

Nuri walked through a wrought-iron gate, and around to the side of the whitewashed building just as the last of the daylight was bleeding away from the sky.

The side entrance led to the basement. No one was there to greet him. He had passed this way often enough that no one paid much attention to him.

Nuri walked back into a rear chamber, inside which was

a small trapdoor that was barred with a padlock. Nuri had
the key, and opened it.

As old as this structure was, it was built on the founda-
tion of an even older structure. Gerwazek had explained
that his building had once been a stop on the underground
railroad during the Civil War. Under the basement was an
old hiding place.

It was dark and damp down here. The walls were thick
and made of local stone. The floor was packed earth. The
only signs of this century were the two bare light bulbs
dangling from the wooden rafters holding up the floor
above, and the stacks of wooden folding chairs.

Nuri wove his way through the narrow passages until he
reached an old oak door blocking off one of the chambers.
He was still a few paces from the door when he heard a
whisper cut through the darkness.

"Nuri," it said. The quality of the word made Nuri shiver.
Stefan had gained the odd ability to be perfectly understood even when his voice was just on the cusp of audibility.

"Yes," Nuri responded, even though it wasn't a question.

"When will you free me?" Stefan's whisper, and its ech-
oes, seemed to fill the space underground.

Nuri stepped up to the door and slid aside the cover on
its small inset window. The room beyond had the same
stone walls, and a single incandescent bulb. A cot sat in
the corner, the only real furniture in the room. The floor
was scattered with dishes from the abortive attempts to
feed Stefan—he was long past solid food.

"We're *trying* to free you," Nuri said.

Stefan laughed, a rattling whispery sound. Stefan turned
his face toward Nuri. He was so emaciated now that it
wasn't until he moved that Nuri could tell him from the
rumpled blanket on the cot.

"Kill me, then," he whispered. His eyes stared into
Nuri's, open pits that were much too large for his sunken
face. They tried to suck Nuri in, but he had enough experience now to avert his gaze. There was something about eye
contact that tried to impose Stefan's will on him.

"We're trying to save you—"

"*Save me?*" Stefan said. "I'm past saving. Melchior took
that from me. . . ."

Nuri shook his head. "We're trying to save you from Melchior."

Stefan laughed, "You cannot save *yourself* from Melchior. I have His blood in my veins. I'm a part of Him. How can you undo that?"

"Tell me more about it," Nuri said. He'd taken out a notebook and a pencil. "About Melchior's blood."

He could hear Stefan lay back into his cot. "The blood is everything to us. Mind, body, soul, the blood contains it all, controls it all. Those of the blood, we call ourselves that because we're bound it, anchored to it. Because Melchior's blood flows in my veins, I have a piece of his damned soul within my own."

Nuri understood. Stefan was what Iago had once called a thrall. A slave to an older vampire. In some sense, that was what Nuri was hoping to free Stefan from. It had to be possible; otherwise there would be no such thing as a free vampire.

"Your own blood flows in your veins, too."

Stefan sighed. "What is my blood against Melchior's power? His will commands my flesh."

"Then why doesn't it command you here?"

"Perhaps he thinks I'm truly dead now," Stefan said. "Maybe I am, and in hell. I suspect that's what hell is, being trapped with this hunger."

"Maybe Melchior isn't omnipotent," Nuri said. "Somewhere you believe you're on holy ground. Maybe that belief holds him at bay. Maybe he can't control you through these walls." Nuri wasn't certain of that. He wasn't certain of anything. He hoped, and the hope now seemed to have basis in fact since Melchior had not shown up to claim his thrall. He was certain that it was Stefan's belief that was the only thing that could save him.

Stefan emitted a tired laugh that chilled Nuri. "Maybe I'm not important enough for Satan to care."

"Melchior isn't Satan," Nuri said.

"You don't know," Stefan said. "You haven't seen him in his glory, you haven't had him in your mind. He killed me, then he killed my soul. . . ."

The conversation spun again, full circle. Every time it led around again to the same point. The talks were a little longer each day, but they always began and ended the same way.

"He isn't Satan," Nuri said. "He's a monster, but he was a man once, just like you."

"Not like me, not like any of us."

Nuri slammed his fist against the door frame, "Why don't you even *try* to fight him?"

There was a long silence before Stefan said, "You think I haven't tried? When I see what he's done, what he's going to do? But even the *thoughts* sear me, like being in this cell, on this ground. Even though Melchior has forgotten me, his blood remembers."

"Fight his blood, then," Nuri said. "Melchior isn't here. It's just you and me. You have a mind, you have a will, *why can't you use it!*"

"Because . . ." Stefan's voice trailed off.

The silence was long and dark. After a few minutes, Nuri said, "Stefan?"

"Leave me," came Stefan's voice.

Nuri spoke again a few times, trying to entice Stefan—then trying to anger him—into talking. Stefan didn't break his silence. Nuri stood by the door for a long time hoping Stefan would change his mind, but he didn't speak again.

Eventually Nuri sighed and left him.

13

Fight his blood.

The thoughts echoed through Stefan's fevered brain.
It was a statement that was pathetically simple, but it
seared itself inside his mind like a revelation.

The blood was the life, the soul, the will, the flesh . . .

And the blood was the chain that bound him.

"Am I evil, then? This your Bible says?"

"You feast on the living."

*"Didn't your savior say to drink of his blood? Eat of
his flesh?"*

Memories flew through his mind as he waited for the
priest. What he wanted was insane, blasphemous, perhaps
even suicidal—but he knew that Gerwazek wouldn't refuse
him. Hunger burned in him as he waited, flaring brighter
than it ever had. The aching lack inside him was worse
than it ever had been. What was left of his pulse throbbed
in his temples.

*"Our will, our soul, everything within us is bound within
the blood. Our blood controls the flesh, moving it to our
will."*

The wait seemed interminable. It seemed that he
drowned in the hunger of his own decision for weeks before
Gerwazek visited him. Every moment of that time was
spent in a mental battle with the parts of himself that
weren't himself. Every shred of his mind, every fragment
of his will, spent every conscious moment holding on to the
decision, keeping it from sliding under the pain of Melchi-
or's will.

Stefan drew some strength from the desperation he felt

in that pain. It was as if the part of Melchior that lived inside him knew what he planned.

And he took bread, and gave thanks, and brake it, and gave unto them, saying, "This is my body which is given for you: this do in remembrance of me."

Likewise also the cup after supper, saying, "This cup is the new testament in my blood, which is shed for you . . ."

The words seared in his brain worse than the image of any cross, or his presence in the house of God. But somehow he held on to the verse in his mind, despite the pain.

When Gerwazek came, it was Stefan who spoke first.

"Father?" he whispered from his cot. He was almost too weak to move his lips, and his body was drenched in sweat from the mental effort he had been maintaining since Nur had left him with his newfound determination.

"Yes, Stefan?" Gerwazek said. His voice was hesitant, as if Stefan had taken him off-guard. Perhaps he had heard something portentous in Stefan's voice.

"I want to take communion," Stefan said.

The resulting silence seemed to last an eternity.

Convincing Father Gerwazek took longer than Stefan expected. Apparently their meeting in the graveyard chapel had made a deep impression on the priest. It took all the strength Stefan could muster to convince Gerwazek that he wasn't going to lose control like that again.

Stefan also had to convince himself of that. The smell of Gerwazek on the other side of the door, the presence of that much living blood, ignited a hunger that rendered what Stefan had felt in the graveyard insignificant by comparison.

While every shred of Stefan's will was concentrated on the burning image of Communion, the well of hunger inside him tore at every fiber of his body. Every cell was pulled by the desire to feed, and the pull was only checked by the image in Stefan's mind, an image that pained him worse than the need for blood.

Eventually the talk ceased. The memory of the words fell away from Stefan's mind, which only had room for the image, the hunger, and the pain. Gerwazek left for a time and for that time the hunger ebbed.

When Gerwazek returned, the hunger returned a hundredfold. When Gerwazek opened the door, the first time it had been opened while Stefan was conscious, the sensation, the *need*, slammed into his brain like a runaway train. The presence of Gerwazek, suddenly within reach, tore Stefan apart inside.

The tattered part of his will, holding onto the sacred image, was briefly torn apart by the screaming hunger from every part of his body. Stefan leaped to his feet, for the moment possessed only by a savage instinct to fill the burning void inside him with the pulsing life he felt moving just beneath Gerwazek's skin.

Stefan grabbed Gerwazek's robed wrist, and their eyes met. Stefan could in a brief moment see everything through the priest's eyes. He saw the fortress of the man's faith, he saw his pity for him, and he saw fear. . . .

Stefan saw the fear, and it gave him enough pause to draw the painful shreds of his will together. Somehow he looked at Gerwazek, at the life flowing through his veins, and feeling the demonic need tearing at every muscle, every nerve, he managed to fall to his knees.

Slowly he unclenched his hand from Gerwazek's wrist and said, "Thank you, Father."

Genuflecting in front of Gerwazek, naked, his bony knees scraping on the stone floor, the bonfire hunger raging inside him, that was the first moment he really believed he might not be completely lost.

That thought, a tiny kernel of faith, gave him the strength to reimagine Christ, reimagine the body and the blood. It gave him enough will to deny the physical hunger.

Gerwazek was visibly shaken as he took the gifts, the wine, the chalice, and the Communion wafer, and began the ritual. Before this moment, the presence of these icons of his lost faith would have been as painful as a brand.

He could look at them now without shrinking away. The pain was there, their presence seared themselves into his consciousness, but now it was as if it was something else inside of himself that was burning, something he could distance himself from.

Gerwazek broke the wafer and raised the chalice, and as he spoke in solemn Latin it was as if the entire room had become a kiln. The pain had progressed a thousand times beyond simple hunger. It was as if his flesh, each individual cell of his body, had burst into a slow fire that burned without consuming. Every muscle tensed and froze, as if it was tearing itself from the bone. Stefan felt as if his skin should blacken, crack and fall away in the presence of the glory. He had lost the ability to move voluntarily, and his body began to vibrate.

The vibration soon came close to a seizure. He swayed in place, kneeling on the floor, his upper body trying to shake itself apart.

Gerwazek held a part of the holy wafer in front of him. To Stefan, through blurred eyes, the wafer seemed to glow with an arc of light white enough to sear the back of his eyes with a purple afterimage.

Gerwazek hesitated.

Somehow Stefan managed to croak the word, "Please."

Gerwazek stepped forward until the only thing that Stefan could see, the only thing he could perceive, was the host. Then it touched him.

The sensation was falling into a molten cauldron of lead, swallowing the metal, having it sear every layer of his flesh from the inside out. Stefan could feel his flesh burn and crack. He could feel jets of flame shooting from deep inside the bone as it carbonized. He felt the consumption of his entire body except for the nerves that transmitted his pain. He felt his soul dragged screaming through every level of purgatory . . .

Then he opened his eyes and saw the light bulb dangling from the ceiling. He rose, every joint an agony to move, but the pain nothing compared to the immolation. He put his hands together in front of him. The skin was intact. Everything he had felt had been inside him, inside his mind.

He said, "Amen," in response to the priest's words he had never heard.

Gerwazek stared at him, and Stefan nodded.

Gerwazek picked up the chalice.

Fight his blood, Nuri had said. With God's help, that was what Stefan was trying to do. What better way to fight the blood of a devil than with the blood of Christ?

It didn't matter now what happened. Stefan had beaten Melchior. He could feel the part of Melchior inside him, screaming. For it, the pain had not yet ended.

Stefan took the wine. Again, it was a scalding heat inside him, but this time was a light and a life far beyond what he could have taken from Gerwazek. It filled the void inside him, pushing aside the hunger. It kept filling, and spreading, pushing through him, displacing Melchior—

Gerwazek said something that wasn't part of the ceremony and crossed himself.

He repeated, "Christ preserve us."

In front of him, Stefan's hands, clasped in prayer, were bleeding. Stefan stood, slowly, feeling the glory burning within him. He separated his hands and saw the open wounds on them, spilling blood, Melchior's blood, pooling in his palms and spilling over onto the stone floor.

Other wounds had opened, on his feet, on his side, on his brow. . . .

He stood in front of Gerwazek, spilling blood from his own stigmata. He looked at his hands, said, "Amen," and collapsed.

14

When Nuri arrived at St. John's, it was nearly three in the morning. He burst into the priest's office.

"What happened?" he demanded before he was completely through the door.

Gerwazek nodded slowly. His skin looked waxy and pale, and he sat behind his desk dressed for Mass. Nuri slowed his approach when he saw that the satin robes were spotted with dirt and blood.

"What happened?" Nuri asked, softer this time. All Gerwazek had said on the phone, about fifteen minutes ago, was that he should come quickly.

Gerwazek looked at Nuri with eyes that were heavy and bloodshot. "Maybe a miracle?" Gerwazek looked down at his hands. Nuri saw a wound on his right wrist and shuddered.

"Did Stefan attack you?"

Gerwazek shook his head. "No, he asked—he begged. After what I had seen, could I deny him?".

Nuri walked around the desk, put his hand on Gerwazek's shoulder and knelt so he was at eye level with the priest. "What happened with Stefan? What did you see?"

"He took Communion." The statement lay heavy on the air. Nuri's mind raced through all the possibilities of what might have happened. A vampire was supposed to cringe from things holy—at least things Christian—what would Communion do to Stefan?

"He took the wafer, and I thought he was going to die. I never thought I'd see a demon possessing someone, but that's what it was. A demon throwing him to the ground, tearing at his own flesh. Then he came back, was rational, took the wine—" Gerwazek shook his head as if he couldn't believe it. "I saw him become the image of Christ. I saw him bleed from the wounds of the crucifixion—"

"He took your blood?"

"He collapsed and begged me for it. How could I refuse?"

"Where is he now?"

"I don't know. I slept, I don't know how long before I called you."

Nuri slammed his fist into the desk. "We lost him! After all this, he's going to fall back to Melchior!"

Gerwazek shook his head.

"He bit you and walked out? Where else is he going to go?"

"He won't return to evil. The Lord has touched him."

Nuri stood up. "How do you *know* that?"

Gerwazek held out his wrist in front of Nuri. "Because I am still alive."

Stefan walked the night-drenched streets of Cleveland, searching for a place to call home. In his wake he left five or six people sleeping, people who had looked into his eyes and couldn't refuse his request.

He was dressed in some of Gerwazek's clothes, old black trousers and a black shirt with a priest's collar. He wore nothing on his feet. Gerwazek's clothes hung loose on him, the cuffs of the trousers dragging on the ground.

Stefan looked out at the night and felt an uncanny sense of freedom. Melchior was a distant ghost to him, a dim memory of the purgatory he had crossed to reach this point.

For the first time since his death, since before his death, Stefan Ryzard felt whole.

As the night sky turned ruddy violet, he stopped. He had reached Public Square. On one side towered the Union Terminal Building, once the headquarters of the Van Sweringen empire. Across from the terminal stood a small sandstone church, walls black with age. The sign above the front of the building read, "Old Stone Church."

Before, when he'd felt himself damned for what Melchior had done to him, being this close to a house of God would have put him in pain. Now, as Stefan looked up at the twin Gothic towers flanking the entrance, he saw it as a refuge.

He walked inside, and hid himself deep in the basement. He stayed there that day, knowing he was safe.

1939

15

"Who the hell is *Frank Dolezal*?" Ness said. "Good Lord, was he ever a suspect?"

A collection of the highest ranking cops in Cleveland were crowded into Ness' office, and Ness stared at all of them in turn. A few looked abashed, a few stared blankly—the ones who hadn't heard about Dolezal yet. Someone said, "The name may have come up in the investigation—"

"Every name in the Roaring Third has come up in the investigation," a cynical voice answered.

Ness stared out at all of them, feeling a near-unbearable frustration. The case was like an albatross, dragging him down with it. When he had finally razed the shantytowns, he had hoped to take away the murderer's prey. Everyone agreed that he preyed on hobos and transients, and Ness had removed the population from Cleveland. The press and the public had blasted him for it, but in the time that had passed, he felt he might be vindicated. There'd been no more murders for nearly a year.

There had been one debatable case where someone found some human bones in a Youngstown dump, but it really looked as if Ness had faced the problem down. The press and the public might have begun to feel that way, too.

Now the damn county sheriff claimed to have gotten what Eliot Ness and the massed force of the biggest manhunt in Cleveland history had failed to get. Sheriff O'Donnell said he had the Torso Murderer, and he was some immigrant named Frank Dolezal.

That was bad enough—

"He went and told the press before he told *us*," Ness said to the assembled cops. He was fuming. "He's running

a circus, and he's done everything to keep the city away
from Dolezal."

Everything to make sure that Ness had no part of the
credit. Worse, it made the effort of last summer look pointless. He had done so much else for this city, why did this
keep haunting him?

"I want detectives going after Dolezal's background. Go
over what we have, the interviews we've taken. If there's
evidence either way, damning him or clearing him, I want
us to get it before the county boys. Everyone understand?
And I want some detectives up at the county jail. We're
going to have a presence there, even if we don't get in to
see Dolezal."

Ness clapped his hands and said, "Let's get moving."

Frank Dolezal sat in a chair while the sheriff and his
deputies walked around and badgered him with questions.
Every time O'Donnell said, "We know it was you, Frank,"
Dolezal felt a tremor of fear shoot through his body. He
was afraid of the words, that his slurred answers weren't
quite right, that in the end they wouldn't believe him.

The room was hot, stifling. They sat him in a hard chair
and refused to let him move. Occasionally one of the deputies would strike him, and the pain would make him forget
the heat, the lack of sleep, and let him concentrate on
the fear.

They had to believe him, or he would lose his chance at
a golden eternity. He managed to keep the denials going.
That was the worst part. Taking the beatings, the heat, the
violent shouts in his face, and still give them denials that
he knew he would recant.

He knew they had the knives in his apartment, he knew
that they'd tracked down the stories he'd been told to prop-
agate. But he knew that they wouldn't believe him unless
he began with denial.

Time was all. He needed to deny everything for six hours
at least, before he gave them a confession. And the confession needed to be convincing. The sheriff needed to believe
he had the Torso Murderer.

If he didn't, Frank Dolezal would lose his chance at
eternity.

So Dolezal sat, drenched in sweat, bruises turning livid

n his body, until his Master's blood moved inside him and
e felt that it was time.

"Okay," he said in a thick accent, "I did it. Just stop."

That got their attention. They began on him, asking for
etails, and Dolezal gave them, feeding them bits and
ieces of the murders just as his Master had fed them to
im. The confessions took hours more.

At the end Dolezal stared blankly ahead of him, the only
motion inside him a desire to fulfill his Master's will.

16

Nuri was given the unenviable job of being present when Sheriff O'Donnell unveiled his big catch. As soon a he got to the county jail and saw all the press, he knew i wasn't going to be good. He was glad he was plainclothes If he wore a Cleveland uniform, the reporters might asl him some embarrassing questions.

A sense of futility hung in the air, though perhaps he was the only one to sense it. Nuri knew for a fact tha Frank Dolezal was at best a fall guy for the murders, a worse he was just an innocent schmo who crossed Sherif O'Donnell's path at the wrong time.

Nuri couldn't even get to talk to the sheriff on behalf o the department. The sheriff was too busy.

So Nuri was stuck in a room with all the reporters, wait ing for the sheriff to throw them all the story he wanted to give.

Eventually Sheriff O'Donnell walked in, a pair of hi deputies leading in a man who had to be Frank Dolezal The room became alive with a chain lightning of flashbulbs Dolezal stared into the flashes as if he didn't quite see the room of reporters.

Sheriff ODonnell spoke to them all, about how he had finally closed this five-year-old investigation, about how Dolezal had given him a detailed confession.

Nuri stared at Dolezal. The man was wide-eyed, staring ahead, looking like an empty husk. As Nuri stared, he thought he could see something in those staring eyes, a familiar depthlessness, as if he were looking into an abyss an abyss which stared back.

The reporters began shouting questions. Nuri didn't lis

en to them. He kept looking at Dolezal. The man was sweaty, unshaven, probably beaten by his captors, and he just kept staring. Nuri moved around the back of the room until he looked directly into the man's eyes.

He hadn't imagined it. Nuri could see it in the man's eyes. A blackness that filled everything behind his eyes. A cloud of darkness more felt than seen. Nuri saw that and knew that the devil had touched this man.

Of course he confessed, Nuri thought. *He was told to confess. Ordered to confess. Willed by the darkness flowing through his veins.*

Seeing that, Nuri was consumed by the same helplessness he had felt when he had lost Stefan. There was a man here, still human, who had fallen so far in the darkness that Nuri couldn't help him even if the sheriff would let him near him. Everyone wanted the Torso Murderer, and Dolezal and his owner had provided that.

All Nuri could do was say they were wrong.

Nuri watched as the legal road to Melchoir was shut down.

17

A deputy sheriff sat at a desk at the entrance to the holding area of the Cuyahoga County Jail. It was during visiting hours, a dull routine of ushering prisoners to the visiting area and back again. One of the prisoners was the Torso Killer, Frank Dolezal.

There was a pause, shortly after lunch, so the deputy's feet were up on his desk, and he was thumbing through the latest copy of *Weird Tales*.

A shadow fell across his magazine, and he looked up.

His eyes met the gaze of Melchior, and his face turned into a slack mask. No words were exchanged, but when Melchoir slid by the desk, the deputy put down the magazine and went off to bring back a prisoner he had forgotten until just that moment. He wouldn't return for nearly half an hour, though he would later insist it wasn't more than three minutes.

Melchoir walked down the aisle of cells, unseen, unnoticed.

He stopped in front of Frank Dolezal's cell. Dolezal stood in the front of the cell, as if he had felt his Master coming. He gripped the bars and said to the shadow walking before him. "It is time, My Lord?"

Melchoir's shadow nodded.

Dolezal's eyes lit with hope, his lips turning with a perverse joy. The beatings had been worth it. He would become one of the chosen now. One of the blood.

A whisper came from Melchoir. "Take those rags." He pointed at a pile of cleaning rags heaped in the corner of Dolezal's cell. "Tie them together.

Dolezal nodded and did as he was told, making a short length with the rags tied end-to-end.

"Fasten it to that hook, here." Melchoir reached to the ceiling of Dolezal's cell, where a rusted hook projected from the concrete. His arm extended, through the bars, more than was natural, until a pale finger touched the metal.

Dolezal did so, watching his Master with wide eyes.

"Loop the other end around your neck," Melchoir said.

The first flickers of doubt crossed Dolezal's face. Melchoir stared at him and repeated, "Do it."

All the force of hell seemed to reside in those two words, and Dolezal found his hands working of their own accord. The doubt was turning to fear as the rags tightened around his neck. His traitor hands had fastened them tight enough that it was painful to croak the word, "Why?"

The rags were slack between Dolezal's neck and the hook above.

Melchoir reached a hand through the bars and rested it on Dolezal's forehead. "Because it is necessary," Melchoir said, and pushed down on Dolezal's head.

Dolezal's legs slipped out from under him and the rags went taut. He clawed at his neck, and kicked out with his feet. He tried to scream, but it only came out as a strangled gasp.

"They will want your body," Melchior said. "Head intact, I'm afraid." He looked down at the struggling form. "Crush the neck long enough, it's as good as decapitation."

No one seemed to hear Dolezal's struggles. Eventually, his body hung slack. Still, Melchior held his hand to Dolezal's head, as if dispensing a blessing.

Melchior stood that way with Dolezal, pressure on the broken neck and windpipe, until he was certain Dolezal wouldn't rise again. When he was certain, Melchior strode from the jail unnoticed by all who saw him.

The suicide of Frank Dolezal marked the end of the official investigation into the Torso Murders. Even with questions about the confession and the bizarre nature of the suicide, even though the case remained officially unsolved, the Cleveland Police had little impetus to continue the case. No more bodies were found. In the eyes of all but a few, it was over.

———❄❄❄———

Book Four

March 1942—October 1944

THE STREETS OF HELL

1942

1

Sunday, March 1

Times were quiet for Eliot Ness. He was easing toward middle age, his career was going forward, and the press and the public thought he was doing a good job. He had the credit for taking one of the country's most dangerous cities and making it one of the safest.

As he sat in his den, reading a newspaper, and drinking a tumbler of Scotch, his thoughts were nowhere near the string of bodies that had begun on the shores of Euclid Beach Park in 1934. His thoughts were on the paper, on Europe. At the moment he thought of all his men that had gone overseas, how they were doing. A lot of his force, firemen, patrol officers, and a few detectives were fighting. He wondered how many of them would be coming home.

His musings were interrupted by a knock at the door.

He looked up from the paper and at a clock on the wall. It was after eleven. Who would be knocking at this time of night?

He wanted to ignore the late visitor, but his wife had gone to bed early and he was afraid that the persistent knocking would wake her. He put the paper aside as the knocking continued and walked to the door.

Angry at the interruption, he was ready to curse his visitor, but when he saw who the man was, the words died on his lips. The tumbler of Scotch he carried slipped out of his fingers.

Standing on his doorstep was Stefan Ryzard.

"What are you doing here?" Ness finally said.

"I want you to listen to me," Stefan said.

He looked into Ness' eyes, and Ness thought he could sense something in his gaze, something dark and inhuman.

Ness tried to shrug off the feeling and bent to retrieve the tumbler. "Listen to you? I should arrest you. Your ex-partner witnessed you at the scene of a murder."

Stefan smiled down at him, and the smile made Ness feel cold, alone, and badly exposed. He began worrying about his wife's safety.

"That must have been a long time ago," Stefan said. "Things have changed."

Ness looked at him, empty glass in his hand. Time seemed to have done well by Stefan. He didn't look any older than when Ness had last seen him. If anything he looked younger. There was an eerie confidence in his face that Ness found unnerving.

"Will you let me in?" Stefan asked.

Ness considered closing the door on his one-time detective. Ness suspected that if he did so, he would never see Stefan again.

He wondered what it was that could have taken Stefan out of hiding. He gestured back into the house, into the den, and said, "Come in, Mr. Ryzard."

Stefan entered, and Ness noticed that he carried a large attaché case with him.

Ness followed him and asked, "What do you want?"

Stefan took a seat and pulled a coffee table toward him. He opened the buckles on the case and said, "I want your complete attention for two hours."

It went much longer than two hours.

"You assigned me," Stefan began, "to gather evidence on Eric Dietrich in relation to the murders of Edward Andrassy, Flo Polillo, and a number of other unidentified people." He spilled the case onto the table in front of him. "I have evidence now, and I am here now because the only cop I trust is overseas."

Ness sat on the other side of the table, mounded high with papers and photographs as Stefan began to tell him about the thing called Eric Dietrich, began to tell him about the creatures of the night. The story was unbelievable, and Ness tried to protest, but every time he met Stefan's gaze, he fell into silence.

All the deaths, every one and more, were either at Die-trich's hands or at his orders. This wasn't a case of a madman murdering transients. Each death was an assassination, with purpose, meant to inspire terror in Dietrich's enemies. In some cases the deaths were followers of Dietrich who dared to defect, in others they were the leadership of Dietrich's main opposition. By the time Ness burned the shantytowns, those shantytowns had been the sole refuge, the remnants of the society that Dietrich displaced trying to leave via the only avenue left them.

When Ness called his forces down on the transient population, he had solidified Dietrich's control of the city.

"Now the only one of the blood here that isn't pledged to him, is me."

Ness shook his head. "You started on this supernatural nonsense before you left. I still don't belie—"

Stefan held up his hand, silencing Ness. As Ness watched, transfixed, the skin darkened and thickened. The fingers lengthened with the sound of breaking bone. Nails grew into black talons as the hand became a weapon capable of tearing Ness' throat out.

"You do not know everything," Stefan said. "Melchior believes he is Satan and destined to rule the Earth, and *he* does not know everything. I have been saved from my fate, and my purpose is only to stop him and his plans. Do you understand? I am here because his darkness hasn't reached you, and his destruction by human forces will be far preferable to the means *I* would have to use." He clenched his demon hand into a fist and it slowly returned to normal.

"Preferable for whom?"

"Every human in this city who would be near Melchior when he dies," Stefan said the words with such gravity that Ness feared for anyone who would be near that event.

"He has prepared himself to regain the kingdom he lost a millennium ago." Stefan pulled a sheaf of documents from the pile and handed it to Ness. "Eric Dietrich is a Hungarian expatriate industrialist. He has become an influential voice in the legislature, in the administration in Washington. He's invisible, but he's taken in thrall major forces in our government. All of this was in preparation."

"Preparation for what?"

"That folder contains an agreement between Dietrich and our government. In return for his resources, and contacts in Europe, the Allies have agreed to install him as the provisional leader of the occupied German Empire."

Ness stared at Stefan, and then looked down at the folder.

"Melchoir knows who will win this war. He was planning this long before the first shots were fired. Before this century began."

The folder was official-looking, and carried markings from half a dozen agencies of the US Government, including the Army. It was marked top secret.

"Where did you get this?"

"I'm invisible," Stefan said.

It went on, and on, and on. How Melchior took over the rail empire of the Van Sweringens, using it as a network to move his influence across the continent. How the killing ground rode on the rails themselves. How every organized force, human or not, was stalled, subverted, or destroyed if it served Melchior's purpose.

Ness watched as Stefan sifted through the mountain of evidence. Deep into the night he asked, "How did you gather all this?"

"I am alone. No one is left to betray me. He might sense others of the blood, or his own thralls, but my nature has become alien to his. I walk on ground he cannot perceive." Stefan stared at Ness. "Do you believe in God?"

Ness nodded. "Of course."

Stefan frowned slightly, as if the answer came too quickly, too facile. "You should. That is all that can protect you from him."

Stefan watched Ness and hoped. Stefan had worked alone, gathering the evidence of what Melchior had done, what he *was* doing. He hoped he could cause something to happen, stop Melchior short of what would be the ultimate solution. Ness had the forces of the city under his command, and through connections in the Treasury Department he could call on many more.

If Melchior's plans were balked, if he were discredited, Stefan hoped it wouldn't end the way he feared it would. If he could take away the human levers that Melchior used to amplify his power . . .

Ness looked at the pile of documents, listened to Stefan's

story, and shook his head, "I don't know what you want me to do, arrest him?"

"Perhaps as a beginning. Even though he is old enough and powerful enough to walk abroad in sunlight, he still relies on darkness and fear. Illuminate him, just a little, and these tangled plans begin to crumble."

Ness gathered up the pages and photographs and told Stefan, "I'll think about what you've said. Look into it. If anything's here, we'll see this guy behind bars."

I hope so, Stefan thought.

2

Eliot Ness spent most of his spare time in the first half of
the week trying to independently confirm the evidence
Stefan had given him. He couldn't double-check more than
a fraction of what he had been given, but what he had
checked seem to pan out. The man named Eric Dietrich
was many of the things Stefan said he was.

Ness was still far from believing in the supernatural.

But confirmation of any part of Stefan's story was unnerving. Deitrich, or Melchior, seemed the center of his
own twisted form of worship. Stefan had given him dark
pictures of ceremonies that twisted Ness' stomach. Even if
there was nothing supernatural involved, there were people
who followed Melchior as if he were the God of his own
religion. After two days going over Stefan's papers, it was
easy to believe that sacrifice was part of it.

By Wednesday, Ness believed that he might be the one
to bring in the Torso Murderer. He might be able to erase
the one dark spot of his term as Public Safety Director.

He was in a good mood as he accompanied his wife to
one of the parties he frequented. As he danced with her,
he felt as if he were just about to reach the high point of
his life.

Driving home, his wife asleep beside him, slightly high
from the party, Ness imagined the headlines when he would
capture Dietrich. It would be a news story of epic proportions, not just here, but all over the country, maybe even
overseas.

The night was dark, the roads slick and icy. The head-
lamps of his car picked out a tiny circle of reality ahead of
him on the road, the rest of the world vanished into black-

ess. Ness suddenly felt a shiver of apprehension and he reached first to touch his sleeping wife, then the satchel that sat in the back seat—

Stefan's evidence followed him everywhere, even to the party. It was too important to let out of his sight.

The road was dead in front of him, the only sound the wind and the engine—

Then, as he rounded a curve, a car appeared in front of him. It appeared suddenly, as if it had been pushed out into the road ahead of him. He slammed into the side of it, his head striking the steering wheel, then snapping back. His car rolled to a stop ahead of the car.

My God, where did he come from? What happened? Ness' thoughts were a haze. He looked in the mirror and saw the other vehicle unmoving by the side of the road, windshield shattered, driver slumped behind the wheel.

Good lord, I've killed someone.

A shadow passed in front of the mirror. Ness looked up to see a figure standing in the darkness between the two cars. Ness wasn't a fearful man. People had often said that he had less fear than was smart. All the threats that followed him throughout his career had left him unmoved—

The figure standing in the moonless night, backlit by the damaged car's headlights, *that* frightened Eliot Ness.

"You broke one of your own rules," Ness heard on the air. The voice was quiet, but as hard and icy as the pavement. "One of your commandments for safe driving. You have alcohol on your breath."

The words slammed into Ness like blows. They left him dizzy, speechless. There was barely time for him to wonder who this figure was, angel, devil, Melchior, or some phantom called up by the blow his head had just taken. All he could think was that his own mistakes had probably killed a man.

The figure stepped up until it was next to Ness' car. Ness couldn't take his eyes away, even though it never became more than a shadow.

It pointed an accusing finger and said, "Your wife needs to be tended to."

Ness looked into the passenger seat, and felt his heart nearly give way. He saw his wife's face as a nearly featureless mask of blood.

He had no time left for thought. He accelerated awa
from the scene. He had to get her to a hospital. He ha
driven like a madman for what seemed like hours, but mus
have only been a few minutes, when he heard her say
"Honey, we need to go home."

Ness turned to look at her and felt a sick wave of disori
entation when he realized that her only wound was a scrap
and a bump on her forehead. There was no sign of th
massive hemorrhage he had seen earlier.

He swallowed and drove home, while through his hea
he kept telling himself that he had to return to the acciden
But he didn't remember exactly where it was any more
and every time he looked across at his wife he felt that h
couldn't trust his own memory.

When he got home, he realized that the satchel with Ste
fan's papers was gone.

When he made sure his wife was all right and in bed, h
started calling hospitals to find the unknown man he ha
collided with. He eventually found him, alive and all right
He hung up without leaving his name.

He knew that wasn't going to be the end of it. H
couldn't live with himself if he allowed himself to becom
a party to a criminal hit-and-run, even if it wasn't his fault
He picked up the phone and called the Central Station.

Afterward, shaking, he walked to the bar in the den an
poured himself a drink. He was picturing different head
lines now. Eliot Ness stared into the amber liquid and real
ized that his career as Public Safety Director had jus
ended.

3

Watching the end of Eliot Ness' career was like watching newsreel footage of a bomber going in extreme slow motion. Stefan read the papers, saw every hit as it landed, read salvos that lasted days.

Ness had been a public hero, but the act of fleeing the scene of a drunken accident was the one thing that would have made the public turn on him. If there had been an accusation of bribery, or corruption, the public wouldn't have believed it. Somehow it was easier to believe in personal hypocrisy, and it was somehow more damning.

Stefan suspected that it had been more than an accident.

He knew it was more than an accident when every move Ness made toward Melchior petered out and eventually stopped. He knew it when Ness resigned.

Stefan sat on a bench overlooking the night-blackened lake and reread the story over and over. There was no choice left. He had spent his time to gather the evidence to support Ness' actions, and with Ness gone there was no one left for Stefan to turn to. The only other ally he could trust was Nuri, and he was overseas.

And Stefan saw that trust was no longer an issue. He could evade Melchior because he was alone. Every time there was anyone else involved, Melchior began to see what he was doing. He had been more than aware of the police and the local gangs, he had manipulated them. Even with a conspiracy as small as him, Nuri and Iago, Melchior had seen through it. Now, the instant he tried to bring some human agency into the picture, the most trustworthy man Stefan knew of, he was removed from any position of authority.

Ness had asked someone the wrong question.

He tossed the paper on the ground, and watched it blow away. He had no choice. The only chance against Melchior was an individual with no one to share his secrets.

It would require more time for preparations, and Melchior's fall would come at a cost that Stefan didn't want to contemplate. He sat and began to pray for forgiveness.

1944

4

Nuri Lapidos walked Euclid Avenue as the night turned to dusk. He was still getting used to being home. More than that, he was still getting used to the absence of half his right foot. He used a cane, but the doctors said that he'd eventually regain his equilibrium. He'd been lucky. The sergeant who'd actually stepped on the land mine behind him lost a more than his foot—some of the shrapnel they'd taken out of Nuri's legs had been splinters from the sergeant's pelvis.

The sergeant had died within minutes, while Nuri spent three months in a hospital fighting off a dozen infections. He had managed to return home a lieutenant, and something of a war hero. He still wore his uniform, as if putting on civilian clothes would deny what happened.

Also, a uniform and a cane gave him more respect than a badge ever did. It occasionally made asking questions easier. That's what he'd been doing ever since he had hobbled off the train, asking questions.

He'd been wondering, since before he was wounded, once he began getting letters from people he knew on the force.

There were rumors about Stefan Ryzard. Nothing concrete, but people said they had seen him. The reports were enticing: stories of Stefan asking questions, lurking around neighborhoods at night. The oddest ones were about people seeing him at nighttime services. He had apparently been at more than one midnight Mass.

When Nuri returned, he felt an impulse to seek him out, to find him once and for all.

What Nuri had found out for himself was more than the

rumors. He had followed Stefan's trail all over the city. He had been visiting junkyards and hardware stores, apparently bribing people out of some items collected for aluminum and copper drives. He had paid cash for a ten-year old Lincoln V-12. Most disturbing was his purchase of large quantity of dynamite.

From there, Nuri struck a dead end. He found no one who could tell him where Stefan was. He appeared, bought what he wanted, and disappeared again. It took a while before Nuri had an idea of where Stefan might be hiding.

Nuri turned off of Euclid and began walking north of East Fifty-Fifth. He was heading toward the Slovenian community on St. Clair. Toward the unpretentious structure of St. John's. Father Gerwazek had retired, and the Church had decided to close down the building rather than appoint a new pastor to the superfluous parish. Everyone in the community went to St. Vitus now.

But the building was still there.

Nuri stopped in front of it and suppressed a shudder. It had only been shut up for a year or two, but it looked as if it had been abandoned much longer. The paint had peeled away, someone had removed the statue of Mary and the sign saying "St. John's" had disappeared, leaving a dark spot of unpainted wood on the side of the building.

But a cross still stood, at the peak above the front door.

A gate stood in front of the church, locked with a rusty chain.

Not knowing quite what to expect, Nuri circled the structure. It was crowded on all sides by turn-of-the-century working-class houses. It hugged its small grounds to itself with a wrought-iron fence that two winters without maintenance had canted at an inward angle, as if it were retreating from the surrounding neighborhood.

Nuri followed a narrow alley, paralleling the fence, all the way to the rear of the church. Another gate stood in the fence, but on this one the chain was shiny, the lock new.

Nuri prodded the weeds around the gate and uncovered the remains of an older chain, the metal still shiny where the links had been cut. Past the gate, Nuri could still see signs of a car passing through—a rut in the weed-shot lawn where the wheel had left the drive.

Nuri looked up at the church, through the bars. There

was a large shed that took up almost all of the church's small back lot. The doors were shut and locked, but Nuri suspected that there was just enough room there to hide a car the size of a Lincoln.

Nuri walked up to the fence, shoved his cane through the bars, grabbed the top, and heaved himself over. He barely avoided impaling himself on one of the ornamental spikes on top of the fence, and landed shoulder first into the tall grass behind the church.

He grabbed his cane and used it to push himself upright.

Nuri stood still for a few long moments, waiting for someone to notice him. The church stayed dark and silent, the only sounds distant ones from the neighborhood around him; a baby crying; a dog barking; two children shouting at each other in the distance; a radio . . .

Nothing came from in front of him, no sound of alarm, as if the building was a tomb.

What do you expect? It's supposed to be abandoned.

Nuri walked up to the shed. The entrance was two swinging wooden doors, securely padlocked. The lock and the clasp that held it were both new. Nuri tried to see through the crack between the doors, but the interior was as dark as ink. He couldn't see anything but flat blackness.

He moved around to the side, where a dirty window looked in on the shed. Nothing was visible there either. Nuri stood and stared at the window. Something was wrong with it. The window was covered in grime and cobwebs, but there still should be moonlight leaking through. He reached up a hand and wiped away some of the grime.

The blackness beyond was too flat. The other side of the glass had been painted so no one could see in.

Nuri tried to open the window, but it refused to move, locked, painted, or nailed shut. After shoving the frame a few times he smashed in one of the panes with the head of his cane. The sound seemed deafeningly loud in the quiet space around the church, and Nuri paused and waited for something to react.

Nothing did.

The glass had shattered, but the cane stopped moving an inch through the window. The cane leaned against something inside as shards of black-painted glass fell by Nuri's feet. Inside was still blackness.

Nuri pulled the cane back and felt through the broken window. The cane had caught on a drape of heavy velvet dark as pitch. Nuri tried to push it aside, but there was too much of it. It felt as if it covered the entire inside wall of the shed.

Feeling around, Nuri found the latch to the window. After a few tugs, it loosened.

The window frame let out squeals of dry, warped wood as Nuri forced it open. Again, when he was done, he waited, listening if anyone heard him.

Again nothing but the nighttime sounds of the surrounding neighborhood.

Nuri pulled himself through the window, sliding behind the velvet drapery. For a few claustrophobic seconds he tried to find the bottom of the drape. He finally got his hand underneath it and managed to duck through to the other side.

Unexpectedly, the inside of the shed was lit, and brightly. All the walls were covered with black drapery, it was even nailed to the ceiling. But from that ceiling hung a very bright bulb, and a reflecting skirt drove all the light on to the car below it.

Nuri stood there blinking for several moments while he tried to make sense of what he saw.

A Lincoln V-12 was here, in the last stages of some major modifications. Both hoods were open and the doors had been taken off the hinges. The glass on the windshield, the rear window, and on the doors he could see leaning against the wall, were all painted black. Every seat but the driver' had been torn out, and in their place stood stacks of wooden boxes piled to waist height, surrounding a metal barrel that reeked of gasoline. In the trunk was the same thing, a drum—this one sidewise—surrounded by wooden boxes. Thick wire coiled from one box to the next, throughout the whole car.

Nuri walked up to the side of the car and gently lifted the lid of one of the boxes. He wasn't surprised by what he saw. In the box, connected by wires to each other, were at least a dozen sticks of dynamite.

The Lincoln was a rolling munitions dump. He felt the same sick feeling in the pit of his stomach that he'd felt when he heard his sergeant step on a land mine.

The room was no longer silent. Something moved behind him. Nuri turned, raising his cane to defend himself. He was too late. Something slammed into his head and he fell into the blackness of the draperies.

Nuri came awake in a familiar room. A single light burned above him, dangling from a wire in the ceiling. He lay on a dirty cot, still in his uniform. At the moment he wished he'd been wearing his service pistol.

He sat up and looked at the stone walls surrounding him and called out, "Stefan!"

From the other side of the door Nuri heard Stefan's voice say calmly, "There's no need to shout."

Nuri sprang up and stumbled on his bad foot. He limped up to the door and tried to force it open, even though he knew it was hopeless. The door had held Stefan, and Stefan had been stronger than him even before he was claimed by the supernatural.

"What are you doing?" Nuri yelled at him. "Let me out of here!"

"I can't, Nuri." Stefan's voice sounded heavy beyond the thick door. Nuri wished he could see him. "I wish it was possible—"

"Just open the door."

"You saw what I was doing. I could stare into your eyes and tell you to forget, but that wouldn't be enough. You would do something—inadvertently I'm sure—that would alert him. I can't let you, not when it's almost over."

Nuri looked at the door and shrank back, thinking of the modified Lincoln. "You're going after him? Good Lord, you can trust me. I'm not going to warn the bastard after all this—"

"It's not about trust," Stefan said. "I've spent years making sure that I was the one person who knows what is about to happen. You found me here. I don't know what you asked, or who, but it might be already too much. Melchior has ears everywhere. I'm also not sure you wouldn't try and stop me."

"Why would I do that?"

"If you knew what it was going to cost."

There was a long silence, and Nuri thought Stefan had

left him. He pounded on the door. "Are you still ou
there?"

"Yes. It's probably a good thing that there'll be someone
left to remember what happened and why."

The way Stefan said it made Nuri freeze. He began to
realize that there had to be someone driving the Lincoln
when it went up.

"Sit down," Stefan said. "I'm afraid that you'll be here
a while. But I might as well tell you, so someone knows."

Nuri tried the door a few more times, then gave up in
frustration. He backed away and sat down. He stared at
the wooden door, and shivered as the cold began to sink
in. He wrapped a blanket around his shoulders as Stefan
spoke.

During the whole monologue, something in the tone of
Stefan's voice kept Nuri from interrupting.

"You saved me, Nuri. If not for your intervention, I
would still be one of his thralls, probably used up and truly
dead by now. He could see in me, and through me, but
you found his blind spot. My presence here, on blessed
ground, blinded him—or gave me the power to blind him.
Father Gerwazek gave me the faith to push him from me.
I died to him, and I gained my soul back.

"But I knew, even as I walked from this place, my redemption wasn't free. I was saved for a reason. What af-
flicts me might not be evil in itself, the thirst given me
doesn't have to kill—but Melchior is an abomination. He
feeds on his own kind. In the end, he wants all the world's
flesh bound to his own.

"The war we're fighting in Europe is a result of his desire
to rule an empire of men, an empire ruled by those of the
blood. If he lives when this war is over, he will gain that
empire. He has become part of the industrial sinew of this
war. He builds munitions, transports them, feeds our effort
in Europe and Asia. He is so tied into the powers of the
allies that he will rule what is left of the axis when the war
is over. That cannot happen. Compared to Melchior; Hitler,
Mussolini, Tito, Franco, they are all angry children.

"I've seen the carnage that supports him and his followers. I've been a part of it. The bodies he left for us, the
ones he wanted to be found, those weren't a hundredth

part of the blood left in his wake. And what he wallows in now is not a thousandth part of what would happen if he is granted what he seeks.

"My redemption won't be complete until that is prevented. I want you to realize what I am stopping. The cost may be appalling, but what would happen without it is unspeakable. I only pray to God that the sacrifice will succeed."

Nuri grew colder and colder as Stefan spoke. He had been in Europe, and had seen the Nazis' handiwork for himself. He knew what the SS was capable of, and he knew stories of things much darker. Imagining something that might be worse gave him a sick feeling in his gut.

It was a while before Nuri realized that Stefan had stopped talking.

"You can't do this by yourself," Nuri said.

"There's no other way I can do this," Stefan said. "I've left you food. You won't see me again."

Nuri sprang up and pounded on the door. *"You can't just leave me here!"*

"Father Gerwazek will be here to let you out on Friday." Stefan's tone became frighteningly cold. "When he does, leave here as fast as you can."

"What are you going to do?" Nuri said, "What happens on Friday?"

"Melchior dies," Stefan said flatly. "Remember, leave here quickly. Good-bye, Nuri."

"Stefan?" Nuri called.

There wasn't an answer.

"Stefan!" Nuri yelled out, to no response. *"What happens on Friday?"* Nuri called repeatedly, into the night.

That was the last time he ever heard Stefan Ryzard's voice.

5

2:10 PM

After four days Nuri was stir-crazy. He had broken his cane attempting to open the door, his throat was raw after hours of screaming for help, and his head ached from the cold and damp. But the room had held Stefan, and it held Nuri. On the fourth day he looked at the last dregs of the food and water Stefan had left for him and wondered if he would ever get out of this small stone room.

But, just as Stefan had promised, on Friday afternoon, Nuri heard Father Gerwazek's voice calling out, "Hello?"

"In here," Nuri yelled, and then erupted in a fit of coughing. The shout tore at his abraded throat.

"I'm coming," Gerwazek said. In a few moments the door pushed open.

Gerwazek entered, looking older and more worn than Nuri remembered. The priest stared at him for a moment before saying, "Detective Lapidos?" There was the sound of surprise in Gerwazek's voice.

Nuri grabbed his shoulder, "Where is he? What's he doing?"

"What?" Gerwazek said.

"He *sent* you here. You have to know what's going on."

Gerwazek looked at him blankly. "All I know is I got a phone call saying that someone was trapped in the basement of old St. John's, and I needed to come here before two. I didn't know it was you."

Nuri shook his head, and pushed past Gerwazek. He hobbled toward the exit. "He's planned something for him. It's about to happen."

Gerwazek followed. "Who? Who's been using this building? Who locked you in there?"

"Stefan, Father," Nuri said as he pulled himself up through the trapdoor. "I've got to find out what's happening."

Nuri stumbled out into a brisk, cloudless, sunlit afternoon. He stood in front of the church, staring at the sky.

Gerwazek came out after him. "What's happening?" he asked.

"I wish I knew," Nuri said. "He's planning something for today. The way he said it, saying I had to leave here quickly when you showed up, it has to be happening now—but it can't be."

"I don't understand."

"You know what he is. He can't be running around in daylight. I've seen what sun does to them." *He'd have to be as powerful as Melchior to walk in the daylight. . . .*

Nuri looked up at the afternoon sun and whispered, "Or be shaded from it."

"What?"

Nuri ran unsteadily around the church to the shed in the back. It took a few moments for Gerwazek to follow him. When he caught up, Nuri was standing in front of the open shed, looking at where the Lincoln used to be. He remembered all the windows painted black.

"It *is* today," he said, staring into the empty shed. "He blacked out the windows so he could go out in daylight."

"Stefan?" Gerwazek said.

"Yes, Stefan. Father, I need to get to a phone. Stefan's riding a bomb somewhere, and I want to find out where."

2:20 PM

Stefan Ryzard checked his watch and then started the engine of the Lincoln. The powerful V-12 roared into life, vibrating the chassis around him. It was time.

He had parked way back from the site of Eric Dietrich's visit. He hadn't wanted anyone in any security capacity, either Dietrich's, or the plant's, to take notice of the car. The black windows were enough to draw attention.

Even with the windows blacked out, even with only a sliver of window open for him to see the road, Stefan

sensed the pressure of the mid-afternoon sun. The light
outside was a numbing presence that he could feel even
inside his pitch-black car. Wherever the light from his sliver
portal touched the skin, it would go numb and dead. Stefan
knew that if such light hit him directly, he would become
a pile of dead meat. His recuperative powers would save
him from a gunshot, or a broken bone, but they were taxed
to the limit by just a thin beam of sun.

It was a measure of just how old and powerful Melchior
was that he could walk abroad in the sun, apparently
unharmed.

The sun also brought a crushing fatigue that Stefan had
spent years learning how to fight. The natural order of
things was for his body to shut down while the sun was in
the sky. Every motion, every thought, required an inhuman
effort to maintain.

Fortunately, while the planning and the secrecy was deli-
cate, the execution was not. All Stefan had to do now was
aim the car down two miles of road, and accelerate. When
the Lincoln came into Melchior's view, Stefan expected that
he would sense one of the blood inside, even though Stefan
had purged himself of Melchior's blood long ago. It was
the nature of the blood that its people sensed one another.
Stefan just hoped that by the time Melchior knew what was
racing toward him, it would be too late.

Stefan pulled out into the road, and began flooring the
accelerator. He dodged slower-moving traffic as the speed-
ometer crept toward ninety.

On the gearshift, Stefan found a button strapped there
with cloth electrical tape. He pressed it down and held it.

There was no turning back now.

2:22 PM

"Look, I know I'm not on the force anymore, I'm asking
a favor as a friend." Nuri stared at the phone in front of
him. He wanted to beg, to plead—mostly he wanted to tell
the officer on the other end what kind of stakes they were
dealing with.

"Look," said the man on the other end of the line, "As
a friend I'm telling you, we're not supposed to be giving
out that kind of information. There's a war on, you know."

Nuri shook his head in exasperation and looked out of

the phone booth. Gerwazek was still there, watching him with a bit of concern, but calmly enough that Nuri realized that none of the unease that flooded him had really touched the priest.

The closest phone they'd found was in a little drugstore on the same block as the old St. John's. The white-jacketed pharmacist was busy talking to some old Slovenian lady.

Nuri took a few breaths to calm himself and said, "Are you suggesting I'm a Nazi spy?"

"I'm saying that—"

"I had my foot blown off for schmucks like you!"

The pharmacist and the old lady both turned to look in his direction.

"What do you want from me?" asked the man at the other end of the line.

"I want to know where Eric Dietrich is, right now. He's a VIP, he gets police protection when he's in public, you have his itinerary somewhere."

"Is that all?"

"Yes, and *hurry*."

"It'll take a minute." Nuri heard the officer set down the phone.

Nuri felt time slide by, oily and slow. The Slovenian lady got what she'd wanted, walked over to Father Gerwazek and started talking in hushed tones, occasionally looking in Nuri's direction. Nuri suddenly realized how he must look. He had slept in his uniform for four days without a shower or a shave. Dirt was smeared all over him, and he must have smelled like the mildewed basement where he'd been kept.

Every minute was marked by an axlike thunk from a large clock above the pharmacist's counter. Nuri stared at the clock, wondering how much time he had before whatever happened, happened. It might be happening now, might have already happened. . . .

The officer came back on the line. "Okay, I've got what you wanted."

Nuri listened with slowly growing horror as the officer told him where the Hungarian industrialist Eric Dietrich was at that moment.

Nuri stumbled out of the phone booth without hanging

up the phone. The old lady stumbled backward like a frightened bird as Nuri grabbed Gerwazek's shoulders.

"What is it?" Gerwazek asked. Some of the fear from Nuri seemed to finally erupt in the priest's face. It was as if everyone could see it, smell it on Nuri. Even the pharmacist stepped out from behind his counter, as if he suddenly felt the sense of menace that had a stranglehold on Nuri.

"He's at the East Ohio Gas Company," Nuri whispered.

"What?" Gerwazek asked.

"Some industrial tour, him, some Congressmen—" Nuri shook his head. "Don't you get it? The natural gas tanks."

Gerwazek stared at him.

Nuri looked at him and said, "Millions of cubic feet of liquefied natural gas, and Stefan's riding a bomb in there!"

The minute hand thunked home. It was 2:28.

2:29 PM

A man in a hard hat led Eric Dietrich and a small horde of followers across the grounds of the new East Ohio Gas liquefication-regasification facility. The tanks towered around them, reaching toward the cloudless sky.

"The first part of the facility," their guide was saying, "was completed in January of 1941. Tanks number one through three." He motioned to a column of spherical structures nested in girders and scaffolding towering nearly sixty feet into the sky.

He motioned around to a different tank, this one cylindrical and somewhat shorter than the others. "Tank number four," he continued, "was built later on, to help deal with the wartime shortages. Despite the fact that it holds a hundred million cubic feet, double any of the others, the design actually uses less material, saving about a hundred tons of steel for the war effort." He looked at Dietrich as he said it.

Dietrich was here in his capacity as a wartime industrialist. In that capacity he had visited innumerable factories and power plants. This was just the latest in a long line. His party consisted of bodyguards and two congressmen who were bound to him by more than party affiliation.

"I am interested in the transportation of natural gas," Dietrich asked. "The feasibility of rail transports is my current concern."

Their tour guide nodded and started to say something hen he was interrupted.

The party stood outside and towards the front of one of ɪe buildings of the Number Two Gas Works. From there ɪey could see the three spherical tanks and the cylindrical ɪnk number four. Also, through the fence around the gas orks, they could see the street that went by the grounds.

One of Dietrich's bodyguards, and one of the cops with ɪem, both shouted that something was coming.

On the road, shooting toward the Number Two Works, ʼas a long black car. It was topping a hundred miles an our as it barreled down the street, weaving in and out of affic. Sunlight gleamed off of its ebony windshield.

Dietrich stared at the vehicle, as if he saw more than a ɪlack shell hurtling down the street. Across his face ran an ⅹpression of first puzzlement, then recognition.

The car swerved so it was no longer pointed down the treet, but angled toward the gas works, toward the group athered around Dietrich.

Calmly and without passion Dietrich said, "Stop that ar."

The cops were still assessing the situation when the triad f Dietrich's bodyguards responded to his command. All hree drew their weapons, braced, and began firing. Sparks oomed across the long hood of the sedan. The ebony ʼindshield sprouted spidery cracks. One of the rear tires ⅹploded, throwing its hubcap across the sidewalk and ⅰrking the car off its course as it burst through the fence urrounding the works.

"Stop shooting!" the tour guide shouted, his voice on the ⅾge of panic.

The bodyguards emptied their weapons into the vehicle s it swerved past them. It slid between the massive storage ɪnks and the main building of the works—its body pep- ʼered with holes, the engine spouting steam, three tires ɪattened.

It was still going near sixty miles an hour as it plowed ɪhrough the supports of tank number four, grazing the mas- ⅰve tank. The impact slowed it enough that it rolled to a top about thirty feet beyond the tank.

The incident had lasted less than a minute.

"My God," said one of the cops.

Their tour guide let out a long exhale. "Thank God.
have to go to operations, and get number four draine
God knows what damage that did." He turned to Dietrich
"If there're any bullet holes in our equipment, you have t
answer for it."

Dietrich paid him no attention. He motioned his body
guards and told the others, police, congressmen, industria
ists, "Stay here, I have an issue with the driver of that car.

The tone was so cold that no one, not even the police
objected. No one would look him in the eyes. Dietric
strode the distance to the car. His stride appeared unhu
ried, but it carried him faster than any man should hav
been able to walk. Every move carried him with a represse
fury that anyone watching could sense.

The bodyguards followed, reloading.

2:31 PM

Gerwazek's response was down-to-earth and sensible. H
told Nuri to call East Ohio Gas and warn them. It was hi
only chance to avoid catastrophe. Nuri kept telling himsel
that Stefan wouldn't do it, wouldn't ignite the tanks there

But each time he thought of what Melchior was, an
importantly, what Stefan thought Melchior was, he knew
what Stefan was going to do.

If Adolf Hitler was in an allied city, would they firebom
the place to kill him? Would we do it if it cost hundreds o
thousands of civilian lives?

Nuri didn't try to answer the question. He knew wha
the answer was. But he was a soldier, and he knew it wasn'
his decision, or Stefan's. The people in this city hadn't con
sented to the war Stefan was fighting.

He reached a desk at East Ohio Gas after several tries
"Hello?" someone said. Nuri heard commotion behind
the voice.

"Please listen. I don't think there's much time. You have
to evacuate the plant and the grounds around it. There'
going to be—"

"You have to speak up, there's a bit of confusion here
An auto accident— What are you saying?"

"You have to evacuate!"

"What?" Nuri heard the voice muffled, talking to some
one else. The voice continued, "No, you've got to be kid

ing." Nuri heard the phone rattle on the desk, and the
voice moving away. Then, distinctly, he heard a different
voice say, *"Holy God, Number Four's letting go!"*

Nuri heard running feet, and the line went dead.

The clock went thunk. It was 2:34.

2:35 PM

No one at the Number Two Works who chose to look
at the direction of tank Number Four noticed Dietrich or
his bodyguards as they strode to the ruined Lincoln. They
didn't notice the ruined Lincoln, pockmarked with bullet
holes and belching steam from its fiercely idling engine.

What captured the attention of every employee who saw
tank Number Four was the cloud of white fog that poured
from a crack that started about ten feet above the ground
and ran halfway to the top of the tank. The fog looked
innocuous under the bright blue sky, like ice smoke or
water vapor.

The sight struck terror in everyone who saw it.

The white vapor was heavy, spilling to the ground, rolling
like a short cloud, spilling in a circle around the tank. All
the employees who saw it began running to put as much
distance between themselves and Number Four as possible.

Dietrich wasn't looking at Number Four, or at fleeing
employees. He was looking at the Lincoln with an inhuman
anger. His bodyguards followed, mindless, following his
will.

But when the rolling cloud reached the feet of the rear-
most bodyguard, he looked down into the rolling white
vapor. He lowered his gun, stopped moving and said,
"What the—"

If Dietrich heard him, he gave no sign. He walked next
to the Lincoln as its engine finally died.

2:39 PM

Stefan lay inside his Lincoln, his body riddled with a
dozen holes. Every strip of flesh seemed in agony as it tried
to knit itself together again. He was nearly blind from the
sunlight streaming through the holes in the car.

Spots of sunlight fell on his body, and everywhere they
landed was a spot of boiling numbness. He couldn't move,
and he thought that one of the bullets must have clipped

356 S. A. Swiniarski

his spine. He tried to force his will into his right hand, which still had a deathgrip on the stickshift, and on the switch he'd taped to it.

However he thought, how much he willed, how much he prayed, his hand would not release the button. What he could see of its flesh was dead and white, washed in a shade of deadly sunlight.

"God forgive me," he whispered through cracked and bleeding lips.

In response, the driver's side door was torn off the hinges, flooding the inside with the lethal sun. Stefan could feel it searing his whole body, driving the life and the spirit from it.

The last sensation Stefan knew was Melchior dragging him from the car, hissing, "No one of the blood opposes me."

Stefan never even felt the tug of his hand coming free of the stick shift.

2:40 PM

When the being called Melchior tore free the door of the Lincoln, white fog had already crept around his ankles. He didn't notice. All he had focus for was rage, a rage that one of the blood would still oppose him. His form was changing as he tore the door away. His arms and legs distorting with the crack of bone, his head becoming fanged and goatlike. The suit he wore tore away, revealing leather skin that was tearing and distorting with the pressure to keep up with the changing body.

He reached in for the one who defied him, his hand sinking deep into the chest of his enemy. He knew that this was one of the blood. He could smell it rank in the air even as his enemy was already dying in the light. His enemy's small will was too fragile to chain the spirit to the flesh when confronted by the sun.

"No one of the blood opposes me," said the thing that was Melchior. He tried to recognize the latest fool who had tried to bring him down.

He pulled the corpse closer, but the name wouldn't come to mind.

As the body came free of the automobile, there was the

ound of a click as a button taped to the gearshift raised
ack into position.

The dynamite went first.

It threw the goat-headed thing back toward the main
uilding of the Number Two Works, the body still clasped
its hands. The explosion blew the tanks of gasoline into
fine aerosol that instantly ignited a rolling ball of flame
at engulfed Melchior as he was still flying backward.

Shrapnel and fire ripped from the car, tearing through
l three bodyguards. Metal pierced Melchior in a dozen
laces before the blast had carried him six feet.

He was still conscious, still alive, his body still repairing
self, when the fog ignited.

Flames shot through the white cloud, and the air around
Melchior turned into a searing hell as the natural gas
urned. The air itself became fire. Melchior tried to will
is body together as he felt the flesh turn to carbonized
sh. It was too much. His breath sucked in fire that seared
way his lungs. His eyes melted. His flesh was consumed
nd the bones beneath cracked apart with the change in
mperature.

He was dead before his remains struck the ground.

Then tank Number Four exploded.

2:42 PM

The floors of the Union Terminal building shook so vio-
ntly that people on the platform looked down the tracks
or a collision. Along Kingsbury Run, the railroad cop who
ad found the head of Edward Andrassy looked up as the
ky to the east turned red. In the Roaring Third, still wak-
g from the night before, a bartender that had known Flo
olillo thought he saw the sun set in the north before the
ind of the blast burned his cheeks and cracked windows
round him.

A hellish wind tore through the Norwood-St. Clair neigh-
orhood. Within seconds everything was burning between
ast Fifty-Fifth and East-Sixty-Third. Telephone poles be-
ame pillars of fire, utility wires whipping tendrils of flame.
he wind turned the walls of working-class houses into rip-
ling sheets of fire. Birds cooked in the air and fell into
ools of melting asphalt. Cars swerved off the road as their

windows shattered and their tires blew out, seconds befo
their gas tanks ignited.

In the basement where Tito, Dante, and Aristaeus ha
played poker, the walls turned red and black-painted wi
dows blew in. In a few seconds, jets of flame whistle
through the floorboards. In the corner of the baseme
where a cot sat, one of Melchior's thralls opened his eye
He had the briefest time to realize that the chains of bloc
that bound him were gone with his Master's death. Then
house of flame collapsed upon him.

The walls of St. John's blistered with the heat as th
windows blew inside. The black curtains burned where th
wind touched them. The cross over the door fell burni
to a blackening lawn. In seconds, the dry wood of the sto
age shed exploded in an imitation of the holocaust aroun
it. The flames spread to the already burning church.

Close to the plant, where liquid fuel had penetrated in
the sewer system, rivers of fire followed the streets fro
the storm sewers and manhole covers. Inside buildings, to
lets and sinks exploded and basements flooded with fir
burning houses from the inside out.

High above, millions of burning fragments of insulatic
from tank Number Four rained down on the neighborhoo
igniting what the blast hadn't touched.

Nuri had been trying to get through to the Gas Worl
again, when the sun rose in the north. Nuri only had tir
to turn around in the phone booth as the windows of th
drugstore blew in. The paper posters promoting the w
effort burst into flames. Gerwazek fell across the old lad
protecting her from flying debris and the contents of th
shelves around them spilled to the ground as the who
building shook. The clock fell from the wall and smashe
to the counter next to the pharmacist.

Nuri pushed out of the telephone booth, into a searin
wind that made him feel as if his skin was on fire. Aroun
him the air roared as if the earth itself was dying.

"My God," Gerwazek said. Nuri could barely hear hin

"We have to get out of here!" Nuri said, grabbing Ge
wazek's shoulder. "Get her to safety."

Gerwazek nodded, helping the old woman up. Nu
limped to the rear of the store to find the pharmacist.

Nuri found him behind the counter, unconscious, his fac

ut and bruised. Fire was rolling across the ceiling as Nuri
ied to revive him, and the air was almost too thick to
reathe. Nuri glanced around and saw that the rear of the
1op was already a mass of flames; it was no use trying to
evive the man.

Nuri grabbed the pharmacist's arms and pulled him over
is shoulder. Then he began walking to the front of the
ore. The air was rank with the smell of burning chemicals.
s he passed shelves, he could see bottles of medicine melt-
1g into bubbling black ooze that dripped flame. Some of
dripped on to his uniform and stuck, burning all the way
1rough to his skin.

Under his feet, the black-and-white linoleum was yel-
>wing, warping, and cracking in the heat. It seemed forever
efore he reached the entrance and what seemed to be
afety.

It wasn't safety.

When Nuri stepped out of the drugstore, he stepped
traight into hell. Flames rolled from buildings on both
ides of the street, the air choked with rolling black haze,
nd the light seemed to come, not from the sun, but from
thousand-foot-tall pillar of fire that burned to the north,
lowing through the smoke.

Nuri looked around and saw Gerwazek's car burning by
ne side of the road, and he saw Gerwazek, hunched over
vith the old woman, running down the center of the street.
Ie was one of what suddenly seemed thousands of people
unning through the street, away from the towering pyre
o the north.

Nuri ran into the street following the crowd, hobbling as
est he could on his bad foot.

6

It would be nearly twenty-four hours before Nuri allowed himself to rest. Initially he was a refugee from the blast, but his uniform and his status as an ex-cop made it easy for him to join the rescue effort as safety officials began pouring into the disaster area. He fell to work helping people out of the rubble, rendering first aid, and helping firemen rig a feed from Lake Erie because exploding water mains had cut off water pressure to the blast zone.

Ten thousand people were evacuated from the area, while in the center, eight square blocks burned to the ground. The fires burned out of control until early Saturday morning.

Sometime during that morning, Nuri began finding more corpses than survivors. It may have been stress, or lack of sleep, but as Nuri worked through the night, he suspected that—despite the fact that the whole area was sealed off— the safety workers weren't the only ones searching the smoking rubble.

Many times before dawn, Nuri would see a set of pale men and women digging at a ruined building. Their clothes were ragged and torn for the most part, as if they were survivors of the blast, but none of the safety workers would approach them.

Each time Nuri saw such a gathering, they were retrieving a body from the wreckage, and sometimes the body wasn't quite human-looking. Whenever one of the safety workers approached them, one of the pale ones would stare at the intruder until he walked away. Nuri would always wonder how many of the blood had died in the blast—and how many survived.

By morning, dozens of safety workers—firemen, police, coast guard, and others—had to be relieved due to fatigue. A large proportion of them had small wounds on their legs, wrists and necks . . .

Nuri worked with the effort until he couldn't go any further, and then he kept at it until someone ordered him home. He got home, exhausted, around three Saturday afternoon. He smelled of ashes, and he looked as if he had worn his dress uniform into battle. Nuri collapsed into a chair and opened the *Cleveland News* he had picked up on the way home.

"71 Known Dead in Gas Plant Explosion," said the headline.

It was conservative.

According to the paper, about 250 homes were destroyed, and at least a thousand people were homeless. Nuri scanned the article until he reached the point where the coroner had asked the county engineer for bulldozers to help search for bodies.

Nuri had to put the paper down.

He sat in his new apartment, barely furnished since his return. He felt an odd sense of guilt at having survived. He slowly balled up the paper, wondering if it had been worth it, if there had been anything he could have done to prevent it.

The bodies he left for us, the ones he wanted to be found, those weren't a hundredth part of the blood left in his wake. And what he wallows in now is not a thousandth part of what would happen if he is granted what he seeks.

Nuri shook his head. Nuri knew that Melchior himself was responsible for many more deaths than the explosion had taken. But he kept feeling that Stefan was wrong, that the deaths were wrong.

If Adolph Hitler was in an allied city, would they firebomb the place to kill him? Would we do it if it cost hundreds or thousands of civilian lives?

Nuri knew the answer.

It was yes . . .

. . . but he would never be able to accept it.

Author's Note

This novel incorporates a number of actual events and peo
ple from Cleveland's history. Nevertheless, this is a work
of fiction, not a work of history, and none of the characters
in this book, even those based on historical personages,
should be considered as representing actual people. In par
ticular, Eliot Ness, the Van Sweringens, Mayor Burton, and
various police and county officials who appear in this book
are all products of my imagination.

While a dozen decapitated bodies were discovered in the
Cleveland area around the end of the Depression, and
while Eliot Ness was Public Safety Director through most
of the investigation of the Torso Murders, the investigation
as portrayed bears little resemblance to the actual events.
I have also taken liberties with the events surrounding the
East Ohio Gas Company explosion. And, of course, most of
the events portrayed in this novel never happened at all. . .

S. Andrew Swann

HOSTILE TAKEOVER

☐ **PROFITEER**   UE2647—$4.99

With no anti-trust laws and no governing body, the planet Bakunin is the perfect home base for both corporations and criminals. But now the Confederacy wants a piece of the action—and they're planning a hostile takeover!

☐ **PARTISAN**   UE2670—$4.99

Even as he sets the stage for a devastating covert operation, Dominic Magnus and his allies discover that the Confederacy has far bigger plans for Bakunin, and no compunctions about destroying anyone who gets in the way.

☐ **REVOLUTIONARY**   UE2699—$5.50

Key factions of the Confederacy of Worlds have slated a take-over of the planet Bakunin . . . An easy target—except that its natives don't understand the meaning of the word surrender!

OTHER NOVELS

☐ **FORESTS OF THE NIGHT**   UE2565—$3.99
☐ **EMPERORS OF THE TWILIGHT**   UE2589—$4.50
☐ **SPECTERS OF THE DAWN**   UE2613—$4.50

Camille Bacon-Smith

☐ **THE FACE OF TIME**   UE2707—$5.95

Tracking down a serial killer in the town of Thorgill, two New
Scotland Yard officers are about to enter a whole new territory
of police investigation. And though one of the detectives and
the townspeople know what is really going on, no one's willing
to let his partner in on the secret. But as ancient rituals begin
to be fulfilled, the two officers find themselves drawn into an
unholy war—facing an enemy more powerful than death
itself. . . .

☐ **EYE OF THE DAEMON**   UE2673—$5.50

All the wealthy Mrs. Simpson knew was that her half brother
Paul was missing, and the ad she was responding to had been
lying on top of the ransom note she found in her dining room.
But these were private investigators of the immortal kind—and
this kidnapping was about to lure them into the heart of a
demonic war. . . .

C.S. Friedman

IN CONQUEST BORN	UE2198—$6.99
THE MADNESS SEASON	UE2444—$5.99

The Coldfire Trilogy

BLACK SUN RISING (Book 1) UE2527—$6.99
Hardcover Edition: UE2485—$18.95

Centuries after being stranded on the planet Ema, humans have achieved an uneasy stalemate with the *Fae*, a terrifying natural force with the power to prey upon people's minds. Now, as the hordes of the *fae* multiply, four people—Priest, Adept, Apprentice, and Sorcerer—are drawn inexorably together to confront an evil beyond imagining.

WHEN TRUE NIGHT FALLS (Book 2) UE2615—$5.99
Hardcover Edition: UE2569—$22.00

Determined to seek out and destroy the source of the *fae*'s ever-strengthening evil, Damien Vryce, the warrior priest, and Gerald Tarrant, the undead sorcerer, dare the treacherous crossing of the planet's greatest ocean to confront a power that threatens the very essence of the human spirit.

CROWN OF SHADOWS (Book 3) UD2717—$6.99
Hardcover Edition: UE2664—$21.95

The demon Calesta has declared war on all mankind. Only Damien Vryce, and his unlikely ally, the undead sorcerer Gerald Tarrant stand between Calesta and his triumph. Faced with an enemy who may prove invulnerable—pitted against not only Calesta, but the leaders of the Church and the Hunter's last descendent—Damien and Tarrant must risk everything in a battle which could cost them not only their lives, but the soul of all mankind.

Prices slightly higher in Canada. **DAW 140X**

Attention:

DAW Collectors

Many readers of DAW Books have written re
questing information on early titles and book num
bers to assist in the collection of DAW editions
since the first of our titles appeared in April 1972.

We have prepared a list of all DAW titles, giving
their authors, titles, reissue information, sequence
numbers, original and current order numbers, and
ISBN numbers.

If you would like a copy of this list, please write
to the address below and enclose a check o
money order for two dollars or the equivalent
amount in stamps to cover the handling and post
age costs. Never send cash through the mail.

DAW Books, Inc.
Dept. C
375 Hudson Street
New York, NY 10014-3658